Even Legends Die

CRIMSON WORLDS VIII

Jay Allan

system 7
publishing

Crimson Worlds Series

Marines (Crimson Worlds I)
The Cost of Victory (Crimson Worlds II)
A Little Rebellion (Crimson Worlds III)
The First Imperium (Crimson Worlds IV)
The Line Must Hold (Crimson Worlds V)
To Hell's Heart (Crimson Worlds VI)
The Shadow Legions(Crimson Worlds VII)
Even Legends Die (Crimson Worlds VIII)

The Fall (Crimson Worlds IX)
(October 2014)

War Stories (Crimson World Prequels)

Also By Jay Allan

The Dragon's Banner

Gehenna Dawn (Portal Worlds I)

The Ten Thousand (Portal Worlds II)
(July 2014)

www.crimsonworlds.com

Even Legends Die

Even Legends Die is a work of fiction. All names, characters, incidents, and locations are fictitious. Any resemblance to actual persons, living or dead, events or places is entirely coincidental.

Copyright © 2014 Jay Allan Books

ISBN: 978-0692220047

Death smiles at us all, all a man can do is smile back.
- Marcus Aurelius, Meditations

Chapter 1

MCS John Carter
Earth Orbit
Sol System

It is beautiful, he thought, staring at the blue and white disk displayed on the main screen…so much prettier than his adopted homeworld's dusty-red visage. Duncan Campbell had been born on Earth, though his childhood memories of the slums of Edinburgh stirred a different set of emotions than the celestial vision he now enjoyed. Despite his ugly memories of violent streets and ancient, crumbling structures, he had to acknowledge that even centuries of war and pollution hadn't completely destroyed the beauty of mankind's birthplace…at least not when viewed from a distance.

Mars, on the other hand, was dusty and generally inhospitable, a hostile place where a man still needed machines to survive a casual stroll on its surface. A century's aggressive terraforming had created a far friendlier environment than the one men first found on the red planet, but there was far still to go. Seas and lakes and walks outside without a respirator and heated pressure suit would be his grandchildren's joy, not his.

For now, however, those grandchildren, and the children who would precede them, would have to wait. Campbell's life was one of duty, and anything remotely resembling a personal life had taken a backseat to his military career. He was enormously grateful to be a Martian citizen, and he was a committed patriot to his adopted home. He knew how fortunate he was to be on John Carter's bridge and not prowling through the squalor of Edinburgh's notorious Cog neighborhoods. He considered it a privilege to serve the Confederation, to give back to the nation that had done so much for him.

"We're getting multiple inquiries on all channels, Captain." Lieutenant Christensen's voice pulled him from his daydreaming. "All of the Powers have requested confirmation of our intentions."

Of course, he thought…they would be concerned, wouldn't they? Earth had been a demilitarized zone for over a century, ever since the Treaty of Paris had imposed terrestrial peace between the Superpowers. War hadn't been abandoned by mankind, nothing of the sort. It just moved out into space, where the constant conflicts didn't threaten the survival of the species quite so severely.

"Yes, I imagine they are a bit anxious right about now." Why wouldn't they be worried, he thought, with the Confederation's newest super-battleship knocking on their door without warning or introduction? Mars wasn't a signatory to the Treaty of Paris, so a warship entering orbit uninvited wasn't a violation of any covenant. But that was a diplomatic fine point, one that didn't make the situation less worrisome to the Superpowers. The Earthly nations were all parties to the treaty, which meant they were virtually defenseless from space. And John Carter was one of the most powerful warships ever built by man, larger even than the Alliance's vaunted Yorktown-class battlewagons and bristling with leading edge weaponry.

The Confederation hadn't been a major factor in the balance of power a century before when the treaty was signed, and the shattered Earth powers were too weak in space then to compel the nascent Confederation anyway. The successive Martian administrations had maintained a relatively neutral stance ever since, though they had steadfastly refused all entreaties to belatedly agree to the terms of the Paris accords. Nevertheless, the fear of a Confederation attack on Earth, while occasionally debated in one Power or another, had rarely been a serious concern. The Martians were the least expansionist of the Powers, committed more to building wealth than fighting wars. They controlled most of the mineral resources of the solar system, and they could deliver their ores to Earth at vastly lower cost than the other Powers' own interstellar colonies. They preferred markets and trading partners to enemies, and they conducted their foreign policy accordingly.

Now, however, all that was about to change. For the first time in history, a Martian ship had come to Earth not to trade or parlay, but to attack. Campbell's mission was highly specific, and he had a single target. But, surgical strike or no, John Carter was here to unleash thermonuclear fury on man's homeworld.

"Maintain communications silence, Lieutenant." You'll know why we're here soon enough, he thought. Then all hell will break loose…but it will be someone else's problem, not mine. Campbell was glad for the thousandth time he was a warrior and not a diplomat. "And I want scanners on full power. We're not expecting any of the Superpowers to have ships near Earth, but that's no excuse for carelessness." Campbell had been awarded the newest and largest ship in the Confederation's navy because of his spotless record, and he intended to live up to it in every particular. He was an odds on favorite for promotion to the admiralty after this tour, and he owed most of his success to his meticulous caution.

"Yes sir." Christensen's hands worked over her board, and the image of Earth moved to the left half of the screen, the right now displaying a scanning plot of local space. There were a few small symbols on the map, cargo ships and a single passenger liner, but no armed vessels. "No warships within scanner range, Captain."

"Very well." He leaned back, thinking quietly for a few seconds. "Bring the ship to battlestations, Lieutenant." Campbell pushed away the extraneous thoughts that had been clouding his mind. Now it was time to do what he'd come to do. "And get me weapons control."

There was a brief pause, no more than a second or two, and the bridge was bathed in a reddish light from the battlestations lamps. Another 3 or 4 seconds then: "Commander Linken here, sir."

"Are the weapons ready to go, Commander?" Campbell skipped the pleasantries. He and Linken had served together for two years, and they worked together like a finely tuned machine.

"Yes, sir." Linken's response was crisp and immediate. "The missiles are fully fueled and ready for launch, and the warheads are cleared and ready." Campbell could see an updated weapon status display appear on his personal screen. "Awaiting your final order to arm them, Captain."

Campbell took one more look at the gauzy blue image of Earth floating on the display, smaller than it had been a moment before when it occupied the entire screen, but just as beautiful. "You may arm your weapons, Commander." Campbell closed his eyes for an instant, pondering the gravity of what he was about to do. The 125 megaton Penetrator warheads were nothing special in terms of ship combat. In the vacuum of space, without atmosphere to carry heat and shockwaves, vessels targeted each other with enormously powerful missiles. Warheads yielding 500 megatons or more were commonplace. But against a ground target, 125 megatons was an enormous weapon, even an inefficient one. Cities were better targeted by dispersed spreads of smaller weapons, which distributed the destructive force far more effectively. Unless you were trying to dig out and destroy a heavily fortified subterranean target, in which case five or six of the big warheads were more likely to do the job. Campbell was about to launch 60 of them…and, in doing so, become the first commander to bombard an Earth target since the end of the Unification Wars.

He sighed, thinking of the significance of the act, the crushing responsibility of what he was about to do. His actions could lead to war; they could provoke reprisals against the Confederation. The attack was targeted at a rogue base, but there was no way to contain the effects of the devastation. Innocents in the area would die and fallout and radiation would affect residents hundreds of miles from ground zero. He was destroying an enemy installation, one that would cause immeasurable harm if it was left functional. But he was also killing men, women, and children who were totally uninvolved, probably thousands of them…as surely as if he stood in front of them and shot them with his sidearm.

But none of that mattered. He had his orders, and duty was first to Duncan Campbell…another factor he suspected had played a role in his appointment as mission commander. "You may arm your weapons, Commander." Campbell's voice was eerily calm. "And launch when ready."

"What the hell is that?" The shaggy old ranch hand pointed toward the sky.

His companions almost ignored him, all but one. The old man was a little crazy, and no one took him very seriously. No one except Gus Hart, who'd been friends with grizzled Chuck Trexler since he'd been an unpopular kid befriended by the bizarre old cow hand. Trexler had been ancient even then, at least to Hart's recollection, but the two had developed a strong friendship, one that endured to the present day.

"What the fuck?" Hart was staring now too, his mouth open in shock. The rest of the group looked up immediately. Hart was the informal leader of the ranch's Cog workers, and everyone paid attention to whatever he did.

"Are those aircraft of some kind?" Gyp Tompkins was the first to look, after Hart and Trexler. His voice was a little shaky, nervous. You didn't see things like this every day in the ranchlands of Dakota.

"They're missiles." Hart's voice was deadpan, his eyes locked on the long white trails in the sky. Most of the workers on the ranch had never traveled more than a few klicks from the pastures, but Hart had served a five year stint in the terrestrial military. Mustered out in one of the periodic downsizing efforts, he returned home with corporal's stripes and a reasonable knowledge of military hardware. "Probably nuclear." And if they airburst, he thought but didn't say, we're screwed. "C'mon…we have to get back to the village." He looked at the others then back to the sky for a few more seconds. "Now."

He turned and started, walking a few steps then breaking into a run. He glanced back over his shoulder. The rest of the group was standing still, transfixed on the rapidly descending smoke trails. "I said now!" he screamed, waving his arm wildly. "We need to move now!"

The group followed this time, running hard on his heels. What the hell is this, he thought...what is going on? What's out here worth attacking? He was in a near panic, but his military training was there too, rising from the back of his mind, telling him their only chance was to keep moving. They were running across the flat plains, Hart looking around desperately for some kind of cover. He glanced back over his shoulder, shaking his head violently when he saw how far the missiles had traveled in just a few seconds. There was no way they were going to make it far enough, he thought...those birds could detonate any second now.

He looked around as he ran, nearly tripping over a rock as he did. There, he thought, scrambling to regain his balance. To the south was a small depression. He knew the spot...the ground dropped off sharply to the banks of a small river. The slope would give some protection from the detonations. "Let's go!" He waved his arm, pointing south. "Get down that hillside there, and hit the dirt when I say so."

His companions were screaming and panicking, but they followed him. The ground on the hillside became steadily more rugged, and Trexler tripped. Hart swore bitterly, but he dropped back, pulling the old man to his feet and shoving him forward. He looked back again. Most of the smoke trails extended behind the hillside, past his field of vision. He wanted to get a little farther, but he knew he was already pushing his luck. "Get down," he shouted, as loud as he could. He dove into the ground, holding his hands ahead to absorb the impact and slow his momentum.

He felt a sharp pain in his arm as he landed, but he tried to ignore it. A broken wrist was the least of his problems now. "Stay down and close your eyes," he screamed.

A few seconds later his eyelids glowed orange. He squeezed them tight, but the blinding light still penetrated enough to hurt his eyes. He clutched the ground, his hands digging into the soft wet grass. He felt the waves of heat, burning his back. The hillside was blocking most of it, but it still hurt like fire. Then he heard the blasts, one after another, a deafening rumble. His hands went to his ears, instinctively trying to cover them, to block out the shattering roar, but it was futile. The deafening blasts kept going…ten, twenty…then he lost count.

The ground shook too, throwing his body up and back down with a jarring thud. He felt himself tumbling, rolling down the hillside as the terrible earthquake continued, fed by detonation after detonation. His burned back scraped painfully along the ground as he slid toward the river edge. My God, he thought, as his broken body finally came to a rest 20 meters from the stream…this is the end. This is the end.

"Weapons control reports 43 missiles successfully penetrated Alliance air defenses and impacted on or near the target." Christensen's voice was a little shaky, but still remarkably calm, Campbell thought, considering she is reporting the results of a nuclear attack on Earth.

"On or near" wasn't the kind of precision terminology Campbell typically demanded from his crew, though he knew she was just giving him a preliminary assessment. More details would follow as soon as she had them. He waited a few more seconds for the follow up and then he pressed her. "Damage assessment, Lieutenant?"

Her hands were flying across her screen. "Working on that now, Captain."

He knew how demanding he was with his people. Christensen was a good officer, and he knew she'd have the data to him as soon as humanly possible. He was just anxious…and he knew the only way to keep a blade sharp was to hone it constantly. He had good people, but he made damned sure they stayed that way by constantly pressing them to do better. And this mission was no place to let those standards fall. Roderick Vance had been brutally clear. Campbell was to launch one attack…and one attack only. Then he was to break orbit and return to Mars immediately. And, no matter what – those had been Vance's exact words…no matter what – he was to make sure that one attack completely destroyed the target.

Still, he thought, don't take your tension out on Christensen. Let her do her job. Duncan Campbell was driven…a creature of duty who took his commitments, especially those of the service, very seriously. But he also trusted his crew and, even as he pushed them, he knew he had to have faith in their own dedication.

His commitment came from a powerful source, something deep within himself. He knew just how lucky he was to be a naturalized citizen of the Confederation…and how many Cogs living in squalor and deprivation in the slums of the Superpowers would kill for the life he had.

Campbell's mother had been his father's housekeeper…and later his lover. A widowed Martian executive, Arthur Campbell was on Earth overseeing his business interests in a manufacturing complex in the Scottish countryside. The Martian magnate took both his lover and their child with him when he returned home, but tragedy cut short their happiness. Duncan's mother had been infected with the X2 virus as a child, and her acclimation to the Martian environment triggered a reversal of the dreaded disease's remission. She died a few months later, despite the best medical care the wealthy – and grief-stricken - Arthur Campbell could buy. A remnant of the biological weaponry used during the Unification Wars, certain mutated forms of X2 remained incurable, even to the cutting edge medical technology of the Confederation.

Broken-hearted, Arthur Campbell doted on his son. But there was trouble in the family. His adult children resented the beautiful Scottish maid they felt had seduced her way into their father's life, and they wanted no part of the half-brother that had resulted from that union. Their intransigence ultimately compelled him to purchase an alternate estate to house the young, illegitimate, Duncan. His father had insisted he would find a place for his youngest son in the family business, but Duncan didn't want his relationship with his half-siblings to become any more difficult than it already was, and he chose a military career instead.

He excelled at the Naval Academy, graduating second in his class, and he followed that up with a distinguished career that took him from one end of human space to the other... and finally out beyond the Rim with Augustus Garret's Grand Fleet. He returned to a decoration and command of the newest battlewagon in the fleet and, five weeks later, the mission to launch a nuclear attack on Earth. How, he thought...how did it come to this?

"Captain, I have the scanning report." Christensen's voice pulled him from his introspection.

He turned to face the tactical officer. "Yes, Lieutenant." He hesitated a few seconds, clearing the residual thoughts away. "Please, continue."

"The attack appears to be a complete success, sir. Based on the parameters provided to us, the AI estimates the total destruction of 99% of the targeted land area to a depth of 3 kilometers."

Campbell was silent for a few seconds, his mind imagining the nuclear fury his missiles had unleashed. How many had he just killed...not just in the base, but in the surrounding areas? It wasn't a heavily populated region, but his bunker busters had burrowed into the ground before they detonated. The resulting explosions were vastly dirtier than airbursts, and the massively toxic fallout would spread for hundreds of miles. Thousands of civilians would die from radiation poisoning, townspeople and farmhands and normal workers who had nothing to do with the plots and schemes of the politicians and soldiers. Cogs like he was, he thought sadly...the lower classes who would be denied the medical treatment that could save them.

He'd fought in space before, and he'd killed enemies in those battles, but this was somehow different. His enemies before were all combatants, just like his own people. This was...different. He felt odd, queasy...guilty. He'd been a warrior before. Was he a mass murderer now?

He exhaled slowly and looked across the bridge. He didn't have time for indulgent self-reflection. The Alliance – and the other Powers – were in shock right now, but they'd all be recalling any ships within range. Campbell was glad he didn't have to sort out the international uproar. Was the Alliance at war with the Confederation now? Would Admiral Garret be recalled from the frontier to lead his fleet against Mars itself? Would the great admiral obey such a command? Campbell didn't know the answers, but he was glad it was Vance's problem and not his.

"OK, Lieutenant, we have our orders." He sighed softly, taking one last look at the perfect blue image of Earth on the main display. "Prepare to leave orbit."

Chapter 2

Saw Tooth Gorge
Red Mountains
Northern Territories, Far Concordia
Arcadia – Wolf 359 III

"Let's go. I want the first column moving out in ten minutes." Kara's voice was raw, determined. She glared at her second in command, a cold determination behind her sparkling blue eyes. "No arguments, Ed. Ten minutes."

Calvin opened his mouth to argue, but he closed it again without speaking. "Whatever you say, Kara," he muttered grudgingly. He turned and walked away, still limping from his injuries and waving his arms as he shouted out commands along the way.

Kara watched him go. She knew he didn't agree with her decision, but he'd go along with it…she was sure of that much. Even Captain Mandrake thought she was jumping the gun. The Marine officer had agreed with Ed, advising her to wait until more information was available. But she didn't need to wait. She knew they were coming. She knew.

It had been just over an Arcadian month since Admiral Garret's fleet burst into the system, driving away the enemy naval contingent and landing a Marine expeditionary force on the planet. The navy also made contact with Kara's Arcadian army and resupplied her. They replaced the planet's destroyed satellite grid too, and for the first time, she and her refugees understood why the enemy had never committed the strength to wipe them out once and for all. They'd been fighting another Marine force all along.

James Teller and his Marines had landed shortly after the native army was driven deep into the Arcadian wilderness, and the enemy had been compelled to pull forces from the pursuit to face the new threat. With the planet's satellite network destroyed and all ground-based communication severed, Kara and her soldiers were completely cut off from their Marine allies, entirely unaware they weren't fighting their battle alone.

Teller's Marines were massively outnumbered from the beginning; they'd never had a real chance to liberate the planet. But they fought hard and held out, week after week, just as Kara's people were doing in the mountains. Teller was just about at the end of his resources when the fleet blasted into the system and landed General Holm and his old vets, armed to the teeth and looking for a fight.

The fleet was gone now, off pursuing the enemy naval forces, but the ground troops remained. The Marines were still heavily outnumbered, but now they had fresh reserves and a complete resupply…and with that, the ability to hold out for a while longer. Perhaps a long while.

For a month that is just what both forces had done. The enemy controlled Arcadia City and most of the developed areas, but the Marines and the native forces remained in the field… and as long as they did, the fight would go on. In the occupied cities, opposition was growing. Scattered acts of sabotage were morphing into organized resistance movements, tying down ever larger numbers of the invaders to maintain control of the areas they occupied. Kara and her commanders had even been considering staging a breakout from their positions, taking the fight to the enemy. Then the signal came.

It was brief, spotty. A fleeting alarm from the warp gate scanner, lasting only a few seconds before the thing stopped transmitting entirely. Something had transited through the gate…that much was certain. But what? Her people had argued ever since, and multiple theories were bouncing around. Was it a malfunction? Could it be friendly ships inbound…reinforcements? The arguments went on all night, but Kara just sat silently. She had no doubts. She knew it was the enemy.

She let them argue until they exhausted themselves, but her mind was made up. Enemy reinforcements were coming, and when they landed, their adversaries would have overpowering strength. The waiting game was over...standing in place and playing for time was a losing strategy. In a few days the enemy would be here. They'd destroy the satellite network Garret had left, cutting Kara's army off again from the Marines thousands of kilometers away. Then they would land fresh troops and hunt down the Marines, her people, the nascent rebel movements...anyone left in arms on Arcadia.

But if they wanted her world, she resolved that they would have to take it from her. They would have to follow her forces into hell itself. The Army of Arcadia was moving out. She'd considered attacking the troops masking her position, hitting them before they were reinforced. It was a tempting idea, but the mathematics hadn't changed. Attacking across the gorge between the armies was suicidal, at least without overwhelming superiority neither side yet possessed.

No, her people wouldn't be moving south into the teeth of the enemy. They would be marching north, cutting across the planet's brutal polar region and out into the largely unexplored wilderness beyond. If they made it far enough, through the bitter cold and titanic storms of the arctic and across the virtually uncharted areas beyond, they'd force the enemy to divert massive forces to pursue them. Eventually, they'd hunt her down, but she would tie down many times the strength of her own force.

They thought she was crazy...all of them. The army would suffer enormous hardships on so difficult a march. Calvin had argued for caution. Mandrake agreed. The Marine captain's platoon was fully-armored, and his 50 men and women would be zipped up, protected from the brutality of Arcadia's savage arctic winter. But the native forces had no powered armor. Her troops would march through waist-deep snow and frigid temperatures. They would traverse icy mountain passes and make their way across the frozen sea. At night they would huddle in their portable shelters, absorbing whatever warmth their heaters and field generators could produce.

She would lose people; she knew that. Dozens would die on the march…maybe hundreds. But as long as she kept her force in the field, the Arcadian cause would endure. And that was all that mattered. She wouldn't let Will's army perish, no matter what the cost…no matter how many of the dedicated men and women who formed its ranks froze in the arctic wilderness or died under the guns of their enemies. As long as the army itself survived, the cause remained alive and, in a way, Will's spirit did too.

"I'd kill for some decent ground defenses." Elias Holm was pacing back and forth in his makeshift HQ, his armored boots scraping along the gravel floor. There was a small table in the center of the room, a shabby makeshift construction put together mostly from scrap metal. It wasn't very plush for the office of the Commandant, but the Marine expeditionary force on Arcadia had to make do with what it could get. Elias Holm had led the largest forces the Corps ever deployed, tens of thousands of crack Marines, supported by Admiral Garret's massive fleets. But that was another time, one that felt very long ago. Most of those veterans were gone now, lost over the years as the Corps faced one savage battle after another. Now Holm led less than 2,000 Marines, half of them battered and exhausted from weeks of fighting against overwhelming odds and the rest a hastily-assembled force of retirees, called back to the flag decades after their service had ended. It wasn't even a tithe of the strength he'd once had at his disposal, just a tattered remnant of one of the greatest fighting forces mankind had ever put into the field.

Holm didn't given it a second thought. He didn't miss luxuries…he didn't need a huge headquarters or a cluster of aides following him around. He was on the front lines again, giving all he had to a desperate battle. He felt alive, in a way he hadn't for a long time. This is where a general should be, he thought…not behind some desk echelons above the actual fighting. His mind

drifted back through the years, from one world to another…
to the planet Columbia, where Colonel Holm and his Marines
fought to hold that crucial world against an overwhelming CAC
invasion force so many years before. It was a situation similar
to the current one, though he faced far longer odds now than
he had then.

It was Columbia that earned Holm his stars, in a battle where
he first met then-Sergeant Erik Cain. It was a desperate struggle, waged at the nadir of the Alliance's fortunes in the war…
and the victory was the start of the turning point.

"We might as well just sit here and let them land." Holm's
voice was grim, lifeless. "It's not like we can do anything about
it. Throw rocks maybe."

"It's not as bad as all that, Elias." Sam Thomas was sitting
on the end of the table, looking up at Holm's agitated expression. "We've got a good supply of the handhelds. We'll take
out a decent number of landers if they come down anywhere
near our positions." Thomas knew it wasn't really the lack of
ground-to-air defenses bothering Holm. It didn't matter how
many enemy landers they managed to shoot down. The Marine
forces on Arcadia were hopelessly outnumbered already…any
enemy reinforcements that made it to the surface were too many.

Holm glanced back at Thomas and felt a sudden pang of
guilt. He'd gone to Tranquility…he'd rallied the old veterans
and led them here. Had he done it just to drag them to Arcadia
to die? To prolong a pointless defense a month or two and
change nothing? Was that all their lives were worth…all they'd
earned after lifetimes of service? To die for a purpose was one
thing, but to waste your life for nothing?

"God damn, you've turned into a gloomy SOB, Elias."
Thomas slapped his armored hand down on the metal table. He
knew exactly what Holm was thinking. He could read it in his
eyes. "Stop wallowing in guilt, my old friend. Every man and
woman who came with us did so because they chose to …and I
wager not one of them would change his or her mind now. Not
if a million enemy troops land on this God forsaken planet."
Thomas sighed before he continued. "I'm older than you, Elias,

but I never had the weight on my shoulders you've borne these last ten years. I knew you had a bright future back in the day, but you've gone beyond anything I imagined. You remember… when I talked you out of resigning after that debacle on Persis? But my God…Commandant!" Thomas' eyes stared out of his open helmet, locking on Holm's. "I'm damned proud of you, kid." He paused a few seconds, his eyes focusing briefly on the wisps of mostly-gray hair visible inside Holm's helmet. "And you're running out of people who can call you 'kid' so enjoy it while you still can."

Holm smiled. "You better be careful. People hear you talking like that you're gonna lose your rep as a crusty old grouch." Holm walked back to the desk and sat down, looking back into the older man's eyes as he did. "Thanks, Sam," he added softly, following it with a gentle nod. "That means a lot coming from you."

Thomas returned the gesture. "So," he added after a few seconds of silence, "I guess we should get back to how we're going to deal with these uninvited guests. Don't you think?"

Holm nodded and looked down at the large 'pad sitting on the desk. "Well…" – he paused as he stared at the map – "…if I were them, I'd bring my main force down right here…"

It was time. Time for the vengeance he had so long been denied. At last, he would put an end to those meddlesome Marines. They had interfered with his plans for the last time.

Gavin Stark sat quietly, looking at the hazy blue disk of Arcadia displayed on his screen. In a few minutes his forces would begin landing, reinforcing the troops already deployed on the surface. His Shadow Legions were the equal of the Marines, at least nearly so. They had the same training, equipment, doctrine. Perhaps, he allowed, they were missing something the Marines had, a spirit, a pride passed to them from those who had come before. But they were close enough, and their numbers would tell, making up for any minor quality gap. And they were his, conditioned to follow orders without question, utterly loyal, from the lowliest private to the highest-ranked general.

Nothing like the cantankerous Marines. And now his soldiers would destroy those troublesome Marines on the surface...and Arcadia and its resources would become part of Stark's new empire.

His plans had been in the works for years. Indeed, he had intended to launch Shadow much sooner, but he'd had to postpone things when the First Imperium burst into human space and started a war. A desperate struggle for mankind's survival. He'd even considered releasing the Shadow Legions at the nadir of that conflict and sending them against the invaders. It would have destroyed his plans for his own dominance, but his clone armies would have done him no good if he was dead along with the rest of mankind at the hands of the robotic enemy. But he'd kept his resolve, betting that the brilliant Augustus Garret would manage a victory somehow. And his bet paid off. Garret did win the war...and at a deliciously high cost. Not only was the First Imperium out of the picture, but the Powers had all suffered crippling losses in the fight. It would be all that much easier to sweep away the opposition.

Mankind would enter a new age...and leave behind its inefficient wars and the wasted productivity and needless destruction that came with them. They would be unified, together, moving forward in lockstep under the absolute rule of one man. Gavin Stark.

It had taken some fancy footwork to keep his secrets. His schemes required enormous financial resources, and he'd met the need by turning the Alliance economy into one giant illusion...a juggling act that was impossible to maintain indefinitely. It had taken no small part of his undeniable genius to keep shuffling things around to maintain the secret...but he'd seen it done. That charade would shatter any day now, and it would cast the world into economic chaos, and that would only aid in the completion of Project Shadow.

Yes, the First Imperium threatened his plans but, in the end, the ancient aliens had done him a favor. The price the Powers had paid to win their victory served him well. Stark had been worried about fighting the Marines on a dozen key colony worlds, but the Corps had been so decimated in the fighting out on the Rim, they struggled to put significant strength on just two planets. And even on Arcadia and Armstrong their forces were pathetic, inadequate. His legions would sweep them away…and into the dustbin of history.

"Number One, Anderson-02 reporting." The comlink pulled him from his thoughts. He'd ordered his staff to identify themselves by name and number in all communications. He'd been assured they would all develop on their own paths after leaving the crèche, as each faced a different set of experiences. But he still found them to be relentlessly alike, even the ones who'd been out the longest. The clones made dependable and capable soldiers, but they all sounded the same to him, even ones from different lines. The cadence of their speech was similar…droning, with an unnatural monotone.

"Yes, what is it, general?"

"All systems are ready to go, sir. Request permission to begin the landings." Anderson-2 was the highest ranking of all the clones, Anderson-1 having been expended in an earlier test. Stark had insisted from the beginning of the project on using clones to fill his entire chain of command. He'd seen enough treachery – he'd encouraged enough - to destroy his ability to trust any other officers. Rafael Samuels was the only non-clone in his ground forces, but he was the one man in all of human space who could never defect to the other side. Stark couldn't imagine what the Marines would do to the greatest traitor in their history if he fell into their hands, but he knew the ex-Commandant had as much reason as he did to want the Marines destroyed.

Samuels was a temporary tool, anyway, far too untrustworthy to be allowed to survive the war. He would serve his purpose, and then he would be eliminated. Gavin Stark did not leave loose ends.

"Permission granted, general." Stark smiled grimly. "By all means, let us begin the final act."

He imagined a similar scene over Armstrong. Erik Cain had managed to defend the Marine's home base, somehow fighting the first invasion force to a standstill. There was a stalemate there now, neither side strong enough to launch an offensive against the other. But that was about to change. The reinforcements should be landing on Armstrong any time now...and General Erik Cain would at last face his final battle.

Stark tried to keep his mind clear and focused, but the thought of Cain stirred a rage deep within him. He hated the accursed Marine...detested him with a fiery passion only another psychopath truly could understand. No one had interfered with his plans more disastrously than Erik Cain. No one except for Augustus Garret. And it had been Cain who'd rescued Garret from Stark's clutches when the hated admiral had been his prisoner during the rebellions.

The reserves he'd sent to Armstrong were more than enough to overwhelm the battered Marines defending the planet, but Stark wasn't taking any chances. Erik Cain was a tactician without equal, and the sooner he was gone the better. He'd hoped to be rid of Cain already, a shot to the head or knife in the dark ridding him of his hated adversary. But Alex still hadn't done the job he sent her – twice – to do. Fucking bitch, he thought, thinking bitterly of his former protégé. Alex Linden was breathtakingly beautiful, and a sexual dynamo the likes of which he'd never experienced elsewhere. But that's no excuse for letting her get to you, he thought. He'd never allowed a lay to get into his head...not until Alex. He'd known he should have killed her when he had her captive...but instead he gave her another chance and sent her back to Armstrong to assassinate Cain. It was a stupid, weak thing to do. Stark wasn't one who normally gave second chances, and it would be a long time before he gave another.

He would have the last laugh though. He wasn't about to let her get away with betraying him twice. He had another assassin on Armstrong, one every bit as talented as sexy little Alex. He already had his orders. He wouldn't falter as she had, distracted with emotional baggage and confused feelings. He would carry out his orders to the letter, coldly, dispassionately. He would assassinate Erik Cain. And then he would kill Alex too.

Chapter 3

Marine HQ
West of the Sentinel Forest
Planet Armstrong
Gamma Pavonis III

"Get your people out of that pocket now!" Cain's voice was loud and raw. The battle had been raging non-stop for three days. For those 72 hours his Marines had held their precarious positions, grimly defending against repeated overwhelming assaults from two sides. It was an astonishing display of will, of what raw courage and determination could achieve. Erik Cain had been everywhere, driving his people to the end of their endurance, leading them by example. But even Cain could only extract so much from human beings, even Marines…and now the relentless mathematics of war was asserting itself. The lines were collapsing, and Cain's army was in mortal danger of being split in two. He'd pulled them back at an angle, shortening his line while still protecting the troops along the river. But he knew he couldn't hold the new position for long. He just hoped it would be enough.

"I mean now, Eliot. Our lines over here are a wreck. You don't have much time." Cain's tone was raw and intense, emphasizing the urgency of the situation. There was a deep fatigue there too, one that showed just how close even he was to the end of his stamina. There were two Erik Cains – the man and the legend. He was well aware of the difference…for all his victories and medals, his ego had always remained firmly in check. Cain used the image of the relentless, invincible Marine for all it was worth, but he never believed the myth himself…and he knew very well that the man was mortal, fallible, beatable. And he knew how close he was to the end of his strength.

The second invasion force had rendered Cain's resistance futile. He knew his Marines had no chance to win this fight. They were too tired, too few, too low on ordnance. They were massively outnumbered and facing an enemy that had just been resupplied. It was over already, save for the formalities. But it just wasn't in him to give up. Surrender wasn't a word he knew, and death was far preferable to surviving failure and defeat. He would fight to the bitter end, until the enemy finally managed to take him down. He knew he would never leave Armstrong.

He put those thoughts out of his head. None of it mattered…he had a battle to wage, and until some enemy soldier put him down he would fight like a demon dragged from the deepest pit of hell. His enemy might finally finish him off, but Cain vowed to himself that his life would come neither cheaply nor easily. The enemy may defeat him, but he would make them pay in blood.

The enemy reinforcements had come down north of the Graywater this time, exactly where he'd expected the first invasion force to land. They quickly compromised his defensive positions along the river and in the Sentinel. Cain and Cooper Brown scraped up every Marine who could be spared…cadres from shattered units, mechanics, orderlies, logistics personnel. Everyone was a combat Marine now, and specialists who hadn't fired their assault rifles in battle for 20 years were in the line. These ragged forces poured into the gap between Storm's people in the Sentinel and the new enemy formations attacking from the west. Utterly overmatched, they desperately held against 30,000 fresh enemy troops. They made the enemy pay for every meter, and they held for far longer than anyone had a right to expect. But now they had reached their limit. Cain knew the end wasn't far away.

To the southeast, Eliot Storm's troops were still defending the riverline, holding back the original enemy force. They had better defensive terrain and were facing troops as exhausted as they were. They had turned every enemy move to cross the river into a bloody shambles. But now they were in grave danger. The withdrawal of Brown's troops exposed their unprotected right and rear. If they didn't get out fast, they'd be hit on the flank by fresh forces and overrun.

"We're falling back now, sir." Storm sounded exhausted. "I've got the remaining Obliterators covering the flank as we retreat." The Obliterators had proven to be extremely effective against standard powered infantry. The four meter tall suits had been designed to counter the First Imperium's giant Reaper robots, and the war on Armstrong was their first matchup against normal armored troops. The massively-armed behemoths had proven their worth, spearheading the assault that destroyed the bridges over the Graywater and cut the enemy force in two. It had been the turning point of the first phase of the battle, but the victory had been bittersweet. It cost the unit its first and only commander, General Erin McDaniels, mortally wounded as she led the final assault on the Graywater bridges to cut the enemy army in two. McDaniels was one of the most popular officers in the entire Marine Corps. Erik Cain had considered her one of his few true friends, and the pain of her loss was hard to bear.

Now the survivors were moving into position, forming a rearguard to cover the retreat of their comrades. The Obliterators were lusting for revenge, straining to get at the enemy that had killed their beloved leader. Cain had whipped them into a frenzy earlier, invoking McDaniels' memory in an emotional - but coldly mercenary - speech, one intended to turn her grieving Marines into relentless killing machines. They would fight better for his manipulation, and probably to the bitter end as well. Cain was repulsed at the idea of using his friend's death as a tool to get her people to fight harder…but he did it anyway. One more reason to hate himself.

"Very well, Colonel." Cain's voice was hoarse, overuse and fatigue beginning to take their toll. "But make sure your withdrawal is speedy. We'll try to cover your retreat, but you don't have much time. Cain out." He flipped off the com channel and turned to look at the ragged line in front of him. It looked weak. It is weak, he thought grimly…that's why it looks that way. But we've got to slow them down. We've got to hold for a while.

He moved forward slowly, glancing at his tactical display. The shimmering blue symbols projected inside his visor gave him an accurate flow of information on unit strengths and positions, but it couldn't tell him what he most needed to know. It couldn't show him the morale of his men and women…which units were faltering…which were most likely to break. It didn't communicate the fear his people felt, the despair and hopelessness…the realization that their cause was already lost, that courage and determination weren't going to be enough this time.

Cain had led thousands of Marines in every manner of desperate stand, but in the end he knew only one way to draw the last scraps of resolve they kept buried deep inside. His men and women followed him for different reasons. Some thought he was invincible, that no enemy could defeat him. Others were driven by the force of his iron will, more afraid of failing him than facing any foe. But one thing they all shared – they knew at the last stand, when all was crumbling to dust and defeat, and destruction surrounded them on every side, Erik Cain would be there, rifle in hand, shoulder to shoulder when death came for them. For all his rank and the legends that preceded him, no Marine doubted that when Erik Cain finally fell it would be in the front lines, standing with his Marines.

He pulled his assault rifle off the harness and checked the cartridge, walking forward toward the line as he did. His people would stand here…they would hold long enough for Storm's Marines to escape from the pocket that threatened to become a death trap. And Erik Cain would stand in the front line with them and make sure they did and, if necessary, die there with them.

Alex Linden crouched down behind the giant tree. She'd never seen a forest like this. The Sentinel was one of Armstrong's great natural treasures, its gargantuan trees reaching hundreds of meters into the open sky. It was not the kind of thing she would have noticed in the past, but she was different now. She didn't completely understand the changes of the last few years but perhaps, given time, she would. But for now, despite the stress, the fear, the uncertainty gnawing at her insides, some part of her mind noted the magnificence of the towering trees. Vast sections of the amazing wood now bore the scars of war, for it was another of the battlefields where man had come to wage one of his many wars. Still, the Sentinel was enormous, and there were thousands of hectares that remained untouched. Alex had taken a wide route around the battlefield, traveling mostly through virgin forest. She'd been stalking Erik Cain, but wandering too close to the fighting and getting blown to bits wasn't going to help her complete the job. Neither was getting picked up by a Marine patrol and sent back to the refugee camp.

She'd resolved to carry out the assassination. She hated the idea. She wanted to stop and drop to her knees, emptying the contents of her stomach on the cold ground. But she didn't have a choice. It would buy her time with Gavin Stark...maybe enough for her to get close to him. Killing Stark was her only chance to survive; she was sure of that. He'd shown uncharacteristic weakness in letting her come back to Armstrong, but she knew she couldn't count on that a second time. Even if she completed her mission, he'd never forget that she'd failed him before. His momentary weakness would pass, and she'd never see it coming. She knew enough from years as one of Alliance Intelligence's deadliest assassins...you couldn't stay vigilant all the time. Offense and defense were not equal forces. With enough persistence, you could get to any target. And no one had more raw stubbornness than Gavin Stark. No...killing the bastard was the only way. And taking out Erik Cain was a necessary step to reaching Stark.

She wasn't sure exactly where she was, but she knew she was getting close to Cain's headquarters. It didn't look like the battle was going very well. She'd ducked into cover half a dozen times as worn looking groups of Marines passed by, heading north, away from the front lines. Most of them were bringing wounded comrades back with them, some staggering along with minimal assistance, others being carried. Their fighting suits were blackened and pitted with the scars of battle.

Maybe the invaders will do the job for me, she thought. She couldn't imagine the legendary Erik Cain surviving a battle where his army was destroyed. If he was killed in the fighting, it would be the same, wouldn't it?

She shook her head slowly. No, that won't work, she thought, feeling the fleeting hopefulness drain away as quickly as it had appeared. She was going to need Cain's rank insignia, ID badge, video of the body, DNA sample…something. If she was going to get close enough to Stark to kill the bastard, she need to be able to prove she had carried out his orders. If he thought she was still defying him, she'd never get in the same room. Gavin Stark had never taken anyone's word for something important in his life. No, I have to get to Cain myself…and I have to do it before the enemy does.

She crept around the tree, moving steadily west toward her objective. She was hungry and tired, but she had a tremendous inner toughness, and she pushed aside her doubts. She'd seen far worse depravation wandering the slums and badlands as a child. She'd survived those hardships to become one of the most powerful operatives in Alliance Intelligence. After the horrors she'd endured, the repulsive things she'd done to climb from the gutter…she wasn't about to let anything stop her now.

She knew she was getting closer. The bands of retreating troops were getting larger and more frequent. They moved slowly, with leaden footsteps. There was a pall over them, a plodding look she hadn't seen before. She watched from cover as each group passed. My God, she thought, they look beaten. They are losing. Erik Cain's legendary Marines are losing the battle.

That could be a complication. How would she get off of Armstrong if the enemy won? What kind of controls would they establish? Could she blend in with the civilians? Should she? Or would the victorious invaders fall upon the helpless population in an orgy of rape and pillage?

She watched the last group move out of sight to the north and then continued on her way. She'd gone 100 meters, perhaps 150, when she saw. It was a Marine, dead, lying behind one of the large trees ahead. There was a smooth, round hole through his helmet. She almost ignored it, but something didn't seem right, and it caught her attention. She'd seen plenty of wounded passing by, and a few bodies too…Marines who'd obviously died of their wounds on the way back from the front. But this wound had been immediately fatal…there was no questioning that. As far as she'd been able to tell, there had been no fighting back this far. Not yet at least. So who had killed this Marine?

She knelt down and examined the body. There was something about the look of the wound that made her edgy. She reached around, trying to pop open the armor. He was lying on his side. He weighed well over a ton in his suit, and she couldn't budge him at all. After a few minutes she gave up and just stared at the entry hole in his helmet. The look was familiar, characteristic…then realization set in. No other weapon left a mark quite like that one. It wasn't military issue; it was highly specialized, developed in great secrecy and used by only one organization. A weapon she'd fired dozens of times…to assassinate well-protected targets.

She looked all around her, scanning the trees carefully…even more so than she had. She felt a wave of cold sweep through her body. Her situation had just changed. There was another Alliance Intelligence assassin on Armstrong.

Chapter 4

Officer's Wardroom
AS Yorktown
Sandoval System

"As we have discussed, the situation is extremely confused." Camille Harmon's tone was hard as steel. "We've sent coded communiques to Arcadia and Armstrong, but we haven't gotten any responses yet." The frustration was thick in her otherwise emotionless voice. "That means we have to be flexible, prepared...with very little knowledge of what we are facing. You're all going to need to be ready to go on an instant's notice. We can't know what to expect or what we will be called upon to do...and that means your people will be prepared for anything." She turned and stared at the officers seated opposite her, fixing her eyes on each for as long as it took to make them uncomfortable. For most of them, that wasn't very long.

"I don't have to remind you that we appear to be moving directly from one crisis into another." She was standing at the head of the table. Her stare was cold, penetrating. "I know you have all been through a great deal in the war with the First Imperium, but as of now that means exactly nothing. You may feel you have earned joyful celebrations and extended leaves, but what you are getting is another war...one we are ill-prepared to fight." Harmon had always been considered somewhat of a cold fish, but now every ounce of pity, of humanity, was gone. "I remind you all that where material and supplies fail, men and women must plug the gap. We will not falter, nor shrink from any fight. Ill-prepared or not, this fleet will do its duty, if every crew member has to climb out on the hull and throw rocks. Do you all understand me?"

There was a short pause before a ragged reply began. "Yes, Admiral," they responded in a ragged chorus. None of them had ever seen her like this. Cold, robotic, relentless. They all knew she'd lost her son in the last battle with the First Imperium. Max Harmon had been stranded with his boss, Admiral Compton, facing almost certain destruction at the hands of a massive enemy fleet. She'd been forced to man her post, to command her task force as it withdrew along with the rest of the fleet, disrupting the warp gate as it did…stranding Max Compton, and 40,000 naval and Marine personnel.

It was a nightmare scenario for a mother, almost impossible to bear. But they hadn't seen a tear from her, nor the slightest sign of sadness or heartbreak. Only a frigid determination driving her relentlessly onward since that day. She didn't eat or sleep that any of them had noticed, and she expected everyone under her to work almost 24 hours a day like she did.

"Then, if there is nothing else, I want you naval officers back at your stations now. We'll be doing complete diagnostics on all systems. This fleet has been through a lot, but it's going right back into battle, and we're going to be absolutely sure everything is first rate and ready to go." Harmon turned her head and gave a slight nod toward Catherine Gilson. "General Gilson, if you would care to further brief your personnel, the room is yours." The Marine general wasn't subordinate to Harmon, but ground commanders usually ceded the top authority to the senior naval officer when aboard ship. Gilson had been silent through the meeting, respectfully listening to Harmon's comments.

"Thank you Admiral Harmon." Gilson rose, nodding back to her naval counterpart then turning her gaze to Harmon's stunned officers. "You all heard the admiral." Gilson's voice was like the sound of a blade drawing from its sheath. The naval officers jumped to their feet and hurried to the door. Admiral Harmon was hard enough for them to take, but Catherine Gilson had been terrifying Marines with her legendary temper for decades now. The two iron-fisted officers together were too much for the naval personnel to handle, and they scuttled quickly into the corridor, grateful to flee back to their stations and the 24-hour shift that almost certainly awaited them.

"I'll be on the bridge if you need anything, General Gilson." Harmon turned and followed her people into the hallway. Gilson caught a glimpse of the admiral's face as she turned, and she could have sworn there was a tiny hint of amusement there. She hoped so. She knew Harmon couldn't keep going the way she had been forever...not without losing her mind. The two of them had long been friends, and now they shared something else. They were bringing back the remaining units that had been left on station at Sigma-4...and that meant they commanded the last significant uncommitted naval and ground forces the Alliance possessed.

She turned back, facing the rest of the Marine commanders present as she spoke. "We don't know where or when we're going to land, but you can be damned sure we'll be doing it somewhere...and it's probably going to be a fucking disaster." Gilson had a reputation for unfiltered speech, one she had more than earned over years of command. She stared at her officers as she spoke. "I know your people are all tired and strung out from the campaign, but our comrades were just as exhausted when they shipped out...and now they've been in the new fight for months. So that makes us the fresh reserves."

She paused, trying to get a read on morale. She didn't expect them to be straining at the leash for more action, not after all they'd been through. Like many senior officers, she tended to believe Marines could do anything if pushed hard enough. But she also knew the Marine Corps that fought and won the Third Frontier War was almost gone, its elite warriors sacrificed in one brutal fight after another. The grim veterans out there fighting somewhere under Cain and Holm were the last of that victorious stalk. Them...and the 7,000 men and women on her transports.

The faces staring back at her were grim, lifeless. These were some of the most seasoned warriors ever to walk a battlefield, but even Marines had their breaking point. They would fight, she knew that…especially to rally to the aid of their brothers and sisters. But she needed that fire, that indomitable spirit that had led them to victory again and again over the years. And she was afraid that spark was almost extinguished, doused by seas of blood. Training, tradition, élan…they were powerful forces. But in the end, men and women were just that, and the last measure of devotion had to come from within, from the stuff that made them who they were. She needed to find that place in each of her people.

"Look," she said, her voice softening a bit. "We don't know what's waiting out there. We'll be outnumbered, for sure…probably substantially. We're worn out, used up, under-supplied. By every reasonable measure, we have no place going into another battle." She paused, her eyes darting from one officer to another. "No place save one. There are Marines already in the fight. Our brothers and sisters who faced the soldiers of the First Imperium at our sides." She stared at each of her subordinates in turn, starting with Colonel Heath. "They are dying, Rod. You know that, just as I do." Heath struggled to keep his eyes locked on Gilson's, her brutal intensity almost overwhelming.

She turned her head slightly. "Our friends, Jack." Her eyes bored into Colonel Mantooth's. "Our comrades. Erik Cain is in the fight as we speak. And General Holm. And all their Marines. They are in the shit right now…while we sit here and talk and moan about how hard the fight on Sigma was." She looked up at all of them. "Are we finished? Used up? Too beaten down to rally to our brothers and sisters?" Her eyes blazed as she stared at each of them in turn. "Do we abandon them?"

"No!" Mantooth shouted first, followed by the others an instant later. "Never!"

She slammed her hand down on the table with such force everyone jumped. "Then don't just say it. Mean it!" She picked up a 'pad and hurled it at the wall. It exploded into a thousand pieces, shards of shattered plastic landing all over the table. The softer, gentler voice was gone, replaced by a thundering crescendo. "Quit this whining and mooning around. You're fucking Marines, God damn it to hell. Act like it!"

The room was silent, the officers stunned by her outburst. "Are you ready to do your fucking jobs now?" Her glare was unrelenting, boring into each of them as her scowling face panned across the table. Her voice became quieter, but no less cold and menacing. "Are you ready to stop acting like a bunch of pussies and do what has to be done?"

The stunned heads around the table all nodded slowly.

"Did you all forget how to answer a superior officer?" Her tone was caustic. "I repeat...are you ready to do your mother-fucking jobs?"

"Yes, General." The response was crisp and clear this time, in almost perfect unison.

"Good." Gilson's voice was back to its normal, only moderately hostile, tone. "I want all your people ready to go on 48 hours' notice. I mean pre-drop intravenous protocols, full equipment diagnostics. The works." She stood at the head of the table, looking down at them all. "Understood?"

"Yes, General."

"Very well." She crossed her arms behind her back. "You all have a lot of work to do, so I suggest we don't waste any time. Dismissed."

She watched them all snap to attention and file out of the room. Finally, the door swished shut behind them and she flopped down into her chair and sighed. They're still more scared of me than whatever is waiting for us, she thought. But who, she wondered sadly, will keep me going?

"As far as I see it, we have two possible destinations." Admiral Harmon sat behind her desk, a large 'pad laying in front of her. She looked exhausted, her eyes red, her face pale. "Armstrong or Arcadia." Gilson could tell she'd lost weight, a good 3 or 4 kilos, she guessed.

Gilson sighed. "The usual suspects. I could have guessed." She was sitting in one of the guest chairs opposite Harmon. "What about Columbia?"

"I've managed to get our data more or less up to date from the Sandoval Commnet station." Harmon's voice was hoarse.

Gilson could practically feel her comrade's fatigue. "We've been able to confirm that Columbia was hit by 15,000-20,000 powered infantry." She paused. "And no help seems to have reached the planet…certainly no Marines."

Gilson nodded sadly. She knew Columbia had the best of the native armies, but there was no way they'd beaten off that many troops armed and equipped to Marine standards. Not without some help from outside. The planet must have fallen by now.

"General Cain led the expeditionary force to Armstrong," Harmon continued. They've been engaged now for several months. The most recent communique suggests that they've fought the enemy to a stalemate." She glanced down at the 'pad. "That data's about two weeks old now."

"At least they have Commnet access. The enemy must have destroyed the stations when they invaded. Has the system been relieved?"

Harmon shook her head. "Not really. Apparently, Admiral Jacobs escorted a medical team to Armstrong before he joined up with Garret's main fleet. The enemy task force had withdrawn, so Jacobs wiped their satcom and dropped a new one for Cain's people. It seems he also put the system's Commnet back online.

"So, Cain has Armstrong under control?"

Harmon handed her the 'pad. "In a manner of speaking. At least as of two weeks ago." Her voice was somber. "But his losses were off the charts. I don't know if he's got the manpower to win in the end, but it doesn't look like the enemy has the strength to destroy him either."

Gilson's eyes widened when she focused on the casualty figures. Cain's army managed to hold out, but it had just about destroyed itself in the process. She was about to look back at Harmon when something caught her eye. "General McDaniels was killed." She pursed her lips sadly, looking down at Harmon's desk for a few seconds.

"Yes, I saw that. I wasn't sure if I should tell you."

"We'd have never won…survived…the First Imperium War

without her. What she did with those Obliterator suits was nothing short of amazing." She sat quietly, dry-eyed but somber. Gilson was an expert at holding back tears, the inevitable result of a lifetime spend mourning dead friends. Her thoughts drifted, memories of McDaniels floating through her mind. The two had become close during the war. She wasn't the first friend Gilson had lost…and it didn't seem likely she'd be the last. But they all hurt.

"Cate…" Harmon spoke softly, her voice soothing. "I'm sorry. I know she was your friend."

Gilson's eyes caught Harmon's, and suddenly she got a grip on herself. She felt a flash of shame for allowing Harmon to comfort her. Camille Harmon was the last person in the fleet she should be burdening with her own grief. "Thank you, Camille." She sucked in a deep breath and pulled her thoughts back to the matters at hand. "I'm OK. Let's get back to work."

"You sure?"

"Yes." Gilson's voice was firm again. "Definitely." She glanced back down at the 'pad. "So, Cain's in a precarious position, but he's holding at the moment."

"That's how I read it." Harmon nodded. "Look, Cate, it doesn't look like we're going right into a fleet action, so this is going to be your call. I'm prepared to defer to your judgment on where to assault."

"But you think we should go to Arcadia, don't you?" Gilson was paging through the stats on the 'pad.

"Yes."

"Well, Cain's certainly got a bigger army…though it looks like he's facing stronger enemy forces too." Her eyes scanned the glowing surface of the 'pad. "But I'm inclined to agree with you. General Holm is on Arcadia with Jim Teller's force and a bunch of vets from the Second Frontier War." My God, she thought, how did we get so desperate? The Commandant of the Corps leading a bunch of 80-something retirees into battle? How did it come to this?

"So we're agreed? We set course for Arcadia?"

Gilson paused. "Yes, we agree." She took a long, deep

breath. "And the sooner we get there, the better."

Harmon nodded and activated her com. "Commander Ronson…" – her voice was firm and commanding, no trace of the warmth she'd shown Gilson – "…plot a course for Wolf 359, and advise the fleet we'll be embarking in two hours." That was a very tight schedule, but she suspected they didn't have time to waste if they were going to save Holm and his people. "And make sure everything is strapped down. We're going to be spending a lot of time in the couches."

That won't be popular, she thought. But the one thing she was absolutely sure of was she didn't give a damn.

Chapter 5

MCS John Carter
Mars Orbit
Sol System

Roderick Vance sat in the large conference room just off John Carter's bridge. He was exhausted, his face drawn and pale. His arms were extended out in front of him, resting on the silvery metal table. Things on Earth were rapidly spiraling out of control, despite his around the clock efforts to prevent all-out war. He'd been optimistic at first, confident he could act as an intermediary between the Powers, resolving their disputes or at least keeping things from going over the brink. But that was before Gavin Stark destroyed the Alliance Intelligence building and framed the CAC for the deed, throwing fuel on a barely-controlled fire. Vance had managed to mediate and prevent immediate declarations of war, but just barely.

The increased tension made it essential for the CAC to lay low…and that wrecked the plan for Li An to destroy Gavin Stark's clone production facility in South Dakota. Another attack blamed on the CAC would almost certainly lead to open war, regardless of Vance's best diplomatic efforts. Grudgingly, he agreed to do the deed with Confederation forces. He knew it would gut his ability to mediate as a neutral power, but leaving Stark's main base intact was unthinkable. Given time, the Alliance Intelligence mastermind would move the production facilities…and the million trained clone-soldiers already there, ready for action. Vance simply couldn't allow that. As bad as the situation was between the Powers, in the final calculus, Gavin Stark was the biggest threat. Vance was sure of that.

Now John Carter had returned, and the diplomatic communiques were ripping back and forth. Vance's ambassadors had managed to forestall the Alliance from declaring war against the Confederation immediately. He flooded Alliance Gov with evidence about Gavin Stark's plot…and the impending economic catastrophe about to result from it. It would take time to assimilate and grasp the true meaning of the documents he provided – and Alliance Gov would be slow to trust his data – but Vance was sure the authorities in Washbalt would eventually comprehend and accept what he had done. Once they calmly reviewed and understood the depth of Stark's activities they would accept what the Martians had done and acknowledge that there was no hostile intent toward the Alliance. But calm consideration was in very short supply now, and Vance had no idea how long reasoned analysis would take. The Alliance had been the subject of two nuclear attacks in less than three weeks. The century-old peace on Earth had been shattered, and they had been the targets of both incidents. Thousands of Alliance citizens were dead, and hundreds of thousands had been affected by the massive fallout clouds from the Dakota blasts. Vance wondered if anyone in their position would be more receptive to explanations. He wondered if he would.

Vance suspected the hesitancy to declare war on Mars had as much to do with the Confederation's current naval superiority in the solar system as it did with any real patience or forbearance. The facts were stark…the Alliance had no way of projecting force to Mars, not without recalling the fleet. The Confederation had no possessions on Earth, nothing substantive the Alliance could reach without naval power. The Alliance could declare war, but that's about all they could do. Wiser heads had prevailed, even if driven only by weakness, but Vance didn't know how long that would last.

He'd have preferred a real diplomatic connection instead of just the fruits of temporary tactical superiority, but he was willing to take what he could get for now. He was playing for time…if he could keep things from going entirely to hell, the

Alliance leaders would realize what had truly happened. Maybe, just maybe, things would cool off then.

The door slid open and interrupted Vance's meditation. Duncan Campbell walked through holding a 'pad in his hand. He didn't look happy.

"More bad news?" Vance looked up, forcing back a sigh as he saw Campbell's expression.

"You could say that." John Carter's captain stopped at the head of the table and stared at Vance. "We just got a communique from Earth, sir. The Washbalt Stock Exchange is down 73%." He seemed stunned at the news, a testament to how well Vance's people – and Li An's – had kept their dark secret. Campbell hadn't been a party to any discussions of the impending collapse, so his surprise was total. "I should say it was down 73% when this was sent. That was barely 30 minutes after the markets opened for trading, and things were still dropping." Campbell stared at Vance, a confused expression on his face. He'd expected the spymaster to be shocked, but Vance had hardly reacted to the news.

When it rains, it pours, Vance thought grimly. He'd been anticipating this for months now, but it couldn't have happened at a worse time. And it wasn't going to stop in Washbalt. "I suspect we'll be getting similar reports from the other Earth markets, Captain." He paused, tapping at the 'pad in front of him, pulling up the pre-market indicators from Ares City. Down over 50% and still falling. He'd been waiting for an economic apocalypse for a long time. It had finally arrived.

"President Oliver, I have all my people working on this, but we just don't have any answers. Not yet." Ryan Warren was trying to maintain his composure, but the president of the Alliance had been firing angry questions at him all morning. Warren had been the head of Alliance Intelligence for all of 13 days, and he'd inherited an organization that had lost half its people, all its leadership, and its main data archives. He was scrambling, trying to discover what was going on while he continued the investigations into the CAC and Martian attacks against the Alliance. He'd slept six hours, maybe seven total since he'd been sworn in as the new Number One. He didn't know how long a human being could get by on stims alone, but he suspected he was going to find out in the days to come.

"Mr. Warren, I appreciate that you have just stepped into your position, and under difficult circumstances, but I want to be sure you understand the enormous gravity of what is happening." Oliver hadn't gotten much sleep in recent nights either, and it showed in his raspy voice and bloodshot eyes.

Warren almost rolled his own eyes, but he caught himself. Shut up, he thought…just listen. Francis Oliver was a vindictive and petty man to begin with, and now he was scared to death. Tread carefully…very carefully. Gavin Stark had been deeply entrenched, his position almost certainly protected by secret files and intelligence reports on everyone of significance in the government. Warren had been thrust up a dizzying number of echelons through the bureaucracy…20 years of advancement in a day. Having your 25 most direct superiors killed in a single instant was an unmatched example of career development, but it tended to leave one scrambling to catch up with things. Warren lacked the store of blackmail he would have procured over decades of normal advancement. He was Number One, but he unprepared and poorly equipped. He commanded a wounded animal, and his grasp on the Chair was tenuous at best. He'd have to take however much shit Francis Oliver sent downhill toward him. At least for now.

"The economy is completely unraveling. For no apparent reason. All financial markets are at a standstill. There are no buyers for any asset classes. The effective market value of all financial instruments is zero." Oliver's voice was loud, but shaky and hoarse. He had no idea what was going on or what to do about it, that much was clear to Warren. The Alliance's president was a bully at heart, and he didn't function well when he felt out of control. "Do you understand the implications of this? We have no idea what is causing the crisis. None at all! I need to know what is going on, and I need to know now!"

"Yes, Mr. President." Warren wasn't sure how many ways

he could say the same thing. His people had no idea what was causing the economic crisis. The more time he could spend working on the problem instead of sitting there as the president's punching bag, the sooner he would be able to uncover some real information. But he reminded himself again he had to tread carefully. Oliver was extremely dangerous in his current unpredictable state of mind. Gavin Stark had easily handled the president, but Warren didn't presume that he was a match for his old boss. He was still struggling to consolidate control and keep the agency operating…and Francis Oliver had buried his own share of bodies in almost 30 years of uninterrupted rule. "With your permission, sir, I will get back to headquarters and put together an updated report for you."

Headquarters…that's a joke, Warren thought. Alliance Intelligence's HQ was a radioactive pit, and he had people scattered all over the government zone, occupying surplus offices and hotel suites. Most of the agency's top experts were dead, their ashes lying in the wreckage of their obliterated building. Warren had been forced to round up replacements from stations all over the world. He'd managed to build a respectable second string in Washbalt but at the cost of gutting efficiency elsewhere. It would be years before Alliance Intelligence matched its former capabilities. It was hardly an ideal situation for an agency accustomed to being the best in the world and working from a highly secure, fortress-like building.

"Yes, I want you to stay on top of your people." Oliver's chair creaked slightly as he leaned back and took a deep breath. "I must have information as soon as possible, Mr. Warren." He stared at the spy with a withering intensity. "I'll expect you at 6pm with an update."

"Yes sir." Warren turned and walked through the door into the outer office. What an ass, he thought…what miracle does he expect me to come up with in five hours?

"Sir, we have received a Code 3 transmission for you. It is in your private encryption and marked extremely urgent." Campbell's voice was loud in Vance's earpiece. He reached up and tapped the comlink, lowering the volume slightly.

"Send it to me here, Captain." What now, he thought, leaning back and rolling his aching neck around on his shoulders… what else could go wrong?

"Yes, sir. At your station."

Vance slid his hand into his pocket and retrieved a small data crystal, slipping it into the port on the table next to the embedded 'pad. It contained the decryption codes for his own data protection protocol. The screen danced around wildly for a few seconds as the algorithm worked on the message, turning it from an impossible jumble into concise, readable text. When it had finished, a short note appeared on the otherwise black screen.

Mr. Vance:

As a result of our continuing efforts to review raw intelligence files forwarded to us by CAC C1, we have discovered the following.

Alliance Intelligence Number One, Gavin Stark had several interactions with Number Three, Alexandra Linden approximately two months ago. Until we discovered this surveillance report, Ms. Linden's whereabouts had been unknown for several years, and we considered her to be missing in action.

After a complete review of all available intelligence data, we feel reasonably confident that Gavin Stark sent Ms. Linden back to the planet Armstrong with orders to assassinate Alliance General Erik Cain.

We cannot be certain about this analysis. There is a large period of time prior to these interactions for which Ms. Linden's whereabouts and activities are still unknown. However, we have assigned the highest confidence level to our conclusion. It is extremely likely that General Cain is currently the target of an Alliance Intelligence assassination warrant.

I have taken no action and await your instructions on this matter.

                    - Simonsen, Lance, Deputy Director Martian
Intelligence

Vance felt his blood run cold as he read the communique. By the time he reached the end, he had no doubts. The analysis was correct. He knew he had to do something. Things were going very badly out in the colonies. Stark's Shadow Legion troops had already sewn up most of the important Alliance colony worlds. The Marines were heavily outnumbered everywhere, unable even to deploy forces to most of the occupied planets.

Vance had planned to dispatch Confederation troops to support the Alliance forces, but the crisis on Earth made that problematic. If Alliance Gov thought the Confederation was moving against its colonies, no amount of diplomacy would prevent all-out war. He reluctantly put a hold on sending the troops.

Vance sighed hard. He had to do something. The loss of Erik Cain on top of everything else would be devastating. Cain was almost certainly the greatest ground tactician in human space. He was irreplaceable...and his brilliance was crucial if Gavin Stark's plans were to be defeated. If Stark managed to take out Cain, he'd be halfway to victory with nothing but an assassin's bullet.

He had to get a warning to the Alliance general. His hands curled up into fists, and he slammed them down on the table in frustration. He was already late. Maybe too late.

He hit the comlink. "Captain Campbell, I need you in here immediately."

The door slid open almost at once, and Campbell came stomping in. "Yes sir," he rattled off as he hurtled through the door.

"We need to get a message to Armstrong right away."

Campbell paused for a few seconds, thinking. "We don't have access to the Alliance's Commnet system, sir. They locked us out after the Dakota attack."

"It'd be too unreliable anyway. We don't even know if the station in Armstrong's system is still functioning." Vance rose slowly. "But we've got a Torch in the landing bay, and it can reach Armstrong in less than a week with a good pilot pushing it to the limit." He looked up at John Carter's skipper.

Campbell didn't say anything, but a doubtful expression crossed his face. He had a feeling he knew what Vance was going to ask…and there was no way Campbell could refuse. But a week was almost impossibly fast for a trip to Armstrong.

"Yes, I know it's a tight timetable." Vance seemed to anticipate Campbell's concern. "But this is urgent. Which is why I need to send the best pilot I've got." Vance was staring right into Campbell's eyes.

John Carter's captain looked back, final realization kicking in. "You want me to go, sir?"

"I know this seems like a job below your pay grade, Duncan." The tension in Vance's voice told Campbell that wasn't the case. Whatever it was, if it had Roderick Vance this edgy, it was probably downright critical. "But this is extremely important. I'd go myself if I could get away from the crisis here. But then I'm not half the pilot you are."

"Of course, Mr. Vance. I'll do whatever you need me to do." Campbell didn't like the idea of leaving his command in time of crisis to play messenger, but if Roderick Vance said it was important, it was a good bet it was a six-alarm emergency. "I'll leave immediately, sir. What do you want me to do?"

"You need to get to Armstrong and find General Erik Cain." Vance spoke grimly, uncharacteristic fear creeping into his voice. "No matter what it takes, Duncan." He stood up behind his desk. "And you need to tell him that Gavin Stark has sent one of his very best assassins to kill him." He paused, eyes fixed on Campbell's. "Her name is Alexandra Linden."

Chapter 6

Base Omega
Asteroid Belt
Altair System

Gavin Stark was livid, his anger almost beyond the considerable capacity of his own iron will to control. Fucking Roderick Vance, he thought, his clenched fist slamming down on the table. It was bad enough the interfering Martian spy had identified the hidden base in the Dakotas, but the son of a bitch had actually launched a massive nuclear attack from orbit and completely destroyed it.

Stark had always known Vance was a capable and dangerous enemy, but he'd still allowed himself to be surprised by the Martian's audacity. He'd always considered Vance to be a genius, but he'd never imagined the Martian spy had balls enough to pull something like this. He was angry at his own failure to consider just how far Vance was prepared go, and he resolved never to underestimate one of his enemies again.

Stark had known he had a limited amount of time before the Alliance moved forces into the Dakotas to investigate. Vance had undoubtedly provided Alliance Gov with the intel his commandoes had collected during their raid. But Stark had given the inbred hacks who ran the Alliance other things to think about... including a nuclear detonation right in the center of the capital.

He had counted on the bombing of Alliance Intelligence HQ to scare the shit out of the politicians...and buy him time to relocate the most vital resources from Facility Q before they sent their forces in and shut it all down. He knew the Alli-

ance bureaucrats, and he'd been sure they would be more worried about bombs taking out their own buildings than seriously
addressing alarmist rants from the Confederation's top spy. He
realized that wouldn't give him unlimited time. He knew he
wouldn't get all his clones out of there, but he'd figured on getting some…and the most vital production equipment as well.
Now it was a total loss. He had battle-ready forces deployed in
half a dozen remote bases hidden around the globe, but Facility
Q was the heart of the Earthside operation. He'd be able to put
at most 200,000 troops in the field now, an 80% reduction in his
projected combat strength.

He'd have to modify the plan. He'd originally intended to
instigate war between the Powers on Earth, and release his million fully-armored clones at the right moment…defeating the
battered land armies and seizing control of each Superpower in
turn. He'd imagined it would be a damaged Earth he would rule
over, but he'd hoped to preserve at least some of the existing
infrastructure and productive capacity. But now he would have
to make certain the Superpowers fought their war to the end,
that their cities were pounded into radioactive dust, their armies
locked in a death struggle until they'd savaged each other into
oblivion. It would mean hundreds of millions more dead and
the nearly total destruction of Earth's civilization, but it was the
only way he could be sure his reduced forces could take total
control. And he wasn't about to let anything interfere with his
victory. He would have total power, no matter what it took. If
he ruled a devastated, depopulated, irradiated world, so be it.
Contamination could be cleaned up, rubble cleared away. Cities
could be rebuilt and populations could be bred back to desired
levels. And it would all be done under the watchful eyes of his
clone soldiers.

Indeed, though it would take longer and involve enormous
work, there might be advantages to a fresh start of sorts. Old
cities, the products of centuries of disorganized growth would
be replaced by new metropolises, designed from the ground
up…perfect models of modern urban magnificence. People,
too, would get a fresh start of sorts. A controlled eugenics pro-

gram might produce a more useful race of subjects than the current mix of genetically inferior Cogs, gutless middle class drones, and inbred political-class cronies. He would steward the creation of a super-race, smarter, more purposeful…and conditioned from birth for total obedience to the state. And the state would be Gavin Stark.

It might take the rest of Stark's natural life to see the rebuilding come to fruition, but what a monument to leave behind. And he would leave it to his own dynasty. Not the chaotic uncertainty of a series of conventional children and grandchildren. Nothing so random and variable. When all the resources and technology of mankind could no longer keep Stark's body alive he would bequeath his power to himself…to the Gavin Stark clone whose rule would follow his.

From the dawn of history man has raged against his own mortality. Great kings erected statues and built gargantuan mausoleums in misguided bids for eternal life. Others left behind historical and scientific achievements that insured their names would live on long after their bodies turned to dust. But Gavin Stark would achieve something orders of magnitude beyond what any historical conquerors or kings had imagined. Mankind would be ruled for eternity by a Stark clone. He would achieve true immortality…or the closest thing possible. In a thousand years…and in ten thousand…men would submit on bended knee to Gavin Stark. He would become like a god ruling over a galaxy of supplicants.

He pulled himself back from his rambling thoughts. His normally rigid discipline had been failing him at times, and he had become prone to fits of anger and moments of wild imaginings. But now he forced himself to concentrate, to regain his focus. Humanity ruled by generation after generation of Stark clones was an appealing image, but first he had to succeed in his bid for power. He had to win this war.

He sat quietly for a few minutes, honing his thoughts, working himself back into that cold emotionless state that had always made him such a successful operator. He'd have to readjust the plan for his intervention on Earth; that much was clear. He had time for that. His other bases seemed to be secure, and his people would maintain security protocols and wait for his word to move. But he had to speed up the timetable on Earth. He'd hoped to secure the Alliance colonies and finish off Garret's fleet and the Marines before pushing the homeworld over the brink, but now he didn't have the luxury of waiting. He needed war on Earth, and he needed it now.

Gavin Stark was a compulsive planner. His schemes had multiple layers and backups…just waiting for the moment they were needed. Like now. A tiny smile crept onto his lips. He might just be able to kill two birds with one stone…and give Roderick Vance a few distractions while he was at it.

He nodded his head slowly as he reached out for the com controls and pressed a button. "Anderson-2…" – he'd kept the command clone as his direct aide – "…please prepare a Commnet transmission to Earth." He took a deep breath. The more he thought about it, the more he was confident it was the right move. "I am activating Operation C6."

Gaston Lucerne stood on the quay, looking out at the turbulent waters of the Mediterranean. There was a storm rolling in, and the ships of Marseilles' fishing fleet were hurrying back to port. The city had long drawn its economic strength from the sea, though for the last hundred years or more, it was the offshore algae fields and not the fishing boats that were the real engines of its economy. The middle class, and the worker classes – la Salete, as they were commonly called by the Classes Politiques, subsisted on manufactured foods, mostly created from pollution-resistant algae grown in the vast offshore farms. The Marseilles algae fields were the most productive in Europe, and the city exported the processed food precursor to finishing plants throughout Europa Federalis.

The fleet plied a different trade, scouring the played out seas and searching through their meager catches, discarding most of the fish, the ones contaminated by the runaway pollution and mutated by the radioactives that had settled into the water. They searched diligently, looking for the few pure specimens that remained.

Most prized were the Red Scorpionfish and the Sea Robin, prime ingredients in the ancient regional dish called Bouillabaisse. Originally a meal made by peasant fisherman, it was now a priceless delicacy, eaten only by the most privileged classes of politicians and corporate managers. The uncontaminated fresh seafood required to make a large batch cost enough to feed a Salete family for months.

The fishermen plying the waters around Marseilles, scavenging for the remnants of a once rich bounty, lived a life different from most of the Saletes in Europa Federalis. Instead of a boring life of sustenance wages, theirs was a wild ride…bounty when their fortunes were good, and deprivation and misery when they weren't.

Lucerne had been born into a family of fishermen, but he'd found a way to escape a life of hardship and poverty. As far as the Saletes of the Marseilles docks knew, he'd traveled throughout Europa Federalis as a seafood buyer, searching for rare catches to serve an elite market. But he had another job too, a considerably more lucrative one…working for Gavin Stark's Alliance Intelligence. Lucerne found he had a talent for espionage, and no cumbersome loyalties to the Europan government to get in his way. He rose quickly to become one of Stark's top agents in Europa Federalis…and ultimately one of the few operatives the Alliance spymaster recruited into his Shadow program.

He walked slowly past the wharves, making his way to his ship. He'd returned to his old home with the cover that he'd lost his job and come back to eke out a living from the sea. He'd been on station for months, the steward of a single operation, going through the motions as a fisherman and waiting for the word from Stark to act.

Finally, that word came. He'd gotten his orders…and confirmed the authorization codes. Operation C6 was a go. He'd had the equipment in place for months, just waiting for him to enter the final arming codes. Now, Lucerne had done the deed. All he had to do was get back to his boat and get out of Marseilles…while there still was a Marseilles.

He walked past the bulk of one of the larger vessels, and Mouette came into view. She was a wreck, or at least she looked that way to the casual observer. Just the kind of ship a destitute fisherman might lease. There was more to her than met the eye, though…high-powered motors, AI-controlled nav system, and enough hidden firepower to sink the rest of Marseilles' fishing fleet.

He climbed aboard, placing his palm on the reader and opening the hatch. He started the engines, and eased the ship back, turning slowly, angling the bow toward the exit channel. The ship sputtered and poured out thick, black smoke…the AI operating the super-powered engines carefully maintaining the illusion of a barely functional wreck. He got one or two odd stares from passersby on the docks. The ships were coming into port now, not leaving. But it didn't matter. They'd all be dead soon anyway.

He cruised slowly out to sea, watching the city disappear over the horizon. He continued for nearly an hour, traveling a fraction of the vessel's potential speed, maintaining the illusion. Anyone watching would assume he was crazy enough to head out into a brewing storm, but they'd never imagine his ship was state of the art, with AI-controlled navigation and enough power to get through any weather. Finally, he stopped the engines and let the boat drift to a stop. He was 40 kilometers offshore, far enough to escape the effects of the hell he was about to unleash.

He flipped a lever, and part of the control panel slipped away, revealing a small workstation. He punched in a code and placed his hand on the palm scanner. He looked out through the small porthole, seeing nothing but open sea, but imagining his bustling hometown. It was late afternoon. The boats would be mostly in by now, fleeing the rough seas and heavy winds of the brewing storm. Children would be scurrying around the wharves, running to greet returning fathers and grandfathers.

He'd expected a wave of regret for what he was about to do, but it didn't come, at least not a strong one. Thirty years of service with Alliance Intelligence had dulled his emotions, especially the useless ones like guilt and remorse. He was already a traitor to Europa Federalis, and 3 decades of working in Gavin Stark's Alliance Intelligence had fundamentally changed his way of thinking. The citizens of Marseilles, the pathetic Saletes infesting the waterfront…they would all die in a few seconds, their miserable existences erased with a blast of nuclear fire. Lucerne realized he didn't care…whatever loyalties he may have had to childhood friends were gone, replaced by the coldly mercenary self-interest Stark instilled in all his people.

He glanced at the chronometer then turned and looked away. A few seconds later, the sky lightened. He knew the Marseilles waterfront was an incarnation of hell itself, the temperatures at ground zero reaching millions of degrees in a fraction of a second. The destruction would go on…firestorms raging for hours and radiation contaminating the entire area for years. But most of the city's people were already dead, those who lived along the waterfront near ground zero simply vaporized, others burned to death or crushed by debris.

He smiled, congratulating himself on a job well done as he watched the huge cloud rise up over the horizon. Marseilles was gone, wiped from the map by 20 megatons of nuclear fury. When the Europan authorities investigated they would find clues…hints Lucerne himself had placed there. That data would point to the Central European League, and almost certainly lead to full scale war between the two bitter enemies. The Treaty of Paris would be shattered, and the European continent would be engulfed by total war.

But there would be other evidence too, indications Gavin Stark had ordered him to add at the last minute. And those clues would suggest Martian involvement as well. He tried to imagine the fallout, especially after the Confederation's nuclear attack on the Alliance. Their pleas of innocence would fall on deaf ears, and everyone would believe they had now attacked two Superpowers. Europa Federalis would probably declare war…and the other Powers would begin to fear and distrust the Martians.

He glanced at the chronometer. The shockwave would take another minute to reach his location. It would shake his little boat roughly, but the AI was well equipped to handle navigating through it.

Stark had planned the operation brilliantly. It would serve his purposes perfectly and hasten the war on Earth that was so crucial to his plans. Lucerne's smile widened as he thought about Stark. He was always impressed by his master's thoroughness, how he considered his actions from every angle. He reached down and hit the controls, plotting a course for Barcelona. He'd lay low in the safe house there for a few weeks. Then Stark would send him further instructions…and get him out of the impending war zone he'd helped to create. Then he would enjoy the rewards of his actions. He would have a high place in Stark's new regime, and he would sit close to the center of power.

He punched the designated coordinates into the nav computer. He was still hitting keys when the AI executed one of its secret files, and the ship's entire fuel supply detonated, leaving nothing larger than fist-sized bits of debris.

Gavin Stark did not leave loose ends.

Chapter 7

North of the Sentinel
Planet Armstrong
Gamma Pavonis III

Cain's HQ was as makeshift a facility as he'd ever seen, just a few small portable shelters and half a dozen workstations. The army had been falling back continually, setting up one hasty defense after another. The desperate stands had cost heavily, but they'd given Eliot Storm's troopers a chance to slip out of the enemy's trap and pull back from the river line all the way through the Sentinel. Storm's people had linked up with Cooper Brown's wing along the northern edge of the great forest, ready to continue the withdrawal. All except the Obliterators. They had remained behind, ready to execute Erik Cain's daring plan.

Cain flipped on his com. "Colonel Clarkson, you may commence your operation whenever you are ready." The words came slowly, sticking in his throat as he forced them out. Clarkson's attack was the right tactical move...Cain was sure of that. The enemy was inexperienced with the giant Obliterators, uncertain how to counter their attacks. Clarkson's people had a good chance of disordering the enemy force and stalling their advance. And if they could do that, the rest of Cain's retreating Marines would have time to march farther south and set up a strong defense. But it was also a suicide mission, and Cain knew he'd be stunned if any of the colonel's people survived.

"Yes sir." Clarkson's voice was sharp, crisp, his enthusiasm cutting through Cain like a knife. "We're moving out now."

The veteran colonel knew what his people were about to do;

he understood the odds. But he also knew there was no other choice. The Marines on Armstrong were hopelessly outnumbered…low on supplies and near defeat. His Obliterators might just buy the time they needed to pull back and set up a last ditch defense north of the capital. It probably wouldn't make any difference in the end, but there wasn't anything a doomed force could do except play for time.

Cain sighed. Sending people to their deaths…it was something he'd done before, far too many times. It never got easier. Clarkson and his people would join the legions of lost Marines Cain knew waited for him. They used to haunt his sleep, their cold dead faces staring back at him in the dark of night, but somewhere along the way he'd made a peace of sorts with them. Most of them, at least. He knew he would join them one day, that one of his many battlefields would be his last. Cain was a cold-blooded butcher, but when he sent his Marines into the meatgrinder he shared the danger with them. They'd seen him in the front lines time and time again, assault rifle in hand, fighting alongside the rank and file. When he ordered them forward into the fires of hell, they knew, all of them, that Erik Cain had been there himself…and would be again. He was reckless for a general, too ready to charge into the thick of the fighting. Earlier in his career he'd been repeatedly ordered to take fewer chances…commands he'd unilaterally ignored. His loss would be a disaster for the Corps, and a crushing blow to the morale of his Marines, but none of that mattered. Cain did what he had to do. He knew it was the only way he could live with himself.

"Good luck, Colonel." Cain's voice was somber, grim. He flipped off the com, closing his watery eyes tightly for a few seconds, indulging his grief. Then he forced Clarkson's people out of his mind and turned back toward the retreating columns moving past him on their way north.

"Cooper, let's speed things up here." He was staring at the retreating Marines as he commed Brown. He could see they were beaten. They walked past him slowly, hunched over, dragging their feet through the muddy grasslands. Their armor was black and pitted, showing the signs of weeks of hard fighting.

He'd been in dozens of desperate battles, but this was the first time he looked out over his men and women and realized they were broken. He couldn't fault them. They didn't lack for courage or dedication. But they'd gone right from the brutality of the war against the First Imperium into the hopeless battle for Armstrong. There was a limit to what men and women could endure, even Marines. And Cain knew his people had reached it.

"Yes sir." Cooper Brown was exhausted too, but there was something keeping him going, helping him deal with the desperation and defeat hanging thick in the air. Brown had fought one of the first battles against the First Imperium. He'd been a retired Marine living on the planet Adelaide when the robotic legions invaded. He led the planetary militia through one of the worst holocausts imaginable. His soldiers – and the surviving citizens – were trapped for months in underground shelters, short on supplies and facing terrible deprivation. He'd been forced to impose strict discipline and rationing on the miserable, suffering civilians, driving them almost to starvation.

Intellectually, he knew he'd saved their lives, but he found it impossible to deal with the hatred they directed at him. He knew it was driven by the suffering they had endured…by the grief and despair over those they'd lost. But it tore at his insides, and came close to costing him his sanity. Adelaide had been his adopted home, and he'd given all he had to pull its people through the horror of the invasion. And now he was the most hated man in the colony's history.

Part of Cooper Brown died in those tunnels. He left Adelaide forever and returned to the Corps, fighting alongside Cain ever since. He found a new purpose, and he was grateful he'd been allowed to serve again with his brothers and sisters. The Corps was the only real home he had, one he wished he'd never left. But he had. Adelaide was part of his life too, and he'd carry the psychic wounds he'd taken there until the day he died. He had originally excused the way the civilians there treated him, but as time passed, he became angry and resentful too. Some days he was proud of the work the Marines did defending the civilians of the Alliance. Others, he was bitter, wondering if they were worth the sacrifices his brethren made every time they went into battle. He found a kindred spirit in Erik Cain, another Marine who gave everything he had to defend a humanity he didn't really believe in. Cain knew there were some people worth saving, but not most of them. Still, when the bugle called, he was there, rifle in hand.

Whatever his feelings and motivations, however, Brown had served well as a returned Marine and contributed his share to the constant fighting. But he felt like he was living on borrowed time. He'd been ready to meet his death since the day he walked out of the shelter and into the light of Adelaide's sun. It hadn't caught up to him yet, but he knew one day it would.

Cain took a deep breath. "Cooper, I need your help." His voice sounded weak, uncertain. Cain was near the end of his endurance. More than anything he wanted to take his rifle in hand and march south toward the enemy. Dying in action would be quick and merciful…a fate vastly preferable to watching the last of his beloved Marines broken and killed.

"I'm with you, Erik." Brown could see Cain's agony. He understood it in a way few others could. "Whatever you need me to do."

"I want you to go north and start setting up a defensive line." Cain's voice was dead, monotone. "They've had it…" – he gestured toward the column of battered Marines marching north – "…and I don't want them to die running." His tone changed, still grim, but with some of his old fire returning. "If this is the end of the Corps, then we're going to make it a fitting one. We're going to make a last stand to be proud of." He turned and stared into Brown's eyes. "You understand?"

Brown nodded. "Yes, General." In that instant he understood the raw determination that drove Erik Cain. He knew Cain had lost all hope of winning the fight on Armstrong. But he still wouldn't give up, not while there was still a breath in his body or blood pumping through his arteries. Brown felt his face tighten, and his hands balled into fists. Erik Cain would never give up…and neither would Cooper Brown. "I understand, sir."

"These three are critical cases. They need to stay in their life support units. We have to find room for them on one of the transports." Sarah Linden stood in the muddy clearing, her head snapping around from one direction to the other. Her hair was tied back in a tight ponytail, but a few dozen hairs had worked their way free, and they blew wildly in the breeze. Her eyes were red and bloodshot, the result of fatigue and way too many stims, and her light blue overalls were covered with dried blood.

Supervising the bug out of the field hospital was enough of a job, but she was in charge of the civilian withdrawal as well. Erik had ordered everyone to evacuate and move north, and he'd put her in overall command of the operation. The Marines were falling back, planning a last ditch defense just north of Astria. That meant giving up the capital, but there wasn't a choice. There was no defensible terrain between the Sentinel and Astria.

"Yes, Colonel." Sergeant Carlyle stood rigidly, his voice firm and confident. "I've got another 5 light transports on the way. They should be here in…" – he glanced at his chronometer – "five minutes. We should be able to get those wounded on them…and another 20 of our staff as well."

"Excellent, Sergeant." Sarah was impressed. She couldn't even imagine where the resourceful non-com had found another 5 trucks, but she was grateful he had. Carlyle had been a workhorse, performing wonders arranging transport for the wounded and her staff alike. He was tireless, and he drove the small force under him mercilessly. He reminded her in many ways of a young Erik Cain. He had the same coldblooded determination, the single-minded obsession with getting the job done…and the same ability to inspire those he was pushing to the limits of their endurance. He wasn't a Marine…not yet at least. But Sarah promised herself if they made it through this battle she'd see him admitted to the Corps and sent to the Academy. Ian Carlyle was just the kind of warrior the Marines needed to fill the depleted officer ranks. If the Corps was going to survive, she thought, they'd have to find a lot of Carlyles.

"What else do you need done, Sarah?"

She spun around, glaring at the hunched-over figure standing before her. "What the hell are you doing out of bed, Isaac?" General Isaac Merrick had led a forlorn hope against the newly-landed enemy forces, buying time for Brown's people to form a defensive line. He was wounded badly in the fighting, but his survivors dragged him back and Sarah patched him up. "I told you to stay in bed, didn't I?" She shook her head. "You're just as bad as Erik," she added, fighting to keep a smile off her face.

Merrick stood in front of her, leaning on a pair of crutches, obviously in considerable pain. "I'm fine, Sarah. At least I can stop being totally useless and help with the withdrawal." He still faced a significant recovery time, but he knew Cain needed every man. He might not be able to take his place in the battle lines yet, but he'd be damned if he was going to lay around in a hospital bed while Marines were fighting for their lives.

She sighed. The doctor in her wanted to send him back to his bed, even if it took half a dozen guards to get him there. But the Sarah Linden who had spent most of her adult life as Erik Cain's companion knew when to compromise. Some brick walls were just too thick to break through.

"OK, Isaac, but only what I tell you to do." She looked right at Merrick, the intensity of her stare leaving no room for discussion. "Because if you tear open those wounds, I swear to God, you can patch them up yourself next time."

He forced a smile. "Got it, Sarah." He tried to straighten up, wincing as he did. "You're the boss."

She grinned, not believing his humble acquiescence for a second. "But first, go see Samitch. She'll give you an extra dose for the pain."

He shook his head. "I'm OK. It's not too bad." Merrick knew they were running low on medical supplies. "Save it. We both know there'll be more wounded before this is done."

She nodded. "OK, tough guy. But promise me if it gets too bad you'll take something."

"Who could say no to you?" He grinned. "If Erik hadn't gotten to you first…"

She smiled. "That'll be enough out of you, General Merrick."

"Very well, Doctor Colonel Sarah. Now, how can I help?"

"Actually, there is something you can do." She paused. "I think I've made a few breakthroughs with our prisoner." Sarah had been working on breaking down Anderson-45's conditioning. She knew the Marines' sole prisoner was the key to understanding their clone enemies. Progress had been slow, but she felt she was starting to get somewhere. "You can keep an eye on our prisoner. Talk to him…about anything. I think the more interactions he has, the easier it will be to get through his conditioning."

Merrick smiled again, amused at Sarah's cleverness. She'd managed to come up with a task requiring no physical activity at all, but one that was too important for him to refuse. "Of course, Sarah." He winked at her. "And congrats, Doc. I doubt I'll work up much of a sweat chatting with our guest. Or tear open any newly fused wounds."

She smiled and leaned in to kiss his cheek. "Well, you looked like shit when they carried you back here. I have to protect my handiwork, don't I?"

"Let's go, people." Clarkson spoke on the unitwide com, his voice raw, angry. "These bastards killed General McDaniels…now let's show them what that's gonna cost. The rest of the Marines on Armstrong are counting on us…General Cain is counting on us." His fingers were curled up into fists, and the servo-mechanicals transmitted the movements to the suit's massive hands. He raised an arm in the air, shaking the huge fist as he shouted into the com. "General McDaniels is watching us, people…she is with us as she has been since the start. Are we going to let her down?"

The com line erupted, the raw screams of hundreds of Marines all saying one thing. "No! Never!"

McDaniels had organized the Obliterator corps from its inception, and she'd been its only commander until she fell in the fighting along the Graywater. Her Marines had fought savagely that day, destroying the bridges the invaders had erected across the river then turning north and tearing through the

enemy forces until none were left on the northern side. They'd
run out of enemies before anger, and they still lusted for vengeance. Clarkson was as bitter and angry as any of his Marines,
but he knew he was also using their emotions to manipulate
them, to work them into a battle frenzy. There was no finesse
in the plan, no elaborate tactics. They would achieve their goals
with aggression, courage, raw savagery. They were death incarnate, and they would kill until the last of them fell.

"Obliterators...attack!" Clarkson surged forward, shifting
the bulk of his huge suit to avoid the trees. His people were on
the very edge of the Sentinel, about to burst out into the open.
The trees were smaller than the ones in the deep forest, but they
were still at least 100 meters tall. In a few seconds his people
would leave them behind, and plunge into a death struggle with
the enemy.

The Obliterators were fearsome killing machines, four
meters tall and bristling with weaponry. They burst out of the
woods into the open fields, smashing into the enemy's flank like
a scythe. They pushed forward, stopping for nothing, firing
away with all their weapons, leaving hundreds of enemy casualties behind them as they did.

Clarkson was in the van, blazing away with his dual autocannons. The massive hyper-velocity rounds tore apart even powered armor, firing a thousand rounds a minute, wiping out entire
squads in seconds.

They'd caught the enemy by surprise. The rest of the Marines
had been retreating north, abandoning all their positions south
of the capital, and the battle had entered a brief lull. The sheer
audacity of Clarkson's attack shocked their adversaries, and they
caught hundreds of them strung out, advancing to the north. In
the first ten minutes, the Obliterators took down thousands and
sliced deep into the enemy formations.

For a few minutes it seemed as though Clarkson's people
might win the battle by themselves. But the enemy was trained
to Marine standards, and they outnumbered the Obliterators
100-1. They suffered heavily, but they kept their discipline and
followed their training. They began to form lines facing Clark-

son's people from all sides. Slowly, steadily, the Obliterators were flanked, then surrounded.

The Marines kept moving, driving deeper into the enemy's position. They knew what they had to do. If they didn't disorder the invaders enough to slow their pursuit, the rest of the Marines wouldn't have enough time to build a defensive position. They'd be hit, outnumbered and in the open…and the last of the Corps would be destroyed.

"Keep moving!" Clarkson's voice was strained. He'd been hit twice, and he was trying to hide the pain. "To the south! Take out their supply dumps!" He angled his hulking suit, jogging south, favoring his injured leg. His people were almost through…it wouldn't be long before they were wiped out. Hitting the enemy's logistics would slow them down more than a few extra casualties. If his people could get to the LZ they could make a real difference. It was the best chance to buy Cain and the rest of the Marines the time they needed.

Clarkson was down to one autogun; the other had taken a hit. It was just as well. He was running low on ammunition, and what he had left would last longer with a single gun firing. He glanced at his display. Less than half his people were still in the fight. Some of them were scattered around, isolated and pinned down in firefights with clusters of enemy soldiers. They were going down quickly as the Shadow forces got themselves organized and brought enough force to bear on each of them.

It looked like maybe 80 were still with him, moving toward the LZ. They were being pursued, but they'd broken through the heaviest resistance to their front. "Arm your grenades." Clarkson couldn't hide the weakness in his voice anymore. He'd be on the ground already if his AI hadn't given him a near-lethal dose of stimulants. "All of them." The grenades were a marginal weapon against powered infantry, but ideal for taking out crates of supplies and ammunition.

He heard a smattering of acknowledgements and glanced again at the display. The Marines at the back were taking heavy losses from the pursuing enemy. He was down to 50 effectives. But the supply depot was just ahead…almost in range. Only a few more seconds...

He lurched forward even before he felt it. He stumbled two or three steps and fell, his massive suit slamming face first into the ground. The fall knocked the wind out of him, and when he tried to inhale he felt a shooting pain, like a blade piercing his chest. The wound was mortal...he didn't have to check his med scanner to know that. His vision was failing, and every shallow breath was agony.

He flipped on the com. "Keep...moving...all..." He coughed, spraying blood all over the inside of his helmet. His voice was weak, throaty, every word a struggle. "Take...out... those...suppl..." His chest spasmed, and blood poured out of his mouth." The pain wasn't bad, but he knew that was only because his AI had flooded his system with painkillers. His eyes caught a glimpse of the tactical display. His Marines were running forward, launching their grenades. He didn't think they would last much longer, but maybe, just maybe, they'd do enough damage.

He lay there another minute, maybe two, unable to speak... unsure, even, where he was. Armstrong, he thought, yes...the battle. He felt himself slipping away into darkness...his last thought...take out those supplies...

Alex scanned the terrain ahead. It was open ground, mostly, and she was trying to stay out of sight. She'd started out stalking Erik Cain, but now she had a different agenda. There was another Alliance Intelligence assassin on Armstrong...she was sure of it.

Stark must have written her off, she thought bitterly, and if he had someone else here already, he'd sent him weeks before, if not months. Alex Linden was nothing if not a realist. Whatever chance she'd imagined she had of getting near Stark was gone. Killing Cain wouldn't do her any good. Most likely, Cain's would-be assassin had her as a secondary target.

She'd had a moment of panic, of uncertainty. Alex Linden always had a plan, but when she first realized what was going on, she didn't know what to do. There was a flash of rage, then

frustration...but she quickly cleared her head and began analyz-
ing the situation. Bit by bit, she formulated a new plan. She
wasn't going to kill Cain; she was going to save him. She was
going to kill the assassin.

Her quarry had to be one of Stark's best, as she had been.
The brilliant psychopath wouldn't send anyone but an elite killer
to go after Erik Cain. That meant she was pursuing a very dangerous foe, one she couldn't underestimate. He wouldn't be an
easy target, but then, of course, he wasn't expecting to be stalked
by another of Alliance Intelligence's crack killers. Indeed, he
had been careless, not expecting to be a target himself. He left
behind a trail she could follow. It wasn't much, but Alex was
one of the best trackers to emerge from Alliance Intelligence's
killing school, and she didn't need much.

Her adversary was better equipped than she was. His rifle
was designed specifically for assassinations. He could take out
a target, even an armored one, from at least 3 klicks. She hadn't
been able to smuggle any weapons into the refugee camp, so
she'd been unarmed when she headed south to find Cain. She
couldn't scavenge anything from the dead Marines she'd come
upon. They were armored infantry, and their high-powered
weapons required the output of the nuclear power plants they
carried on their backs. But finally she found a cluster of dead
planetary regulars...unarmored troops with standard weaponry.
She grabbed an assault rifle and a pair of pistols, along with a
particularly nasty-looking survival knife. Her arsenal was a weak
one to face powered infantry, but more than sufficient to kill a
single unarmored target.

She moved cautiously, stopping every couple hundred meters
and listening carefully. There were more Marines passing by
and larger groups than before. The army was clearly retreating.
That was bad news for the battle...and for her prospects of
escaping from Armstrong when her job was done. It was also
slowing her down, forcing her to spend precious minutes staying hidden. She needed to make better time. If she didn't, her
enemy would get to Cain first.

She was struggling to stay focused, to keep her emotions in

check. She had killed hundreds of times, coolly and without remorse. But now she was anxious, upset. She thought she'd been ready to kill Cain, but now she wondered if she would have gone through with it. Alex wasn't sure who she was anymore, but it was clear the cold-blooded Alliance Intelligence operative was gone. She had doubts someone like her had any kind of chance at redemption…she wasn't even sure she wanted it. But she knew one thing. She was going to save Erik Cain.

"We've got him stabilized, Doctor Linden." Elaine Samitch was one of the Corps' best doctors, and she'd effectively commanded the field hospital while Sarah was busy trying to unravel the mystery of Anderson-45 and his cohorts.

Sarah walked down the neatly graded path, heading toward the critical care ward. The field hospital had been hastily erected at the new location. It was a cluster of prefabricated shelters linked by a series of pathways. The setup was only half done, and many of the non-critical patients were still outside, lined up on portable cots.

"And he asked for me?" Sarah had been busy at the old hospital site when the patient was brought in. He'd come down in an escape pod and crashed just north of Astria. He didn't have any identification, and all he said was he was looking for Erik Cain. When they told him Cain was unavailable, he asked for Sarah.

"Yes." Samitch hurried her pace to keep up with Sarah's purposeful gait. "I came to get you immediately. I thought you'd want know."

"Of course, Elaine. You did the right thing." Sarah slapped her hand on the palm reader. She was impatient and didn't make enough contact. The reader flashed red and rejected her ID. "Fuck," she muttered under her breath as she pressed her palm against the glass and held it firmly in place.

The door slid open, and she ducked through. She strode swiftly down the corridor and into the last room on the right. The patient was lying on the bed, his eyes closed. He was connected to half a dozen machines and his face was deathly pale.

He'd been critically injured in the crash, but he was out of danger now. It would take some time to recover fully, but Samitch had treated all his major injuries.

"Hello, I'm Sarah Linden." She was stressed and impatient, but she'd been treating wounded men and women for years. The harshness in her tone fell away, and she spoke softly, kindly. "You wanted to see me?"

The patient opened his eyes and slowly turned his head, staring up as if trying to reconcile her appearance with a description. "Colonel Linden?" His voice was weak, his breathing labored. "I am Captain Duncan Campbell, Martian Confederation Navy. I have a message for you from Roderick Vance." He was trying to speak louder, but all he could manage was a tortured whisper.

Sarah felt her stomach clench. Roderick Vance was a trusted ally, but not one to waste time or resources. If he had sent one of his people into a war zone to find Erik, something was wrong...probably disastrous. "Yes Captain?" She was trying to stay calm, but the tension was obvious in her voice. "What is it?"

"It's about your sister, Colonel." He took a deep breath, trying to focus his strength. "Alex Linden is an Alliance Intelligence agent. She is Number 3 on their Directorate...or at least she was."

Sarah stared in disbelief, almost unable to process the words she was hearing. She had known there was something in Alex's past, something dark. But she'd never have imagined her sister had been Alliance Intelligence. Is that why she'd turned up looking for her long-lost sister? To spy for Gavin Stark and his band of murderers? What had she reported on? Had Marines died because of things Sarah had let her learn? She felt sick... she wanted to drop to her knees and vomit.

Her first thought was to doubt what Campbell was telling her, to argue that it was some kind of mistake. But somehow she knew it was true. It all made sense. She took a deep breath, struggling to regain her composure. "So she is here to spy on us and report back to Gavin Stark?"

Campbell looked up at Sarah, his watery eyes meeting hers.

"No, Colonel." He took a deep raspy breath and continued. "She is here to assassinate General Cain."

The slim figure hovered over the dead Marine. He was at the very edge of the Sentinel forest, watching, waiting. Once, his name had been Vincent...Thomas Vincent. But for two decades he'd been known only as Cobra. He was an assassin, one who could boast he'd never failed to kill a target. For 20 years he had murdered at the orders of Gavin Stark. He'd taken out politicians, scientists, soldiers...but this would be his greatest kill. General Erik Cain was famous throughout the Alliance, the Marines' invincible veteran commander, a warrior of unquestioned ability.

Cobra felt a kinship with his target. By all accounts, Cain was as cold-blooded as any assassin, a man who killed en masse... who unflinchingly sent his troops to march off to certain death. Anything to secure victory. Cobra felt he could understand a man like that. But whatever kinship he felt toward his victim it wouldn't affect the job. Cobra never let anything get in his way...no more than Cain himself ever did.

He reached into his pocket, pulling out a small egg-shaped device. It was a miniature hyper-EMP generator. Its battery could only power it for a few minutes, but that would be enough. It would interfere with all communications and create chaos over a 500 meter zone. He'd find a suitable vantage point, a firing position with good coverage of Cain's HQ. Then he'd activate the jammer...and wait for Cain to show himself.

Marine armor looked alike...officers didn't strut around the battlefield advertising their presence to snipers. But Cobra had Cain's transponder code. Alliance Intelligence and the Marines were on the same side, at least they were supposed to be. There were advantages to going after your own. Even through the jamming, Cobra's scanner would confirm Cain's presence...and an instant later, the veteran assassin would put his target down.

He scrambled slowly down a small hillside, crouching low, his camouflage blending with the scrubby grass and fallen leaves of the forest floor. He paused, looking around the last few trees and out into the open plain. There it was...Marine HQ. It was small, almost deserted. The Marines were pulling back, and it looked like most of the command personnel had already gone.

Cobra wondered if he was too late, if Cain had already left, but he quickly dismissed the concern. Everything he knew about Erik Cain suggested he would be among the last to leave. Being on the retreat, staring defeat in the face...it had to be the Marine general's worst nightmare. Yes, he thought, Cain will still be there.

He jogged up a small rise and crouched behind a large spur along the trunk of one of the trees. It was a good spot, giving him a view of the small central quad between the HQ structures. He checked and double-checked his rifle. Everything was ready. It was time to kill Erik Cain.

He scanned the area, cold eyes acclimating himself with the layout of the HQ, covering every centimeter, every possible contingency. Then he took a deep breath and pressed the button on the jammer.

Chapter 8

Brooklyn Docks
Midtown Protected Zone Cargo Terminus
American Sector – Western Alliance
Earth – Sol III

"There's a huge crowd just outside the fence." Bill Quinn walked back onto the dock where his crew was unloading a massive cargo barge. They'd been listening to the screams and chants while they worked, and his people were nervous. He'd tried to ignore it, but finally he went to make sure the security forces had things in hand. "But the guards have it under control. The gates are closed and locked."

Things had been deteriorating rapidly. The crash spread quickly beyond the financial markets, and economic activity of all sorts was coming to a halt. Throughout the Alliance, money flows had ceased entirely. The Cogs who did the menial work weren't getting paid, and when their income stopped, their families began to starve. Few of the Alliance's lower classes had any type of savings, so when their pay stopped, they ran out of food almost immediately. The ghettoes where they lived became even more dangerous than they had been. Walking down the street with a bag of groceries was enough to virtually guarantee an assault. Then the food stopped coming entirely. The workers began to stay home to try to protect their families instead of reporting to jobs that had ceased to produce income.

Things were bad in Brooklyn, and riots had swept from one neighborhood to another. Even for those few who had money, there was no food to be found. The stores had been looted, cleaned out by the gangs. The rioting mobs got what little the gangers had left behind. And no shipments were making it to the ghettoes...none at all.

Quinn and his people were lucky. Their jobs were necessary to maintain the flow of food and other materials to the privileged classes in the Midtown Protected Zone. Their pay wasn't coming through either...all monetary transactions in the Alliance had come to a halt. But they were being paid in food, enough for them and their families to survive. And they were picked up at their homes and dropped off by armored security vehicles.

There had been talk of relief...of government convoys bringing food and medicine to the Cog neighborhoods, but Quinn hadn't seen any sign of that yet. In truth, Alliance Gov was having enough trouble getting vital shipments to the upper classes. Any relief for the poor was going to be long in coming...if it ever materialized at all.

Quinn watched his people carrying boxes from the barge and loading them onto the cargo monorail that would whisk them north, across the radioactive wasteland of lower Manhattan to the walled bastion of the Midtown Protected Zone. They worked alongside half a dozen robots, all that were left of the forty or more they'd had when the crisis first hit. The Cogs were cheap labor, and the only way automation could compete was by skipping maintenance and working equipment well past its normal useful life. The robots at the Brooklyn docks were ancient; they required constant repair...and the parts needed to keep them functioning were no longer available. One by one they malfunctioned, leaving only 6 still working alongside the sweating Cogs.

His people labored ceaselessly, carrying boxes or dragging them on carts. The trucks and loaders were out of fuel, and there was no more coming any time soon. The Alliance was on the verge of war with the CAC, and the military had first claim on vital supplies...after the Political classes, that is. But the politicians and corporate masters, ensconced in their plush and heavily guarded neighborhoods, didn't give a shit if Quinn's

Cog crew had to carry the cargo by hand. Not as long as they did it and the supply of food and other essentials continued to reach their wealthy enclaves.

Quinn's people didn't complain. They knew very well they were among the few residents of Brooklyn who had something to eat, and they weren't about to risk their positions. They would work without argument, carry boxes until they dropped from exhaustion. Anything to keep their families fed.

A loud crack echoed through the cool morning air, then another. Quinn's head snapped around, looking back toward the gate. He couldn't see what was going on; his view was blocked by a cluster of warehouses. The communal screams became louder and the shots steadier. His crew had mostly stopped in their tracks, looking anxiously at the buildings between them and the gate.

"Get back to work, all of you," Quinn growled. "I'll go back and see what's going on." He jumped down off of the platform and started toward the main gate. He'd gone about ten steps when he heard a loud crash. He stopped in place, listening to the sounds of the angry mob getting closer. My God, he thought…they must have smashed right through the gate.

He started to turn back toward the loading dock when he saw them come around the end of a warehouse. There were hundreds of them, thousands. And they were screaming murderously. The ones at the front were carrying some kind of large objects, passing them back and forth. It took a second or two, but Quinn suddenly realized they were bodies. Bloody and mangled, but still recognizable. The guards, he thought, his blood running cold as he did.

He turned and ran back toward the dock. "Run…the mob's inside the gates." He shouted as loud as he could, but the crowd was on his heels, and their deafening shouts drowned him out. He got back to the dock and started to climb up when he felt the first hands reach out and grab him.

He screamed, begged for mercy, shouted as loud as he could that he, too, was a Cog. But the crowd was past listening to reason. It was a mindless creature now, an incarnation of pure rage…and Quinn was the enemy. Cog or no, he and his people had gotten preferential treatment. Their families had eaten while the others starved. It was pure elemental rage, and right now it was targeted at John Quinn and his loading dock crew.

Quinn felt hands grabbing him, the strength of 4 or 5 men pulling him down off the concrete pier. He was lifted above their heads, pushed back, deeper into the screaming, surging mass. Then he fell, pushed to the ground, while they beat and kicked him. Fear and pain drove everything from his mind. He knew he was going to die. The crowd was worked into an orgy of hate and anger. No reason, no pleas for mercy would reach them. He felt a hard kick to the stomach, then another. He coughed, and blood welled up out of his mouth, pouring down his face. Tears streamed down his cheeks as the enraged Cogs – his neighbors since the day he'd been born – beat him to death.

Hans Werner looked out over the cloudy waters of the Rhine. The river was one of the most polluted on an Earth that had been treated contemptuously for centuries. The once prolific life that had teemed in its waters was long gone, and the great river was a dead zone from 100 kilometers below its sources in the Southern Alps to its terminus at the North Sea.

Many things had changed in the past few centuries, the nations along its lengthy path to the sea combining and splitting and finally merging to form two great Superpowers. But one thing remained the same. For most of its history and much of its length the Rhine was a border between bitter enemies.

Werner looked back over his shoulder. The main battle tanks of his battalion were dug in along the rolling grasslands, with squads of infantry entrenched between the massive Leopard Z-9s. They were on a Red-1 Alert. Werner had been an officer for twenty-five years, and this was the first time he'd ever seen the CEL's top alert level invoked. War is imminent. That's what a Red-1 declaration meant. Not war is possible, or even likely. Imminent. The word itself suggested an inevitability… as if battle had already commenced.

The German-dominated Central European League and

Europa Federalis had been enemies as long as the powers had existed. But for more than 100 years, both had adhered to the terms of the Treaty of Paris. They had fought half a dozen wars in space, mostly inconclusive feuds over the same few border colonies. But they'd maintained the peace on Earth. Until now.

The CEL had steadfastly insisted it had nothing to do with the destruction of Marseilles, but the Europans kept uncovering evidence, and most of it pointed right at Neu-Brandenburg. The RIC had tried to mediate talks between the two governments, but they'd gone nowhere…and had finally been abandoned entirely when the evidence against the CEL piled up. When the Russian diplomats gave up and returned to St. Petersburg, war became an inevitability.

Werner and his soldiers – and millions like them – were preparing to fight a conflict they had long trained for but never really expected. The Treaty of Paris had held for so long, the prospect of open war seemed somehow unreal. He knew his counterpart was somewhere on the other side, probably staring across just as he was. He wondered what was going through the Europan's mind. He's my enemy, Werner thought, but I wonder if he isn't thinking the same things I am right now, staring across at me and wondering what war will be like.

"Colonel Werner, we have a priority communique coming in." Captain Kohl was standing in front of the com tent and shouting nervously. The battalion was a front line armor unit, well-drilled but without combat experience. The prospect of actually fighting the war they'd trained for was daunting. No CEL tank unit had seen combat for a century. An infantry formation may, at least, have fired its weapons putting down civil disturbances, but the heavy armored units existed for one reason…to fight Europa Federalis. For over a hundred years they'd stood vigil, but they'd never really believed the balloon would go up. Now, that confidence had been shattered, and the soldiers of the 11th Heavy Armored Battalion waited for the orders they'd never expected to receive.

Werner jogged toward the com tent, his stomach twisted into knots. He ducked through the open flap and grabbed a headset, holding it to one ear. "Colonel Werner here."

"Werner, this is General Beck." Werner knew as soon as he heard Beck's tone. "Invasion is imminent. I repeat...invasion is imminent."

Werner swallowed hard. "Acknowledged, sir." He croaked his reply, the best he could manage. His chest tightened, and he felt nauseous. It was unseasonably cold, but he could feel a trickle of sweat sliding down the back of his neck.

"Protocol C is in effect."

Werner was startled. He'd expected to be purely on the defensive, but Plan C was a hybrid strategy. It called for leaving the Rhine bridges intact and allowing the enemy to cross. His battalion would engage the invaders, driving them back and then counterattacking. When the Europans retreated Werner and his people were to invade Europa Federalis. Protocol C was no limited tactical response...it was a total war scenario. Whether the CEL was behind the destruction of Marseilles or not, clearly the high command had decided to solve the Europa Federalis "problem" once and for all.

"Understood, sir." Werner clamped down on the fear welling up inside him. He had a job to do, and his peoples' chance of getting through the next few days depended heavily on him keeping his shit together. "Enacting Protocol C directives."

The line was silent for a few seconds. Finally, Beck spoke, his voice soft, tense. "Good luck, Colonel." Then the line went dead.

Werner stood still for half a minute, breathing deeply and getting control over his emotions. Finally, he turned toward the com tech. "Sergeant, please advise all company commanders to prepare for imminent contact with the enemy. Protocol C directives are in effect."

"Incoming!" The shout came from just outside the tent. Werner couldn't tell who it was, but a second or two later the warning was repeated. Then he heard the first explosion...followed by a second, and a third. He ducked outside the tent and saw his soldiers running around, hurrying to their defensive positions.

It was a moment of tremendous historical significance. A century of worldwide peace had just been shattered, and the implications were almost unimaginable. But Werner wasn't thinking about any of that. To him there was only one thing that mattered. Europa Federalis was coming.

Axe sat on the edge of the crumbling brick wall, staring out across the ancient buildings and pockmarked streets of Brooklyn. He had another name once, one given to him by a mother and father he'd almost completely forgotten. He had abandoned it years before...when he left behind the life that went with it. Now he was just Axe.

He'd been born a Cog, like almost everyone in Brooklyn, but he rejected the life to which his birth had consigned him. He possessed a level of initiative and street smarts that allowed him to break out of the life he'd been fated to live. He'd risen through the ranks to become the leader of the largest gang in Brooklyn, a man who was feared and respected by all the other New York gangs...and the half million pathetic Cogs who lived in the areas he controlled.

His people terrorized the Cogs and stole from them what little they possessed. The Gangs were predators, feeding on the helpless sheep, oppressing them more completely than the government could ever manage. The Cogs were afraid of the government, but they were even more terrorized by the gangs.

The gang members clashed with the police from time to time, but the law enforcement agencies mostly ignored what went on in the ghettoes. Major conflicts were usually limited to gang incursions into the upper class areas like the Protected Zone. The gangs ran the illicit drug trades, and the police waged a half-hearted war against their influence in the elite neighborhoods. It was all a charade of sorts...the wealthy wanted their drugs of choice, whether legal or not, and they relied on the gangs to keep the supplies coming.

Axe glanced at the small reader, his eyes moving slowly down the screen. Nothing. Still no response. He sighed, frustrated that he couldn't get through to his contact.

The gang leader cultivated an image of course, one of uneducated brutality. But there was more to Axe than met the eye. He was extremely intelligent and quite literate. He'd taught himself to read, and he had a voracious appetite for knowledge. He planned the operations of his gang meticulously, considering its actions from multiple points of view. He was far from the typical gang leader.

The Cogs knew the gangs well, but there was one thing they couldn't have imagined…a bit of knowledge that was known only to the highest ranking gangers. The gangs were allied with the government.

The liaison was handled through Alliance Intelligence, and it was a pragmatic arrangement. The government wanted the Cogs compliant and obedient, and the gangs were in a position to keep the working classes terrorized to the point of impotence. The gangs also siphoned off the likeliest leaders of any civil disobedience, giving the most aggressive members of the Cog class a route to prosperity that didn't involve rebellion against the government.

The two sides allowed a certain amount of conflict to occur between the gang rank and file and the police, mostly for appearances, but the gang leadership was guaranteed safety in exchange for keeping the Cogs under control. It was a bizarre arrangement, but one that had worked well for decades.

Now, however, the tables had turned, and the gangs were seriously threatened by their former victims. The starving Cogs had taken to the streets, a surging, bloodthirsty mass, killing all in its path. Fear was a powerful tool, but its effectiveness waned when the victims lost the last of their hope. The Cogs were starving; they had nothing left to lose. Without the restraint of fear, generations of repressed rage emerged. The Cogs, so long downtrodden, now exploded in an orgy of violence and hatred. They swarmed into the streets, killing, burning, laying waste to everything in their path.

Axe had lost track of most of his people. He knew a lot of them were dead already, murdered in the streets by the masses of Cogs they had victimized for so long. He'd been staying out of sight, avoiding the vengeful mobs. That's why he was still alive. He'd tried to reach his contact at Alliance Intelligence, but there had been no response. The Alliance was falling apart, its economy a shattered wreck and its armed forces on full alert, waiting for word that they were at war with the CAC. No one gave a shit what happened to the gangs. The Cogs were driven by justifiable hatred, and Alliance Intelligence had more important matters to handle. Now, Axe realized that the gangs had never had a real partnership with the government. He and his people been an easy means to an end for Alliance Gov, but they'd always been expendable.

Most of the gang members were like stupid, vicious children. They'd come from the ranks of the Cogs and gone feral, feeding on those whose natures were less predatory. But Axe was different. He was as savage as any banger, but he was a lot more intelligent than most…smart enough, at least to know it was time to get out. Loyalty was a quaint concept, but not worth getting torn to shreds on the streets of Brooklyn.

He would leave as soon as it got dark. He'd considered slipping away alone, but now he was thinking he should take a few of his people with him. He didn't expect the roads outside New York were going to be safe. It was clear the entire Alliance was unraveling, and a couple extra guns could be the difference between getting out of a jam and ending up a rotting corpse along some abandoned highway.

Chapter 9

CWS Sulieman
Deep Space
Avalon System

"Nothing. Absolutely nothing. We've been sitting here a month, and we haven't been able to reach Admiral Garret. Or General Holm." Admiral Abbas sat at the end of the conference table, a frustrated scowl on his face. "Wherever the Alliance fleet is, they've gone deep, somewhere without Commnet access." Or, he thought grimly, the brilliant Augustus Garret had finally been defeated. He kept that thought to himself, though he was sure Khaled was thinking the same thing. Abbas didn't want to seriously consider the prospect, but a lifetime at war had taught him never to discount anything.

Ali Khaled sat on the side of the table to Abbas' left. He'd been staring down at the polished metallic surface, but now he looked up, gazing at the admiral. "It is clear that Alliance space is experiencing some kind of extreme disruption. There has been fighting in many systems. We cannot even know the status of their Commnet chain. Perhaps the integrity of the system had been compromised. It is possible that our communiques are being blocked or intercepted at some point, even that we have been fed inaccurate data. Or, more likely, the system has simply been cut between us and the Admiral."

"That is true, Lord Khaled." Abbas leaned back in his chair, returning the Janissary commander's stare. He always addressed Khaled formally, as the general did him. The two had learned to work together battling the First Imperium, and they'd been pushed to ever closer cooperation by their joint escape from assassination, but they weren't friends. In truth, neither man particularly liked the other, though they did share a sort of mutual respect. Each knew the other was skilled and reliable, and both subscribed to a rigid code of honor. There was trust between them but no warmth, admiration but no camaraderie. They were both gifted officers and, despite their differences, they made a highly effective team.

The two sat quietly, each deep in thought. They had to decide what to do next. For decades, Abbas and Khaled had been loyal Caliphate officers, but now they were fugitives, fleeing from a nation that had put them both on a proscription list and sent agents to kill them. The whole fleet and most of the Janissary corps had rallied to them, throwing in with their beloved and long-time commanders. They fled the Caliphate, leading their people to the temporary safety of deep space. They had no home anymore, no flag to follow, no place to go. But they did have their counterparts in the Alliance, long-time enemies now become friends of a sort. They'd fought the First Imperium War alongside Garret and Cain and the rest of the Alliance forces. Now those new friendships would be put to the test. Where they real…strong enough to erase years of enmity and war? Would their new allies stand by them now that they were renegades? Or had the cooperation between their forces been a passing expediency, a last-ditch necessity to fight off an overpowering enemy trying to destroy them all?

Finally, Khaled broke the silence. "I believe that we need to investigate what is happening to the Alliance. We must determine once and for all…does our future lie along a path of friendship and cooperation with Admiral Garret and his people? Or are we truly on our own?" He exhaled loudly. "From the communications we have intercepted, it is clear there has been considerable fighting, but we have no idea who it is they are battling…or who has the upper hand. We must find out exactly what is taking place." He paused, thinking silently for a few seconds. "Is it possible they are experiencing a second series of rebellions?" The two renegade Caliphate officers had watched with considerable amusement as the Alliance had almost torn itself apart a few years before. They'd been enemies then, drawing satisfaction of a sort from their adversaries' distress. But things had changed enormously in the years since. The Caliphate officers were themselves rebels of a sort now, commanding a powerful renegade fleet. They possessed a force of enormous capabilities, but with no support, no bases, no home.

Abbas stared down, watching the reflection of the ceiling light dance on the polished metal of the table. Finally, he raised his head and turned back toward Khaled. "Do you think it is possible that whatever is happening in the Alliance is related to…to what happened with us?" His voice was halting, uncomfortable. The two had hardly discussed the events that led to their flight from Caliphate space. Neither of them wanted to seriously consider the fact that they'd been betrayed by a government they had served brilliantly and loyally for decades. They had both suppressed the rage they felt, and the guilt at leading the thousands of naval crew and Janissaries in the fleet into a life as fugitives. There was no place for doubt and recrimination, not now. There would be time for self-flagellation later, if they survived. Now they both needed all of their wits. There were decisions ahead, cold-blooded ones that would determine if their people lived or died.

"It is certainly possible." Khaled paused, uncomfortable even at the mention of the proscriptions that almost took their lives. "The entire unfortunate action was unexpected. It never occurred to me that there would be a plot against us. We haven't discussed it, but let us now ask the question…what could have instigated the whole sorry affair? I am aware of nothing we did that could have caused our loyalty to be questioned." Khaled was addressing something the two had pointedly avoided discussing. His voice was becoming sharp, strained. He struggled to control his anger, to suppress the part of him that wanted to take the fleet back to Earth and challenge at gunpoint whoever had ordered the purge. It was probably that miserable bitch, Li An, he thought, his hands subconsciously curling into fists as he did. The CAC was involved too. It had butchered its own commanders…and whisperings of treason from the murderous head of C1 would find sympathetic – and paranoid – ears within the Caliph's inner circle. Perhaps the sequence of events leading to their flight had their roots in Hong Kong.

He took a breath, centering himself, forcing his focus back to the matters at hand. "Clearly, there is more going on than we are aware of." His eyes bored into Abbas'. "The Alliance government is at least as capable of perfidy as the Caliphate's. Do you think it is possible they have made a similar move against their own military leadership?"

Abbas returned the gaze but didn't answer right away. Certainly, he thought, Alliance Gov and its brutal intelligence agency were capable of anything the Caliphate was. It was possible that Garret and Cain and the others were unreachable because they were fleeing Alliance assassins. Indeed, perhaps they were already dead, the victims of a successful proscription. But it didn't feel right. Admiral Garret and Generals Holm and Cain were unquestionably the most capable military leaders in the service of any of the Superpowers. The Alliance's command structure was their greatest military asset, the primary factor making them the preeminent power in space. Would they be so quick to sacrifice that advantage, the one factor that made them unquestionably the strongest force in the international balance of power? And even if the Alliance had inexplicably decided to assassinate its gifted commanders, Abbas wondered what kind of professional killers could manage to outwit both Augustus Garret and Erik Cain. He had a hard time imagining either of the brilliant but paranoid Alliance commanders falling into a spy's trap.

"I don't know…I just don't know." Abbas spoke slowly, considering the situation from all angles as he did. "But we're not going to find out here." He reached out, running his fingers across the large 'pad on the table in front of him. It displayed an image of crisscrossing lines representing the warp connections between systems. "From the communications we've been able to intercept, we now know that a minimum of 21 Alliance colonies have been invaded. Whether these operations were conducted by an outside enemy or internal Alliance forces, we do not know."

Khaled sat upright in his chair, his posture rigid as always. "Before we analyze the situation further, we must make a fundamental decision. There is clearly a widespread conflict underway. We are sorely lacking details about the nature and the status of the fighting, but there is no doubt it is occurring. The question we must answer is essentially a simple one...are we prepared to involve ourselves in this struggle?"

Abbas took a deep breath. "That is the crucial decision, isn't it?" He sat quietly for a moment then asked, "What is your opinion?"

"We do not have sufficient information to make a rational decision. Nor do we have any way to obtain it within a reasonable timeframe." There was a touch of nagging uncertainty in Khaled's tone. He was a deliberative man who typically approached problems in a sober and unemotional way. He wasn't comfortable making uninformed choices. But he was a realist too, and he knew this decision was going to be made on a hunch, not on a review of facts. "We know we cannot go back to the Caliphate. And we cannot remain indefinitely in deep space. Our supplies are finite; our ships will need maintenance and repair." His chest heaved with a deep breath. "If we eliminate the non-options, I do not believe we have a choice. Our Alliance allies – if indeed they remain such – are our only real hope. We must trust to the friendship of those we have bled alongside. We must seek them out and aid them in whatever struggle they now face."

Abbas began nodding as Khaled finished. His comrade's words had reached him, shook him to action. "You are quite right, Lord Khaled...quite right indeed. We have wasted enough time dithering...and sitting here in the hope that some answer will come to us." He waved his arm, a directionally vague reference to the Commnet station the fleet had surrounded for almost a month. "The time for waiting is past, as is the time for timidity." He looked back at Khaled. "Admiral Garret... and General Cain...they have acted with honor in our dealings together. Far more than our own high command has shown in its actions toward us." The emotion in his voice, usually so tightly controlled, was escalating. "It is time to trust to new friends…and hope they prove more honorable than old ones."

Khaled nodded. "Then we are in agreement. But the question remains…where to go? I do not believe it prudent to divide our forces."

"Nor do I." Abbas' tone was strong, definitive. "We must concentrate our strength and remain as well prepared as possible for any eventuality."

"Then only one question remains to be addressed." His eyes drifted to the large 'pad on the table displaying the starmap. "Where do we go?"

Chapter 10

Columbia Defense Force HQ
40 Kilometers South of the Ruins of Weston
Columbia, Eta Cassiopeiae II

The hospital tent was crowded, rows of cots lined up against each of its four gray fabric walls. There were two cords draped across the ceiling, a row of lights suspended from each. They flickered every minute or two as the power cut in and out. The field hospital's electricity came from portable generators, and the operating and critical care tents got preferential feeds. When the surgical equipment drew too much power, the lights flickered everywhere else.

The hospital in Weston had been state of the art, with first rate surgical theaters, well lit and equipped patient wards, and an onsite nuclear plant providing a surplus of power. But most of Weston was radioactive ash now, the pride of Columbia blasted into an incinerated and poisonous ruin. The battered Columbian forces had retreated 50 kilometers to the south, bringing their wounded and supplies with them, and the small tent city was the best General Tyler had to offer his injured and dying soldiers.

"It's no uglier than it was before. That's something, isn't it?" Reg White was sitting on a small metal stool next to his friend's cot, playfully mocking his wounded comrade. He wore a fresh set of brown and green camo fatigues. It felt good to be out of his armor for a while. His suit was with the tech team getting an overhaul. Weeks spent on the line was hard on men, but it wore down equipment too. The Columbian militia had powered armor units, something few other colonies could boast. But their suits were 40 year old surplus units, leftovers from the Second Frontier War. He knew the maintenance was none too soon to keep the antique functioning. He hoped the armorer had time to do a complete overhaul…he suspected he'd be back inside the suit before long, and his survival prospects were much better if his gear was fully functional. "The doc did a helluva job on that hairy pygmy arm. Patched up that scratch real good."

Tony Paine managed a fragile smile. He was lying on his back wearing a white hospital gown and looking uncomfortable. "Yes, you're very funny, Reg." He pulled himself upright on the bed, his good arm struggling to shove the pillow higher up his back. "Why exactly are you here anyway? Didn't I get to smell you enough on the line?"

Paine laughed. "If you could smell me right through my sealed armor you better let the general know. He can transfer you to the bloodhound corps." He reached around White's head, pulling the pillow up for him. "Besides, I'll have you know I finally managed to get a shower. It took some scrubbing, but I'm actually clean."

Paine and White had been friends for years, long before they joined the militia. Paine was an effective enough soldier, but White was a natural warrior and an extraordinarily skilled killer. He was proficient at every aspect of soldering except one. He was a notorious hothead, one who constantly struggled to control his temper. He'd been promoted several times, only to have his rank stripped from him over one infraction or another. He had been a private for the third time when the invasion hit, but now he was wearing brand new sergeant's stripes.

White had struggled in his relationships with the non-coms and junior officers of the militia during peacetime, but General Tyler was well past worrying about minor behavioral issues. When he heard about a gunner who'd killed so many of the enemy they'd begun to direct their attacks around his position, he signed the promotion order immediately and sent Reg White both a new set of stripes and his profound thanks and congratulations for his work in the field.

"So when are they letting you out of here anyway?" White was staring at his friend's bandaged arm. "I've been curious how long you could freeload off a scratch."

"They told me a week." Paine frowned. "The suit did a decent job of managing the wound, but apparently running around for a ten days with a bullet in your shoulder is not conducive to quick healing."

"Who would have thought?" White laughed. "Well, I'm sure you'll be as good as new when they're done." He stood up. "But it's not vacation time for all of us, I'm afraid. I've got to report in. Time to get back to work. I don't want to be late." He looked down at the stripes on his arm. "I think I'll try to keep these this time."

"Try not punching out any officers." Paine smiled. "That'll probably help." He was silent for a few seconds, the grin slowly fading from his face. "Take care of yourself, Reg." He looked up, his eyes meeting his friend's. "I mean it. I don't like you being out there without me."

"You know me, old friend," White responded teasingly. He paused for a few seconds and looked down at his friend. The humor drained from his voice. "I will, Tone. I'll watch my ass until you're back to watch it for me." He reached out, firmly clasping Paine's good hand. "You get better. Listen to the doctors and don't be a pain in the ass. You gotta get back on your feet." He slowly released his friend's hand. "We're gonna need you out there."

Jarrod Tyler sat alone in his command tent, a sliver of bright light slicing through the partially open flap onto the dirt floor. He was silent, brooding, thinking about what to do next. He was also struggling with a crushing fatigue. All he wanted to do was walk out of the tent and keep going…deep into the countryside. He longed to shed the responsibilities that weighed so heavily on him, to turn his back on his obligations and run away.

His nuclear attack on Weston had been an enormous success. He'd caught the enemy completely by surprise. They had moved into the city in force, on the heels of the retreating Columbians, rushing right into Tyler's trap. As soon as the last of the native forces cleared the minimal safety line, Tyler ordered the bombardment. Three-quarters of Weston disappeared in a few seconds, consumed by the nuclear fire of 24 tactical warheads. The enemy had been heavily concentrated, packed together chasing his people through the city streets.

The bombardment inflicted enormous casualties on the enemy, almost wiping out the attack force and sending the few survivors reeling in ignominious retreat. The latest casualty estimates exceeded 5,000 enemy dead. Entire units were wiped out, and hundreds of soldiers were wounded and exposed to dangerous radiation levels.

The invaders had been pushing his people back since they landed, but now an uneasy stalemate had settled over the battlefield. The enemy retreated from the ruins of Weston and were reorganizing their shattered formations. The respite gave Tyler got a chance to give his exhausted soldiers a badly needed rest… and to set up a new defensive line. As badly as he'd hurt the invaders, they still outnumbered his force at least 2-1…and they were 100% powered infantry facing his own hybrid force. They were shocked and disordered by the unexpected repulse, but he knew they'd be back on the offensive soon. And he was damned sure going to be ready for them.

The enemy hadn't responded in kind to his nuclear attack, at least not yet. But he still had his forces dispersed, organized to face atomic weapons. He figured it was only a matter of time. Adopting nuclear battlefield protocols presented a serious challenge. He had to spread his troops over a wider area to minimize vulnerability to nuclear bombardment, but that weakened their defensive strength against a conventional attack at any specific point. He'd been trying to set up a defense in depth but, however he organized his forces, their flanks were vulnerable. The deeper his formations, the narrower…making it easier for the enemy to slip around the flanks and attack in enfilade.

He'd been moving units around his tactical map all morning, but all he'd managed to do was increase his frustration. He just didn't have enough troops...the enemy was still too strong. When they resumed their offensive, his people could slow them down, but he knew they weren't going to stop them.

His eyes slipped away from the display and settled on the floor. Tactically, his plan had been a stroke of brilliance. If he hadn't inflicted such a heavy blow against the enemy, his army would have been defeated by now, crushed by the invaders' numbers and material superiority. When the fighting was raging he didn't doubt himself, but the lull had given him time to think. Too much time. Weston was the most cosmopolitan city in all of mankind's interstellar domains, a symbol of a bright future, one marked by unparalleled growth and prosperity. Now, the city was a smoking, radioactive ruin, destroyed by a single command from Jarrod Tyler. Was it, he wondered, a symbol now of man's more probable future...self-inflicted devastation instead of wealth and happiness?

The weight of his temporary dictatorship was pressing down on him, the responsibility almost more than he could bear. He was charged with defending his home world...of somehow saving it from subjugation by an enormously powerful enemy. But did that charge entitle him to act like God, to destroy whatever he saw fit? Was a Columbia in ruins, its people starving in refugee camps, its soldiers dead on the field, worth saving? Did the price of freedom exceed its value?

"Can I interrupt the general's deep thoughts for a minute?"

Tyler recognized the voice immediately. He jumped to his feet. "Lucia!" He walked over and threw his arms around her. She was his oldest friend, his companion since they'd been two kids exploring the hills and woods around Weston. She was also the president of the Republic...or had been until she turned over her powers to Tyler, investing in him absolute authority for the duration of the crisis. The Columbian constitution strictly limited the power of the government, except in time of war. A battlefield in all three of the frontier wars and in the rebellion, Columbia had been repeatedly devastated by invaders. Its people, scrappy and protective of their freedoms in most areas, placed the highest priority on defense. When they drafted their constitution, they borrowed from ancient Rome, providing for a single general to assume dictatorial powers during times of extreme crisis.

Jarrod Tyler was the first officer invested with that authority, and he had used it to destroy the capital and force hundreds of thousands of Columbians into refugee camps. He wondered how they felt about the constitution now...whether his name had become a curse yet, spoken in angry tones in the cold and rain-soaked shelters that housed most of his people.

She held on to him for a long hug, and then she looked into his eyes and smiled. "How are you, Jarrod?" There was kindness in her tone, but also concern. She felt the tension in his body when they hugged, and she could see it in his eyes too. He had assumed an overwhelming burden, and it was taking its toll.

"I'll survive, Lucia." He managed a smile for her, the first one to cross his lips in weeks. "Hard times. For everyone."

"Harder for you, my old friend." She walked over to the makeshift table he was using as a desk, sitting down on the end. "So let me ask you again, Jarrod Tyler – and no bullshit this time - how are you?"

He sat back in his chair and looked at her silently for a few seconds. He couldn't fool Lucia; he'd never been able to slip anything past her. She always saw through his bravado. "I destroyed Weston, Lucia. Our people are sleeping outside, fleeing from camp to camp ahead of the enemy's advance. Half my soldiers are dead or in the hospital, and I don't know what's been keeping the others on their feet." His eyes slipped from hers, dropping down to look at the floor. "I can't do this, Lucia. I'm destroying everything. I'm failing."

She reached out and put her hand on his cheek, gently lifting his face until he was looking at her again. "You listen to me, Jarrod, and you listen good." Her voice was kind and sympathetic, but strong and forceful too. "Weston was bricks and steel. Nothing more. We can build it again; we can build it better than it was."

He started to turn away again, his expression turning sour. She put her other hand on his face and pulled it back to her.

"Cut the shit, Jarrod. Your soldiers would follow you into hell if you led them there, and if you think our people would trade their freedom to save some buildings, then I need to slap some sense back into you." She stared at him, holding his face in her hands. "Jarrod, those people in the camps aren't Earthers... they're Columbians, by God. Do you think sleeping in tents is going to break their spirit?"

He gave her a forced smile but didn't say anything. He knew she was trying to help him, but he had trouble seeing beyond the blood on his hands and the crushing burden that was his alone. He'd made the enemy pay dearly, but he still didn't see a path to ultimate victory. Once his forces were finally defeated, would things just be worse for the people? Would the enemy exact revenge for their losses? He imagined the Columbian civilians paying the price for the casualties his actions had inflicted on the invaders.

"Listen to me, Jarrod. You're my oldest friend, and I would do anything for you. But I am also the president of Columbia." Her voice became firmer, more authoritative. "I tell you now that, seeing what you have done with the power I gave you, I would not hesitate to do it again. I am proud of you and, as a Columbian, I will follow you wherever you lead. If we do not prevail then we will at least keep our honor. I would welcome death if it comes defending all that we value...and I would prefer it a thousand times to a craven life as a slave." Her voice was loud and defiant now, all traces of friendliness and familiarity gone. "And so would the rest of our people."

He stared back at her silently, deeply affected by her words, but still not entirely convinced. She leaned in and kissed him softly on the lips, holding it for just a second. "Now get back to work, General Tyler. All of Columbia is with you."

She stood up and turned around, slipping out of the tent without another word. He sat still, watching her slide through the tent flap and out of sight. He smiled as he thought of what she had said. She was part of his earliest memories. He'd know her his entire life, his closest friend and his companion in any adventure. There had never been anything romantic between them in those many years, just unconditional friendship. He had been there for her when her short-lived marriage failed, and she'd lived at his bedside when a rare Columbian pathogen almost took him down. There wasn't a major event in his life she wasn't part of.

All those years, he thought...the adventures, the hours-long conversations, the joy of just being together. When, he wondered...when did I fall in love with her? He wanted to run out of the tent and tell her, but he knew it wasn't the time. He didn't have the strength now to deal with his emotions if she didn't feel the same way. And if she did, what could he give her now except more misery. He knew very well the odds his forces were up against...and if his army was going to die in the blood-soaked fields of the war zone, there was no way in hell Jarrod Tyler was going to survive to mourn it. No, he was not going to give her more grief. If they both made it through the fighting, if they lived to see peace again...there would be time enough then to tell her.

He took a deep breath, and slammed his fist down on the table. No more despondence, he thought, no more self-doubt. Only one thing mattered now. Victory. He was fighting for duty, for honor...for his home. But mostly, he was fighting for Lucia. And he wouldn't fail, no matter what it took, what it cost him. He couldn't disappoint her, and he wouldn't leave her defenseless against a conquering enemy. The thought of her, alone and afraid...beaten, raped, murdered by the victorious invaders...it was more than he could stand to imagine. He felt the rage inside, the savage energy coursing through him.

He stared back at the tactical map, his eyes poring over every terrain feature. He imagined every line of advance the enemy might take, every scrap of ground where his people could set a trap. There had to be a way...something...and he would find it. He would find a way, somehow, to win this war. He would destroy every invader who dared to sully the ground of his beloved homeworld.

Chapter 11

Sub-Arctic Tundra
2,200 Kilometers North of Arcadia City
Unassigned Territories
Arcadia – Wolf 359 III

Kara Sanders sat on a large boulder deep in thought. She was on the edge of the column, staring off across the semi-frozen plain that stretched out of sight in all directions. They'd marched 25 kilometers since she had roused the army at dawn, and she was determined to make another 25 before dark. But right now she was taking a few minutes to herself while her soldiers rested.

Ed Calvin had come over to make sure she was ok...and Captain Mandrake too. She'd told them both the same thing. She was fine...she just wanted a few minutes alone. They'd respected her wishes, but she knew they were both worried about her. She'd become quiet and withdrawn over the last couple months. She obsessed over the army and its operations, seeing personally to her soldiers' every need, but otherwise she kept to herself. The Kara who sat around the heater talking far into the night was gone, replaced by the grim creature she'd become.

She spent most of her time thinking about how to keep her disintegrating army together. The march across the planet's polar region had been nothing short of a nightmare. She lost people every day to the brutal cold, a constant toll that sapped the army's morale. The whole thing was a horror. They rose early each morning, breaking camp and continuing their unending march. They left those who died where they fell. The ground was frozen solid, making burial almost impossible. And they couldn't spare fuel to burn the bodies. The dead lay frozen in the snow, marking the path the army had followed.

But she wasn't thinking about the war this time, at least not directly. Her mind drifted back to Concordia, to her son, Will Jr. She'd left him behind when she fled with the army, in the care of one of her oldest friends. She knew she had to join the fight to save Arcadia, no matter how hopeless it was. But she wasn't going to expose her child to that danger. Young Will had lost his father to the battlefield, and before this was over he might lose his mother too. But he would be safe...she had made sure of that. She and Gwen had been close since childhood, almost like sisters. If Kara failed to come back from war, Will would have a loving home and a chance to grow up. Whether he did that in freedom or under the rule of an oppressive regime depended largely on how the fight for Arcadia progressed. Things looked bleak now, but Kara held on to a shred of hope. As long as her soldiers were in the field, freedom wasn't dead.

The army had adopted Kara as its leader and, to a man, they followed her orders as if they were commandments from heaven. She was all that remained of Will Thompson, and he had been the father of the Arcadian forces. He'd raised them and trained them and led them against the federal armies that had come to crush the rebellion. He died leading them...he'd died before the victory was won, before Arcadia became free. He endured all the suffering the revolution could heap on him, but he never had the joy of seeing the triumph, of watching free Arcadians elect their own leaders. He lived on in his soldiers' hearts, though...and in their devotion to Kara.

But Kara Sanders was more than Will Thompson's lover and the mother of his son. She was a force in her own right, and the survivors of the Ice March, as it had come to be called, began to see her differently than they had. Pain and suffering – and the loss of hundreds of their number to the brutal conditions she forced on them – had dulled the unconditional affection they felt. But in its place, respect grew, almost awe. Wherever the army had gone, she had been there in the forefront, enduring everything her soldiers had. She marched through thigh-deep snow at their head and huddled with them around the portable heaters through the frigid nights. She shared their meager rations and walked among them while they rested, making sure everyone was fed and the sick and wounded got what care was available. She was becoming a legend in her own right, cold, hard, invincible…the symbol of Arcadia's strength and spirit.

She was looking down at her 'pad. She only had one picture of little Will, and she knew she should delete that one. If she was captured, she didn't want to lead the enemy to the boy. But she couldn't bring herself to cut that last small connection to her son. She knew her chance of ever seeing him again was small.

The tundra was considerably warmer than the polar hell the army had just crossed, but it was still damned cold. She knew the temperatures would continue to rise as the army marched south…and the hard, frozen ground would turn into a muddy quagmire. That would be another challenge, one nearly as difficult.

She put her hands on the rock and slid herself off. It was time to get the troops back on the move. They had to keep going. She knew they were being followed, and she was determined to stay ahead of the pursuit. She had a plan, one she hadn't shared with anyone yet. She knew all her army could achieve was to distract and disorder as many of the enemy as possible…and hope General Holm and the Marines could exploit her diversion. And she knew that distraction had to be a big one to do any good. The army wasn't just marching aimlessly as she'd allowed them all to think. They were heading to Arcadia City…and when they got there they were going to launch a surprise attack and retake the capital.

It was a gamble of epic proportions. She had no intel, no idea how many enemy troops garrisoned the city. But she was determined to make a difference in the fight for her home world. She knew the Marines were facing most of the enemy's strength…and much of the rest was pursuing her force. Maybe…just maybe, they'd left the capital weakly protected.

Holm and Teller's people were all veterans, but they were

massively outnumbered. They'd put up a hell of a fight, but in the end their situation was hopeless. Unless Kara's people could stir things up.

Her army wasn't strong enough to make a conventional difference, at least not in a straight up fight. But if she was right, if the enemy had left Arcadia weakly garrisoned, maybe they could accomplish something. A surprise attack might just succeed… and create enough disruption to give the Marines a chance to hurt the enemy.

She started walking back to the column. My God, she thought, glancing at her soldiers slowly lining up for the march… they look ragged. Men and women can only give so much, she thought, even patriots. "Not much longer," she whispered to herself. "Soon it will be over, my soldiers. One way or another."

"Keep up the fire!" Elias Holm walked all along the trench-line, watching his Marines gunning down the enemy charge. They'd repulsed a dozen attacks in the last two weeks, killing thousands of the enemy. But even successful defenses had a cost, and slowly, surely his force was melting away. The enemy could lose 10 men for every one of his people they killed and still be ahead on the exchange.

Holm had been the Commandant of the Corps since the rebellions, and for years before he'd been the CO of the massive operations that closed the Third Frontier War. Now he was on the front line, commanding a force that would normally rate no more than a brigadier…or even a colonel. But he felt exhilarated to be so close to the action again.

He was scared, certainly. It was widely believed in the Corps that he felt no fear, that he never had. His cult of cold-blooded fearlessness was second, perhaps, to Erik Cain's, but that was only because Cain was widely believed to be a little crazy too. No one would say that about Elias Holm. He was as rational an individual as could exist in such insane circumstances.

Holm found it amusing, and he wondered what his Marines would think if they could know how scared he was in battle. Still, it was a useful fiction. Indeed, he wondered if that wasn't why the rank and file created such legends around their leaders. Did it help them find their own courage, to march boldly into situations that would make a sane man turn and flee? Whatever the true motivation, Holm saw no reason to strip his Marines of their mythologies and stories. Every man had his own way to bolster his courage.

"Pour it in to them, Marines." Holm kept walking down the line. He was leaning forward, keeping his head down below the berm his people were defending. He couldn't think of anything worse for morale now than the CO getting his head blown off… and Holm preferred to hang on to it if he could.

"They're moving to the flank, General." It was Sam Thomas. The old Marine and his pack of retirees had returned to form, and they were savaging the enemy forces on their section of front. Thirty years of farming, fishing, sitting on the porch… it didn't seem that it did anything to take the Marine out of the Marines. They were hardcore veterans, and it showed.

Holm looked at his tactical display. He saw the move immediately. The enemy had been assaulting his position frontally, expecting to overwhelm his outnumbered forces. But his people showed the attackers just what Marines could do. Finally, the enemy was moving around the flank. Holm sighed. It was what they should have done weeks ago…and it was going to be a lot harder to deal with.

He flipped the com to Teller's channel. "James, I need you to pull your people out of the line and move to the right flank." He was staring at the display as he spoke. "Fast."

"Yes, General."

Holm flipped back to Thomas' channel. "Sam, I'm sending Teller's people to the flank. I need you to thin out your lines and cover his frontage.

"That's going to leave us pretty stretched out, sir." Holm was uncomfortable every time Thomas called him 'sir.' He had tried to get his second in command to address him informally, but the old Marine simply wouldn't do it. The last time the two had seen action together, Holm was a junior captain, and Thomas was a full colonel, a hero of the Corps on the cusp of promotion to general rank. That was on Persis, at the end of the Second Frontier War. Thomas abruptly and unexpectedly retired soon after, ending his celebrated career much earlier than anyone expected. Holm knew why the veteran colonel had called it quits, but that was a story for another time.

"I know, but we don't have a choice." Holm was trying to sound positive, but it was fake, and Thomas heard right through it. They both knew the enemy could keep extending the length of the front line. Eventually, the Marines would be too stretched out to mount a credible defense. The enemy would slice through the weakened lines at will...and that would be the end of it. "Just do your best, Sam."

"There it is. Arcadia." Kara didn't add the 'city' like she often did for the benefit of offworlders. Her people were all Arcadians, and they knew when someone meant the capital city instead of the planet itself. "To the south the Marines are fighting to destroy the invader." She really had no idea where the Marines were...or even if they were still in the field. But she needed her people to believe right now.

"Now is the time. We are here to take back Arcadia! The enemy is away, facing the Marines, and the capital sits naked, barely defended." Another baseless guess. She really had no idea how many enemy soldiers were in the city, but she doubted it was 'barely defended.' She was gambling that most of the invaders' strength was to the south, massed against Holm and his army. It was a reasonable guess, but a guess nevertheless. But no one else needed to know that. "It is there, waiting for us to take it back, to liberate its people...and to show the enemy that Arcadians will never yield!"

The cheers began along the front of the formation, but it quickly worked its way back. In a few seconds, thousands of Arcadians...farmers, mechanics, engineers...were shouting her name. "Kara...Kara...Kara..." They surged forward, breaking as if there was an invisible barrier around her, until they formed a vast circle with her at its center. "Kara...Kara...Kara..."

She stood silently before them, her arms raised high above

her head. She let them chant and scream for a few minutes then she lowered her arms. "To your posts, my brave Arcadians. We attack immediately...and we shall not stop until Arcadia is ours again, and every enemy soldier who soils her streets and houses is dead!" She threw her arms up again. "Prepare to attack!"

The noise was deafening. They kept shouting, even as their officers pushed and pulled them into attack formation. She moved to the front of the army, her fingers clasped around the worn grips of her assault rifle. Captain Mandrake led his 50 Marines to the front of the formation, his fully-armored men and women shaking out in a long skirmish line. The Marines were the professionals, veterans of the First Imperium war, and men and women who had seen some of the most desperate battles mankind ever fought. But they, too, were moved by Kara's words, and they stepped forward grimly, silently...the sharp tip of Arcadia's spear.

Kara knew the defenders in Arcadia could see her army. They knew the attack was coming. There was only one question. Were there enough of them to defeat her? She would have an answer soon, very soon.

"Arcadians and Marines...attack!"

Holm stood behind his wavering line of Marines. The enemy had breached the defenses in 3 places. Holm had scraped up the last of his forces to plug the holes. When the next attack broke through, his reserve would consist of one man...him.

His people had been holding the line for weeks, but for the last 3 days, the enemy had been throwing themselves at his troops incessantly. He didn't know what had changed - perhaps a general over there had lost his patience – but the urgency level had ramped up considerably.

The enemy had been moving to stretch out the line and work around his flank, but then they just stopped the maneuvering and started pounding straight at his positions. Across the entire line, they launched massive wave attacks. They were taking horrific losses, but they were wearing down the dwindling Marine force too. Holm was going to run out of people before they did.

Holm had no idea what had changed to send the enemy into a frenzy of suicidal charges, but he knew his army was on the edge of the abyss. The attackers' numerical superiority was just too great to overcome. If they were willing to take enough casualties, they could overrun the Marines.

"General Holm…" – it was Sam Thomas, his normally emotionless voice sounding surprised, almost shocked – "…the enemy is pulling back. All across my frontage."

Holm felt his tension spike. What the hell, he thought, what are they up to now? They had him. They were on the verge of bagging the whole Marine force. Why pull back now after taking 10,000 casualties to get to the threshold of total victory?

"General Holm…they're retreating. All across the line. It's a miracle." There was as much surprise in Teller's voice as Thomas'. More, even. "I can't explain it, sir, but they're running."

"I can explain it General Teller." It was a woman's voice, blasting through on all of their coms. "I've got a few Marines with me…and man are they pissed about being left out of the party.

Holm let out a deep breath. He knew the voice immediately. It was Cate Gilson and her Marines, back from the frontier and on their way down to the surface. He glanced at his tactical screen just as a wave of landing craft moved onto the edge of the display. "General Gilson…are you a sight for sore eyes!"

Chapter 12

North of the Sentinel
Planet Armstrong
Gamma Pavonis III

Cain was sitting at his desk. Really, it was just a box, a sur-plus plastic crate that had once held ammunition. There was a label on the side, partially faded but still readable...2,500,000 hypersonic rounds.

He was wearing his battle armor, but he had the visor retracted, and he was enjoying the fresh air. Protocols called for sealed suits in the combat zone...it was too easy for an enemy to deploy chemical weapons or for a Marine to get too close to a radiation hotspot if things suddenly went nuclear. But there was no one to scold the commander-in-chief, and he'd had just about enough of breathing air that stank of Erik Cain.

Long battles were always a challenge. His people were well beyond the suggested maximums for continuous armor usage. The plutonium in the suits' reactors would keep them function-ing almost indefinitely, but performance would degrade as men and women were pushed beyond their endurance. It was just one more thing to worry about, but there was nothing to be done. There was no sign of any respite for Cain's Marines, so they were just going to have to tough it out. He knew he'd start seeing psych cases soon, but he'd just have to deal with them the best he could.

Cain knew he shouldn't be this far up...not now, not when his people were pushed so close to the end of their endurance. He'd ordered most of the staff to withdraw to the new HQ, but he intended to stay at the forward headquarters until Carlson's people made it back. It was the kind of thing General Holm would have scolded him about. But Holm was lightyears away. Cain didn't even know where the general was. Isaac Merrick did a good job of filling in for Holm, trying to keep Cain from getting too reckless, but he rarely succeeded. Merrick didn't outrank Cain like Holm did, and that was a huge disadvantage. It was hard enough to get Cain to follow orders he didn't like. But simply persuading him was damned near impossible. But now, Merrick was wounded and in the hospital, and Cain was alone with half a dozen junior officers, all too scared of him to do anything but jump a meter in the air when he snapped an order to them.

Cain was on the com with Jake Carlson. "OK, Jake, everybody else is heading south. Let's get your people moving." Carlson had been a sergeant on Adelaide and the initial man to confirm that the First Imperium's soldiers were robots. He'd been part of Adelaide's militia at the time, but now he was back in the Corps and wearing a major's insignia. He'd fought in every significant engagement of the First Imperium War, and he'd become one of Cain's "go to" officers, a stone cold veteran who could be trusted to handle the toughest assignments.

Carlson's 300 Marines had been given just such a mission. They were the rearguard, trying to slow down an enemy that outnumbered them 50-1 while their comrades retreated and formed a new defensive line. It was hard business, and costly. Carlson had lost a third of his strength, but he'd gotten the job done. The rest of the army had extricated itself from a potential trap and fallen back into the new position. The outlook was still grim, but at least the fight would go on. Now Carlson had to get his survivors out…and no one was holding the enemy back for them while they did it.

"Yes, General." Carlson's voice was calm, even. Cain had never seen an officer as cool under fire as Jake Carlson. "We're trying to break off now."

"Don't worry about making it pretty, Jake. Just get the hell out. If you need to bolt and run for it, do it." Carlson's people had done a good job of making a lot of noise and convincing the enemy they faced a large force. But the trick had only been effective for so long. The invaders had briefly slowed their advance, but now they were coming hard, and they were right on Carlson's heels.

A loud blast of static erupted from Cain's com unit. "Jake?" Nothing but interference. "Jake? Can you hear me?" Nothing. He flipped through the com channels, trying to reach Carlson, the new HQ…anyone. But all he got was static.

He got up and walked through the door and into the open area between the small portable shelters. Captain Claren was coming out of the other building, on his way to report the com failure. Cain motioned for him to open his visor.

A few seconds later, the reflective hyper-glass visor pulled back, and Claren shouted to Cain. "What's happening, sir? I can't raise anyone on the com."

"Somebody's jamming us." Cain didn't know what was going on either, but none of the options he could conceive were good. "It's got to be an attack coming in. Tell Evans and Barts we're pulling out. We can't get a fucking thing done with no com."

"Yes, General." Claren spun around…then all hell broke loose.

Cobra sat still, silent. It was motion that usually gave away an assassin who was this close to the target. People didn't think, didn't realize how easily a little movement could undo everything the best camo could achieve. It was patience more than anything that separated the great killers from the others. Cobra had stalked targets for months, even years, waiting for that one moment when the victim was exposed. Erik Cain had been his most daunting assignment…but now the great general was vulnerable, in a crumbling war zone with just a few aides around him. It was time.

His rifle was resting on a large root that branched out from the giant tree. He was crouched in firing position, his eye looking through the weapon's scope. He had a good view of the target area and a perfect line of sight. Now he just needed Cain to show himself. One shot was all it would take. Not even Cain's state of the art armor would stop a shot from this rifle. And Cobra never missed.

He'd just activated the jammer. That would shake things up in the camp. He didn't need much…just a second or two with Cain out in the open. There were two large shelters…Cain had to be in one of them. He waited…watching.

Cobra was as meticulous and cold-blooded as any killer who served Alliance Intelligence, a natural sociopath whose inborn tendencies were exploited and encouraged under Gavin Stark's tutelage. But even he felt a tightness in his gut, a warmth around his neck. Erik Cain was one of the Marine Corps' most accomplished killers, a man who had taken down hundreds of enemies himself…and led forces who had killed tens of thousands. His legend was one of invulnerability, of almost superhuman ability. Even Alliance Intelligence's top killer couldn't help but feel awed.

He was watching…silently, intently. He saw the door slide open in one of the shelters…and almost simultaneously on the other as well. A figure stepped out of each, both clad in Marine armor. They walked toward each other.

Fuck, he thought…they look identical. His mind raced, trying to choose a target. He could take them both down, but the second target would have a brief warning, a chance to run, to duck for cover. He was almost sure he could take them both out, but there was a small doubt. And trying to kill Erik Cain and leaving him alive seemed like a really bad idea.

He flipped a coin in his head, moving the sight to the figure on the left. "Time to die, General," he muttered softly as he squeezed the trigger.

Cain stood watching as Claren turned to carry out his orders. The captain had proven to be the best assistant he'd ever had. Claren was smart, efficient, fearless…and he'd mastered the tricky art of handling Erik Cain. Cain knew he wasn't easy to work closely with, and he appreciated the synergy he had with Claren. The two worked seamlessly together, and that benefit-

ted the entire army. Cain would have promoted the captain long
before, but he didn't want to lose him…not in the middle of
a situation like this. He felt guilty about not giving Claren the
rewards his service had earned, but he promised himself he'd
make it up to the captain. If they both made it off Armstrong,
Cain had already decided he was going to bump the erstwhile
aide right to colonel and give him his own regiment. He'd need
General Holm's approval for that, but he didn't think that would
be a problem.

But now Cain was thinking about the current situation, not
the things he would do if he made it through the battle. He was
trying to make sense of what was happening and, no matter how
he figured, it just didn't add up. It took a lot of energy to jam
Marine coms over a wide area. A lot…the kind of energy fusion
plants put out. There was no way the invaders could be jamming
his HQ this effectively. Carlson's people were still in the field at
least 3 klicks away. Could there be another force onplanet, one
much closer to his HQ? Did the enemy get around Carlson's
flank? Unless it was a very small area being targeted. But that
would mean…

Cain was still looking right at Claren when the aide's head
exploded into a cloud of red mist. His blood went cold with
horror. Decades of combat experience shoved the emotions to
the recesses of his brain, but he was still sick, nauseous. He felt
a rush, no, a double rush of adrenalin - his AI, Hector, injecting
a supplement to his body's own blast.

Claren was dead. He knew it immediately; he didn't have
to check. But there was no time for grief now. His muscles
tightened; his body tensed. He knew he would live or die in the
next few seconds.

The world was moving in slow motion as he reacted rapidly, effectively. The captain's body was still falling when Cain's
battlefield instincts took over. He shifted his weight, moving
his head down, diving for the cover of the shelter behind him.

Alex prowled through the brush, hiding behind the massive trees whenever possible. She knew she was running out

of time, but she needed to stay hidden. Her quarry was better equipped than she was. If she gave herself away, he'd just turn his attention to her. She was a gifted killer too, but she couldn't match her adversary's weapons and technology. He could take her down before she got close enough to fight back. Unless she remained hidden.

She'd originally set out to kill Cain herself, but now she was determined to save him. Alex Linden had been eleven years old when her parents were murdered by government thugs. She'd escaped by fleeing into the crumbling ghettoes and, later, into the semi-abandoned suburbs and countryside. Even now, she didn't like to remember some of the things she'd done to survive, the horrors she'd endured. By the time she ended up at Alliance Intelligence, she was beyond angry, beyond bitter…just the sort of promising young psychopath Gavin Stark's recruiters salivated over. She cursed the world and everyone in it, and she did whatever she had to do to get her job done. Emotionlessly and utterly without pity. She rose rapidly through the ranks, leaving a trail of efficiently dispatched victims behind her.

Then she found out her sister Sarah was still alive. She'd hated her older sibling for years, blaming her for everything that had happened to the family. That hate had served a purpose over the years, channeling the horrors she couldn't face, giving her a focus for her rage. A dead sister blamed for all the ills that had befallen her was a useful psychological device. A live one who awakened all kinds of suppressed emotions and memories was far more complex and confusing.

Alex Linden, Alliance Intelligence's stone cold killer, was buried under a deluge of emotions, memories of a happy eleven year old with a close and loving family clashing with recollections of decades of murder and remorseless scheming. She had struggled enormously with it, descending into drug addiction and despondency before pulling herself back from the brink.

Now, suddenly, she had clarity. She had no delusions about the things she had done, and she wasn't going to beg anyone's forgiveness. Atonement wasn't her goal. What she had done, she had done. But she was going to save Cain. She was going to do it for Sarah, for the sister she'd wrongfully hated for so many years.

She slipped around the tree and moved slowly to the next, carefully scanning the thinning woods ahead. Then she froze. She caught a hint of movement, maybe 200 meters from where she stood. She stared, letting her eyes adapt…scanning every millimeter. Was it him?

She slowly pulled her own rifle off her shoulder, creeping forward as she did. She took each step with care. One small twig, one pile of dried leaves could give her away. She needed to get closer.

One hundred fifty meters, one hundred twenty-five. She paused, taking a deep breath, holding the rifle in front of her as she carefully continued ahead. One hundred meters. She stopped again, scanning the area. She was about to step forward when she heard a loud crack.

A cold feeling swept through her body. She lunged forward, running as fast as she could, bringing the rifle to a firing position as she did. She started shooting, aiming as well as she could at a full run.

She couldn't hear if her target had fired again over the noise of her own rifle blasting away on full auto. She saw the target move, turning toward her. He raised the rifle in her direction. She pivoted, zigzagging as she ran toward the assassin, still firing.

She felt the pain…a bullet grazing the top of her shoulder. Nothing serious, she told herself as kept running forward. She was almost there…only a few more meters. The assassin was just ahead, his eyes focused on hers. His shirt was bloody… she'd hit him at least once. She lunged forward, reaching around and grabbing the knife hanging from her belt. It was time to finish this.

The hovercraft zipped along just above the ground, racing to the north. The army didn't have many vehicles left, and the few it did have had been assigned to assist with the relocation of the hospital. This one had been scheduled to move south with supplies when Sarah got Campbell's message.

She'd run outside and ordered the supplies thrown out of the transport. There were no armored Marines nearby, but she grabbed half a dozen of the walking wounded and climbed aboard. She ordered the pilot to redline the engines, and the craft raced toward Cain's headquarters.

She spent the few minutes of the trip on the com, desperately trying to reach Cain. Nothing…all she got was static. She tried to get Claren too, but it was the same. No response at all, just heavy interference. She tested the hovercraft's com, and it worked perfectly. Whatever was wrong, it was on Erik's end.

She struggled to hold back the wave of nausea that almost overcame her. How could she have been so blind? She hadn't been able to spend a lot of time with Alex before the First Imperium War tore her away from the reunion with her long-lost sibling. She knew her sister had some troubles…a past she didn't want to discuss. But the truth was more than Sarah could bear. Alex was one of Gavin Stark's murderers? It was almost more than she could grasp, and it made her feel sick.

Oh my God, Erik, she thought…I can't lose you, not like this. She reached to her waist, feeling around for the sidearm Erik had insisted all rear-area personnel wear. I'm coming, Erik. I'm coming.

The projectile blasted through the air at five times the speed of sound. It had been aimed at Cain's head, but one of Alex's rounds hit the shooter just as he was firing. It wasn't enough to send the round completely off-target, but the shot hit Cain's shoulder instead of his head. It tore through his armor, ripping through the lean muscle and bursting out the other side.

Cain felt the pain and the kinetic impact, sending his body spiraling down to the ground. There was a rush of relief, even while he was still falling…Hector pumping painkillers into his bloodstream. He hit the ground hard, felt the wind knocked from him. He rolled the instant he fell, reaching around with his good arm, pulling his assault rifle from its harness. Erik Cain was a veteran's veteran. He ignored the wound in his arm and prepared to fight off whatever enemy had fired at him.

He flipped over onto his belly and crawled behind a large crate, staring toward the forest. He wasn't sure exactly where the shots had come from, but he had a general idea.

There was nothing. No more shots, no one visible. Wait, he thought. He saw a figure stumbling forward. He pulled up his rifle and took aim, but something held him back. It was a woman, and she was clearly wounded. He could see blood on her now, and she was stumbling, struggling to stay on her feet.

"Don't shoot...I'm here to help you." She had her hands in the air, showing him she had no weapon drawn. He was suspicious, but he held his fire. She looked familiar, but he couldn't place her at first. She resembled Sarah...no, not just a resemblance...she was almost the image of his lover. Then he remembered...Carson's World...the last battle of the Third Frontier War. He'd seen her there...the spitting image of Sarah.

"I'm Sarah Linden's sister, General Cain," Alex shouted, just as he was trying to figure it out. "I killed your assassin. I want to help." She ran the rest of the way toward Cain, her clothes soaked in blood. Some of it was hers, but most was Cobra's. She'd hit the assassin with two rounds from her assault rifle and then finished the job with her knife. The two had struggled mightily until Alex managed to shove the blade into her adversary's neck. He fell back, choking on his own blood and she finished him off, driving the knife deep into his chest. She'd neutralized the enemy...but he'd gotten two shots off. Her first thought was to get to Cain...to see if Cobra's aim had been true. She felt a wave of relief when she saw him moving.

"I'm relieved you're still alive, General. The man sent to kill you rarely misses." She heard a noise to the south, and her head snapped around. It was a long sleek craft, some kind of transport vessel. She reached for her pistol, unsure if these were friends or enemies arriving...

The hovercraft's hatch opened and Sarah leapt to the ground, followed by her six Marines. She stood there for an instant, the wind taking her hair and blowing it back in a confused tangle. She looked across the 50 meters of flat ground, and her blood ran cold. There she was…her sister Alex, crouched over the fallen form of an armored Marine. There was a gun in her hand.

"NO!" she screamed, her arm reaching down for the pistol at her side. "Get away from him." There was anger in her voice, uncontrollable rage. She ran toward Alex, pulling the gun up in front of her as she did.

Alex looked up, seeing her sister running toward her. "Sarah…" Her eyes caught the gun in Sarah's hand. "No, Sarah…"

The first shot took her in the chest. She fell to her knees, wide eyes looking right at Sarah as the second hit her neck.

"Sarah, NO!" The voice was familiar, but it took a second to work its way through her rage, her focused fury. It was Erik. He was alive. But why was he shouting no?

"NO!" he screamed again. "It wasn't her. She saved me, Sarah. I'm OK." His voice was weak, but he put every bit of strength he had into his scream.

Sarah stopped, looking down in front of her in horror. Erik was lying on his back. He had a nasty-looking wound on his shoulder, but she didn't see anything else. Alex had fallen on top of him. She was lying face down across the legs of his armor.

My God, she thought, what have I done? She ran over and turned Alex onto her back next to Cain.

"Stark sent an assassin, Sarah…this woman saved me."

Sarah felt the tears welling up in her eyes, the awful realization of what she had done. Her instincts took over, decades of experience as a battlefield surgeon directing her every move. She leaned over Alex, tearing open her shirt, surveying the wound. There was blood everywhere.

Her hands moved rapidly. She tore off a section of Alex's shirt, wadding up the material and pushing hard on the wound, trying to slow the bleeding. She knew it was hopeless, but she couldn't bring herself to stop. She had to save Alex. She just had to.

She felt something against her arm. She looked down, seeing Alex's hand reaching up to her. Sarah was still leaning forward, pressing hard on the makeshift bandage, but Alex was slowly shaking her head.

"It's…ok…Sarah." Her voice was weak…it took an enormous effort to speak, and there were gurgling sounds when she did. Her neck wound was bleeding too, and she was struggling to breathe.

"I'm so sorry, Alex. My God, I'm so sorry." Sarah was leaning on the wound with all her weight, but the shirt was soaked in blood. There were tears streaming down her face. "You'll be OK."

"No…" - she grabbed onto Sarah's arm and squeezed gently - "…it's…over…Sarah…"

"No," Sarah yelled, "No…"

"Sarah…I…am…sorry."

Sarah looked at her stricken sister. Her face was soaked with tears. She'd shot her sister…for no reason. And Alex was apologizing to her?

"I…did…terrible…things…Sarah." She spasmed hard, spitting blood all over herself. She coughed, struggling to speak. "I…hated…you…for…so…many…years." Her eyes glistened with tears as she looked up at Sarah. "I…saved…him…" She sucked in a deep breath, coughing and trying to clear her throat. "I…saved…him…for…you. Be…happy…Sarah…I…love… you…sister."

"I love you too, Alex." Sarah grabbed onto her sister, holding her tightly. "I love you too. I'm so sorry. I'm so sorry." She was sobbing uncontrollably. She felt Alex draw a last deep breath and then fall back, lifeless.

Sarah held onto her sister's body, still sobbing and repeating, "I'm so sorry…"

Chapter 13

Front Line – Europa Federalis-CEL Conflict
25 Kilometers West of Stuttgart
Baden-Wurttemberg Sector – Central European League
Earth – Sol III

Hans Werner poked his head out of the massive Leopard Z-9a command tank. He had a full scanner suite inside the armored protection of the behemoth vehicle, but sometimes nothing replaced a good old fashioned look around.

The CEL army was a week into its first war in a century, and they'd been driven back by the invading Europan forces. The army of the German-dominated CEL had long considered itself more than a match for its enemies, but that confidence had been seriously shaken by the ferocity of the Europan attack. The CEL had repeatedly denied any involvement in the nuclear destruction of Marseilles, but the incident proved to be a rallying cry for the Europan forces nevertheless.

Half his initial tanks were gone, but he'd received reinforcements the day before. The new vehicles were Leopard Z-7s, older models operated by reservists. They weren't a match for the tanks and crews he'd lost, but he was glad to have them anyway.

He watched as a platoon of infantry repositioned, moving into supporting range of his front line of tanks. Armored vehicles were primary targets on the battlefield, and serving in one was difficult and dangerous. But right now he pitied the foot soldiers more. He couldn't image how miserable they were in their heavy rubberized CBN suits. The war hadn't gone chemical, biological, or nuclear yet, at least not on the south-central front. Still, everyone knew it could at any moment, and they had to be prepared at all times. Both sides were massively armed with enhanced munitions, and all it would take was a single order from the high command to unleash their fury on the battlefield. The tank crews could button up and seal off their monster vehicles, but the infantry had to be ready for whatever happened.

There were rumors the two sides had exchanged tactical nuclear strikes to the north, but nothing was confirmed. Communications had been spotty, with few reports on the status of other battle fronts. Werner's people had very little idea what was going on outside their small section of the battlefield, but if things were just as bad everywhere else, he knew the CEL was in trouble.

"I'm getting a recon drone report, sir. We've got enemy tanks moving up the old E52 highway." Lieutenant Potsdorf was yelling the warning from inside the tank. Potsdorf was in charge of the command tank, and he doubled as an aide to the battalion commander. "It looks like a large move, sir."

Werner didn't respond immediately. He took a last look around and ducked back inside the tank's cockpit. "Close hatch." He snapped out the order to the armored vehicle's AI as he eased back to his command chair. "OK, Lieutenant…" – he turned to face Potsdorf – "…let's get the battalion ready for action. I want all units at full alert."

"Yes, Colonel." Potsdorf had proven to be a good aide. He'd come from the working classes and, lacking any substantial patronage, he'd advanced largely through his own ability…a rarity in any of the Superpowers. Obtaining a commission was a huge burst of upward mobility for someone from his background, one guaranteeing him at least a sustenance-level pension when he retired. Few of the lower classes in the CEL had any kind of retirement income or safety net. When they became too old or sick to work, they were forced to rely on their families. Those without children or relatives who could care for them often starved…or reported to one of the population control centers for voluntary euthanasia. But a veteran of the Heer with a lieutenant's stipend was guaranteed a modestly comfortable retirement. The CEL took reasonably good care of its soldiers, unlike powers like the Alliance where disabled and discharged veterans were sent back home with a few credits and virtually no continuing support.

"All units report ready, sir." Potsdorf turned from the scope and looked back at his CO. "Project contact imminently."

"All units are to fire at will." Werner's voice was firm. He entered the war as a colonel with no combat experience, but six days in hell had changed all that. He'd heard of other commanders losing control over the last few days, panicking in action. Werner and his colleagues were drawn mostly from the lower echelons of the privileged families, usually younger siblings with no other prospects. Few of them were truly prepared to face the harsh realities of battle. But Hans Werner felt invigorated by combat. He was scared too, but the tension and the fear honed his mind. His battalion had suffered heavy losses, but they'd held firm. In the end, his people had only been forced back because the units on their flanks retreated.

Potsdorf repeated the order over the unitwide channel. "Here they come, sir." The lieutenant had been cool under fire, but Werner could hear the tension in his voice now. "Looks like regimental strength. As far as I can tell, they're all Napoleons, sir. C-class."

Damn, Werner thought. Where are they getting all these tanks? The Napoleon Class behemoths were the Europans' state of the art main battle tank, and they just kept coming. His front was supposed to be a secondary one, with the real battle fought to the north. But it was starting to look like the enemy had different ideas.

He heard a loud crack…one of his Leopards firing. It was followed by another…and another. He smiled. The CEL's railguns made a distinctive sound. His people had gotten off the first shots. They had performed well since hostilities began, his focus on peacetime training paying benefits now that war had finally come.

Now he was hearing Europan fire too, though only regular

shells. The Europan tanks had railguns too, but those were line of sight weapons, and he had his people hull down in good cover. The Europans were going to have to get close – very close – to get good shots with their primary weapons. He stared at the tactical display. He had a company of tanks deployed at the end of a small ridge…good cover that offered line of sight to targets moving up the highway. It was an obvious trap, but the enemy was over confident, and they blundered forward right into it. Werner's forward position took out three of the enemy tanks in a few seconds…and stalled the entire advance.

"Lieutenant, put in another request for air support." Werner didn't expect anything to come of the request, but it was worth a try.

"Yes, Colonel." Potsdorf's voice suggested he was no more optimistic about seeing CEL planes any time soon.

No one in Werner's battalion had seen an aircraft – either CEL or Europan – for days. They'd heard rumors the two sides were locked in a titanic struggle for air superiority up in the north, and every resource had been committed to that battle. Werner didn't know what was going on, but if the CEL air force would defeat the Europans and gain supremacy in the skies, it would go a long way to stabilizing the crumbling front.

"Infantry teams forward…NOW!" He snapped out his order and listened as Potsdorf relayed it. Running around MBTs wasn't a safe place for infantry to be, but the Europan tanks were disorganized, trying to reposition from the highway and bypass Werner's forward positions. His rocket teams would have a good chance to take out a few more of the monster battlewagons, and Werner needed everything he could get to even the score. If he could hit the enemy hard enough before they reformed, maybe he could stop them here. If not, Stuttgart was as good as lost.

"We've picked up another contact, sir." Lieutenant Barrington was staring at the scanner as he spoke. "That makes 42. Including 9 heavy battleships."

"Very well, Lieutenant." Admiral Dave Young sat in the

command chair on Chicago's flag bridge. "The fleet will continue on the same heading." Young was nervous, but he was trying not to let it show. He'd been in the navy for 25 years, but he knew he owed his position to his family's political influence more than any particular aptitude. He'd been given a ship command after only 12 months service, and he took over a task force within five years. He'd been commanding fleets ever since, and he eventually worked up to the largest of all, the South Pacific Command. The fleet had a single but crucial role...to fight the CAC if war broke out between the two powers. But aside from hunting down a pirate or two, Young had never seen a shot fired in anger.

The Alliance's wet navy differed enormously from its fleets in space. The interstellar navy was mostly a frontier organization now, drawing the majority of its recruits from the colonies and, since the rebellions, operating largely independently of Alliance Gov's day to day influence. Since Augustus Garret had taken command – and achieved living legend status defeating the First Imperium – few in the Earth government dared to challenge him. But the sea navy, like the rest of the Earth-based forces, was firmly under Alliance Gov's thumb. And that meant patronage and corruption governed virtually every aspect of its operation, including who filled its officer postings and top commands.

Young's family was among the most influential in the Alliance, one of the original political dynasties. The family controlled an almost unprecedented three seats in the Senate, as well as a complex collection of Directorates and judgeships. Dave Young was the youngest of seven, however, and his cousins were almost as numerous as his siblings...and all older than him. With no suitable political office available, Young had opted for a military career. His position and influence had almost guaranteed him a quick route to an important command.

Young's exalted rank was predominantly the result of his fortunate birth, but he had at least made an effort to learn his craft, something few of the other officers from prominent Political Class families bothered to do. He'd studied naval history and the campaigns of the great admirals. But mostly, he read and reread every account of the last war he could find. It was often hard to filter out the lies and political adjustments made to the records, but he knew the fighting those navies had done was the closest to what his might be called on to do. The fleets that fought in the early stages of the Unification Wars had been much like those from past battles, consisting largely of surface vessels. But destructive power had outpaced defensive capability, and by the end of the wars, barely a naval vessel was still in action. The fleets the Superpowers rebuilt consisted entirely of hybrids...capable of fighting on the surface, but designed primarily for submerged operations. So, for all Admiral David Young gleaned from the histories, the next war would likely be a dramatically different affair from any that had preceded it.

"The lead elements of the fleet will close to the 20 kilometer line in three minutes, Admiral." Barrington's tone was edgy. The fleet was about to cross the border the CAC had drawn across the South Pacific. The Alliance and the CAC had disputed ownership of the Philippines for over a century, and they'd had soldiers deployed facing each other across artificial borders for that entire time. The CAC controlled roughly two-thirds of the land area, but there were over 100,000 Alliance soldiers dug in all around Manila and southern Luzon, and Young's fleet was offshore, facing the CAC's assembled naval strength. The CAC had issued an ultimatum, a line they would not allow the Alliance fleet to cross. But Barrington's orders were clear. He was to call their bluff, to lead his fleet over that line...and if so much as a single CAC ship fired on him he was to engage and destroy the entire enemy fleet.

"Very well, Lieutenant." He struggled to keep his voice firm. Young took his position seriously, but he wasn't a warrior at heart. He'd grown up surrounded by almost unimaginable luxury, and the transition to military life was a jarring one. He had managed to learn his trade, at least after a fashion, but he'd never really expected to put those skills to the test. Now he was 1200 meters below the surface of the ocean...and possibly minutes away from the first major naval battle in a century. He was trying to play the role of the fearless commander, but deep down he was scared shitless. "Order all ships to battlestations. Attack boat crews to their positions."

"Yes, Admiral." Barrington passed on the order, some of his own fear pushing through and showing in his voice. A few seconds later, Chicago's battlestations lamps lit, casting a reddish glow across the bridge.

The CAC was still denying any involvement in the attack on Alliance Intelligence HQ in Washbalt, but relations between the Powers had continued to fray…and the crisis only escalated further when Alliance operatives discovered that the CAC had previously begun mobilizing a portion of its Earth-based military. News of the military buildup cast further doubt on Hong Kong's protestations about the Washbalt bombing. The two powers were already at war in space…and it seemed like fighting would break out on Earth at any time.

"We will cross the red line in one minute, sir." Barrington was staring at his scope, counting the seconds. An instant later: "Sir, all attack squadrons report ready to launch."

"Very well, Lieutenant." Young strapped himself into his command chair. He stared ahead, breathing deeply, trying to ignore the sweat pouring down his back.

"Thirty seconds, sir."

Will they fire, Young wondered…do they really want war? Is there a commander over there who thinks I am bluffing? He sat rigidly, holding his body motionless. I guess we're going to find out, he thought nervously.

"Lead elements crossing the red line now, sir." Barrington stared into the scope. The seconds passed by, each one slow, agonizing.

Young sat in his chair, looking over at his tactical officer. He was waiting for the word the enemy had attacked…that they were at war. But there was only silence.

"No readings, sir. The entire fleet has passed the red line, and I've detected no…" Barrington stopped abruptly. "Sir… scanners are picking up multiple launches from the enemy fleet." There was urgency in his voice now, and unmasked fear. His head spun toward Young. "It's confirmed, sir. The enemy has fired torpedoes."

Young sat silently for a few seconds. He felt like he was going to vomit, but he clamped down on his emotions. Now, he thought…now is your test. Are you really an admiral worthy of leading this fleet? Or are you just the spoiled youngest son of a wealthy family, good for nothing at all? He took a single deep breath and exhaled hard. "All ships are to open fire immediately. All attack boat squadrons…launch."

The Alliance and the CAC were at war.

"We've got to keep going. We're still way too close to the city." The sun had been down for half an hour, and dusk was giving way to total darkness. Axe was walking along the crumbling wreckage of what had once been a major highway. It was mostly broken chunks of ancient asphalt now, with huge sections of exposed dirt showing in places. There were deep holes in some areas, where the upper structure had collapsed to reveal utility lines and other mechanicals below.

He would have preferred to head west from the city, where they would have had more choices on where to go. But it just wasn't an option, not from where they started out. His small band would have had to cross two rivers just to get out of New York, and the old New Jersey waterfront was a notoriously violent slum, even worse than Brooklyn…and run by rival gangs instead of his own. Besides, the mobs of angry Cogs were rampaging all along the Brooklyn waterfront…and there were still dangerous radioactive hotspots in lower Manhattan. In the end he decided heading east, farther out onto Long Island was the only practical thing to do.

The lands east of Brooklyn had once been a massively-populated suburb, inhabited by millions, but it had long since been virtually abandoned. Alliance Gov liked to keep people centralized where they were easier to watch, so they encouraged people to move to the cities. At first, they used persuasion and enticed them with promises of better jobs and homes. But eventually they just withdrew all civil services and unleashed the gangs on the holdouts. The areas of the island east of the city had been virtually abandoned for close to a century. The perfect place to hide…and wait and see how things played out.

"What the hell is going on, anyway?" Tank was loyal to Axe; there was no question about that. It was why he was part of the small group the former gang leader took with him when he fled Brooklyn. He was a hulking bull of a man, which Axe knew would come in handy if they ran into any fighting, but no one was going to confuse Tank Jones with a genius.

Axe sighed. Sometimes he wished Tank would just shut up and not try to think. "The economy is crashing. Everything's shutting down. They're having trouble keeping the Politicos fed and supplied…which is why the Cogs in places like Brooklyn are getting nothing. And that's why they're in the streets." He paused, feeling a chill when he thought of the staggering rage now ruling the mobs back in Brooklyn, and probably everywhere else. The Cogs had been so docile, so easy to intimidate. But that was when they still clung to their miserable but sustainable lives. They never had much, but it was enough for most of them to survive. Now they were truly desperate, faced with the prospect of watching their families starve to death. All the anger they'd repressed, the hatred that had grown deep inside them…it was all coming out, erupting like a volcano that had long been building pressure. "He glanced over his shoulder back toward Brooklyn. "And that's why we're getting the hell out while we can."

Chapter 14

Martian Command Bunker
Garibaldi Base
Mars, Sol IV

Roderick Vance sat at the end of the table rubbing his temples with considerable force. His head was throbbing. The bad news just kept coming, like water pouring from a broken floodgate. Vance had a reputation for being cold and efficient, but he was worn down and exhausted…and that was something he knew he couldn't afford. If someone was going to stop Gavin Stark it was probably going to be him, and he'd need to be at his best to have a chance. Garret, Holm, and Cain were incredibly capable warriors, but Vance was the only spy in the group. A psychopath as brilliant as Stark couldn't be beaten by force alone…not without overwhelming superiority Vance knew his allies didn't have. Stark was too smart, too careful…his plans would have backups and contingencies to cover the backups.

Vance looked down at the table, his expression grim. He had come to the realization that even he had underestimated Stark. He'd known the Alliance spy was ruthless, willing to sacrifice thousands to achieve his goals. But now he saw there was no limit to what the bastard would do. Stark was willing to see millions die, even billions, if that's what it took to secure his final victory. Vance realized he faced an enemy who would do literally anything to accomplish his goals.

To make matters worse, war was breaking out on Earth, largely through Stark's machinations. Vance had hoped to leverage the good feeling from the victory against the First Imperium to usher in a new era of greater cooperation between the Powers. But Stark had masterfully manipulated the situation, destroying Vance's work and turning the camaraderie and good feeling into mistrust and hatred.

Europa Federalis and the CEL were already locked in a death struggle, their entire border a brutal war zone. There were hundreds of thousands of casualties already, and the battle was still escalating. Vance doubted the CEL had any part in the destruction of Marseilles, though the evidence certainly suggested their involvement. He smelled the stench of Gavin Stark behind that tragedy too, but he hadn't been sure...not until additional evidence from the blast area began pointing toward Mars as well as the CEL. It was fairly thin, but the Superpowers were all leery of the Confederation after the attack on Stark's Dakota base. Paranoia was running rampant through the capitals of Earth, and any suspicion was blown enormously out of proportion and given the status of proven fact.

His eyes drifted back to the screen...and the dire message it displayed. More bad news...possibly the worst yet. The ocean navies of the Alliance and the CAC had clashed in the South Pacific with massive losses on both sides. The Alliance Senate had declared war on the Central Asian Combine, and the CAC Committee responded in kind within an hour. The next morning the Caliphate issued a declaration against the Alliance, responding to its treaty obligations, and the Pacific Rim Coalition did the same and declared war against the Caliphate and the CAC.

In less than two weeks, six of the eight Earth Superpowers were at war. The Treaty of Paris was in tatters, and a generation of political leaders who had no living memory of the horrors of the Unification Wars prepared to unleash their armies for the first time in a century. The war between Europa Federalis and the CEL was largely a regional affair, offering some hope of containment, but now the 4 most powerful Superpowers were locked in a global death struggle, one that could very well lead to total apocalypse.

Stark had tried to contact Li An, but the CAC's top spy was

nowhere to be found. He knew Li had been against war with the Alliance, working behind the scenes to defuse tensions. But what would she do now that conflict was a reality? Li An was smart, cunning, willing to go to considerable lengths to achieve her goals. But he knew she'd never do anything that endangered the CAC. Vance didn't doubt Li An's loyalty to her homeland. If war was unavoidable, however much she might have been against it, she would do her best to help the CAC win it.

Maybe she had cut ties with him, unsure where Mars would end up in the rapidly-expanding conflict. Or perhaps she had continued to counsel peace and been eliminated by the pro-war forces in the government. He found it difficult to imagine anyone outsmarting Li enough to successfully assassinate her, but he had to remind himself that no one was invincible. And Li An was very old now and well past the peak of her abilities. Perhaps she'd finally slipped up enough and paid the price. Or even decided she had no desire to see the final war through to its inevitable conclusion. He had a mental image of her sitting at her desk, peacefully sipping on a Scotch as she allowed her assassin to penetrate her inner sanctum.

Vance didn't know. He was used to being a master operator, the one pulling the strings. But he'd never faced off in a death struggle against an adversary like Gavin Stark. What freak of genetics, he wondered, produced a monster of such amorality and stunning ability combined? Vance was not a religious man, but he had trouble imagining Gavin Stark as nothing more than an accident of genetics and environment. It was almost easier to think of him as an antichrist or some other great beast from man's ancient religions, come to punish him for his many sins. "Stark is just a man," he muttered to himself, forcing his thoughts back to cold reality. He sat at his desk, fists clenched in frustration. "He is just a man, and he can be defeated." He paused. "And we will find a way to beat him…" – he stared grimly ahead – "…to destroy him…whatever it takes."

Vance breezed into the room, his hurried steps not quite a run, but certainly a jog. Roderick Vance - who admired punctuality, who demanded it of his subordinates, who had broken agents' careers over habitual tardiness – was late.

"I'm sorry for my lack of punctuality." He flopped down into his chair with considerably less grace than usual. "I'm afraid there was more news on the Alliance-CAC engagement, and I wanted to be fully briefed for our meeting. It was a reasonable excuse for being late, but he couldn't help but flash back to more than one occasion when he'd castigated hapless agents who'd offered equally valid explanations. He felt a twinge of regret… and a passing thought that maybe he had his own touch of the sociopathy that ruled Gavin Stark. Perhaps all successful spies did. But he put it out of his mind immediately. There was no time for self-indulgent soul searching. Not now.

"Don't give it a second thought, Roderick." Sebastian Vallen spoke in a soothing tone. He, better than anyone, knew the workload Vance had taken on himself. The last thing he wanted – the last thing any of them could afford right now – was for Vance to waste time and attention on foolish protocols. Vallen had been the younger man's mentor for decades, and he knew Roderick Vance was a genius. He was also well aware his protégé suffered from an epic case of OCD. The Martian spymaster would be facing his greatest challenge in the weeks and months ahead. They were going to need him at his best if they were going to have any chance at all to salvage the rapidly deteriorating situation. Vallen had confidence in Vance, and he believed deep down that his friend could defeat Gavin Stark. If he didn't lose his mind first.

Vallen leaned back, deliberately telegraphing a relaxed mood. "So what do you have for us this morning, Roderick?"

Vance nodded at his oldest friend and then glanced down at the 'pad he'd placed on the table. "Let's begin with the wars on Earth. We must consider these conflicts to be the greatest danger." He knew what Stark wanted…that the wars on Earth were his idea of a diversion. But 99% of mankind still lived on the homeworld, and the Powers possessed enough weapons to kill them a hundred times over. It took a mind like Stark's to consider that a diversion.

Vance looked out over the table at the oligarchs, the men – and one woman - who effectively ruled the Confederation. Each of them could trace a direct line of descent from the original settlers. Mars prided itself on being a fairer, more open society than any of the Earth-based Powers. That was true, but only a point. Those who had been there first had managed to reserve the real power to themselves…and their descendants. Mars was a free society of sorts, but only by comparison with the statist regimes that ruled on Earth.

He paused for a few seconds and then cleared his throat. "First, the conflict in Europe. Europa Federalis and the CEL have continued to fight along their entire border. The combat has been high intensity, and casualties have been extraordinarily heavy. Fortunately, the war has remained largely conventional. There was a brief exchange of tactical nuclear weapons, but both sides quickly de-escalated."

His eyes dropped to glance at his 'pad before continuing. "Unexpectedly, the Europans seem to have gained the upper hand, and their forces have penetrated 10-40 kilometers into CEL territory." He paused, noting the surprised looks around the table. "Except in one small area on the southern end of the front. It appears the CEL forces have stopped the Europans cold in that sector."

"What happened there?" asked Vallen.

"It is hard to be sure. Our details at that level are limited. It appears that a battalion commander was instrumental in turning back a heavy Europan attack." Vance's voice was tentative… the facts he was disclosing were unconfirmed rumors at best… and wild guesses at worst. But it was all he had, so he continued. "Subsequently, it appears he was made acting brigade commander, after which he launched a successful localized counterattack." He glanced down at the 'pad again. "It remains to be seen if his axis of advance will expand or if the salient his attack created will be pinched out."

"Perhaps we should hope that his victory is short-lived." It was Katarina Berchtold. "While my sympathies are with the CEL…" – Berchtold's ancestors had emigrated from old Germany – "…the greater good may be served by whatever leads to a swifter victory – for either side."

"Perhaps, Katarina, but I am not so sure." Vallen was speaking to Berchtold but looking at Vance. "That conclusion is dependent on the losing side accepting defeat and ceasing hostilities…instead of unloading its nuclear and biological arsenals on the prospective winner."

"Which is precisely what I would expect them to do." Vance's tone was grim. He'd studied the geopolitics of Earth extensively, and the CEL was not a power likely to yield easily. Worse, the current regime was one of the most hawkish of the last century. Vance didn't doubt for a second that they would use every weapon they had before they accepted defeat. "If the CEL is pushed against the wall, they will escalate." He looked down the table at Berchtold. "Our best hope is for a stalemate. That is the strongest chance to keep the fighting conventional. The two sides might eventually yield to mutual exhaustion, but a Power near defeat is a dangerous loose cannon."

Vallen nodded, followed by the rest of the council. Finally, Berchtold signaled her agreement. "I defer to your greater knowledge, Roderick. Unfortunately, it looks like Europa Federalis may be on the way to winning a quick victory."

"That's not very likely, Katarina." Vallen beat Vance to the punch. He had headed up the Martian intelligence services before his protégé took over, and he knew the realities of the Earth Superpowers better than the rest of the Council. "I think the Europans will find it hard to maintain their momentum as casualties mount and supplies run low. There is a tendency in war for things to bog down." His eyes flicked toward Vance then back to Berchtold. "The Europans may maintain an edge, but it is quite a different thing to overrun another Superpower. It is a possibility, of course, but certainly not the likeliest source of disaster." He paused for a few seconds. "I fear we must look to the Alliance-CAC conflict for the greatest danger of catastrophic escalation." He paused for a few seconds before continuing. "Perhaps we should shelve our discussion of the Europan-CEL conflict and discuss the situation with the Alliance and the CAC." Vallen stared at Vance expectantly. "You mentioned some new intel?"

"Yes." Vance's tone left no doubt the news was bad. "The CAC and the Alliance were already at war in space, as you all know. My operatives report that the CAC navy has been ordered to find Admiral Garret and engage his fleet." Vance spoke slowly, deliberatively.

"Did they give them a blindfold and a cigarette?" It was Katarina Berchtold again. She was the matriarch of one of Mars' oldest families and a woman of immense ability. But she was the least experienced in military matters, and it was showing. She glanced around the table, noting the somber expressions both Vance and Vallen wore before she pressed on. "Do we really think whatever admiral the CAC placed in command after the purge can defeat Admiral Garret?" Garret had become a legend throughout all the Superpowers. He was regarded as the man who'd defeated the First Imperium, though Garret himself objected strongly to such singular characterizations.

"It's not that simple, Katarina." Vallen spoke up, sparing Vance the task. "Certainly Augustus Garret is the most capable naval officer serving any of the Powers. But there are other considerations. Garret only has part of the Alliance fleet with him. Admiral Harmon was left in command of considerable forces on the frontier to confirm no First Imperium forces could cross the Barrier." He paused for a few seconds. "Additionally, Admiral Garret is cut off from all his bases. His fleet has not been able to refit or resupply. He has only the armaments he brought back after the final battle on the Rim. Worse, he has since engaged a portion of Gavin Stark's fleet, which had to further deplete his limited stores." Vallen's eyes looked down at the table. "And there is another factor we must at least consider. He lost his best friend and long-time colleague…worse, he gave the order that trapped Admiral Compton beyond the Barrier." He paused briefly. "We cannot know how that will affect him. Garret is a man who has always been willing to make the necessary sacrifices and take well-chosen gambles. But every man has his breaking point. We must wonder if Admiral Garret is still the man who achieved the victory against the First Imperium."

Berchtold looked across the table at Vallen. "Are you saying that Admiral Garret might be defeated by the CAC fleet?"

"No, Katarina, not necessarily." Vallen was returning her gaze. "But we believe the CAC fleet was able to fully replenish itself. If the two forces engage, Admiral Garret will be at a substantial disadvantage." He paused again. "We cannot know whether Garret will be able to overcome such a deficit. At some level of material disadvantage, even Garret's skill and courage will be insufficient to counter the enemy's superiority. His crews cannot throw rocks at their foes."

Berchtold nodded slowly. After a long pause she said, "Shouldn't we aid him then? I cannot imagine how Admiral Garret's defeat can be anything but disastrous for the Confederation."

"You are right, Katarina." Vance sat motionless in his chair, staring across the table at her. "However it is a more complex situation. Indeed, the Alliance is on the verge of declaring war on the Confederation over the Dakota attack. And Europa Federalis is a concern as well. If Gavin Stark managed to place any more false evidence of our involvement in the destruction of Marseilles, it is very possible that Paris will also make a declaration against us."

He glanced at Vallen then back to Berchtold. "While I am confident that Admiral Garret would refuse to obey any orders to attack the Confederation, I have no doubt the Europan space forces will do so. If the Europans order their fleet to commence operations against us, we must have ships in place to defend Mars. Indeed, it is not just Mars we must consider. We have possessions throughout the solar system…and interstellar colonies as well. If we are to defend all our people, what force can we spare to aid Admiral Garret?"

The room was uncomfortably quiet for perhaps 30 seconds. Finally, it was Vallen who broke the silence. "Not that we need more bad news, but I don't believe you have shared with us the latest dispatch from Earth. The reason for your…ah…tardiness." Vallen frowned, immediately regretting the misplaced attempt at humor.

"Yes, you're right, Sebastian." Vance stared around the table, settling his gaze on Vallen. "Before I left my office for this meeting I received a flash communication from one of our deep cover agents in the Alliance." He hesitated, but only for an instant. "CAC and Alliance fleets have engaged off the coast of the Philippines. The engagement was a pyrrhic victory for the Alliance fleet." He moved his eyes across the table again, pausing for an instant on each of his colleagues. "The two Powers exchanged declarations of war, after which the PRC and Caliphate honored their respective treaty obligations." He took a deep breath and exhaled. "Six of the Earth Superpowers are now at war."

Chapter 15

Outskirts of Arcadia City
Capital District
Arcadia – Wolf 359 III

Kara stood on the top of the hill and stared out across the valley. There it was…Arcadia. The capital city looked serene, though she knew that was an illusion. The enemy almost certainly knew her army was there, and they were undoubtedly dug in, waiting for her attack. She squinted through her mags, scanning carefully, trying to pick out the defensive strongpoints. There was a rocket battery emplaced just outside the city limits, tucked in behind a small cluster of houses, but otherwise, she couldn't see anything significant. There were probably troops deployed in and among the buildings, but no large formations or heavy weapons.

"Are you ready?" Captain Mandrake walked up behind her, his visor retracted. "I assume your plan is still a go?" The Marine captain smiled. He'd come to admire Kara over the last few months, and the thought of her backing down, giving up on her plan, was almost inconceivable.

"You still think I'm crazy?" She was still looking straight ahead, the mags glued to the front of her face.

"I never thought you were crazy." There was a warmth in his voice, a gentleness the veteran Marine didn't show very often. He respected Kara immensely. He suspected he'd be very fond of her…that is if she ever let her grim armor down long enough for him to really get to know her. "I just suggested that you consider the difficulties of marching your army through a polar wasteland."

She lowered the mags and turned to face him. She didn't say anything at first, but he could see the guilt and hurt behind her eyes, a rare glimpse past her defenses to her inner self. The army had left over 500 of its number behind, a trail of frozen corpses marking its journey like footsteps. Mandrake thought for an instant she might open up, show some real emotion. But she just looked at him and said, "You know better than anyone, Captain, that war has its cost."

"Yes, I certainly know that." And one day my dear Kara, he thought, you are going to unravel. There was a limit to how much one person could internalize. He just hoped she didn't lose it in battle, when it would get her – and a lot of her people – killed. He looked over at her. He couldn't argue with the validity of her plan. It certainly looked like the capital was lightly defended, and he couldn't imagine another strategy that offered as much chance to help out the Marines to the south.

"Well," she said emotionlessly. "We've got bogies on our tail, so there's no point in wasting time." She tapped the comlink clipped to her collar. "Ed, let's finish getting everyone formed up for the attack."

"Yes, Kara. They're almost ready." Calvin was technically the army's commander, though he'd expressed no reservations about acting as Kara's second. He knew she'd want to attack as soon as possible, and he had the troops almost set to go. "We can advance in a few minutes."

She stared quietly across the valley, her eyes fixed on the center of Arcadia. She could see the spires of the Capitol, rising just above the surrounding structures. She couldn't see the park she knew sat right across the street, but her memories filled in the missing details. Independence Park...it was just a patch of grass around a small central square. She closed her eyes for a few seconds, imagining the simple bronze statue that stood dead center in the square, the image of Will Thompson looking out over the nascent Arcadian government he'd helped to create. Her mind drifted back, thinking of Will, of how things could have been if he'd survived. Or if she hadn't wasted the time they'd had together.

Kara shook her head, dragging her mind back to the present. She took a deep breath and turned to walk down the hillside, motioning for Mandrake to follow her. "Let's go, Craig."

Mandrake stood motionless on the hilltop. "Wait, Kara."

She stopped and turned. "What is…"

Mandrake held his hand up and jacked the volume on his com. "Attention all Marine forces, this is General Catherine Gilson." Kara stared at him dumbstruck, listening to the tinny sound coming from his helmet. "We are currently conducting landing operations." There was a brief pause then the com crackled to life again. "Attention all Marine forces…"

Kara turned abruptly, slapping the com on her collar. A Marine relief force was landing! "Ed, I want everybody moving now. All units…attack!"

"Black Dragons…attack!" Lieutenant-Commander Elisa Haroldson angled her sleek atmospheric fighter-bomber toward the enemy troop concentrations, her squadron tucked in just behind. The Black Dragons, otherwise known at the 87th Atmospheric Assault Squadron, was one of the best, built from the veteran survivors of the fleet's decimated formations. The campaigns against the First Imperium had been costly, not only to the Marines, but to the fleet and the support services as well. Haroldson had served in three other squadrons, each decimated in turn during the planetary assaults and defenses that had ultimately turned back the First Imperium. She'd built the Dragons from the shattered remnants of other units, and her people were all Admiral Harmon had available to send in to cover the Marine landings.

She pulled back slowly on the stick, leveling her craft at an altitude of less than 200 meters. "Prepare to strafe enemy positions." Her planes were coming in with FAEs and autocannons only. Arcadia was a friendly planet, and Harmon had taken nukes and chemical weapons off the table.

She was flying parallel with the enemy's primary line of battle. There was some sporadic fire from the ground, but nothing serious. She wished the fleet had more air assets...the enemy didn't appear to have any serious defenses against aerial attack, and a proper air wing would have a banner day. But her job wasn't to daydream about what she didn't have; she was here to get as much as she could out of what was actually available.

They were coming in over a major enemy concentration. "Fire at will, Randi." Randi Anders was Haroldson's gunner... and one of the best in the fleet.

"I'm on it." Anders voice was scratchy, gravelly. She was bent over her scope, her fingers primed above the firing controls. Crack! The sound of the FAE nodules being released reverberated throughout the cockpit.

Haroldson flipped on the ship's belly cameras, watching the target area for a damage assessment. One by one she saw flashes as the thermobaric bombs detonated, an initial charge disbursing their concentrated fuel, mixing the highly flammable explosive with atmospheric oxygen. An instant later, a second charge detonated, igniting the now-aerated explosive, creating a fiery holocaust. Against unarmored targets, the FAEs were nearly as destructive as nukes, but they were also effective against powered infantry. The heavily protected troopers were unaffected by the weapons' pressure wave and the subsequent localized vacuum, but the temperatures near the center of the firestorms reached levels well beyond what the fighting suits could endure, and their occupants were literally cooked in their armor.

Haroldson banked the bomber hard, clearing the FAEs' area of effect. She angled toward another enemy concentration, smiling as she heard the autocannons engage. The enemy's armor was almost useless against the fighter-bomber's heavy 20mm autocannons, and Anders fired them with merciless efficiency, their massive iridium-coated rounds tearing the powered infantry apart.

"Alright, people, one pass is all we get. Back to the fleet." Haroldson vectored upward, the g-forces of her ascent slamming her crew into their acceleration couches as the bomber streaked up into the sky. The Dragons had done what they could. Now it was up to General Gilson and her Marines.

"Let's go, Marines." James Teller was shouting into his com, his tortured voice cracking as he urged his exhausted men and women into action. "Those are our brothers and sisters landing out there, and by God, we're going to cover them while they deploy." He glanced at his tactical monitor. There were symbols all over the flickering map, hundreds of landing craft descending on the battlefield.

Teller's people had been on Arcadia for months. They'd lost more than half their number, and most of the rest of them were walking wounded. By any textbook definition, his force was combat ineffective. But the books couldn't quantify heart…or guts. His Marines would dig down; they would find the strength to launch one more attack. He didn't have a doubt.

"We're going to attack…and we're going to keep attacking until we hook up with General Gilson's people." Teller was on the opposite flank from the LZ. The more enemy troops they could tie down, the easier time Gilson would have landing her people.

"Follow me, Marines." Teller leapt out of the shallow trench, and headed toward the enemy positions. He was crouched low, sheltering behind a fold in the ground as he jogged forward. The air strike had disordered the enemy, and he wanted to get his people in position before they had a chance to pull themselves together.

He was moving diagonally across the front, heading toward the enemy's flank. There was decent cover about half the way, but the rest of the charge would be across open ground. He was counting on the enemy being further distracted by Gilson's landings, but he knew his people were likely to take heavy losses going in.

"Heavy weapons teams deploy." He was at the edge of the covered approach. He'd culled all the SAWs from his squads, and he was going to set them up on the reverse slope, with decent cover and a good line of fire on the extreme left of the enemy line. "I want you all firing in two minutes."

The rest of his force was stacked up behind him. He flipped

on the unitwide com. "We're moving forward as soon as the heavies start firing." His tone was determined, even harsh. "There is no room for hesitation now. When I give the order, everyone goes. We'll have 32 autocannons giving us covering fire, and the faster we get where we're going, the more of us are going to make it." He paused, letting the words sink in. "Do you understand me, Marines?"

"Yes sir." Three hundred voices responded almost as one. They were exhausted and hurt and low on supplies. But they knew this was their best chance for victory…for survival. The training taught that and, for most of them, the experience as well. And they knew one more thing. When they leapt out from behind their cover and headed across that open ground, one man would be in the front, leading the way…James Teller. These 300 men and women had been through hell with their general, and they were ready to go wherever he led them. If they were fated to die in this battle, they were resolved to a man that they would do it in arms following their general…and not in some miserable POW camp.

"Major Barnes, are your teams ready?" Teller had placed his number two in command of the autocannons. The major had objected strongly, insisting he should join the charge, but Teller had been firm. He needed everything he could get from the autocannons. If they didn't keep the enemy suppressed, the charge would be a bloody disaster. And he knew he could trust Barnes to see it done.

"Yes, General. We are ready." Barnes' voice was somber, sullen. He'd obey his orders, but he didn't have to like it.

"Then you may commence fire, Major." There was another reason Teller wanted Barnes there…in case the charge was repulsed. He wanted the veteran major in place to rally whatever was left of the command. Because Teller was sure of one thing. If the charge failed, he wasn't coming back. "Let's go! Charge!" He leapt forward and headed toward the enemy lines, 300 Marines right behind him.

Kara crouched behind the corner of the building, her assault rifle gripped tightly in her hands. They'd all insisted she stay back…Ed, Captain Mandrake, half the officers with ranks high enough that they dared to argue with her. She'd listened, or at least pretended to listen, to what they had to say. Then she ignored them all and placed herself at the head of the army. Her army. She was done with her amorphous role, half civilian leader, half military officer. If she was going to command this army she was going to do it like a soldier.

She was staring down the street when three enemy soldiers burst into the open. She fired, almost instinctively, and she kept her finger depressed, emptying her clip at full auto. The first enemy went down almost immediately; the second stumbled and fell just as she was firing the last few rounds. The last dove behind one of the buildings at the end of the street.

Kara ducked back behind her cover just as the surviving trooper opened up. The hyper-velocity rounds tore into the masonry, obliterating the corner of the building and sending shards of shattered brick flying all around. She instinctively covered her face as she was pelted with chunks of masonry.

There was a sharp pain in her side. She swore under her breath as she looked down and saw a 10 centimeter shard of brick protruding just above her waist. She reached down and grabbed it, tears streaming down her cheeks from the pain as she slowly pulled it out and tossed it aside.

She was leaning against the wall, trying to catch her breath. She started to reach around for another clip, but the pain was unbearable, and she couldn't get her arm all the way. Her eyes were fixed on the corner of the building. If her enemy came this way she was a sitting duck. She reached down to her waist and pulled a pistol from its holster. She didn't know if the side-arm could even penetrate powered armor, but it was the best she could do.

Finally, she looked down at the wound on her side. It was an ugly sight. There was blood everywhere, and she realized immediately she had to do something. She grabbed her knife and reached down, cutting a swatch of fabric off the bottom of her shirt. Every move was an agony, but she knew there was no choice. She grabbed the swath of fabric and pressed it hard against the wound. When she looked down again she realized it was much deeper than she'd first realized. I've got to slow this bleeding, she thought, or I'm in trouble. She pressed harder wincing at the pain as she did.

She was trying to stay alert, but she felt weak, groggy. Her arm holding the pistol ached, and she rested it on her knee. There was no sign of the enemy soldier, but that didn't mean he was gone. He could still be out there, waiting, ready to charge her at any moment.

She could hear the sounds of battle all around. Her people had advanced far into the city's center, pushing the enemy garrison back with the ferocity of their assault. She glanced down at her comlink, wanting to call for help, but refusing to distract her people when the battle was still being decided. She was going to make it on her own – or not – but she wasn't going to divert so much as one of her soldiers from this battle.

She was lying against the wall when it happened a few seconds later. She heard the sound of heavy metal boots on the shattered gravel. Fear gripped her insides, and her body went cold. She raised the pistol, ready to fire at anything that came around the corner.

It happened in slow motion. The enemy soldier swung around the corner, his massive armored bulk almost totally filling her field of vision. She fired, then again...and again. The rounds just ricocheted off the dense osmium-iridium alloy of the soldier's armor. She saw his assault rifle swing around, moving toward her head.

She sat, frozen in place, transfixed on her own imminent death. She held her breath, waiting for the kill shot. But it didn't come. She heard fire, but it came from behind, not from the figure standing in front of her. Her enemy fell back, half a dozen hyper-velocity rounds tearing into his chest. She was confused, uncertain. She tried to swing around, to get a look behind her, but the pain was too severe, and she fell back against the wall.

Everything was hazy, surreal. She heard something...a voice. It was somehow familiar, and it was calling out to her. "Kara?"

A pause then again. "Kara? Are you ok?"

Her eyes slowly focused. Captain Mandrake was leaning over and looking down at her. His visor was open, and he called to her again. Kara, it's Craig Mandrake…can you hear me?"

"Craig?" She was looking up at him, but she was still disoriented.

His eyes dropped to her wound. Her hand had slipped off, and the makeshift bandage had fallen to the ground. It was soaked with blood. "Sergeant, get me a spare medkit." He reached behind him as one of his companions handed up a small pouch.

He ripped open the kit, pulling out a vial with a long needle at the end. "Sorry, Kara, but this is going to hurt." She looked back at him dreamily, not really understanding what he was saying. He jammed the needle hard into her side. She screamed and tried to jump up, but his armored hands held her rigidly in place. "It's OK, Sarah. Just try to relax." He knew she wasn't understanding him, but he continued anyway. "That was a nanobot injection, Kara. It will stabilize the wound." He stared into her eyes for a few seconds, but she didn't respond.

He turned toward the hulking figures standing behind him. "Corporal Lasky, take General Sanders to the aid station." It was the first time anyone had called Kara 'general.' It wouldn't be the last.

"Yes sir." The heavily armored Marine scooped her up like a feather."

Mandrake watched him head back toward the field hospital. "And hurry, Corporal." He paused, a worried expression on his face. "Hurry."

General Catherine Gilson felt the locking bolt retract, and she hopped off the lander, reaching around and pulling her assault rifle from its harness. She looked down at her tactical display, scanning the immediate area for enemy contacts. She knew her AI would have warned her if there were hostiles near, but Gilson wasn't the trusting sort, and she was a relentless double-checker. She tended not to believe anything unless she saw it for herself. And even then she was suspicious.

Her caution was particularly justified on this drop. Gilson was bringing her forces down right in the center of the action. It was a high risk strategy, but her scanner reports had shown her just how outnumbered and against the wall Holm's and Teller's people were. That was all she had to know. Any risk was worthwhile if it saved other Marines from being overrun.

Most of her people were down, but the last waves were still landing. In another ten minutes all of her 7,000 Marines would be on the ground. The enemy still had overall numbers, but they were exhausted and strung out from months of combat. Gilson knew her Marines were the last reinforcements coming to Arcadia…and she had no interest in simply prolonging the struggle. She was there to win. And that meant there was only one strategy that she'd considered. Attack.

She expanded the tactical display to cover most of the primary battlefield. She could see her forward elements were already on the move, advancing on the enemy positions. They would be engaged in a few minutes. The plan was simple… attack, attack, attack. There was no elegance, no needless complexity. Her people were fresh and fully supplied, at least compared to their enemies. Now they had to do the work.

She checked the clip in her assault rifle and headed up toward the front. Back in the shit, she thought as she jogged forward. Back home.

Chapter 16

Rhine Bridgeheads
Baden-Wurttemberg Sector – Central European League
Earth – Sol III

Hans Werner was still getting used to the shiny new stars on his collar. He'd just gotten word that his battlefield promotion had been approved by the high command. As of the day before he was officially a brigadier, though he'd already been acting in that capacity for two weeks…ever since his battalion had stood firm, breaking up the whole Europan southern advance.

Things up north were still bad. The Europan forces had lunged across the border from the Belgian Federal Zone and cut deep into CEL territory. The CEL northern armies had been twice defeated, and now 1,200,000 demoralized and exhausted troops were trapped in the Dusseldorf-Cologne pocket. The high command was throwing in everything it had up north, trying to break the siege before the encircled troops were forced to capitulate.

Werner's success in the south was a welcome piece of good news, and the high command was determined to make the most of it. The CEL finally had a genuine hero in a war that had so far been an almost unmitigated disaster. They were determined to make the most of it…through Werner's promotion, and his subsequent orders to go on the offensive.

There were troops moving forward in a steady stream, reinforcing his growing command. He'd had a brigade equivalent before he even gotten his stars…now that his status as brigade commander was confirmed he was leading a heavily reinforced division…almost a small corps.

"Major Kimmel's batteries are in position, sir." Potsdorf was standing right behind Werner, monitoring the attack force's communications. Werner had pulled his erstwhile aide from his tank and taken him along when he was promoted. He tested his newfound influence by requesting – and receiving – a bump up to captain for his assistant.

Werner stood silently, staring off toward the river. The last of the Europan forces had pulled back to their side, destroying the bridges behind them as they fled. The retreat had become somewhat of a rout as Werner threw fresh forces into the pursuit as quickly as they reached the front. In the end, the Europans had abandoned tanks, vehicles, and supplies as they fled for the relative safety of their side of the Rhine.

Werner had been surprised when he saw how quickly the victorious enemy had collapsed into a fleeing mass of fugitives. Now, staring across the river and contemplating his own imminent attack, he understood. There wasn't a real combat veteran in either army. The forces were well equipped and trained, but the Superpowers had not fought a war on Earth in over 100 years. All the training, all the equipment in the world cannot fully prepare men and women for the realities of combat. The armies fighting this new war were large, and they had immense stores of weaponry. But they were fragile instruments. Victory would sustain them, but defeat would shatter their morale quickly. He'd seen it happen with the Europans…how rapidly their momentum had broken when his people stood firm. Werner knew his own forces would be just as brittle.

He didn't want to cross the Rhine. He'd requested permission to fortify the eastern bank and form a defensive line, but he'd been denied and ordered to attack at once. The northern forces needed a diversion, and invading the enemy's territory was the fastest way to provide one. If his attack made progress, he would quickly be in a position to threaten the Europan capital of Paris…and that would force the enemy to reposition strength from their own northern offensive.

"Advise Major Kimmel he may commence fire." There was

no point in delaying. If he had to attack, it was best done while the enemy was still disorganized...before they could be reinforced and resupplied. "And the air wings are to begin their attack." The battle for air superiority had turned into an exercise in mutual annihilation, and both sides had lost most of their effective strength. But the high command had diverted a few precious squadrons to support Werner's attack, and he intended to get the most he could out of them.

"Yes sir." Potsdorf relayed Werner's orders, his voice a little shaky.

"Engineering companies are to commence bridging efforts immediately." Crossing a major river into the teeth of the enemy was a difficult proposition. If his artillery and air strikes didn't keep the Europans occupied, they would slaughter his engineers, and his attack would be stopped before it even got started.

"Yes, Col...General...sir." Potsdorf was still having trouble getting used to the rapidly changing situation. It had taken him 20 years of exemplary service to rise from the ranks and get his lieutenancy. Now, less than a month after the fighting began, he was a captain and Werner was a general. He had lived all his life under a stifling bureaucracy where everything moved at a glacial pace. Now the rules were changing. Rapidly.

Werner turned toward his slightly discombobulated aide. He understood what Potsdorf was feeling...he was feeling it himself. "Don't worry, Heinrich." He put his hand on the captain's shoulder. "We will get through this. Even if we have to figure it out one step at a time."

Potsdorf nodded, staring back wordlessly – and gratefully - at his commander.

Werner flashed a brief smile and nodded. "Now let's get the engineers up to the bridgeheads."

"I want the entire approach screened." Admiral Young was leaning forward in his command chair barking out orders. "If that means we've got some damaged ships on the line, so be it." He was angry and tired of getting excuses from his ship commanders. "And if the captains don't like it, tell them I'll see how the first officers feel about it." The convoy from Australia was his main concern right now. The Alliance army outside Manila needed those reinforcements and supplies, and if the CAC was able to intercept them, the ground battle in the Philippines was as good as lost.

"Yes sir." Barrington was exhausted. Young was determined to do his duty, but most of the ship commanders were members of the petty political classes. They'd joined the service for reasons similar to Young's, but they lacked the commitment of their admiral. Most of them were more concerned with getting back to their comfortable lives in one piece...and the savagery of the battle had shaken them up terribly. They'd been arguing with every command, driving Barrington crazy.

Young's ships had engaged the CAC fleet and driven it back, but not without cost. The ferocity of the battle and the losses incurred by both sides had come as a shock to all the combatants. Young's victorious fleet was almost shattered, and the fact that the CAC forces were in even worse shape was cold comfort. War had come, and the horror of it had exceeded his worst fears.

Despite the victory, he knew he had a tougher situation in the long term. The combat zone was close to the CAC's main bases, while the Alliance fleet had to rely on the resources of the Oceania Sector for most of its support. Australia and the rest of the Alliance possessions in the southern Pacific had been virtually destroyed during the Unification Wars, and a century of moderate growth had still not restored its prior population levels. There were bases in the area, especially in Australia proper, but nothing sufficient to sustain major combat forces indefinitely. Not against a CAC that had all its mainland resources within supporting range.

Young knew his enemy was going to be reinforced before he was, and that was going to be a big problem. His orders were to hold at all costs and support the ground forces around Manila. That job was likely to get damned difficult long before his own reinforcements could make the journey across the Pacific from the New Frisco Naval Base.

He didn't know when – or if – those reserves would get to

him. The war was global, and Alliance Command would have calls on its resources coming in from multiple combat zones. The Alliance's terrestrial military was a massive organization with considerable reserves, but ships and planes and troops were still finite. If there were enough hotspots around the globe, there simply wouldn't be adequate support to go around.

He had a better chance of getting help from the Alliance's PRC allies. The Japanese-dominated Superpower was geographically closer, and it was a bitter enemy of the CAC. The PRC could be counted on to throw most of its strength against the Chinese-led Combine. But the Caliphate had entered the war too, and their relations with the Alliance were just as caustic as the PRC-CAC rivalry. They were likely to reinforce their CAC allies…and to attack the Alliance in other theaters, diverting forces from the CAC war zones.

Young turned his focus back to the current situation. Making wild guesses about reinforcements and the progress of the war was a waste of time. All that mattered now was getting those reserves through.

"Odds, fall back." Captain Davies stood in the trench, knee deep in sopping mud and screaming into his comlink. The battle wasn't going well…in fact, it was going like shit. The Alliance forces had been falling back for days, and the CAC troops kept coming. Davies knew the Alliance was outnumbered in the Philippines, but he didn't realize by how much until he ended up on the front line facing charge after charge.

Jungle fighting was brutal, and it was more than just the enemy. His troops had to deal with the heat, the constant rain, bugs the size of small birds…even poisonous snakes. It was the closest thing he'd seen to hell on Earth. And he had no idea what he was doing there.

Davies' father was a local Magistrate in the St. Louis Metroplex. The family was not particularly influential, but it was still part of the Political Class, and Davies had grown up surrounded by considerable luxury. He had attended a Political Academy, but the family held only a single office, and it was earmarked for his older sister when his father retired.

Bored and not anxious to spend his life hanging around the family estate with nothing to do, he accepted a captain's commission and joined the army. He was dazzled by the idea of a fancy uniform and seduced by the thought of ordering around a bunch of soldiers. But once he reported for duty he found the good assignments went to those from more influential families. He'd imagined himself in some pleasant posting in the US or English sectors, preferable someplace with good weather. If he'd known he would end up in the fucking jungle dancing around bugs and snakes – not to mention enemy troops – he'd have stayed home and lived on his family's resources.

His company was facing at least a CAC battalion, and they'd been falling back for days. The enemy had been attacking aggressively, especially since their navy got the worst of the offshore fighting. The first success had gone to the Alliance, and the CAC generals were determined to even the score. Besides, if the fight on the ground was lost, the naval victory would be rendered almost pointless. Davies tried to work himself up into a patriotic frenzy, but he just couldn't get himself to give a shit about who controlled the Godforsaken Philippines. But he knew he didn't want to end up a prisoner of the CAC…and the only alternatives to that unpleasant outcome were victory or death in battle. Victory sounded a lot better than death, so he resolved to be the best combat officer he could.

"Odds, covering fire. Evens, pull back." He climbed out of the muddy, rain-soaked trench, reaching down to pull his boots out of the muck. He could see most of the evens running to the rear. There was fire from the newly repositioned odds, but it was sporadic, maybe half what it should be. Davies knew that meant half his troops were cowering in their foxholes…or just running outright. His troops were well-equipped and organized, but the morale of the Alliance's rank and file was poor. Drawn from the Cog populations, they received decent training and usually had enough to eat, but they had no combat experience… and few were commanded by officers who cared about much beyond their own comfort. The Alliance had fielded veteran armies during the Unification Wars but, like the armed forces of the other Powers, a century of peace had atrophied their effectiveness.

He scrambled toward his fallback position, crouching low, giving the enemy as small a target as possible. The first time he jumped out into the open, he almost pissed himself with fear. It seemed an impossible thing...to flex his legs and leap out of the cover of a foxhole, to trust to fate that he wouldn't be torn to shreds by the enemy fire crisscrossing the field. He knew he hesitated that first time...but he also realized he had only exposed himself to greater danger by holding back. Every second brought the advancing enemy closer, every instant he cowered in a trench instead of moving his ass only increased the fire he would have to survive. It was a hard lesson, but one Davies learned quickly...his first step toward become a veteran soldier.

He swerved around, avoiding the water-filled craters and shell holes from the enemy's bombardment. He lost his footing more than once, and with it, precious time. But he got back up and kept moving forward, doing his best to ignore the sounds of bullets streaking by.

There was a small berm ahead...the target position. He lunged forward, leaping over the small bump in the ground. He landed behind the cover, sliding a few meters in the sopping mud before he stopped. He scrambled around and crawled back to the edge of the berm, looking out as the rest of his soldiers were jumping into the cover.

"Evens, deploy. Prepare to provide covering fire." It felt like his people had been leapfrogging back across the entire island, but he knew that was going to stop soon. They were barely a klick from the main defensive line in front of Manila. There was no way Alliance command was going to give up the city... not without a fight. And that fight promised to be a nasty one.

"Evens, covering fire." His voice was scratchy and raw. Their supply run was late, and his canteen was empty. He didn't dare drink any of the water in this Godforsaken jungle...not unless he wanted the shits for two weeks. He cleared his throat and put more force behind his words. "Odds, fall back."

"Lieutenant Simmons, deploy your troops along this line." Captain Wendell stood next to Simmons, staring out over the surreal landscape of lower Manhattan. He looked over the Crater, about a kilometer and a half south of their position, and beyond to the crumbling towers of the abandoned Financial District. It was a ghostly panorama, a visual record of a troubled and tormented history. It had been almost 150 years since the nuclear explosion that dug out the Crater, but the surrounding area was still moderately unhealthy...enough, at least, that Wendell's troops wore their protective battlefield gear.

"Yes, Captain." He flipped his com to the unit's command channel. "Form your lines," he barked to his squad leaders. He was calm, almost relaxed. War was breaking out around the globe, and army units were being sent to some very unpleasant places. He couldn't believe his own luck when the captain told him they were going to Manhattan to deal with a bunch of Cogs running wild. Facing an unarmed mob was a hell of a lot better than dealing with Caliphate or CAC regulars. He almost pitied the poor SOBs that were on their way to the war zones.

The company was spread out in a long firing line. Gunning down a bunch of Cogs didn't require complex strategy. A few volleys and the ignorant animals would lose heart and run. Not many of them would make it back across the river, though. Wendell's orders were clear on that.

He turned his head and looked south again. He could just about hear the roar of the mob as it approached. "Prepare to fire." He had positioned his company about a kilometer south of the Wall, in a mostly-open area where the abandoned buildings had been levelled. It provided an ideal field of fire.

The crowd was surging northward, pouring from the blocks of ancient, abandoned buildings and out into the open area. Wendell stared in shock for a few seconds. There were tens of thousands of them...hundreds of thousands. His arrogant calm began to slip away. "Fire," he screamed into the com, a bit of panic sneaking into his voice. "All units, fire!"

The line opened up, the deep blast of the assault rifles mixing with the staccato cracks of the autocannons. Along the front edge of the mob, hundreds fell, their bodies torn almost to shreds by the automatic fire. But the crowd surged ahead, trampling the bodies of the fallen, screaming madly for blood.

Wendell was stunned when the mob kept coming. "Keep firing!" he shouted into the com. "Keep firing!"

Hundreds more fell, thousands. But nothing broke the momentum of the screaming, incensed mass. One of Wendell's soldiers fell…then another. The mob wasn't totally unarmed. They'd killed guards on their rampage, and they took what weapons they'd found, mostly semi-automatic pistols and rifles.

Wendell watched with growing panic as the rampaging Cogs got closer. Then it started. One of his troopers threw down his assault rifle and ran back toward the Wall…then another… and another. In a few seconds, the entire company, including its commander, was fleeing north, desperately trying to reach the relative safety of the Protected Zone.

Wendell got to the Wall and looked up in horror. The gates were closed. His people threw themselves at the massive structure and clawed at the closed portal, screaming for the guards inside to let them in. But there was no response.

Then the mob reached them. Dozens of hands grabbed each of his men, pulling them back into the crowd like some hideous beast dragging prey to its fanged mouth. The cries of the dying soldiers were drowned by the screams of the bloodthirsty mob. Wendell felt the hands on his shoulders, on his arms. He was pulled back, thrust upward and carried into the depths of the crowd.

He felt the blows, hands first, and then he was on the ground being kicked and stomped. The pain was unbearable. He curled up, protecting himself as well as he could, but it was hopeless. He screamed in pain and mindless terror, and then he felt the darkness begin to take him.

Chapter 17

Field Hospital
North of Astria
Planet Armstrong
Gamma Pavonis II

"Sit still, or I'm going to fuse your shoulder to the side of your head." Sarah Linden's voice was cold, emotionless, her mind focused on what she was doing.

Cain was lying on the table, stripped out of his armor and wearing only a pair of blue Marine Corps shorts. Sarah was leaning over his shoulder, moving the cell-rejuvenator slowly over his wound. He twitched as the rays worked their magic, accelerating the repair and healing process. It didn't hurt, not really, but it was an uncomfortable feeling. And it tickled. The rejuvenator couldn't repair a major wound, but Cobra's shot had gone right through the fleshy tissue of Cain's shoulder. There was no bone or nerve damage, and with a quick rejuv treatment, he'd be able to get back on the line almost immediately. Not that Cain would have stayed off the line even if he had multiple slugs in his chest. Not now. His people were about to make their final stand, and healthy, sick, or dying, Erik Cain would be with them.

He angled his head so he could see Sarah...or the back of her mane of red hair, at least. He'd tried to get her to take some time to herself, told her that one of the other doctors could fix his shoulder, but she wouldn't have any of it. "I'm fine," was all she had said, in a tone that didn't invite further comment.

Cain knew the kind of pain she was feeling. He'd lost countless friends, as well as the thousands of his Marines who had died following his commands. The guilt from that responsibility was immense, and over the years it had made sleep a very hit and run affair. But one had been worse than the others, orders of magnitude worse. Darius Jax had been a brother to Cain, closer even than most siblings. The two had fought together, risen through the ranks together…lived, ate, and slept together. Corporals Cain and Jax had been friends…just as they remained when both wore general's stars. Then Jax died, killed in action early in the First Imperium War. Marines die, and losing a friend is never an easy thing. But Jax's loss was uniquely painful, not just because they were so close, but because his death was Erik Cain's fault.

Cain hadn't listened; he'd let his arrogance get the better of him. And Jax paid the price. He plunged into the gap, saving the day…but at a terrible cost. Cain never forgot the crushing grief and guilt. He never really dealt with it either. Like he usually did, he buried the pain, focusing on the battle ahead rather than the heartache from yesterday. He knew he would pay for it all eventually; one day he would have a reckoning with all the sorrow and anger he'd submerged deep in his mind. And General Darius Jax would lead that charge.

Cain could face the prospects of his own emotional reckoning, but he couldn't imagine Sarah suffering that way. He had long ago resigned himself to his fate…he deserved his torments. He was a butcher, a stone cold killer. All he knew how to do was kill, destroy. He didn't warrant anything better, not in his own estimation. But Sarah Linden had spent the last 20 years saving lives, often putting her own in grave danger to do it. He couldn't bear the thought of her suffering such pain, and he raged against the unfairness of it all.

But he knew better than to argue, to try to coax the tears from her. She was as much a professional as he was, and there promised to be no shortage of broken Marines for her to repair. She didn't have time for personal pain right now any more than he did, and she wore as effective a mask of emotional invulnerability as he ever had.

He'd tried to talk to her about it on the ride back to the hospital. She simply stared at him and replied, "Alex killed people for Alliance Intelligence for 20 years. What happened was an accident, but she wouldn't have been there at all if she hadn't come here initially to spy on us. And kill you." Cain started to reply, but Sarah but her hand on his lips. "No more," she said. "We both have jobs to do." He frowned uncomfortably, but he let it drop. For the moment.

"You're all set." Sarah's voice pulled him from his thoughts. "You need to rest for a few hours, but Sanchez is still servicing your armor anyway." She paused, pulling her gloves off and taking a last look at her handiwork. "Try not to tear it all apart, OK?" She leaned over and kissed him on the cheek. "I'll give Hector a list of injections once you're back in your armor. It's going to be tender for a while, but nothing a few shots won't control."

He looked up at her. "Sarah…" He couldn't find the words, and he just stared up at her.

She looked at him, her eyes focused like two lasers. "I told you, I'm fine." Her voice was cool, professional…and utterly without emotion.

He sighed softly. Yeah, he thought…you're just fine. He knew she was anything but.

"Even out that spacing." Isaac Merrick walked up and down the line, shouting out orders to the Marines preparing to make their last stand. "And move that autocannon 10 meters to the right. Your field of fire's partially blocked where you are." Merrick had talked with Cain and the two agreed completely. The army wasn't going to retreat another step. They would make their last stand – and live or die – where they were. And they were going to give the enemy the toughest fight possible. Fatigue, fear…none of it was an excuse. If this was to be their last battle, that was all the more reason to make it their best.

Merrick had been sitting with Anderson-45, getting to know the enigmatic prisoner, when word arrived that Cain had been wounded. He didn't know how badly Cain was hit, but he knew he had to get back to the line. Immediately. If Erik was out of commission, he was in command. And he wasn't going to sit in the hospital like some convalescent when Cain needed him to be out in the field.

He'd taken charge of the redeployment and the fortification of the new line, but Cain was only gone for a few hours before he returned and resumed command. But Merrick was back on the line now, and he had no intention of slinking back to the hospital. The Marines were getting ready to make their last stand and, by God, he wasn't going to sit in a hospital bed while they did it. The entire force had worked non-stop for three days, but they'd gotten the defensive line ready…just a few hours before the enemy attacked.

He was tired…no, that was a horrendous understatement. He was exhausted. The only thing keeping him awake was the steady dose of stims his AI pumped into his system. But as long as the chemicals kept him on his feet he could fight. And that was all he had to do.

The new line was tough, multiple echelons of trenches with strongpoints placed in targeted spots. It was the best defense the battered Marines could offer, and an engineering marvel under the circumstances. No one seriously thought it would be enough, but if the enemy wanted the victory, the Marines were going to make them pay for it.

"Isaac, I want you to take charge on the left." Cain's voice was firm, resolute. Merrick knew the Marines' commander well. Cain's doubts came in the quiet hours, when the fighting had briefly subsided and given him time to reflect. But now the enemy was advancing and battle would soon be joined. The doubts, the fatigue, the hopelessness…it was back in the deep recesses of Cain's mind, and Merrick knew the unstoppable warrior was in control again. "I'll take the right."

"Yes, sir." Merrick's tone was grim, hard. He was ready for the final battle.

"We should be engaged in a few minutes, Isaac. We stand here, no matter what. We don't move a centimeter. Understood?"

"Yes, Erik." Merrick pulled his assault rifle from its harness and slammed in a fresh clip. "Understood."

"Good luck, my friend." Cain's iron voice softened slightly. It was a flash of weakness, fleeting and barely noticeable. Anyone who knew him less well than Merrick did would have missed it. But Merrick knew. Cain expected this to be their last battle.

"We have the scanning reports." Abbas walked into the ready room carrying a large 'pad. "It appears we have arrived just in time. The Marines are heavily outnumbered. They appear to be under extreme pressure even as we speak."

Khaled was stripping out of his uniform, handing his garments to an aide as he did. "Then we must waste no time. Commander Farooq's orta group is ready to launch immediately." He looked up at the admiral. "I will give him the order at once. Are we agreed?"

Abbas nodded somberly. "We are agreed."

"May I?" Khaled motioned toward the 'pad.

"Certainly." Abbas handed the device to his companion.

Khaled looked at the small screen, his face twisting into a frown as he did. "The Alliance forces are certainly outnumbered. Indeed, they are facing a sizeable enemy army." He handed back the 'pad and sat on a small bench, pulling one of his boots off. "I will bring the remainder of the forces down as quickly as possible after Farooq's vanguard." He paused. "I believe we should commit all of our ground forces immediately. The situation on the surface appears to be quite desperate."

Abbas was silent for a moment. Finally, he exhaled and said, "I am inclined to agree. My initial thought was to hold back a considerable reserve, but it appears that all of your people will be needed if we are to affect the outcome on the surface. There is little point in squandering half our strength to die alongside the Marines in defeat." I could even the score considerably with an orbital bombardment, he thought. But he knew that wasn't an option. Armstrong was a major Alliance colony, and the home world of the Marine Corps. Blasting it to radioactive dust was probably a bad way to foster a growing friendship with Garret and Cain and their people.

"Then I will bring the rest of the Janissary corps to full

alert." He pulled off his other boot, handing it to his aide. "If you will have your people prepare the landing craft, I believe I will look to organizing a second assault wave."

Abbas nodded, and he bowed slightly, the Caliphate equivalent of a handshake. "Fortune go with you, Lord Khaled."

"And with you, Admiral Abbas." Khaled returned the gesture. He had no doubt he cut an amusing figure bowing solemnly to the formally clad Abbas, wearing only a pair of shorts. "And to all those who serve you." Khaled rose slowly, maintaining eye contact with Abbas as he did.

"And to those who serve you, Lord Khaled." Abbas turned abruptly and strode back toward the corridor.

"May fortune go with all of us, Admiral. With all of us," Khaled whispered to himself as he walked toward the clamshell of his waiting armor.

"We've got recon drones coming in everywhere." Merrick was looking at Cain. He'd been posted on the left of the army, commanding the flank, but when he started picking up the drones, he ran over to Cain's position. The two officers had their visors retracted, and they were talking face to face. "It looks like a pre-landing sweep."

Cain sighed. He had spent his career staying cool in the face of disaster, but every man has his limits…and Cain was close to his. He'd been trying to stay focused on the battle, but his thoughts kept drifting back to Sarah. She was acting as if nothing had happened, but he knew she had immense pain waiting for her. And Erik Cain, the master of suppressing guilt and pain and horror, had no idea how to help her.

But the bad news just kept coming. It wasn't enough for the situation to be hopeless…it had to be utterly hopeless. "How could they possibly have more reserves incoming?" His eyes bored into Merrick's, though he knew his second in command had no answers to offer him. "Why would they even bother? They've got more than enough to finish us off now."

"Maybe it's just a naval force in orbit updating their scouting data." It was a plausible suggestion, but Merrick didn't sound like he believed it any more than Cain did.

Cain forced a fleeting smile. "Nice try, Isaac. But you know a pre-assault scan as well as I do." He slapped his hand on his exec's shoulder. "If I don't get a chance to tell you in the next day or two…or whatever we've got left…" – Cain's voice was somber, emotional – "…it's been an honor serving with you. I'm glad you found your way to us."

Merrick's route to the Corps had been a bizarre one. He had first encountered the Marines as an enemy, commanding the Federal forces sent to crush the rebellion on Arcadia. After the rebel victory, Merrick was scapegoated for the failure and, even though his influential family protected him from any serious persecution, his career was over. He chose to emigrate rather than remain at home in disgrace, and he eventually linked up with the Marines and aided them against the First Imperium. By the end of that war, he was a Marine general and he'd won over the rank and file to become one of the Corps' most popular officers.

"Home, Erik." Merrick stared back at Cain with moist eyes. "I found my way home." He took a deep breath. "And we're not done yet. Not until the motherfuckers kill every one of us."

Cain managed another smile. "I couldn't agree with you more, my friend. I couldn't agree more." He looked down at the ground for a few seconds then back up at Merrick. "You better get back, Isaac. The party's about to start."

Merrick nodded. "Yup." He turned halfway, still looking at Cain. "Take care of yourself, Erik."

"You too." Cain watched Merrick start walking away, and he yelled after him, "And not one step back, Isaac. Not one."

"No, sir. Not one step back." Merrick turned and trotted off to the east.

Cain looked up toward the line. He had one-third of his strength in the first row of trenches. Those Marines would put up a sharp fight, and then they would fall back, pulling the enemy forward, deeper into the trench network. Cain had no intention of abandoning the overall position, but he definitely planned to suck the enemy farther into the killing zone he'd created. Each layer of entrenchments was stronger than the previous one. If all went as planned, the enemy would push forward, breaking through the front line everywhere except the strongpoints located every 500 meters or so. Then they would hit the next, stronger line, while the surviving forts along the front enfilading the advancing troops. The defense was Cain's masterpiece…everything he'd learned about killing distilled into one fortified position.

But now he had to deal with the incoming enemy reinforcements as well. If they came down to the south of the line, they'd just be so many more troops overwhelming his defenses. But if they came down to the north they could sweep through the almost unprotected hospital and refugee camps and hit his lines from the rear. Whatever happened in the next few hours, he had to have something posted north of the civilian camps. He had to at least slow down any landing force. He didn't have anything to spare from the line, but he pulled out 2 battalions anyway…and sent them north with the 28 Obliterators who'd somehow managed to survive Clarkson's charge. They'd suffered 92% losses in that fight, and it took everything Cain had to order them north as a forlorn hope against the enemy invasion force. He'd never seen a group of warriors that better deserved a rest. But he didn't have anything to spare. Everyone would fight this last battle.

He looked up at his tactical display. The enemy was close. His front line would be engaged any minute. He took a deep breath and reached for his rifle. "Hector, give me another stim." He figured he'd be lucky if he didn't need a liver-kidney regen by the time he was done mainlining uppers. But that didn't seem very important at the moment. He felt the rush of energy, the alert feeling taking hold. Sometimes you didn't know just how tired you were until you got a big shot of stims.

"Alright, General Cain," he said softly to himself. "Time to fight one more batt…"

"Attention Alliance Marines…attention Alliance Marines… this is Janissary Commander Farooq." The words blared out of the speakers in Cain's helmet, and he shut up and stared ahead in disbelief. "We are here to assist you in your struggle."

Cain had seen the landers coming in on his scanners a few seconds before, but it never occurred to them they were friendlies. He didn't think there were any friends left out there, at least not ones with any strength to spare.

He recognized Farooq's voice, and now that the landers were closer, he ID'd them as Caliphate Crescent-class invasion ships. But it still seemed unreal. How the hell, he thought, did Khaled and Farooq get permission from the Caliph for this? But it didn't matter. Allies were allies, and beggars couldn't be choosers. And the Janissaries were the best ground troops in space. After the Marines, of course.

The enemy picked them up as well. They'd been about to launch a massive attack, one that almost certainly would have crushed the Marine defenses, but now they were falling back, waiting to see what the new arrivals would do. Cain couldn't believe what he was seeing. He was a pessimist to the bone, but he knew he was looking at a genuine miracle. And he was grateful.

"Commander Farooq, please allow me to welcome you to Armstrong." Cain had a hundred questions, but nothing he was going to discuss on an open line. "I look forward to showing you the sights."

Chapter 18

CAS Kublai Khan
Epsilon Indi System
Inbound From Xeta-3 War Gate

"Still no confirmed contacts, Admiral." Captain Wu stood at rigid attention as he made his report. Many in the navy thought of Fleet Admiral Zhu as a capable commander, while others considered him a pompous fool who owed his position entirely to the influence of his powerful family. But all agreed he was a rigid martinet who had broken officers for the slightest infractions of protocol.

"But you think the Alliance fleet is in this system?" Zhu turned his head slowly, his gaze falling on the tactical officer. "Do you not, Captain Wu?"

Wu fidgeted uncomfortably. He did suspect Garret and his people were hiding in the Epsilon Indi system, though it was nothing but baseless conjecture...no more than a feeling. Admiral Zhu tended to demand facts, not intuition, and Wu had seen the consequences of angering the terrible officer with wild suppositions.

"Speak freely, Captain." Zhu glared at Wu, his eyes penetrating the nervous officer like two lasers. "We appear to have no facts, so we are forced to rely on guess work."

"Yes, Admiral." Wu was still nervous, but he was trying to hide it as well as he could. "As you know, our analysis of the warp gate shows a residual energy signature from the recent passage of a considerable number of ships. I am unaware of any other sizable formation operating in the area save for Admiral

Garret's fleet."

"But Garret has clearly been following someone." Zhu continued to stare at Wu as he spoke. "Thus, we can ascertain that there is another fleet operating in the sector, can we not?"

Wu shifted his feet uncomfortably. "Yes, sir. But we have been closely pursuing the Alliance fleet for nearly a month now, and we have had no contact with any other force. It does not appear that Admiral Garret has engaged in any major battles in that time." Wu hadn't intended to elaborate so much, but the admiral kept pressing him. He was nervous about Zhu, afraid the notorious officer would disagree with his conclusions and rip into him. Zhu's reputation had preceded him, greatly exaggerated of course, as most things of that sort tend to be.

"I agree with your analysis, Captain." Zhu was still glaring at Wu, but his tone lightened slightly. "And if we have indeed caught up to the Alliance fleet, do you in turn agree with my conclusion that Admiral Garret will engage us here…in this system?"

Wu hesitated, uncomfortable about making even more unconfirmed projections. "Yes, Admiral…I certainly consider that a serious possibility." Another pause. "Indeed, if he is pursuing another enemy, I would expect him to want to avoid encountering them with us so closely in pursuit."

"I agree again, Captain." Zhu finally broke his stare and ran his eyes across the flag bridge, pausing for a few seconds before he said, "Please bring the fleet to secondary alert. All vessels are to prepare for imminent combat."

"Yes, sir." Wu turned to his workstation, relaying the alert to all fleet units. He was focused, but it still felt strange preparing to engage an Alliance fleet. For most of his career, it would have been the most natural activity imaginable. He had battled against Alliance forces since he graduated from the Naval Academy. But then the First Imperium attacked, and the former adversaries fought together for the first time, saving mankind in the process.

He couldn't imagine what had gone so wrong so quickly to cause this new confrontation. The more he thought about it, the more troubled he became. But there was nothing he could do. He had his orders…and there wasn't the slightest doubt Admiral Zhu would throw him out an airlock if he refused to carry them out. I'm sorry, Admiral Garret, he thought sadly, remembering how the Alliance's great commander had led the combined fleet against the First Imperium enemy. He wished their forces were still together, facing a common enemy. But that wasn't his decision, and thinking about it was pointless. Now, they were heading into battle, about to confront their former allies. And Admiral Garret was the most dangerous adversary in human space.

Augustus Garret sat quietly in his command chair, staring at the main display. He wasn't an optimist by nature, nothing of the sort. But sometimes he couldn't help but give in to amazement at the unending pile of shit the universe could dump on his people.

He'd done the best he could to put Terrance Compton and the other 40,000 naval crew and Marines he'd abandoned out of his mind. What he'd done in the X2 system would haunt him until the day he died, but he'd sworn not to let it interfere with his duty or degrade his effectiveness. Compton would have been the first one to scold him if he did.

Gavin Stark was behind whatever was going on…Garret was certain of that. He'd been combing Alliance space, hunting down the miserable SOB's fleet. Whatever Stark was up to, Garret wasn't going to leave him so much as a functioning life boat to carry it out. Stark's ground forces appeared to be strong and numerous, but Garret was going to strand them wherever they were and cut off their supplies. He didn't want to think of what it would cost to dig them out of so many Alliance worlds, but that was tomorrow's problem. First he had to find Stark's ships. And that was proving to be a difficult task.

Then he got the communique from Alliance Gov. The Alliance and the CAC were at war. Garret had to read it three times before it sunk in. He didn't think much of the inbred politicians who ran things on Earth, but he couldn't imagine how even they had managed to expend all the good will from the First Imperium victory and blunder into war so quickly.

Despite the news of war, Garret couldn't imagine Admiral An leading his fleets against him so soon after they'd fought side by side. An was a cantankerous old warhorse, but deep down he was an honorable man. Then Garret got the news. An had been removed from command and replaced by Admiral Zhu. And Zhu was a world-class prick.

Garret was determined to hunt down Stark and his renegade fleet, but the CAC forces had been hot on his trail. He'd tried to shake them, but now he realized that wasn't going to work. The last thing he wanted was to end up stuck between the two hostile fleets. So he reluctantly decided to turn and face the pursuing CAC force before continuing after Stark's ships.

Normally, Garret wouldn't be overly worried. Zhu was a somewhat competent officer, but he was unimaginative and deeply immersed in the conservative orthodoxy of the CAC navy. In a straight up fight, Garret was sure he could take Zhu, and probably keep his own losses at least moderately under control. But it wasn't a straight up fight. He'd left Admiral Harmon and a third of the Alliance fleet out at X1, with orders to stay in place and make sure nothing was able to penetrate the Barrier. Worse, all the Alliance bases in the sector had been destroyed or occupied by Stark's Shadow forces, leaving the fleet low on supplies and ordnance. He didn't doubt that Zhu's ships were fully stocked and loaded to the teeth with weapons, and that would give Zhu a big edge.

"Get me a direct laser com to Admiral Jacobs." When Garret decided to fight the CAC fleet, he ordered Jacobs to take his task force into the asteroid belt and find a good place to hide. Garret was going to have to face an enemy that had parity in hulls and a massive superiority in logistics. He was going to counter that with strategy or, more accurately, trickery.

"Yes, Admiral." Tara Rourke was the best tactical officer Garret had ever had. If she survived her battles, he had no doubt one day she'd be sitting in his chair. But for now, he was glad he had her on Pershing. She turned toward him. "I have Admiral Jacobs on Ticonderoga, sir."

"Mike, are you in place yet?" Garret hadn't worked closely with Jacobs for all that long, but he recognized natural talent when he saw it. He'd relied on Compton as his number two for decades and, apart from the overwhelming personal grief at his friend's death, Garret was feeling the loss operationally as well. Terrance Compton had been the one officer Garret trusted and understood completely. It had been like having an extension of himself.

Jacobs wasn't a replacement for Compton...no one ever could be. But Garret had been pleasantly surprised how well the two synced. Now, he was about to see how that synergy translated into action. If Compton had been there, he would have been hiding in that asteroid belt. Now it was Mike Jacobs, with some big shoes to fill.

"Yes, Admiral." Jacob's voice was firm, confident. He'd seen some rapid advancement over the last few years, entering the First Imperium War as the captain of a fast-attack ship. In the estimation of virtually every highly-ranked naval officer, his performance during the war rated every promotion he'd gotten. Jacobs himself, long in awe of commanders like Garret and Compton, had more trouble believing that, but whatever job he was given, he knew he would give it all he had. "I found a spread of asteroids with high-density radioactive ores, and I've got the task force positioned in tight behind them." The radioactivity of the ores would mask the minimal energy outputs from his hiding ships, making it tougher to spot his force.

"Perfect." Garret was impressed. He'd always felt that there was an X-factor to the most capable officers, an understanding they possessed that others didn't, an instinct that gave them the insight their less gifted peers lacked. Most officers could be trained, and they could learn by experience. They could rise to fleet command and perform perfectly well. But the very best officers had that mysterious natural ability. Garret had it; Compton had it. Garret suspected Tara Rourke also had it. And now it looked like Mike Jacobs might as well. "Just lay low until I give you the word." Garret paused for a few seconds. "And Mike, if you think things have really gone to hell out here, and you haven't heard from me…I'm authorizing you to use your own judgment." Garret had come to trust Jacobs more quickly than he would have thought possible a few months before.

"Yes, sir." Jacobs' tone softened a little. There weren't many officers who weren't deeply affected when Garret brought them into his inner circle. The admiral's reputation had achieved legendary status, and an entire generation of younger officers had come up emulating the brilliant officer's exploits. "You can count on us, sir. We'll be ready when you need us." Jacobs couldn't explain Garret's magnetism, but he knew one thing. He would die with every one of his ships before he would disappoint the admiral.

"Very well, Mike. Good luck. Garret out."

Garret leaned back in his chair and thought silently for a few minutes. Finally, he took a deep breath and exhaled hard. It was time. He looked over at Rourke's workstation. "OK, Tara…if you would be so kind, please bring the fleet to alert."

Zhu sat staring at Kublai Khan's main screen, watching the Alliance fleet in dumbstruck wonder. The admiral was a hardliner who generally bought into the notions of CAC superiority the government endlessly promoted. But facing Augustus Garret was a sobering test for his cultural orthodoxy. Even Zhu couldn't convince himself Garret was an inferior. Deep inside, beneath the bravado and the jingoistic conditioning, he was scared to death facing the Alliance's terrible admiral. And now he was watching in stunned silence as Garret's ships headed off in a dozen different directions, breaking into small task forces. Fleeing.

It didn't make any sense. It defied every maxim of war in space. But the master didn't make foolish mistakes, which meant those ships were doing what they were doing for a good reason. But Zhu had no idea what that could be. Unless…was it possible Augustus Garret's dreaded fleet had finally been driven too far? Were his people running for their lives?

It was going to reduce the effectiveness of his own missile barrage…that much was certain. None of Zhu's attack plans had envisioned the Alliance fleet simply scattering, and most of his missiles were already moving at velocities too high to effectively change vectors and pursue Garret's dispersing ships.

But it still didn't make sense, at least not tactically. The Alliance fleet would escape one missile attack, but their units would be scattered across half the system, out of supporting range of each other. The CAC fleet could engage them piecemeal, destroying each in detail before moving on to the next. Perhaps Zhu's earlier thought was correct...maybe the Alliance fleet's morale was broken...or even Garret himself. Had he lost his nerve and ordered his people to flee?

Was it possible? Could the legendary Garret have made a grave error, lost control of his fleet? Zhu's mind drifted, imagining himself as the commander who finally defeated the legendary Augustus Garret. He would go down in history as one of the greatest naval leaders who'd every lived...the man who had destroyed the colossus. The image pleased him immensely.

His eyes focused on the screen, watching the clusters of Alliance ships accelerating on their scattered vectors. He was pinpointing a small group of blue circles, one of them with a small flag next to it. Pershing. Garret's flagship...alone with only two other capital ships and a dozen escorts nearby.

Zhu punched the keys on his own workstation, calculating distance and vectors. If he gave the orders now...if he committed totally...he could bring massive superiority to bear on Pershing's small task force. He could destroy the Alliance flagship. And with it Fleet Admiral Augustus Garret.

"Captain Wu, the fleet will concentrate on these coordinates." He tapped a few keys, sending the flight plan to his aide.

Wu was staring down at his screen as the figures came through. His eyes widened as he read them and plotted them on his tactical map. He looked up, trying hard to suppress his surprise. "The whole fleet, sir?"

"Yes, by God, the whole fleet." Zhu snapped the response in a tone that discouraged any argument.

"Yes, sir." He gulped hard but didn't argue. Zhu's order would concentrate the fleet just as Garret's perfectly plotted missile strike came into range. The losses would be horrendous. Then the trajectory would take the surviving ships right past most of the Alliance fleet. And directly at Garret's flagship.

Wu understood Zhu's thinking, but he had a terrible feeling it was wrong. Horribly wrong. The CAC admiral was betting the Alliance fleet would disintegrate if they lost their brilliant admiral, that their morale would collapse if they heard of Garret's death. But Wu knew the Alliance spacers better than Zhu did. He'd served alongside them in the desperate battles on the Rim. He knew firsthand how sharp a blade Garret had forged. Zhu expected the Alliance fleet to rout and flee if Garret was killed. But Wu knew that was folly. The Alliance crews would go berserk if they lost Garret…and they would fight like demons from hell for vengeance, ignoring losses, ignoring fatigue. They would come at the CAC ships with death in their hearts and a fury the terrified captain couldn't even imagine.

Wu knew the admiral's plan was ill-conceived. But he also knew he couldn't argue. If he did, he'd be relieved at the very least. And possibly much worse. Zhu wasn't an officer who would listen to reason, not once he'd made a decision. Wu held back a sigh and sent the order out on the fleetcom. "Flight plan has been transmitted to all ships, Admiral." He tried to keep his voice professional, but his mind was grim. And he was afraid.

Pershing's landing bay was eerily quiet as Chad Gravis made his way to his fighter-bomber. Gravis had served under Greta Hurley throughout the First Imperium War, initially as a squadron leader and later in command of a strike wing. He'd learned his trade from Hurley, and he'd learned it well.

Hurley was the unchallenged master of small-craft battle tactics, the officer who'd led the most massive bomber attacks in history against the fleets of the First Imperium. But Hurley wasn't there to command the strike force. She'd been attached to Terrance Compton's half of Grand Fleet during the battles at X2, and she was trapped with him behind the Barrier…consigned to whatever fate the universe had bestowed on the Alliance admiral and his people.

Gravis felt the shadow of Hurley looking over him, the massive shoes she'd left behind for someone to fill. Now he would have to try those shoes on...he was about to command a ragtag remnant of those massive attack wings she had led.

The squadrons had suffered crippling losses during the desperate battles on the Line and out on the frontier. There had been no time to train pilots or build bombers and, as the allied fleet contingents departed when Grand Fleet dispersed, they took their own decimated wings with them.

Most of the surviving Alliance fighters had been trapped with Compton's fleet, and Gravis had only a few hastily-organized squadrons he could put into space. This battered cadre was all Admiral Garret had available, a vague shadow of the forces Grand Fleet had put into space a year earlier. But Garret wasn't one to waste time thinking about what he didn't have, and Gravis wasn't either. There was a job to do, and they would both have to make do with what they had.

He stopped under one of the bombers, reaching up and climbing the ladder into the cabin. He pulled himself up and walked to the command seat. The "Lightning" fighter-bombers were over 50 meters in length, but most of the space was occupied by fuel, engines, and weapons. The cabin itself was a cramped affair for the four-man crew.

The other three members of the crew were already in place, strapped in and ready for launch. All 37 of Gravis' ships were fully crewed, and now that the commander had boarded his craft the strike force was ready to go.

Gravis scooped up his helmet and snapped it into place over his head. He climbed into his harness and clipped the belts. "Lieutenant Fitz, advise fleet command we are ready to launch."

"Yes, sir." Fitz relayed Gravis' report. He was a veteran, like every other crewman in Gravis' tiny attack force. They were all survivors of the First Imperium War, seasoned flight crew who had been trained and led by Admiral Hurley. They were laughably few, but they were determined to earn their keep.

"Commander Gravis..." – Tara Rourke's voice came through on the com just a few minutes later – "...you may launch your squadrons when ready." There was a pause, just a few seconds, and then she added, "Good luck."

Mike Jacobs sat on Ticonderoga's enormous flag bridge, trying hard not to be overwhelmed by the scale all around him. There were almost 20 stations in the control center, with support staff busily working at each monitoring the status of the entire task force. Garret had assigned him the massive battlewagon as his flagship as soon as he returned from Armstrong... and gave him a third of the fleet to command.

Jacobs was honored, touched deeply by the show of confidence from the man virtually every living human considered the best naval commander in space. But he also wanted to vomit. The responsibility was overwhelming for an officer who still thought of himself as a ship captain playacting as an admiral. He'd commanded Scouting Fleet in the final campaign against the First Imperium, but this was the first time he'd led a powerful battle fleet. He had never even served on a capital ship before Ticonderoga. Mike Jacobs had been a suicide boat rider from the day he left the academy until command of Scouting Fleet forced him onto a cruiser's bridge. But a cruiser wasn't a battleship, and Jacobs was still fighting to grasp it all.

It wasn't just the staggering power of the task force under his command, it was the importance of his mission. Jacobs had been a student of Garret's tactics his entire career, and he knew his hidden force was the admiral's primary maneuver element, the sledgehammer the brilliant tactician planned to use to crush his enemy. Jacobs wasn't privy to Garret's overall plan, but he knew his ships would have a key role in the decisive combat to come, and probably the key role. Jacobs was trying to stay focused on his tasks, but his stomach was tied in knots. He could think of nothing worse than letting Garret down. And failing Garret would be failing the entire fleet.

He was waiting for the transmission...for the single word Garret had promised him. "Go." That simple command, flashed via direct laser com, would set his force in motion. His orders were simple. His ships would burst out of the asteroids and slam into the flank of the enemy fleet. They would launch a single missile volley as they emerged from their cover, and then they would close to energy weapons range. After that it would be a fight to the death, bare-knuckled and brutal.

His ships were ready. Everything had been checked and double-checked. They were on radio silence, their only job now to remain hidden, to shield themselves behind the asteroids until they got the word to attack. They were sitting, waiting for the decisive moment, for Admiral Garret to unleash them on the enemy.

"Receiving a laser transmission from fleet command, sir." Commander Carp had been with Jacobs since his days commanding a single suicide boat out on the extreme frontier. "The message is 'go,' sir." Carp was a gifted officer, cool and decisive. He was young too. He'd still be a lieutenant if the First Imperium hadn't invaded human space, but fate had given him the chance to excel…and he'd been fortunate enough to serve under another upwardly mobile officer like Jacobs.

Jacobs swallowed hard. It was time. "Very well, Commander. The task force will execute Plan Javelin."

Garret stared at the scanner, watching as his task groups decelerated and changed their vectors inward. Slowly, surely, they were moving behind the CAC fleet, even as Jacobs' forces were coming out from the asteroid field and engaging. Garret was a student of all military history, but certain things resonated with him more than others. He'd read the histories of Hannibal's war with Rome many times, mesmerized by the Carthaginian general's crushing victories against the legions. He'd often wondered if a victory of annihilation like Cannae could be recreated in space. He'd considered the problem for years, but he'd always discounted any attempt as too risky…until now. But now Garret wasn't looking just to defeat the CAC fleet. He intended to destroy it utterly.

He'd paid a price to set the stage for his Cannae. The fleet had scattered, following his meticulous maneuver plan and leaving the enemy to concentrate on Garret's own small task force. He'd put himself out as bait, and it looked like Admiral Zhu was playing along. Garret had micromanaged the defense against the incoming CAC missile barrages, sweating over each of the hundreds of warheads coming at his ships. Anti-missile ordnance exploded all around the incoming CAC barrage and, closer in, the electromagnetic catapults blasted out their "shotgun" rounds, spraying the warheads with hyper-velocity blasts of uranium and osmium shrapnel.

But the CAC attack waves were too massive, even for Garret's skilled leadership and razor-sharp crews to fully counter, and the fleet paid the price. His ships began to take damage as enemy missiles entered the effective zone. Many of the 500 megaton thermonuclear warheads expended their fury without effect, too far from any target to inflict significant damage. The massive weapons of destruction were visible only as quick flashes of light against the blackness of space. But some of them detonated close enough to bathe Garret's ships in radiation and heat their hulls enough to cause significant damage. For all the unimaginable energy released by nuclear explosions, most missile duels were exercises in tearing ships apart bit by bit or killing their crews with blasts of radiation from near misses.

A direct hit would destroy any vessel, but the probability of actually contacting a ship with a missile across the vastness of an interplanetary battlefield was remote. It did happen occasionally, with catastrophic results for the unfortunate vessel involved, but it was far too infrequent to base tactics upon.

The CAC volleys hadn't scored any direct hits, but Garret's small task group had taken enormous damage nevertheless. The capital ship Naseby was a total loss. Riddled with hull breaches and almost entirely non-functional, she'd lost her captain and 90% of her crew before the exhausted survivors abandoned her in the escape pods.

Two cruisers and a dozen destroyers and fast attack ships had also been destroyed, and most of the rest of Garret's central force had taken heavy damage. The CAC ships closed hard, firing volley after volley of missiles before entering energy weapons range. Now, they were moving in for the kill. Just like

Garret had planned.

The energy weapons duel was a standoff at first, the extraordinary skill of Garret's crews momentarily matching off against the numerical advantage of their adversaries. But Garret knew that couldn't last. Numbers would tell, sooner or later. And probably sooner. It was time.

"Send a flash laser communication to Ticonderoga, Commander Rourke." Garret stared straight at the tactical display, eyes blazing as he spoke. "Code word, 'Go.'"

Francisco Mondragon sat still and silent in his chair, staring at the tactical map displayed across Omdurman's bridge. The battleship was in Jacobs' vanguard, and she was bearing down hard on the flank of the CAC fleet. Omdurman had launched her missiles already – the entire task force had – and now she was leading the rest of Jacob's ships right at the enemy.

"All laser batteries, prepare for action." Mondragon was trying hard to shed his Basque accent, but his English was still far from perfect. "Prepare to fire immediately after missile detonations." The Europan officer had bonded with his new allies, and when Grand Fleet dispersed, he appealed to Jacobs to find a place for him in the Alliance navy. He was deeply disillusioned with Europa Federalis and enormously impressed with the standards and skill of the Alliance fleet. Garret approved the request and commissioned the Basque officer on the spot, assigning him to Jacob's task force. He'd expected to have a diplomatic mess to clean up after the fact, but things on Earth had gone to hell so quickly, it never came up. Mondragon was an Alliance captain now…and MIA as far as the Europans were concerned.

"Yes, sir." Commander Jenkins was Mondragon's tactical officer. "Detonations projected to commence in 30 seconds." Before the First Imperium War, an exec like Jenkins might have objected to serving under an officer he considered foreign. But Jenkins had fought in the war, and he'd seen firsthand the bravery and sacrifices of the Alliance's multi-national allies. Besides, everyone knew about Francisco Mondragon and his service under Admiral Jacobs in Scouting Fleet. Mondragon was a genuine hero as far as Jenkins was concerned, and the Alliance officer considered himself lucky to serve a commander of such ability.

Mondragon's ship, along with the rest of Jacob's task force, was coming in right behind the missile volley. Jacobs had been ordered to conserve ammunition and launch only a single barrage, and he'd held it until the last minute before firing. By the time the missiles blasted off, his ships were clear of the asteroid belt, and they had a point blank firing solution on the surprised enemy.

"Very well, Commander." Mondragon took a deep breath and trained his eyes on the huge main screen. There were clouds of tiny dots on the display, the hundreds of missiles fired from the ships of the task force. A few centimeters behind them was a row of larger symbols, Jacobs' ships. At the very front of the formation, less than 10 light seconds behind the line of missiles was a small triangle...Omdurman.

The small dots winked out and disappeared, one at a time at first, then in bunches. Out in space, around the enemy ships, 500 megaton warheads were detonating. To anyone watching, only an impossibly bright, but very short-lived flash would be visible. Most of the energy of the massive nuclear explosions blasted out in the forms of x-rays and gamma rays...massive pulses of deadly radiation.

Any ship actually hit by a 500 megaton bomb would simply disappear, its structure and crew vaporized in an instant. But none of the missiles in Jacobs' barrage scored direct hits. Many of the bombs expended their fury too far away to damage any enemy vessels. But the ones that got close, within a few kilometers, wreaked havoc on the CAC vessels and their crews. Explosions close enough to a target ship could vaporize or melt sections of its hull, tearing the vessel apart bit by bit. The massive dose of radiation inflicted could also overload the shielding, injuring and killing crew members as it did.

Jacobs' targeting had been true, and the CAC units nearest the asteroid field were savaged by the nuclear devastation his volley unleashed. Thousands of their crewmen were killed or incapacitated, and entire systems were knocked offline. All but the most heavily damaged ships could be at least partially repaired by damage control teams...but the CAC task force didn't have the time. Jacobs' ships were bearing down right behind their missiles, about to rake the stunned and battered enemy forces with laser fire before they could regroup or get wrecked systems back online.

"All laser batteries, lock on Macau." Mondragon's eyes focused on the largest of the CAC battleships. He pulled up the scanning report on his display. She'd been damaged by half a dozen missiles, and Gravis' fighters had hit her too. She was in rough shape and streaming air. Mondragon's eyes narrowed into a feral expression. Now he was going to finish off the big capital ship. "Fire."

Admiral Zhu sat in his command chair, silently staring at the disaster unfolding on his tactical display. How was it possible? He'd had Garret. A few more minutes, and he would have destroyed Pershing...and become the man who defeated the greatest admiral in space. A victory like that could have taken him anywhere he wanted to go...even to a seat on the Committee. Now, he'd be lucky to get out of this system alive.

"We've got more enemy contacts, Admiral." Captain Wu's voice was hoarse, ragged. He understood better than the admiral just how dire a situation Zhu's folly had gotten them into. "They're englobing us, sir."

The notion of surrounding an enemy was as old as warfare itself, but no one had ever managed to completely encircle an enemy in the three-dimensionality of space. Until now.

Garret's fleet had appeared to scatter, small groups breaking off in random-seeming vectors, trying to avoid the CAC missile volleys. But there was nothing arbitrary to the actions of those ships...this was no panic-based flight. Garret's vessels pulled themselves back together as they moved past the enemy fleet, each group executing a meticulously crafted thrust plan and maneuvering toward its assigned station. They were almost done, and the CAC fleet was under laser fire from all sides. Over a third of their ships were already lost, and Garret's forces were steadily closing the globe.

"We've got to pull back." Zhu was starting to panic, and it was obvious in his voice. "All personnel to the tanks. Prepare for full thrust back toward the warp gate."

It was far too late for that command, and Wu knew it. They'd be blasted to radioactive dust before they got everyone buttoned up. He was piecing together Garret's strategy, even as he watched it unfold. The brilliance...the brutal truth of it all was becoming clear. None of them were getting out of the system. Maybe a scattered ship or two, but the CAC fleet itself was doomed. Garret had tricked Zhu, suckered him into a trap...an ambush so complete it was going to destroy the entire CAC navy. Almost half of their ships were already destroyed or battered into barely functioning wreckage. It wasn't going to be long before Garret's victory was complete.

"I gave you an order, Captain Wu!" Zhu was really losing control, his terror obvious to everyone watching.

"Sir, it's too late for that." Wu didn't give a shit about humoring Zhu anymore. He figured he had maybe 10 minutes to live, and he wasn't going to spend it kissing the pompous fool's ass. "You've managed to lead us into a deathtrap. You were so focused on getting Admiral Garret...and he used it to trap us, you fool!"

"You will follow my commands, Captain Wu!" Zhu's voice cracked with rage.

"There is no time to escape, Admiral." If he was going to die, Wu didn't want it to be in the tanks. He'd seen that before, and it was a gruesome way to go. If he was going to die, better it be in action, at his station. "All we can do is fight it out here." That wasn't going to be enough, but Wu couldn't think of another alternative.

"We must surrender then! At once!" Zhu had lost all veneer of discipline or courage. He'd become a pathetic mewling creature, worried only about his own survival.

"Fleets do not surrender, Admiral." There was disgust in Wu's voice, and hatred. Hatred for the sniveling creature standing on the flag bridge...and for those who had ordered the removal – murder – of Admiral An.

Individual ships sometimes surrendered when a battle was in its final stages. Damaged vessels unable to retreat often gave up rather than face certain destruction. But an entire fleet had never before surrendered while the battle still raged. It was just too dangerous for the victorious side to show mercy. There were a hundred ways a surrender could be a trick...and no reliable method to ensure that the yielding ships had truly powered down their engines and weapon systems. No fleet surrender had ever been accepted in a century of interstellar combat.

Maybe, Wu thought...maybe if it was an officer who knew Garret, who was close to him during the fighting on the Rim. But C1 had destroyed that possibility when it murdered the highest echelon of officers. Admiral Garret might have trusted Admiral An...or at least heard him out. But he certainly wasn't going to give any weight to Zhu's promises.

No, he thought again, feeling a flush of rage...Garret will never listen to Zhu. If there was a chance...any chance at all, Zhu had to go. Wu acted quickly, almost on instinct rather than thought. His hand dropped to his side, gripping his sidearm. He pulled it from the harness in one quick jerk, and leveled it at Zhu's head.

"What are you doing, Cap..."

A single crack echoed across the otherwise silent flag bridge. Zhu's body fell back, blood pouring from a single hole in his forehead.

Wu turned slowly, panning his eyes from station to station, waiting for someone to act...to pull a weapon and shoot him. But there was nothing except motionless silence. Everyone on the flag bridge stared at him in shock, waiting to see what he would do next. He slowly put the pistol back in its place and walked over to the command station.

"Attention Alliance fleet, attention Alliance fleet." His English was far from perfect, but he did the best he could instead of allowing the AI to translate. He wanted his tone, his emotions to come through. It was their only chance...and it was a longshot.

"Admiral Garret, this is Captain Wu. I served with your forces at Sigma 4 and X2." And you have no idea who I am, he thought grimly. "Admiral Zhu has been relieved of command, and I am offering..." – he sucked in a deep breath and exhaled hard – "...I am offering the unconditional surrender of all naval forces of the Central Asian Combine now present in this system."

He punched in the fleet com frequency, while maintaining the transmission to the Alliance flagship. He wanted Garret to hear this. "All units...this is Kublai Khan. Cease fire at once. Cut all thrust and engine output to zero and reduce power levels to the minimum necessary for life support."

He had no idea if they'd obey. The rest of the fleet had heard his broadcast to Garret...they knew he was trying to surrender them. No one except Kublai Khan's flag bridge crew knew Zhu was dead, but Wu had no idea how the ship captains would respond to his attempt to surrender them all. It would only take one of them to destroy whatever fragile chance there was. It was a longshot Garret would bite under any circumstances, but if anyone continued to fire, there'd be no chance at all.

Wu leaned forward toward the microphone. "Attention Admiral Garret. This is Fleet Captain Wu. I am offering the unconditional surrender of the CAC fleet, effective immediately. I have ordered all vessels to cease fire at once and power down. Please respond."

Wu sat in the admiral's chair and let out a deep breath...and waited.

Chapter 19

Base Omega
Asteroid Belt
Altair System

Gavin Stark stared at the bare rock wall. It was a considerably different view than the priceless wood paneling and floor-to-ceiling windows that had adorned the walls of his office in Alliance Intelligence Headquarters. Omega Base was built with security and defense in mind, not comfort. Bored into the depths of a large asteroid, it could survive almost any bombardment, even one by the heavy burrowing nukes that had destroyed his base in the Dakotas. But defensibility came at a cost, and Omega was a claustrophobic hole in the ground, utterly devoid of luxury.

Stark was breathing deeply as he sat alone in his bare office, suppressing his anger and frustration. Overall, things were still going well, but there were trouble spots too, and they were getting worse, not better. For one thing, Erik Cain was still alive, and his miserable fucking Marines remained in the field, fighting as hard as ever.

Stark was mostly in control of his rage, but he still couldn't keep his hands from balling into fists as he thought about Cain. How, he thought...how is it even possible? Cobra had never failed on a mission. Neither had Alex before he'd sent her after Cain. What force was looking over the accursed Marine general, confounding Stark's every move?

There were other problems too, including at least a few new ones. Stark had known, of course, that General Gilson commanded a force of Marines out on the frontier. He'd anticipated her eventual return, but he had expected to have both Arcadia and Armstrong long secured before she did. She commanded a sizeable force, but nothing capable of assaulting either of those key planets once his own people were in charge and dug in.

But the fighting on Arcadia dragged on just like it did on Armstrong. Elias Holm was the problem there. Cain's mentor had scrounged up some veteran Marines Stark hadn't accounted for – he still wasn't sure where they'd come from - and managed to keep the fight going months longer than even the worst projections. Long enough for Gilson and her 7,000 veterans to land and throw the entire battle into chaos. A few weeks earlier he'd been getting confident assurances that the victory was imminent. Now he was getting frantic appeals for more troops.

He stared at the strength figures and casualty reports from the various colonial operations. His forces had easily swept away the planetary militias of the other worlds – everywhere except Columbia. But when his armies faced the Marines on Arcadia and Armstrong, their attacks bogged down, despite their numerical superiority.

His Shadow Legion forces fought with extreme discipline and courage…yet it was becoming apparent they were still no match for the Marines, at least not without a considerable advantage in numbers. He couldn't understand. They had the training and experiences of veteran Marines implanted directly into their brains, yet somehow, when they faced the real article on anything close to equal terms, they failed. Time and time again, he'd seen the outnumbered Marine forces hold his legions back, despite sometimes massive numerical mismatches.

He tried to put the mounting frustration aside, focusing instead on how to solve the problem. What could it be that made the Marines so effective in battle? It was a question he'd been asking himself for years. He'd always assumed it was their training…and the experience their veterans passed down to the new recruits. But now he could see there was more to it than that. It was strange, some hidden factor that seemed to strengthen the Marines as their situation become increasingly dire. As his legions drove closer toward victory, the Marines seemed to become ever stronger, more resolute. It made no sense, followed no logical pattern…but he'd seen it happen again and again.

He'd initially expected his Legions to fight better than the Marines, not underperform them. His soldiers had all the knowledge and training the Marines did, plus they were conditioned to be fearless, never to lose focus in battle, to ignore losses and methodically, relentlessly follow their orders. No matter how he tallied his mental spreadsheet, it came up the same. His troopers were superior. Yet report after report from the battlefields proved the opposite conclusion.

Gavin Stark was a genius, but he was a sociopath too. His brilliant, but twisted, mind had blind spots, aspects of human motivation he simply could not comprehend. It was a weakness that had caused him to underestimate his adversaries again and again. The Marines didn't behave as his perversely logical mind expected them to. They fought as a single whole, not just in their maneuvers and formations, but also in spirit. They were driven by tradition, by the memories of their Marine forefathers, who'd passed to them a history…with an expectation that they would add to that record and then pass it to the next generation. They felt the obligation to those who had come before to never bring dishonor to the Corps. They fought for the men and women next to them in line, those other Marines they thought of as brothers and sisters, just as they knew those comrades would give their all for them. They were a brotherhood, a single whole made up of the individual warriors themselves.

Stark's forces were trained in Marine tactics, the nuts and bolts of their way of battle. They even had the partial memories of veteran Marines replicated in their own minds. But they were still actors playing a part. The motivations, the thoughts and emotions deep within a Marine that made him behave as he did…these were foreign ideas to the Shadow Legion soldiers, just as they were to their commander. Something they could try to copy but never truly comprehend.

Stark stared down at his desk, trying to understand, but

failing utterly to grasp the difference between his soldiers and Marines like Erik Cain. He was a cold, calculating machine, almost devoid of human emotion, and for all his enormous intelligence, he simply couldn't understand certain basic motivations. Only two people had ever drawn any kind of real feeling from him. Alex had been one of them. Something about her seduction was irresistible. He told himself he'd fallen prey to her sexual charms, that it had been weakness of the flesh only, and not true emotion. But something about the cool, intelligent beauty had reached him on another level, one deeper than pure lust. Briefly, fleetingly, in his deepest thoughts he'd allowed himself to see her as a female version of himself, a fit consort for the man who would bring all humanity under his rule. But Alex had betrayed him, let herself be derailed by useless emotions… and his affection for her had turned to rage and hatred, further fueling his evolution into what he had become.

Jack Dutton was the only one who'd ever really been able to control Stark's behavior. He had been Alliance Intelligence's longest-serving agent…and Gavin Stark's mentor. The old man had been the only real friend Stark ever had and the sole restraining influence on his megalomania. The ancient spy had known how to handle Stark, to channel his energies. But Dutton was five years dead now. Even the Alliance's master spy hadn't been able to cheat death forever. And with Dutton died the only chance of restraining Gavin Stark's ambitions. Indeed, the loss of his only confidante had accelerated his progression into the pure monster he'd become.

Stark was brooding grimly when the com sounded, and Anderson-2's nearly monotone voice came through the speaker. "Sir, we have an incoming transmission." A brief pause. "It is marked Priority One, sir."

"Send it down at once," Stark snapped, shaking himself out of his thoughtfulness.

"Yes, sir."

A few seconds passed…decryption, Stark thought. Then his screen filled with decoded text. He stared down at the report. The news was staggering. The CAC fleet had finally engaged

Garret's Alliance forces in a climactic battle...and Garret had annihilated them. He hadn't just won a victory. He'd completely obliterated the CAC fleet. No more than 4 or 5 ships escaped; all of the rest were destroyed or captured. For all practical purposes, the CAC navy no longer existed.

Stark had mixed feelings as he read the communique. It was what he'd planned...what he needed. Stark had rid him of the CAC fleet, just as he'd expected, and opened up CAC space to invasion. But the victory was so decisive, so complete it left Stark with an uncomfortable feeling. He reminded himself what a dangerous enemy Augustus Garret truly was. He had wanted Garret to defeat the CAC...but he'd never considered the prospect of such total and complete annihilation.

He looked at the estimates of the Alliance fleet's losses. They were considerable. That was good news, certainly. And Stark knew Garret's weapon stockpiles had to be close to exhausted. Still, he wondered if Garret could ever be beaten. Was the admiral simply too brilliant, too perfectly attuned to war in space for anyone to defeat him?

He sat staring at the monitor, a small grin working its way onto his face. Stark answered his own question. Garret was the closest thing to an irresistible force in space combat. Admiral Liang was a perfectly competent naval commander, but Stark was a cold-blooded realist. He knew the renegade CAC admiral could never defeat Garret, not without a massive superiority in arms he knew he couldn't provide.

Stark's grin widened. He'd always planned for Liang to deal with the Alliance fleet. But he had never intended to have the former CAC admiral face Garret. No, that was something Stark had seen to himself. Augustus Garret would die before the decisive battle...right on his own flag bridge. He would die never having guessed one of his own officers was actually one of Stark's pawns.

But he wasn't done with Garret yet, and there was other work to do. He'd managed to keep his fleet out of Garret's reach while he instigated the war that sent the CAC navy after the Alliance admiral...and ultimately to its destruction. He had intended to wait it out, and then send his ships to destroy Garret's battered survivors. But it wasn't time yet. First he had to take other action.

He leaned over and hit the com. "Anderson-2, activate Plan R immediately." Now that the CAC fleet was gone, Stark's hidden strike forces would invade and occupy five of the Combine's most valuable colonies. The CAC would almost certainly blame the Alliance, and any chance to prevent escalation of the war on Earth would be gone. Its fleet destroyed, the CAC would have no way to strike back except to escalate the war on Earth. And Stark's interstellar empire would gain the resources of five more handpicked worlds, every one of them a treasure house of priceless minerals.

"Yes, sir." Anderson-2's perfunctory response.

He smiled. Another useful intensification of the war on Earth. Stark needed the CAC and the Alliance to destroy each other. He needed all the Superpowers in ruins before his plans could succeed. His agents had already instigated a tactical nuclear exchange between the CEL and Europa Federalis, but the two powers managed to pull back from the brink. He hadn't expected the first incident to spark the final battle, and he was confident his plans for Earth would come to fruition. He had more schemes in place, backups after backups. Whatever it took, he would see to it that Earth's Superpowers savaged each other in an orgy of destruction.

When it was over, the terrified survivors crawling through the wreckage wouldn't have a chance to resist his Shadow Legions. They would bow down before his soldiers, swear their eternal allegiance to him in return for scraps of bread. Mankind would willingly sell itself into eternal slavery.

Stark smiled broadly, thinking of his plan. But his grin began to fade as his thoughts drifted. The terrified masses of Earth, picking through the radioactive debris would be far easier to break than the colonists. His expression soured further. It was always the damned colonists. They were naturally rebellious, especially on the Alliance worlds. None of them knew how to do what they were told. He wondered how many he would have to kill…in the war certainly, but afterwards as well. How many would his soldiers have to drag from their homes to disappear in the night before the will of the survivors was finally broken? He didn't know, but he intended to find out.

But first, there was one thing he had to do. A problem he had to solve once and for all. He leaned over the com. "I want the reserve legions activated immediately." He was committing his last available forces. The rest of the inactive troops were hidden on Earth or committed to the CAC strike forces. He had no way to get the terrestrial legions into space, and he needed them where they were anyway. He'd already lost the Dakota force, and he had barely enough strength left to take control after the Superpowers destroyed each other.

"Yes, sir." Anderson-2's response was vaguely monotone as usual. A few seconds later: "Orders transmitted, sir. Force readiness estimated in 4 hours."

He looked around the room, seeing only the bare rock walls, but imagining the asteroid field all around…and the battlefleet he had hidden among those boulders and planetoids.

He would take that fleet, and the reserve infantry…and he would finish things on Armstrong. He would destroy the Marines, all of them. And he would find Erik Cain and rid himself once and for all of the accursed Marine. Personally.

Chapter 20

Columbia Defense Force HQ
40 Kilometers South of the Ruins of Weston
Columbia, Eta Cassiopeiae II

"Let's go, Hernandez. How the fuck long does it take you to reload that thing?" Reg White was firing his own autocannon as he barked out orders to the other three gun crews under his command. The enemy was making a big move, and White's guns were cutting into them, killing hundreds. The action had been hot and heavy for the last two days. Whatever was going on, the lull was definitely over. The enemy was back, and they meant business.

"Almost done, Sergeant." Hernandez' answer was slow, distracted. White knew he and Sand were loading the autocannon as quickly as they could. But it still pissed him off how slow they were.

When he first got back to the front, he found that he'd already been reassigned. The army's new position was a series of trench lines, connected by heavier strongpoints every three-quarters of a klick. White was in charge of the fort on the extreme left. His four guns were backed up by a squad of powered infantry. It was quite a jump in responsibility for a discipline case who'd been a private just a few days before, but for the first time in his life, White was focused, serious, disciplined...determined not to let the army down.

He was on the opposite flank from where he had been, and his command was drawn from a different unit entirely. There were no familiar faces, no old comrades to greet him when he arrived. He didn't know anyone assigned to him, but he could see immediately he was in charge of the most vulnerable spot on the line. His stomach heaved a little when he realized how crucial his small force was to the overall position, but he adapted quickly and took charge. Now the enemy was pressing them hard, trying to force the flank. And Reg White was pushing his small unit, determined to stand no matter what came at them.

"Now, Hernandez." White was impatient...and completely disgusted with the standards his inherited gunners displayed. Did these guys ever fucking practice, he wondered to himself, or did they just sit on their asses until the enemy came knocking? "If I have to come over there and do it for you, I promise you've never been that fucking sorry." It felt strange giving orders again. It wasn't new...he'd been a sergeant before. But this was the first time he'd ever commanded anyone in action. White was wearing stripes for the third time, though he had promised himself his big mouth and volatile temper weren't going to get him busted back down again.

"Yes, Sergeant. Firing now." There was a pause, at least ten or twelve seconds, before White could hear the autocannon firing. Hernandez had bullshitted him a little, but there was no time to worry about it now. Later, maybe...if they both survived.

The enemy had launched a series of direct frontal attacks, all of which had been decisively repulsed. But now they were moving to the flank, trying to get around the Columbian left. And White and his gunners were the extreme end of that flank.

White had positioned his own gun slightly back from the front, with a field of fire covering any attempt to move around. He'd been hosing down the area, inflicting heavy losses on the enemy formations as they came around. But he couldn't kill them all...and that meant the enemy was going to get through... and outflank the whole position.

He flipped his com to the HQ line. "This is Sergeant White reporting from strongpoint 9."

There was a short delay then: "Sergeant White...hold for General Tyler."

White was stunned, and he had to force the words from his suddenly-dry throat to acknowledge. General Tyler? He'd expected to speak with an aide or a tactical officer. What did the army's commander want with a sergeant on the line?

"What's happening, White?" It was Tyler's voice, crisp, calm, demanding.

"Uh, sir…" – White had no idea what he was doing talking to the general, and he could feel the nausea in the pit of his stomach – "…sir, I want to…"

"Relax, White. I was a sergeant once too. Just tell me what's happening. I'd rather hear it from you up on the line than through six echelons of bullshit." White didn't know it, but Tyler had given him his stripes…and handpicked him to command the strongpoint at the end of the line, overruling the former private's immediate superiors, who still considered him a discipline problem. But he was an unmatched fighter when he was in action, and Jarrod Tyler needed men who could kill the enemy.

"Yes, sir." White took a deep breath. "The enemy is maneuvering around our left flank. We've inflicted heavy casualties, but they have a substantial advantage in numbers…and now they are widening their axis of advance." White paused and took another breath. "They are now moving considerable forces on an arc outside our effective range and around the flank."

There was a brief pause on the line…Tyler digesting what White had told him. "Alright, Sergeant. I want you to keep up the fire as hot and heavy as you can." A short pause. "We're going to try to hit the enemy flanking force with a counter-attack, so I want your people to be careful about firing at friendlies…you understand?"

"Yes, sir." White snapped off his reply. He had no idea where Tyler was going to scrape up the troops for a counter-attack. But, he thought, I guess that's why he's got those stars.

"And White?"

"Yes, sir?"

"When the enemy pulls back…I want your guns to rip them a new asshole."

"Yes, sir….with pleasure, sir."

"Attention, Columbians." Tyler stood on top of the body of the battle-scarred tank. The main gun had been torn off, and the autocannons were all twisted wreckage…but the thing still functioned as a vehicle. Without weapons, it wasn't much good on the front lines, so he'd swapped it for his command car and its fully-functional dual autoguns. His army didn't have resources to waste. If it had some kind of weapon, it was up on the front lines, not serving as the commander's glorified taxicab.

He'd managed to organize a counterattack against the enemy flanking force, driving them back into the maelstrom of White's guns. It was a nice little victory, but he knew his people couldn't do it again. He'd put everything he had left, teams of reassigned mechanics marching along limping groups of walking wounded. They'd done the job, but now they were finished. Many of them were dead, the rest wounded, exhausted, broken. The next time the enemy attacked the flank, they would succeed. Their troops would stream around the end of the line and roll up his entire army. There was no choice. Stubbornness would only bring certain defeat. He had to abandon the line. And that meant giving up everything…the camps, the field hospital. Everything.

"Attention, Columbians," he repeated, shouting as loudly as he could. The mic relayed his words to the speakers set up around the crowd, but he knew there weren't enough to relay the message to the tens of thousands gathered around. Some would hear his words directly; the rest would have to rely on their friends and countrymen to pass the message on. "Your army is fighting 10 kilometers north of where we stand, battling against an army that outclasses us in both numbers and equipment. They have fought this war with everything men and women can give…with their blood, their bodies, their hearts."

He gazed out over the mass of people. His people. They were staring up at him silently, attentively. "I cannot lie to you, Columbians, and tell you we can hold that line forever. We cannot." He felt his own voice begin to falter. But then he looked out over the faces closest to him, those pressed right up against the tank...and he saw defiance. Lucia was right, he thought. These are Columbians, by God.

"Our enemy is too strong, their resources too vast. We have lost half our numbers...and inflicted horrific losses on the invader. But now we must make a difficult choice. Do we yield to our enemy, surrender and give ourselves over to their will?"

The crowd roared, "No, never!" Tyler looked out as thousands of Columbians, tens of thousands, pumped their arms in the air as they shouted, "Never, never, never..."

He waited for the screaming to die down. He knew the hardest part was still to come. It was easier to cheer mindlessly, but far harder to face cold realities. "Then we must flee to the Badlands. We must seek refuge in that untamed wilderness... make our enemy pursue us onto terrain that becomes our ally. This will become a guerrilla war. Behind every thicket and in every swamp our soldiers will be waiting. If the invader pursues us, we will turn the Badlands into their graveyard. If not, as long as we stand together, we will keep our freedom alive until help arrives."

The crowd shouted again, though with considerably less enthusiasm this time. The Badlands were enormous, a vast wasteland full of swamps and scraggly forests...and Columbia's most aggressive native fauna. It would be hard to sustain the planet's population there, probably even impossible. Thousands would die, perhaps hundreds of thousands. Famine and pestilence would run rampant. It was easy to shout defiant cries, quite another to embrace a plan so desperate and dangerous.

The comment about help arriving bought its own rumble from the crowd. When the enemy first invaded, the Columbians expected the Marines to come, as they always had before when enemies attacked. But the weeks of combat turned into months, and no one came...no relief force, not even any word. They sacrificed their capital to nuclear devastation to damage the enemy and buy time, and still no one came. The Columbians were beginning to lose faith; they were coming to believe their world had been abandoned. That they were truly on their own.

"Will you follow me, Columbians? Will you come with me to

the Badlands…to face whatever hardships and sufferings await us? Will you battle at my side until our world is ours again?" Tyler had his arm high in the air, hand balled tightly into a fist.

The crowd hesitated, staring up as Tyler stood before them, his uniform torn, a bloodstained bandage wrapped around the arm he held aloft. It started with a single voice from deep in the crowd, a lone, 'yes,' barely audible across the vast sea of people. Then it was joined by another…and another…until the whole surging mass was screaming as one, "Yes…yes…yes…"

Tyler pumped his fist and encouraged the cheering. But his thoughts were dark. It was one thing to rally the crowd, to incite defiance, standing here in this plain. He knew their morale would quickly diminish when they were marching through the swamps…when they started to run out of food. They would begin blame him, he knew, and this show of loyalty would quickly transition to disappointment, then to despair… and finally to hate. They would chant his name at first, swearing loyalty and support. But later, when they had suffered enough, saw their friends and neighbors dying around them, they would shout his name as a curse. If the exile went on long enough, he knew a dread day would come…when he had to turn the rifles of his army on his own people. He knew he would do it when he had to…the alternative would be to fall into disarray and defeat. But he didn't know if he could live with it afterward.

Is this the right thing to do, he thought…or am I leading them all to their deaths? It was the right choice for him, certainly. He had no doubt of that, none at all. If defeat was his destiny, he knew he had no wish to survive it. Jarrod Tyler had no stomach to live as a slave, to meekly do the bidding of his conquerors, to watch his soldiers led away as defeated captives. He would choose Valhalla first, to die in arms resisting the enemy to his last breath.

But did he have the right to make that decision for almost two million people, the men, woman, and children who called themselves Columbians? Was he their war leader, encouraging them, bolstering morale, cultivating their strength until victory was theirs? Or just a butcher leading them all to certain death?

Chapter 21

CAC Committee Command Bunker
South China Sea
Earth - Sol III

Li An sat back in the plush leather chair taking in the luxurious surroundings. She'd last seen the room on an inspection tour a decade ago, but it had been maintained in perfect condition over those years, waiting until a crisis made it necessary. It was furnished with priceless rugs and antiques. The walls were covered with rare teak paneling worth a king's ransom. The facility had been spec'd out at least 30 years before, and she wondered if the trees that yielded the precious boards even existed anymore. C1's chief wasn't a botanist, and she didn't spend much time thinking about trees, but she knew many rare species were lost each year. The Treaty of Paris had pulled man from the brink of extinction, but the damage done to the Earth by centuries of war and abuse wasn't so easily reversed. Recent events suggested it might not be so easy to keep man from extinction either. The Treaty of Paris had held for a century, but now that peace was in ruins. Earth's Superpowers were at war again.

She couldn't help but feel the extreme luxury was misplaced in a wartime shelter, but most of the CAC's leaders were the sons and daughters – mostly sons – of the previous generation of Committee members. They'd never known anything but unimaginable luxury and phenomenal excess. The sparse, sustenance-level lives most of the Combine's citizens lived would be unimaginable to them. They would retreat to an undersea bunker to protect themselves in wartime, but that refuge had to befit their stations. Li knew firsthand the Committee could argue about such things with as much vigor and emotion as major matters of state. She recalled an ancient parable with grim amusement. If Nero did, indeed, fiddle while Rome burned, she thought, depressingly little had changed in two millennia.

Li An was a rarity in the CAC hierarchy. She had not been born to privilege; she'd grown up in the notorious Shanghai ghettoes, surrounded by a level of violence and deprivation no one in the government class could truly understand. She'd pulled herself up by her own skill and initiative, something nearly impossible in the CAC. But Li had a brilliant mind and a flexible attitude toward morality, the perfect attributes for a career in espionage. With her knack for information-gathering and her sleek, petite figure, she rose quickly, using the two tools that were highly effective for the upwardly mobile – sex and blackmail. The young Li An had been one of the most wanted women in the CAC, and she used her appeal with ruthless efficiency. Her secret files had struck terror into the heart of the highest government leaders for almost three-quarters of a century. Her data – and the fear of what information she might have – formed the basis of her power, and it had taken her from starving street urchin to the only woman on the Committee.

Her office in the undersea command bunker was smaller than her palatial quarters at C1 headquarters, yet it would have been accounted plush enough for an ancient duke or prince. She leaned back in the priceless chair, her head sinking into the buttery soft leather. Li An was facing her own failure, trying to understand what had gone so horribly wrong. How, she thought…how did things get out of control so quickly?

Stark. The name floated around her mind like a curse. Alliance Intelligence's brilliant mastermind had been killed in the explosion that claimed his headquarters…at least that was the official story. Li An didn't believe a word of it. Not for a second. More than likely, it was Stark himself who had blown the building. The CAC had taken the blame, but she was certain no one in the Combine had been involved. She knew none of her people had done it...and it was inconceivable any other CAC personnel could have pulled it off without her knowledge. But the evidence was real...and damning. She couldn't imagine anyone other than Stark who could have framed the CAC so effectively without her people finding out about it.

She was certain Stark was behind other events that had fueled the rapid slide into open war. The destruction of Marseilles, the nuclear exchange in the North German Plain...she saw Stark's fingerprints on all of it. She had no real proof, but there wasn't a doubt in her mind. Nearly a century's experience in the field further fueled her intuition. She leaned back and sighed. Yes, she thought...it's Stark. All of it. But what can I do to stop him?

She wished she could talk with Roderick Vance. She was sure the Martian spymaster would have come to the same conclusions she had. But communications in and out of the secure bunker were controlled by the Chairman's personal security. And that made contacting Vance difficult and dangerous, a gamble she wasn't ready to take. At least not yet.

Huang Wei had allowed himself to be swayed by the hawkish party on the Committee, and he'd grown less and less receptive to her counsel of caution. There wasn't a doubt in Li's mind that the foolish CAC mobilizations Huang had insisted upon made Stark's job vastly easier. The CAC chairman later pulled back, paused the preparation for war. But a mobilization that size left evidence, information Stark undoubtedly used to help move the Alliance to war.

Now, however, Huang was in a state of paranoia and near-panic. Committed to his hawkish rhetoric, he found it had taken him down a path he now feared. He'd locked down all communications and ordered Committee members to remain in the bunker at all times. The generals and admirals were running the war now, while the politicians who'd destroyed the peace hid under ten kilometers of seawater and solid bedrock.

Li had operatives in the Chairman's security team, of course, but only a few. They were extremely valuable assets, and she couldn't risk exposing them simply to get a pointless message through to Vance. The Martian intelligence chief undoubtedly had plenty of his own problems now. Li admired Vance, but she also knew his interests and hers had diverged. They'd shared a desire to preserve the Treaty of Paris and avoid war. But now that war was a reality, the likelihood of stepping things back seemed remote at best. Li hadn't wanted war; she'd done everything she could to prevent it. But now, she realized the only way she could serve the CAC was to try and find a way to win it. If winning was even possible.

She looked down at the reports piling up on her desk. There was rioting throughout Hong Kong…and most of the other major cities. The economy had collapsed entirely, but the government was so focused on the war, it was doing almost nothing to deal with the problem. The wealthy neighborhoods and government districts were cordoned off, garrisoned by army detachments and provisioned by special armed convoys. But a mob was a hard thing to control. Killing a few sometimes put enough of a scare into the rest to send them flying back to their homes. But these masses were starving, facing slow and painful deaths if they disbanded. It wouldn't be long, she knew, before they lost their fear of the soldiers and tried to break through to the elite areas.

The Committee members and their families were safe in the command bunker, but there were plenty of influential politicos left in Hong Kong and the other cities…well within the reach of the mobs. The CAC couldn't function without those legions of bureaucrats. If the armed checkpoints failed to keep the political neighborhoods safe the CAC itself could collapse. And Li and the rest of the Committee members would be nothing but a bunch of windbags hiding under the South China Sea.

She sighed and looked at the chronometer. So many problems, so little time. The Committee meeting was about to begin. She held onto the armrests of the chair, pushing herself painfully to her feet. She could feel her strength slipping away almost daily. Why, she wondered, couldn't I have faced my worst crisis when I was younger and stronger? Why did this happen now, when there is so little of me left? She knew there was no answer. Crises chose their own moments, and those affected could only do their best to cope.

She grabbed her cane and moved slowly toward the door.

The Committee Chamber was considerably smaller than the ruling body's magnificent meeting place in Hong Kong but, for a facility buried deep below the seabed, it was breathtaking. The rulers of the CAC had been preparing their wartime refuges since the day the Treaty of Paris was signed. The CAC elites demanded both safety and comfort for themselves and their families during wartime, and the undersea shelter southwest of Hong Kong addressed both concerns admirably. It had been the primary bunker marked for the wartime use of the Committee for 50 years...half a century during which there were one or two scares, but no major crises. Now it was in full operation... the wartime seat of government for the Central Asian Combine.

"We must strike a major blow against the Alliance. We must drive them from our sphere of influence at the very least." Deng Chao was one of the oldest members of the Committee. Autocratic and arrogant, he'd been the unofficial leader of the hawkish party for the last twenty years. "We can no longer tolerate the enemy's presence in the Philippines." He paused, then added, "Or Oceania."

Li held her tongue. Let him finish, she thought. His words will make your case. She had been Deng's primary opposition for years, urging restraint in dealings with the Alliance. Li was as cold-blooded as anyone in the CAC, but she knew what war would be like, and she'd done everything in her power to maintain peace between the Powers, at least on Earth. Too many Committee members had forgotten the horrors their grandparents had suffered to forge the CAC from the gutted ruins of China and half a dozen other wrecked nations. The early leaders, those who ruled from Hong Kong in the early days of the peace, knew firsthand how close they had come to the brink. Their capital was a devastated ruin, the process of rebuilding just beginning. They had considered it unthinkable to risk the renewal of war on Earth. But time had virtually wiped away living memory of the horrors of the wars, and slowly, steadily, the fear that reinforced sanity faded. The leaders were afraid of war on Earth, but not the same way their grandparents had been.

"We must not blindly fear controlled escalation." Deng slapped his hand on the table in front of him. "We cannot crawl before the Alliance, fearing their military might, checking our every move for concern over their response. Indeed, it is time for us to take the initiative, to strike hard against our enemies and allow the Combine to achieve the true greatness that is its just due upon the world stage."

Li heard the applause begin at scattered locations around the Committee table, and her heart sank as the cheering grew louder and more energetic. Deng was playing to patriotism, to national – and racial – pride. She was amazed, not for the first time, how emotional appeals could cripple even the most intelligent and capable individuals. There were men present she knew to be smart and highly educated, yet they were ready to yield to foolish, reckless arguments.

She rose slowly and waited for the cheers to die down before she began. "I have argued these points many times, my friends and comrades...urged this body to moderation." Li tried to hold herself steady without her cane. The pain in her legs was worse than ever, despite the heavy dose of pain meds. "I have but one request...that you all ask yourselves a single question. Why are we here...in this shelter? Is it not because, regardless of jingoistic flag-waving and self-serving speeches, we all fear this war will quickly escalate?" Her voice was weak, throaty. She swallowed hard, trying to increase her volume. She needed to be at her best now, but she knew her strength was almost gone.

"We have not utilized nuclear, biological, or chemical weapons yet; neither have our adversaries. We have not yet invaded any home territory of the Alliance, nor have they done so to us. The fighting to date has been confined to the Manila Perimeter and the sea zones in its immediate area...a location that has been claimed by both parties for over a century. Yet, despite all of this, we have fled the capital, and we cower beneath the

South China Sea, hiding from the massive nuclear strikes we all fear will come. Whether we allow our conscious minds to admit that dread or not, each of us knows it is possible, perhaps likely. Or we would still be in the Committee Chamber in Hong Kong, would we not?"

She stared at each of the Committee members in turn as she spoke, not expecting an answer to her question. "Is that what we want? To see Hong Kong and the other great cities of the Combine turned to poisonous ruins? To see the great industry of our nation reduced to radioactive slag?"

She looked around the room and immediately realized she'd gone too far. There were those in the room receptive to arguments for caution, but none who liked to be told they were 'cowering' in their undersea refuge. Li was angry with herself. Her argument was sloppy, too direct. She'd been careless and alienated those she needed to court. She was about to try and salvage things when Deng jumped to his feet.

"We, too, have the power to destroy our enemies, to burn their cities into toxic dust." Deng spoke out of turn, a breach of normal protocol. But emotions were running high, and tensions were showing, even in the Committee's closed chambers.

"Yes, what our esteemed colleague says is indeed true." Li strained to raise her voice. Deng was a fool, she knew…but that didn't mean his views wouldn't prevail. "But what ultimate purpose does that serve? Does Washbalt destroyed compensate us for the loss of Hong Kong? Will the annihilation of London or New York make up for the obliteration of Shanghai or Nanjing? Or Macau?" Li knew she sounded desperate, but she didn't know what else to say. "Is mutual destruction a victory for either side?"

Deng raised his hand and interrupted again. "I understand Minister Li's protestations." He stared at Li as he spoke, his eyes a pointed warning. "No one has served the Combine longer or more faithfully than Li An." He turned toward Huang. "Mr. Chairman, esteemed Committee members…I'm sure I join with all of you in wishing to express my profound appreciation for Minister Li's lifetime of service to our great nation." A soft murmur of agreement worked its way around the table.

Li stared at Deng. She knew what he was doing, but she didn't know how to counter it. Any rebuttal to his tribute would appear irrational and only further damage her political capital. She could hear his next words, even before he uttered them.

"Perhaps Minister Li has taken too much on herself for too long. I submit that we, as a governing body, have demanded a greater workload from our esteemed colleague than anyone, no matter how intelligent and capable, can carry."

Deng's voice was kind, compassionate. And Li knew every word of it was pure bullshit. It was a warning shot, and she knew it. A glance around the room was all she needed to see that she had a good chance of losing C1 if she pushed too hard. She knew Deng didn't want that fight; he was well aware that Li An was always a formidable opponent even when she seemed at her weakest. But he had the upper hand, and they both knew it. Her heart told her to argue, but her intellect - and her instincts, her unmatched years of experience - urged her to stay silent, to allow Deng to win this round. To survive to fight the next round.

"The current situation requires unprecedented strength of resolve. We must move forward without fear, without hesitation. We must meet our enemy with courage and determination...and we must never waver." He paused, glancing toward Li An as he continued. "Or allow ourselves to be ruled by caution when the situation calls for boldness."

Li sat silently, her expert eyes reading the reactions of the Committee members. Deng had the majority; she had no doubt about that. The war was new, and for all the talk of the horrors of the Unification Wars, that nightmare had been over a century before. Conventional wisdom and stories handed down don't carry the same weight as remembrance. Li An knew the truth, and she realized it applied to the other Powers as well. People no longer had enough fear of the horrors of total war. They talked of quick victories and gaining the upper hand... not of utter devastation and extinction. Her biggest problems weren't Deng's actions...they were the same things that had caused mankind to repeat mistakes again and again. Time and forgetfulness.

She had a few remaining weapons up her sleeve, but if she used them now and failed, she'd be finished. Without C1, she'd lose most of her power. She would become a helpless old woman, watching from the sidelines as her world collapsed. She knew letting Deng have a free run now would only make things worse, but she didn't see any way to stop that. At least if she preserved her power base there would be a chance later… assuming there was a later.

"I have had extensive discussions with Admiral Chen." Deng turned from Li and looked out across the huge conference table. "As you are all aware, our fleet suffered a considerable defeat off the coast of Luzon." He paused, his face twisting into a scowl. "A travesty for which Admiral Dao's incompetence was fully to blame. And for which he has paid the price."

Li winced slightly. Her thoughts drifted away, Deng's ongoing monotone reduced to a barely perceptible buzz in the back of her mind. Admiral Dao had been dragged off his flagship and shot without trial, his body unceremoniously dumped into the sea. Li hadn't agreed that the admiral was to blame for the lost battle. The Alliance fleet had the edge in both hulls and tonnage. But Dao was another victim of expediency. Li knew she couldn't defy the Committee's orders, not without provoking a power struggle she would almost certainly lose. So she had done what she had to do and dispatched the kill team as ordered, just as she had with Fleet Admiral An when he and his officers were proscribed. That had been another mistake, she thought, though that one had been Chairman Huang's alone.

"The Alliance fleet is carrying substantial reinforcements and supply from Oceania bound for their armed forces manning the Manila battle zone. Without these fresh troops, I am assured the Alliance lines will collapse within the next several weeks." Li An was listening again, certain she'd missed nothing important. "We must prevent these forces from reaching their destination." He paused, staring at a few key members of the Committee as he did. "I therefore propose that Admiral Chen be authorized to launch a targeted nuclear strike against the Alliance vessels carrying the reserve force." Another pause, and more pointed glances around the room. "Since Admiral Dao's failure left the fleet in no condition to launch another attack, I do not believe we have a useful alternative. If we do not act and the Alliance troops on Luzon are successfully reinforced, we will be bogged down in an ongoing stalemate in the Philippines… and any longer term offensives against Australia and the rest of Alliance Oceania will be stillborn."

Li listened grimly, surprised at Deng's audacity. Nuclear strikes? Invading Alliance Oceania? He was speaking of massive escalations of the conflict. She felt the tension in her gut, and she knew they were marching toward the cliff…just as Stark wanted. She knew Deng's plans were foolish, a series of tragic mistakes. But she was also aware she couldn't stop them. It was time to look to the next crossroads. If she had another chance to stop things before it was too late she resolved to be better prepared. But for now, she waited silently for the proctor to call her name. She couldn't stop what was happening, but just maybe she could position herself better for next time. "Yes," she said quietly, unable to mask the despair she felt as she voted to authorize the nuclear attack.

Chapter 22

North of Astria
Planet Armstrong
Gamma Pavonis II

Cain walked across the blackened, battle-scarred ground, his visor retracted and a rare smile on his face. "Farooq, you son of a bitch, it's good to see you." He took the last few steps toward the Janissary commander and threw open his arms.

"And you, my friend." Farooq returned Cain's embrace, as much as that was possible in powered armor. I am pleased to be fighting at your side once again."

Cain winced as he extended his arm. The shoulder wound was still a little tender. "I don't know where you came from, but you got here just in time." Cain released the Caliphate officer and took a small step back. "But what the hell is going on? What are you doing here?"

"It is a long story, my friend, and one that requires more time to tell than we have to spare at present." Farooq nodded slightly. "For now, let me just say that the Caliphate fleet and the Janissaries it carries have - how shall I say? – severed themselves from the Earth government."

Not much surprised Cain, and even when it did he rarely showed it. But his mouth dropped open and he stared back at Farooq. "I know I've been cut off here, but..."

"The Caliph ordered a proscription against the senior officers of the fleet and the Janissary corps. Lord Khaled and Admiral Abbas found out in time to thwart the effort, and they took the fleet renegade rather than submit a rather large list of officers…" – he gestured toward himself – "…including this humble personage…to summary execution." Farooq looked a little uncomfortable as he returned Cain's gaze. He still had mixed feelings about the whole thing.

"I am sorry, my friend." Cain's expression softened. "I know that must have been a difficult time." He was very fond of the Janissary commander, and he could see the pain in Farooq's eyes. Cain had gone into the struggle against the First Imperium with deep prejudices against his former adversaries. But years of struggling against a common enemy had forged strong bonds, especially between Farooq and Cain.

"We will speak of it in greater detail one day, Erik." Farooq managed a fleeting smile. "But for now, let us focus on ridding Armstrong of the enemy."

"Fair enough, my friend." Cain nodded. "Are your units ready for action?"

"We are ready, General Cain." Farooq was standing rigidly at attention. "Where do you want us?"

"The 6th Legion will pull back immediately. We are abandoning the capital and moving back to the Sentinel." Rafael Samuels stood on a small rise, staring off toward the south but seeing nothing except his own grim thoughts. The battle had gone on far too long. When he arrived with the second wave, he'd expected to sweep the battered Marines from the field in a matter of days. But it was one thing after another. The Marines fought for every centimeter of ground as they pulled back, and then they sent in their giant Obliterators and devastated his supply base.

Samuels knew it was going to be a bad day when he finally found himself standing before Gavin Stark. Number One did not take bad news well…he'd seen it many times. Samuels had at least expected to have the chance to complete the conquest before he had to deal with Stark. For all the delays, he never doubted his forces would ultimately prevail. Until the Janissaries landed.

"Yes, General Samuels." Anderson-5 was Samuels' field

commander and second-in-command. "The 4th Legion is reporting enemy forces moving around its flank. The enemy is advancing behind a barrage of Smoke shells."

More fucking Janissaries, Samuels thought, clenching his fists in frustration. The first landing had been bad enough…4 ortas, about 5,000 troops. Like the Marines, the Janissaries were all veterans of the brutal battles of the First Imperium War, and they went immediately into action. He'd finally had Cain and his fucking Marines on the brink when the Goddamned Caliphate troopers slammed into his legions and halted their advance. Then more Janissaries landed…wave after wave. By the time they were done, there were almost 25,000 of their elite powered infantry on the ground, backing up Cain's 10,000 remaining effectives.

Samuels didn't understand. His last communique had confirmed that the Caliphate had joined the CAC in its war against the Alliance. What the hell were the Janissaries doing on Armstrong fighting alongside the Marines? It didn't make sense. He'd had no word from Stark, not since that fucking Alliance naval detachment burned his satcom. What was going on?

But sense or no, it was reality, and Samuels didn't know what to do. He still had a slight numerical edge, but his forces were exhausted, and the destruction of his supplies cut down on his options. The Janissaries were fresh, and they were hitting his positions hard all across the line.

Samuels doubted he could win an even battle. His legions were supposed to be as good as the Marines, but despite Stark's assurances, it just wasn't the case. The clones were good soldiers, reliable and well-trained. But they weren't the equals of the Marines, not by a long shot. And not of the Janissaries either, Samuels suspected he would soon find out.

He'd had his doubts all along. Samuels had been a Marine too, one who'd served almost 40 years. Stark's manufactured soldiers were a technological marvel, and his ability to produce them in large numbers made them a very potent weapon. But they still needed numerical superiority to defeat the Marines, an advantage they'd had until the Janissaries intervened.

He looked up at his tactical display. His people were retreating across the line, but there were no routs, no breakdown of discipline. The Shadow Legions were falling back, but they weren't beaten. Not yet. Conditioned from ear to ear to ignore pain and fear, his battered units still had fight left in them.

His eyes moved toward the large dark area on the edge of the display. The Sentinel. That's where he would make his stand. Erik Cain had used the forest's cover to tremendous effect earlier in the campaign. Now it would be Cain's turn to drive an attack through the dense, towering woods, while Samuel's people defended behind every tree and hillside.

"Let them come," Samuels whispered to himself. But, despite the forced bravado, he could feel the fear in the pit of his stomach.

"Move it! Deploy and commence firing immediately!" Jake Carlson was waving his arms, directing his newly-arrived autocannon teams into position. The enemy was pulling back all across the line, and Carlson's people were right on their tail. They were just north of Astria now. This was the last vantage point for his heavy weapons before the enemy reached the city. Carlson had intended to pursue them right through Astria, but General Cain had put a hold on that. There were Janissaries poised to attack and retake the capital, and the Caliphate troops were fresh. But whether it was Marines or Janissaries going in, Carlson wanted to take out as many of the enemy as possible before it came to street fighting.

He switched his com to the support channel. "This is Major Carlson. Commence air attack immediately." The Caliphate fleet that landed the Janissaries had already left the system to search for Admiral Garret and the Alliance naval forces. But before they departed they sent down two squadrons of atmospheric attack craft…all they had left from the bloody campaigns on the Rim. And now those fighter-bombers were going to hit the enemy as they retreated to Astria.

Carlson looked down and saw his reserve teams were already in place and firing, sweeping the plain north of the city. The approach to Astria was mostly flat, open ground…the primary reason Cain had fallen back so far from the city when his forces were retreating. Carlson's gunners were raking the withdrawing enemy troopers, taking down hundreds of them and reducing their formations to disordered mobs.

Carlson couldn't keep a wicked smile from his lips. Only a few weeks before he had been leading the forlorn hope, a few hundred Marines trying to hold back the enemy advance while their brethren escaped the crumbling position south of Astria. Now they were pursuing the enemy back through that same country, gunning them down as they ran back the way they had come.

Once, his pride would have rejected utterly the notion of the Marines being rescued by the Janissaries. It seemed almost an absurdity. But now he was glad for friends…any friends. Still, he couldn't help but wonder how the universe worked at times. If there was a God out there somewhere, he had a twisted sense of humor.

"This is White Tiger Squadron leader to Marine commander. We are commencing our attack run." The Caliphate pilot's voice was loud and clear as it blared from Carlson's helmet speakers.

"We've got incoming air support," he snapped on the unit-wide com. "Keep your heads down." His people were pretty close to the enemy, especially for what he knew was about to come down. "Those birds are dropping FAEs, and I don't need any of you barbecued."

The Caliphate atmospheric fighters were slightly smaller than the Alliance models, with a sleeker, more attractive form. They looked like great birds of prey swooping down on a herd of fleeing animals as they vectored toward the retiring enemy formations.

They came in fast, and it was hard to follow them visually. Carlson watched on his display as the small triangles moved across the tactical map. One by one, a line of tiny dots appeared on the display just behind each plane. FAE canisters.

"Everybody grab some dirt." Carlson shouted into the com as he dove forward, sliding himself down as far as he could behind the small berm his people were using as cover. "Now!"

The FAEs came down all along the disordered enemy line, exploding in a series of massive fireballs. Anything unarmored out on that plain, any enemy soldiers whose suits had been holed or compromised, died instantly from the pressure wave and subsequent vacuum.

The powered infantry, sealed up in their suits, had some chance to survive the attack. Those caught in the center of the firestorms literally roasted in their armor, as the intense heat overloaded their suits' capacity to compensate or the temperatures exceeded the melting points of their osmium-iridium alloys. The ones on the fringes of the primary impact area survived, their blackened and pitted suits enduring the ferocity of the onslaught. The survivors ran toward Astria, leaving half their force behind, dead on the scorched plain. Carlson was impressed as he watched the withdrawal. They were running toward the cover of the city, but there was no panic, no crazed stampede. They were not routing, despite an air assault that would have sent most formations into panicked flight.

He saw something that looked like a streak of fire rising up from the enemy position and the last of the bombers pitched to the side and tumbled end over end, slamming hard into the ground in a massive explosion. Neither side had much anti-air capability, but the enemy had managed to draw blood with one of their small handheld launchers. It was a lucky shot, and it cost the Marines and Janissaries one of their precious aircraft.

"Major Carlson, this is Commander Farooq." The Janissary commander's voice blared out of Carlson's helmet speaker. "My forces are ready to advance."

"Very well, Commander." Carlson turned and looked out over his line. He flipped his com to the unitwide frequency. "Cease all fire." He paused, listening to the sound of the shooting subside before he flipped back to Farooq's channel. "You're clear to go, Commander. And good luck to you."

Anderson-112 ducked behind a section of shattered building, looking out at the strange green clouds floating across the field. He knew it was Smoke, and he had shadowy memories of facing it before, though the fighting on Armstrong was his first campaign. They weren't his own recollections, not really, but they were real nonetheless. It was confusing, unsettling. But still, somehow he couldn't quite explain, he understood how to deal with the situation.

"Concentrate fire on the clouds." He snapped out the orders, almost by reflex. The army was retreating south, but his regiment had been ordered to hold the northern perimeter of Astria while the rest of the units made it through the city. "They're inside those clouds. Keep firing."

He looked out over the blasted plain. The Janissaries were advancing across the blackened ground where he'd lost two-thirds of his strength to the enemy's devastating air attack and murderous autocannon fire. He felt strange about losing over 1,200 of his soldiers in matter of minutes. There was the usual detachment, the normal cold analysis. But there was something else too. Not in the forefront of his mind, but deeper, where the other memories resided. It was unsettling, an unfamiliar feeling, unpleasant and distracting. A horror at watching so many of his troops die in such a terrible way. Anderson-112 tried to push it aside. But it was still there, just on the periphery of his consciousness.

He'd been on the edge of the FAE bombing run. His armor was blackened and scarred, but he'd been outside of the primary kill zone when the bombers struck. Unlike most of his men. He tried to focus on his training, his conditioning. But the sight of so many of his soldiers writhing in the flames as they roasted inside their armor was still there.

The Janissaries started to emerge from the Smoke clouds, rushing his positions. They were shooting as they advanced, raking his shallow foxholes with deadly-accurate fire. But his people were firing back, and the Janissaries were out in the open. They started falling in clumps as the Shadow troopers savaged their lines with autocannon fire.

Explosions erupted all along the Shadow line…incoming grenades from the attacking Caliphate troopers. The Janissaries were well-trained in the use of grenades, a weapon the Marines regarded as a secondary system. They didn't inflict heavy casualties on powered infantry – it pretty much took a direct hit to take out an armored combatant with a grenade. But it made lots of noise and churned things up. The Janissary way of war was a highly theatrical one, designed to instill terror in the hearts of the defenders. It was highly effective against colonial units and second line troops, but less so when they had fought the Marines. The Shadow troops were conditioned to feel no fear, nevertheless, they found it distracting.

Anderson-112 could see immediately his lines weren't going to hold. The grenades were more effective than expected against his unit's shallow foxholes and the wrecked buildings they were using as cover. They were taking casualties they couldn't afford...not after the devastating losses inflicted by the air strike and Carlson's autocannons.

The Janissaries were assaulting in considerable strength. Fresh units were advancing behind the battered first line, and it looked like a second full orta was emerging from the Smoke clouds behind the vanguard. They swept forward, quickly closing the distance between the bilious green clouds and Anderson-112's thin line.

The defenders maintained their discipline, firing at the advancing Caliphate forces. They were making the Janissaries pay, but they weren't going to stop them. They might have driven back a militia unit or a force of colonial regulars, but the Janissaries were every bit as elite as the Marines...and their Shadow Legion imitations. They took their losses and grimly advanced, firing point blank into the foxholes and storming the small defensive clusters around each building.

Anderson-112's orders were clear. Under no circumstances was he to retreat. He knew his unit was to be sacrificed, that he was expected to fight until his regiment had been completely wiped out. He understood, and the conditioning worked at his mind, demanding compliance. But there was something else there, something deeper...from the other thoughts. Anger, outrage at seeing his men wasted so callously. He was sweating, despite the perfect climate control of his suit, and his hands were balled into armored fists. NO, screamed something inside him, something he couldn't fully understand. But he realized he couldn't just watch his men die, sacrificed to a lost cause.

He looked up at the tactical display. The Janissaries were slicing through his lines in half a dozen places. Soon it would be too late to pull back. His thoughts waged a war in his head, pulling him back and forth, between his conditioning and the borrowed memories of a Marine long dead. Slowly, despite his efforts to hold back, his hand activated the unit-wide com. "All forces, retreat at once. Pull back through the city immediately." The words felt almost involuntary as they came out of his mouth, but he still repeated them. "All forces, retreat to the south of the city and regroup."

All along the line, the Shadow troopers climbed up out of their foxholes and ran to the rear. The advancing Janissaries gunned them down as they fled, but the survivors kept going, ducking behind the cover of the buildings as they entered the city.

"Anderson-112, this is Command Central." The voice was as monotone and without character as those of the rest of the Shadow troopers, but there was a sternness to it as well. "Your forces are conducting an unauthorized withdrawal. You are instructed to rally and advance back to your previous line."

"No." Anderson-112's reply was soft but firm. He didn't elaborate.

There was silence on the line. Then the same voice repeated the command. "Anderson-112, you are ordered to rally. Cease your retreat and hold your assigned defensive position."

"I said no." Anderson-112's head had become a warzone, old memories rising out of the darkness…recollections that were somehow a part of him, though they weren't his. They struggled with his conditioning, taking control. Whatever happened, he couldn't see his men thrown away, their lives wasted for nothing. It was somehow…unthinkable, something he just couldn't live with, whatever the consequences.

There was a long pause on the line. Then a gruff voice

replaced the monotone droning. "Anderson-112, this is General Rafael Samuels. You are ordered to maintain your position."

"No, General. I will not. My unit will be destroyed to no effect if I do." His tone was respectful, but firm. He didn't understand why, but he was resolved to see his men escape from this trap.

"Anderson-112, this is your last chance. Obey your orders now!" The anger of Samuel's voice blasted out of the com.

"I'm sorry sir."

There was a pause, ten seconds, perhaps 20. Anderson-112 was watching his forces run past him, fleeing into the cover of the city. He felt a pinprick on his neck, and his vision blurred almost immediately. His breathing became heavy, and in few seconds, he sank to his knees...then fell on his back. He didn't understand how, but he knew he was dying. His heavy eyes panned over to the tactical display. He could see the blurry icons, his troopers. They were too far back now...there was no way to get them back on the line. They had taken heavy losses, but some of them would escape the deathtrap. He smiled. Some of them will survive, he thought.

He felt the other thoughts bursting out of their place in his mind. He imagined himself other places, fighting on steaming jungle worlds and on the glaciers of a frozen ice planet. There were other forces all around him, similar to his own men, but different too. And there was a flag...the banner his enemies carried. The standard of the Alliance Marine Corps. He slipped away, floating in a sea of a dead Marine's dreams.

Cain walked down Astria's main street toward the looming hulk of the Marine hospital, a pack of officers and guards following behind. The city was cluttered with the detritus of war, but the buildings themselves were mostly intact. The Marines had retreated right through the city, and now the Shadow forces had done the same.

He was glad as he gazed at some of the familiar sights. Bricks and mortar would never matter as much as the vast amount of blood that had been spilled, but it was somehow reassuring to see something recognizable survive. It was nice to believe you were fighting to preserve something, Cain thought darkly, even when you know it's mostly bullshit.

The tide had definitely turned. Farooq's Janissaries went into action immediately, and their savage attacks shattered the Shadow force's lines, sending the invaders streaming back south toward the Sentinel. The lightning attacks were reinforced by the additional Janissary forces Ali Khaled brought down after Farooq's vanguard.

The Shadow troopers were attempting to reform in the cover of the Sentinel. The wondrous forest had already been a battlefield, and thousands of its priceless, millennia-old trees had been battered into matchsticks. Now it looked like the scourge of war had made its way back to the vast natural wonder.

Cain was wondering how to finish the battle. Was he going to have to kill every last enemy soldier on the planet? They didn't seem to react like normal human beings, subject to fear, to the realization of hopelessness. Would they rout if pressed hard enough? Would they surrender if certain death was their only other option? Or would they fight on mindlessly to the last man?

Their leadership didn't seem to countenance surrender. Farooq's and Carlson's advancing forces had found thousands of wounded who'd been poisoned by their own AI's when they were too badly hurt to retreat out of the path of the enemy. Would any force that murdered its own wounded accept that a battle was lost and surrender to prevent useless bloodshed? Cain doubted it profoundly.

Cain had fought many enemies, and he'd never been troubled by dispatching them in any way he could. He'd always considered each adversary slain one fewer left to kill his own people. But there was something about the Shadow forces, about his talks with Anderson-45, that made him queasy. The single enemy captive was so reasonable, so rational. He didn't seem like an enemy. Cain knew it wouldn't feel right to kill Anderson-45, even in the heat of battle. Were all the Shadow forces like him?

Sarah was back working with the prisoner, trying to unlock his conditioning. If she could find a way to truly understand Anderson-45, perhaps she could develop a method to reach the thousands like him…soldiers that were still fighting the Marines and Janissaries tooth and nail. It wasn't just about the Shadow forces. It was going to cost thousands of lives to finish this battle, especially if they had to wipe out all the enemy soldiers on Armstrong. And Cain had seen enough of his people die.

Ali Khaled walked briskly toward the communications tent, clad in armor, his helmet fully retracted. He reached out his arm and pulled the flap open. "You have a communication for me from the orbital force?"

The com tech rose abruptly and bowed before the Janissary lord. "Yes, my Lord Khaled."

Khaled was already waving off the formal greeting. "Yes, yes, there is no time for that." He reached out and grabbed the headset, wrapping it over his ears and nodding to the nervous tech. "Put it through," he snapped.

Khaled watched as the technician pressed a few buttons on his panel. "You are connected with Fleet Captain Yusef, sir."

"Captain Yusef, this is Ali Khaled. What's going on up there?" He paused, waiting out the brief delay that was an unavoidable part of ground-to-orbit communications.

"Greetings to you, Lord Khaled, and fortune to you and those who follow you."

The captain responded with the formal greeting, but there was something wrong…Khaled sensed it immediately. He could hear it in the captain's voice. "Yes, and good fortune to you as well." Khaled stopped midway through the prescribed response. "We have no time to waste, Captain. What is happening up there?"

"Sir, we have a large fleet inbound from the warp gate. We have identified fourteen capital ships…over 100 hulls in all so far." There was fear in the captain's voice, though he masked it well. But Khaled was a master at reading such things.

"Have you been able to identify them, Captain?" Maybe it

was Garret, Khaled thought fleetingly. If he hadn't gotten any of the communiques Khaled and Abbas had sent, the Alliance admiral wouldn't expect to find a Caliphate naval force in Armstrong's system. He would likely consider them hostiles.

"Negative, sir. We've identified some of the vessels, however. Many are Alliance ships, but there are CAC, Caliphate, and PRC hulls as well." There was a short pause then, "All vessels that were undergoing repairs at the Alliance's Wolf-359 facility, my lord."

Khaled's heart sank. Stark, he thought grimly. Enemy reinforcements. "You must retreat at once, Captain. Your force will not have a chance against an enemy fleet of that size."

"Negative, Lord Khaled. Admiral Abbas was clear that I am to remain here and provide orbital support to your forces." Abbas had departed with most of the fleet after the Janissaries landed, searching for Admiral Garret and his forces.

Khaled sighed hard. Pointless gestures, he thought angrily… why is war so full of them? "Captain, listen to me. You will serve no purpose throwing away your command and the lives of your crew here." Yusef had four cruisers and a dozen destroyer-equivalents. It wasn't a time to be throwing away irreplaceable hulls and crews for no gain. "Get your ships out of here immediately. I will accept all responsibility with Admiral Abbas." Khaled and Abbas were of approximately equal rank, though the Janissary lord had no official authority over fleet operations.

There was a long silence. "Sir, I don't know if…"

"Now, Captain," Khaled snapped, interrupting the stammering naval officer. He knew he was going to have to intimidate Yusef if he was going to save the 5,000 naval crew manning those ships. If they stayed, they would die for nothing. "I told you, I will accept all responsibility with Admiral Abbas." He paused then added, "Do you really want to explain to the admiral why you refused my order?" A pointless argument…Khaled had no right to issue orders to Yusef. Besides, if the captain and his people stayed in the system, they'd never live to see Abbas again anyway. But Khaled was desperate.

"Uh…very well Lord Khaled." Yusef sounded uncomfortable, but he was giving in.

"Transmit your full scanner data on the incoming fleet, and then get the hell out of here." He paused for a few seconds. "Now!"

"Yes, sir."

Khaled turned toward the com tech. "I want that data transmitted to me the instant you have it." He stared at the sweating technician. "Understood?"

"Yes, Lord Khaled."

"Very well." He turned and walked out into the hastily cleared mud streets of the camp. Now I have to go find Erik Cain, he thought...and try to figure out what we've got coming at us.

He flipped on his com. "General Cain...Commander Khaled here." He stifled a sigh. "We need to talk. Right now."

Chapter 23

Red Hills
South of Arcadia City
Arcadia – Wolf 359 III

"The enemy is abandoning their position and pulling back in disarray, General." Colonel Heath was staring out over the broken plain watching his Marines move forward. The fighting had been intense, the enemy forces continuing to resist, even after Heath's Marines had outflanked their position.

"Well done, Colonel." General Gilson's voice was tired, strained. Her forces had been in action non-stop since they'd landed 3 weeks before, and everyone was exhausted. She had no idea where these enemy soldiers had come from, but they seemed almost without fear. Her forces repeatedly outmaneuvered them, but still they held, regardless of losses. They fell back from compromised positions, but only far enough to regroup. Then they kept on fighting, seemingly ignoring even crippling casualties. Only in the last day's combat had their morale begun to fail, and savaged units started falling back in disarray. "Pursue them, Rod. Keep on their tail or they'll just pull back and reorganize."

"Yes, General." Heath's voice showed his excitement. His forces had advanced relentlessly, but the enemy maintained their order as they fell back. He'd almost lost hope the enemy would break. But now it felt like victory was truly possible. "We'll be right on their asses."

"That's where I want you, Rod. I don't want them to take a breath." She paused then added, "Go get 'em. Gilson out."

Heath stared out over the blasted terrain to the left. It looked like it had been a sparse area of woods once, or maybe an orchard, but the trees were gone now, blasted to kindling by the nonstop fighting. Only a few blackened trunks remained to offer a hint at what this ground had been before the armies came.

"Captain Zimmer, take your company to the left. Put some pressure on their flank." Heath had been holding Zimmer's people in reserve, but the enemy line was showing signs of solidifying, and that was the last thing he needed. Breaking the enemy's lines and forcing them to retreat had been a costly exercise, not one he cared to see repeated. His job was to keep the pressure up, prevent the enemy from rallying or forming a strong defense. And that was turning out to be a 24/7 job.

"Yes, Colonel."

Heath could hear the sounds of Zimmer's people forming up behind him, even as the veteran captain acknowledged the order. Zimmer's people had fought at Sandoval and at Sigma 4. They were veterans who'd marched relentlessly into the teeth of the First Imperium's robotic legions. Heath was confident they could do the job here too.

Don't underestimate this enemy, he thought...they are trained and equipped just like Marines, and they are clearly disciplined and courageous. "We've got them off balance now," he muttered softly to himself, "but if we give them a chance, they'll pull it together and come right back at us."

He watched as Zimmer's lead platoon swung around the flank and headed toward the enemy. There were a few shattered buildings along their route, probably where a small village or a good-sized farming operation had stood. Some cover, at least, Heath thought.

"Captain Linz, I want your people to hit the enemy line with grenades. One full spread per man. Keep their heads down while Zimmer's people get into position." Heath looked across at the enemy position. "I have a surprise for you," he whispered softly, imagining his counterpart trying to pull his disordered units back together.

Heath's Marines had something special. Something far more effective than the standard issue grenades...the newest weapons system from General Sparks' miraculous laboratory. Sparks was still at Sigma-4, studying the ruins of the First Imperium facilities there. But he'd finished a limited number of his new thermobaric grenades and given them to General Gilson before her force left the frontier. And Gilson had given them to Heath.

"Yes, Colonel," Linz snapped back. "Commencing fire at once, sir."

Almost immediately, he heard the distinctive sounds of the grenade launchers. They each fired six shots, one after the other. The popping sounds were nearly synchronized, but not quite, as each squad fired off their spreads.

The grenades were a high-trajectory weapon, taking a few seconds to reach their targets. Heath was staring right at the enemy line when he saw the first bright flash. Then another... and another. In an instant, the entire enemy line was engulfed in massive, billowing flames. Inside the raging hell, he knew the temperature exceeded 3,500 degrees. Dozens of enemy soldiers died, roasted alive inside their suits. Others fell to the ground, imprisoned in disabled, partially melted armor.

Heath looked across the field in stunned surprise. Like most Marines, he tended to discount the usefulness of the grenade launchers built into every suit of armor...at least against other powered infantry. But watching Sparks' thermobaric creations wreak havoc on the enemy changed his mind on the spot. They would be a tremendous addition to the Marine arsenal once Sparks got back and put them into mass production. But Heath's people had been assigned only two spreads each, all that were currently available, and he'd ordered Linz to save the last one for an emergency.

"Captain Zimmer, your people are to fire a single spread of thermobaric grenades targeting the last half klick of the enemy flank." Linz's attack had been so effective, he wanted to see what Zimmer's people could do, focusing on a truly concentrated target area.

"Yes, sir." Zimmer's acknowledgement was immediate.

"We're in position and commencing fire now, sir."

Heath could see the launches from Zimmer's company, and a few seconds later, the enemy line was again engulfed in a nightmare of searing white fire. The attack was as effective as Linz's, and the enemy was wavering in disorder over a kilometer of front.

Heath flipped the com to the unit command channel. "Captain Zimmer, Captain Linz...your strike forces are to advance immediately and assault the enemy line." Heath stared out at the slowly fading hell he'd unleashed on the enemy position, and a small smile crossed his lips. The effectiveness of the grenade attack had created an opportunity. Yes, he thought. Time to hit them hard.

Kara stood in front of the Capitol, staring up at the building's battered remains. The façade was still standing, but she could see that whole sections on the side and rear were gone. The fighting had been fierce throughout the city, but the enemy had made their last stand there. Hundreds of her people had died within 75 meters of where she stood. Half her army had been killed or wounded in the two weeks of seesaw fighting it had taken to liberate the capital, and nowhere had the combat been more desperate than where she was standing...and inside the shattered shell of a building in front of her.

She was trying to ignore the pain in her side. The doctors had almost physically restrained her when she tried to leave the hospital, but she had work to do, and lying around in a makeshift bed wasn't going to get it done. The wound had been fused shut and the lost blood replaced with a synthetic. She might be sore, but she was patched up enough to do her job. At least in her own judgment...which was all that counted as far as she was concerned.

The early fighting had been bloody, but her people quickly gained the upper hand against their outnumbered foe as they drove into the city's center. But then the enemy diverted reserves from the south and counterattacked, pushing her forces back...and almost expelling them entirely. She'd managed to rally the army and lead them back one more time, fighting their way block by block toward the Capitol.

She'd been wounded during that fighting, and she missed the final assault on the Capitol. It was the climactic struggle of the battle, and there were only a handful of enemy survivors left when it was over. They fled the city and retreated south. Arcadia City was Arcadian again, a victory the cold and suffering citizen soldiers couldn't have imagined just a few weeks before when they were trudging across the frozen wilderness.

But victory was rarely without cost, and this time that loss struck close to home. Among the hundreds of dead and wounded from the final assault was one very dear to Kara. Ed Calvin had led the final charge, bursting into the Capitol itself and driving the enemy out room by room. The battle was almost won, and he was one of the last to fall...at least that's what Kara had pieced together from the multiple versions of the story already circulating.

He'd been pulled out alive and brought back to one of the aid stations. When Kara found out, she leapt out of her bed in the field hospital, practically assaulting the doctors and nurses who tried to stop her. She rushed over to see Calvin, but he died before she got there.

Ed Calvin had been a loyal compatriot and a dedicated friend, and the pain of his loss hit her hard. He'd loved her, of course. She'd known that for a long time. She had even tried to return the feelings for a while. But they just weren't in her anymore. Kara could be a friend, a confidante, a comrade in arms, but she knew in her heart she'd never love anyone again. Not like she had Will Thompson.

She would give all she had to see Arcadia free, fight each battle with everything she had. But, apart from her son, she knew she would never truly love again. Her passions existed now for her country, for Arcadia, and that was where she would channel them.

She stood in the center of the street, near the spot where her grandfather had been gunned down early in the war. She wanted to cry for him...and for Ed Calvin. For the thousands – soldiers and civilians - who had died in the fighting. But there was nothing there, only a cold numbness.

She turned away from the wreckage of the building, looking over at Independence Park. It was still there…the statue of Will Thomson, standing tall in the center of the small square. She'd half expected it to be gone…torn down or defiled by the enemy, but there it stood, proud and defiant. She gave herself a minute to stare at the statue and remember her lost love. Then she turned and walked back toward headquarters.

Her army had fought itself to exhaustion, but now she was going to ask more of them. There was elation over the liberation of the capital, but the fight for Arcadia wasn't over yet. It was time to wake her people from their exhausted slumber, to pull them from well-deserved celebrations. They were heading south…back into the battle. It was time to help the Marines in the final struggle to drive the invaders off Arcadia.

Catherine Gilson stared at the large 'pad on the table, nodding in satisfaction as she scanned the glowing symbols spread across the display. There were blue triangles extending in a semi-circular formation across a 10-kilometer front…her forces, pushing back the enemy on the flanks. Behind the main line there was another, smaller cluster of triangles…Holm's and Teller's exhausted Marines, now forming a tactical reserve while they rested and reorganized.

Red squares denoted the positions of enemy formations. There were more red symbols on the screen than blue, but the small squares had been moving back, as the enemy abandoned position after position under the relentless assaults of her Marines.

But now there was something else, a small cluster the AI had arbitrarily chosen to display as gray ovals…Kara Sanders and the Arcadian army. The group of gray symbols was the smallest of the three forces, but it was right behind the red line, marching directly on the enemy rear.

Gilson's face wore a narrow smile. She'd never met Kara Sanders, but she still had a healthy respect for the Arcadian leader. Erik Cain had mentioned her a few times when he returned from Arcadia after the rebellion…and anyone who could impress Erik Cain was worth taking a look at.

"General Sanders is quite a leader, wouldn't you say, Cate?" Elias Holm walked into the command tent, his armored helmet retracted, and his filthy, matted hair blowing softly in the breeze whipping in through the open door. "I would say she is offering us a chance to end this now." There was satisfaction in Holm's voice, but exhaustion too. The fight on Arcadia had been long and brutal, and it wasn't over. Not yet, at least. But the enemy army was bracketed between two forces. It was time to finish things.

"She is very impressive, sir." Gilson was one of the toughest screws in the Marine Corps' tool chest, but her voice was soft, pensive. "I can't imagine what her forces have been through, General. I can't begin to understand how she held them together. They're only militia, after all. At least most of them."

"I think we sometimes underestimate what good men and women can do when they're fighting for something important, don't you, Cate?"

She looked over at Holm and nodded gently. "Perhaps, sir." Gilson wasn't quite the cynic Cain was, but she was close. She didn't tend to expect much from most people…outside the Corps, that is.

He smiled. "Don't get me wrong, Cate…there is nothing like the Corps, at least not anywhere I've seen. But I think sometimes true patriots tap into the same sources of strength our people do." He took a few steps and pulled out one of the low, stubby stools that passed for chairs for powered armor. "Look at Kara's people. They spent almost a year in the field, low on weapons and supplies. They marched halfway across the planet and then back through a polar hell. They suffered thousands of casualties, but they stayed together…and when they had the opportunity, they liberated the capital and immediately marched down here to help us."

"It's still going to be a brutal fight, sir." She looked toward Holm as he slowly eased his armored bulk onto the stool. "And not the least for her people, unarmored and poorly equipped as they are. I don't think any of us expects the enemy to give up without one hell of a fight." Her eyes moved involuntarily upward. "And there's no escape for them...not with Camille's ships up there. So if they aren't going to surrender, they're going to fight to the bitter end."

"No, they won't surrender, at least not right away..." – Holm glanced across the table at the 'pad – "...but we have them caught between two lines. They'll fight like hell, but I think we've finally got them." He paused for a few seconds. "You're right that Kara's people will probably take heavy losses, but they're fighting for their homes...and if we win this last battle, they'll have taken their homes back, driven the invader from their world.

"Victory within our grasp?" Gilson wondered if there was truly any such thing. She'd won her share of battles, but the triumph had always been fleeting, without permanence. Every battle won just seemed to lead to another, harder, more costly one. "How many more of our people – of General Sanders' soldiers – will die before that victory is won?"

"You'll know the answer to that when the fight is over. You know that, Cate." Holm looked over at his longtime subordinate and nodded solemnly.

An orderly ducked his head through the open door. "Excuse me, sirs, but General Sanders has sent a communique. Her people are ready to attack at any time."

"Thank you, Lieutenant," Holm answered sharply. "That will be all." He turned back to Gilson and nodded again. "Well, Cate..." – he started to stand as he spoke – "...shall we go finish this?"

Gilson stood up brusquely, pushing her doubts aside and snapping to attention. "Yes, sir." The grim hardness of her battlefield persona was back, and it was clear in her voice. "Let's end this now."

Chapter 24

Outskirts of Nancy
French Sector, Europa Federalis
Earth – Sol III

The heavy guns shattered the pre-dawn stillness, the echoes of their fire bouncing kilometers across the valley. Hans Werner, now major general of the CEL and commander of the south-central front, stood on a nearby hill and watched the shells smash into the fortified outbuildings near the city of Nancy.

His forces had pushed their way across the Rhine and sliced deep into Europan territory. Nancy was on the line to Paris, and Werner's orders were clear. Advance directly on the city, ignoring losses.

Ignoring losses…that part didn't sit well with him. He'd three times requested permission to pause in his advance and regroup his weary and strung out forces, but each time he'd been denied…and urged to push harder, faster into Europan territory. He was winning the CEL's first victory of the war, and the high command wanted him to keep it going.

He stood unmoving as explosions erupted behind and next to him…the enemy artillery returning the fire. The Europan batteries were weak…his forces had captured large numbers of their guns as they fled across the border. He looked to the east, where his forces were sheltering on the reverse slopes, waiting for the word to advance.

The bombardment wasn't going to last long; he was sending the attack in shortly. He had 300 Leopard Z-9s massed, the last of the front line MBTs. Behind them, there were 70,000 infantry in the first attack wave, and another 85,000 reservists after that. Even the troops of the first wave were mostly replacements and second-line troops, but they'd all been blooded, at least, in the advance across Lorraine. The reserves were pure rookies, just arrived at the front. He wondered for an instant how many troops from his original battalion remained in the line, but he decided he'd rather not know.

Werner tried not to think about casualties, but that didn't keep him from running a rough count in his mind. At least 100,000 soldiers had been killed or wounded under his command, and possibly twice that. It was almost impossible to accurately determine how many were MIA or AWOL. But losses didn't matter. His sector had been the most promising when things were disastrous on the other fronts, and the high command kept feeding him more troops...meat for the beast.

The enemy started pulling forces from the northern front, moving them to face Werner's growing threat. Then the trapped CEL front line armies burst out of the Dusseldorf-Cologne pocket and launched a counter-offensive that put the Europans on the defensive in the north for the first time since the war began. Werner had heard rumors of the casualties in the massive northern battles. He didn't want to believe them, but he suspected the reports of 2,000,000 lost on each side were accurate.

The tide had turned, and the CEL was seizing the initiative, but they were paying for every meter with rivers of blood. He tried to imagine the countryside up around Dusseldorf. What does a battlefield look like after 4,000,000 men and women had been killed or wounded? What about the civilians? Had they fled eastward? He knew enough about the CEL and the way it was run to be sure the refugees were a low priority for supplies. Would the displaced civilians starve? Would they run wild across the countryside, rioting and stealing to survive?

"General..."

Werner had been so deep in thought, he didn't hear Potsdorf running up the hill toward him."

"Yes, Captain?"

"The forward elements are ready to go, sir." Potsdorf had been running around all morning, and he was breathing hard.

Werner stared out over the small valley between his army and the city. If his forces broke through the enemy defenses and took Nancy, the Europan lines would be compromised. His army would be one step closer to Paris. "Commence the attack, Captain."

"Yes, sir." Potsdorf pulled up the unitwide channel. "Attention all units…attack."

"I want a full report, Captain. Any further progress on those subsurface contacts?" Admiral Young's voice blared through the open com, and the impatience in his voice was obvious to everyone listening on Norfolk's bridge.

"No further sightings, sir." Captain Harcourt switched to his private com link. "Not since the first two, sir." Harcourt was not an officer who took his duty as seriously as Young did. He was another privileged hack from a political family but, unlike Young, he'd have been happy to sit around and spend his family's money with nothing to do. But his father had been a naval officer, another younger sibling who'd only ended up taking the family's Senate seat when his older brother died suddenly from the X-2 virus. He insisted all his younger children serve as he had, and so far, at least, Harcourt's older sister remained perfectly healthy and ready to take the Seat. It was an unfortunate situation as far as he was concerned, but there was nothing he could do about it.

Life as a naval officer had been barely tolerable before war broke out, but having enemies shooting at him was more than he could handle. And dealing with Admiral Young and his gung ho bullshit was really starting to wear on him.

"Well, they're out there somewhere, Captain, and I expect you to find them. If we lose any of those troop transports, I will hold you personally responsible. Do you understand me?"

Harcourt almost felt Young's eyes boring into him through the audio-only connection. He'd have tried to bully the fleet commander to get him off his ass, but Young's family was even better connected than Harcourt's, so that was a non-starter. "Yes, sir." Harcourt tried to keep the whining out of his voice, with only marginal success. "I understand."

"Very well, Captain. I'll let you get to it. Young out."

The com unit went silent, and Harcourt stared angrily around Norfolk's bridge. His gaze settled on the officer at the scanner station. "Well, Commander...have you got anything for me yet?"

"No, sir." Commander Simorino started to look up from his scope when he froze suddenly. "Wait a minute, sir..."

"What is it?" Harcourt's tone was dripping with impatience.

"Sir, I have eight enemy contacts." Simorino's voice was distracted, and his face was pressed against the scope as he spoke. "It almost looks like they're preparing to launch..." His voice stopped dead.

"Launch what, Commander?" Harcourt snapped.

Simorino hesitated another few seconds. Then his head spun around, and he stared at the captain. "The enemy is launching cruise missiles, sir."

"What the hell do they think eight ships are going to accomplish..." Harcourt felt realization grab him like a cold hand gripping his spine. He poked at his com panel, connecting again with the admiral. "Admiral Young...I believe we have an incoming nuclear strike on the convoy."

The hypersonic missiles streaked rapidly over the roiling waves, heading for the Alliance fleet at eight times the speed of sound. They would cover the nearly 300 kilometers from their launch platforms to the convoy in less than 100 seconds. By the time the Alliance fleet could react and get any significant interdictive assets into the air, they would have closed most of the distance.

Their flight pattern had been designed to bypass the escort ships deployed around the transports as much as possible, but the salvo couldn't avoid them all. About halfway to their targets, the sky began to fill with clouds of metallic shards fired from the railguns of the Alliance warships. Missiles began to explode in midair. At almost 3,000 meters per second, it didn't take much mass to obliterate one. But for every intercepted weapon, two made it through the defenses and continued on to the targeted ships.

The cruise missiles followed a zigzag pattern, trying to throw off the enemy defensive systems as they closed on the target zone. The random vectors were a highly effective defense mechanism during the early stages of the approach, but the Alliance commanders guessed that the troop convoy was the target, and they were able to get anti-missile ordnance up in a perimeter around the transports. The defensive rockets homed in on the approaching cruise missiles, knocking another 20 out of the sky while the target vessels submerged as quickly as possible.

But a third of the 200 missiles made it through the defenses and dove into the water after the target ships. They slowed abruptly just before breaking the waves, and the weapons split into 6 super-cavitating torpedoes, each one tipped with a 500 kiloton warhead.

The Alliance forces launched countermeasures and underwater interdiction systems, but it was too late to stop all the incoming warheads. They spread out, bracketing the target area and began detonating.

A massive plume of water rose from the surface, followed by another a kilometer south. Then another…again and again, until 138 nuclear explosions had roiled the South China Sea. Underneath the massive waves, submerged vessels were buffeted by shockwaves and their hulls were breached. The troopships were armored, but not as heavily as warships, and one after another they were torn open, their rent hulls quickly sinking to the sea bottom, 4,000 meters below. Every one that went down took 122 crew and 1,040 soldiers with it.

Damage assessment would be difficult and approximate at first, but two things were immediately clear. First, the CAC had seriously hurt the Alliance's resupply efforts for the forces dug in outside Manila. And second…they had just massively escalated the conflict.

Francis Oliver sat at his desk, his head resting in his hands. There was nothing but bad news, wherever he looked. The Cogs were running wild in half the cities of the Alliance, and it was just a matter of time before that became every metropolis. The economic crisis had shut down their food supplies, and the government simply didn't have the resources to replace them... not while keeping supplies flowing to the Political and middle classes too.

It was bad enough in Washbalt, but things were completely out of control in New York. The mobs had overrun an army unit sent to drive them away, and the murderous Cogs were right outside the gates of the Manhattan Protected Zone. He'd dispatched air transport to ferry the important families out of the city, but there were still hundreds of thousands of middle class residents – and the less influential Political families too, cowering in their apartments as the city police manned the Wall.

The police knew they'd be among the first the mob ripped to shreds, so they were grimly determined to hold the Wall. They mounted every heavy weapon they had along the top of the 20-meter bastion, and they blasted anything that came within half a kilometer.

The mob had lost thousands in the fighting against the army units, and hundreds more from the police fire from the Wall. But every loss just fueled their anger further, increased the brutal savagery and suicidal courage of the Cogs. The crowd was like an animal now, with its own will, its own white hot rage. It didn't want to argue, it didn't want to negotiate. Generations of brutal repression had turned to hatred, freedom so long denied now burst out of them as savage cries for vengeance. Oliver had originally tried to find food supplies to divert to them, but now he doubted it would matter. Things had gone too far, and it was going to take more than a few rations to put the Cogs back in their place.

The war had gotten off to a promising start with the naval victory in the South China Sea, but then things went downhill sharply. The Caliphate forces in northern Africa had launched an assault on the Alliance-owned provinces in the south and broken through in several places. The Alliance forces had withdrawn over 300 kilometers, and they were on their third commander.

Then, a CAC hunter-killer pack had targeted the Philippines troop convoy and its escorts with a nuclear attack, launching over 200 cruise missiles. The attack was clumsily executed, and almost half the transports survived to land at Manila, but that was cold comfort. The ship and troop losses were still severe, and the CAC escalation left him with a very difficult decision about his next step. Admiral Young was requesting an unlimited release to use nuclear warheads, and General Simpson on Luzon was insisting he be allowed to launch a chemical strike on the attacking CAC ground forces.

Oliver had forgotten how many aspirin he'd taken, and he threw back four more, washed down with cold coffee. He had just put his head back down when the buzzer sounded.

"I have Number One here, sir." The voice of his chief of staff sounded loud on the speaker, though he suspected it was the pain in his head and not the actual volume.

"Send him in."

The door opened and Ryan Warren, Alliance Intelligence's new Number One, came walking in, his shoes snapping hard on the polished wood floor. He was hunched over with fatigue and moving slowly as he made his way to the president's desk.

"Thank you for coming, Mr. Warren." Oliver's voice was pleasant, respectful.

Warren knew immediately the president was scared...that he didn't know what to do. That fact might have comforted him more with regard to their power dynamic if he himself had any ideas.

"Please have a seat."

My God, Warren thought, he looks like hell. He took a breath and wondered if he looked as bad. One glance at Oliver's expression told him he did. "Thank you, sir." Warren flopped down into the chair with considerably less grace than he'd normally have shown in the office of the president. "Where shall we start, sir?"

"With the Cogs, Ryan." The war was far away, at least for the moment. But there were two million Cogs rioting just outside the Washbalt Core…and it was the same at the other cities. "We have to do something to deal with these mobs."

Warren leaned back into the chair. The soft leather was so comfortable, he had to resist the urge to yawn. Sleep was a dim memory, something he remembered doing ages ago… before popping stims had become his daily routine. "Well, Mr. President, I believe the time for half-measures has passed." He paused. "I know the combat forces are in need of reinforcement on multiple fronts, but I propose we divert a large contingent of army gunships to deal with the Cog problem."

"Genocide?" There was concern in Oliver's voice, but Warren knew better than to ascribe it to any moral concerns. "I am not overly fond of the Cogs, Ryan, but we do need them back in their factories if we are going to pull the economy out of this depression and maintain the war effort."

"Do we, sir?"

Oliver stared across his desk. "We don't have times for games, Ryan. Nothing is being produced right now. The factories and mines are idle. With the Martian situation and the wars on Earth and in space, no shipments are arriving from the colonies. How can we restart the economy with no factory workers?"

"I'm not suggesting we kill them all, sir." Warren reached inside his jacket and pulled out a data crystal. "We have known for some time that there is a surplus population of Cogs, above and beyond the numbers needed to perform required menial tasks." He reached out and placed the crystal on Oliver's desk. "I believe that we can return to pre-crisis production levels with less than half the current population. My predecessor commissioned the study on that data crystal. It takes into consideration an increase in cost-effective mechanization and a more efficient deployment of Cog labor." He paused as Oliver reached out and picked up the small crystal. "The conclusion was that a minimally acceptable Cog population would be less than 45% of current figures." He was calm and businesslike, as if he were discussing a factory's need for raw materials.

"So you are saying we can kill half the Cogs and still revive the economy back to its pre-collapse levels?"

"Yes, sir." Warren's voice was eerily unemotional for someone proposing the mass murder of 60,000,000 human beings. Gavin Stark had chosen his people carefully, and moral ambivalence was one of the primary characteristics he looked for. "The mobs will have no defense against air attack...they will be forced to disperse or face annihilation." A small smile crept onto his lips. "Culling out the population will also reduce the food supplies required to sustain the survivors. And losing so many of their number will be a lesson those who remain won't soon forget."

Oliver leaned back in his chair. "Very well, Ryan. You choose the units to be deployed, and I will sign the orders." He looked up and stared at Warren. "But make sure they don't get carried away. We need half of these animals back at their jobs... and we need it soon."

"Thank you, sir. Yes...I will make sure the proper...ah... restraint is used." He hesitated, but when Oliver remained silent he took the initiative. "May I assume you also wish to discuss the escalation in the South China Sea?"

Oliver sighed. It had been one thing after another, and it showed no signs of stopping anytime soon. "Yes, I would like your opinion on an appropriate response to the CAC nuclear attack."

"In my opinion, sir, we have little choice." Warren's face hardened. "It is dangerous to show weakness to the Cogs...to show it to the CAC would be suicidal. We must leave them no doubt that any escalation by them will trigger a greater response from us."

"What do you propose?"

"First, I think it is essential to authorize Admiral Young to utilize any weapons he sees fit. The enemy fleet has gone nuclear. We cannot leave the admiral's hands tied when he must face an enemy who is already using atomic weapons."

"I am inclined to agree with you." Oliver didn't sound as

convinced as Warren.

"I also believe we must authorize General Simpson to utilize both chemical and tactical nuclear weapons." He could see the surprise on Oliver's face. "Sir, the enemy escalated at a time and place of their choosing, when their attack could cause the maximum damage to our war effort. We must respond in kind. Admiral Young is not facing imminent enemy attack, but General Simpson is. With the loss of almost 50% of his expected reinforcements, he is in a difficult situation trying to hold the Manila perimeter. If the enemy strikes first again with enhanced weapons, they could shatter his line and seize Manila before we are able react. The conquest of the Philippines would be a fait accompli."

"So, you are suggesting we escalate first in the Philippines? Launch an enhanced strike of our own before the enemy can?" Oliver understood the rationale…he even agreed with it. But he was afraid too. Things were beginning to move too quickly. He could feel the situation slipping out of his control.

"If we do anything else, we telegraph weakness, sir. We invite an even greater escalation."

Oliver ran his hand slowly through his greasy, disheveled hair. It felt like an age since he'd had time for a shower and a fresh change of clothes. He turned and looked out the window at the Washbalt skyline. There was a nasty scar on the majestic image, the gaping pit where Alliance Intelligence headquarters had been. He imagined CAC ICBMs streaking down from the sky, their megaton warheads obliterating the Alliance's magnificent capital with nuclear fire. Was that where the escalation would lead?

He sighed and wrestled with his own frustrations and fears. Finally, he looked right at Warren. "OK, Ryan. We will authorize both Admiral Young and General Simpson to deploy any tactical-ranged enhanced weapons in their arsenals at their own discretion."

"Yes, sir."

"And Ryan?"

"Yes, sir?"

"I'm implementing plan Stonewall. Prepare your A-team for evacuation to the Bunkers.

"Yes, Mr. President. Immediately, sir."

Chapter 25

Near the Sentinel
Planet Armstrong
Gamma Pavonis II

"It looks like a significant force, General Cain." Ali Khaled spoke calmly, but Cain could hear the grave tone in his voice. "Our best estimate of the transport capacity is two Alliance divisions." Khaled stood outside the portable HQ shelter, his massive, armored form silhouetted against the setting sun. The Caliphate armor was bulkier than the Marine equivalents, and the alloy was slightly different, giving the metal a darker look.

Cain sighed softly. Another 30,000 enemy troops, and they'd reach Armstrong orbit in two days. He felt a wave of anger and frustration. He and Khaled had finally pushed the enemy back on the defensive, and now the bastards had fresh reserves and resupply on the way. "That will stop our offensive dead in its tracks." Cain turned to face Khaled, his expression troubled. "You came to our aid, Lord Khaled, as a true friend...yet I fear you have now become embroiled in a fight to the death...with no means of escape."

"Were there such means, I would refuse them utterly. I would not live at the cost of abandoning a friend and ally. Death would be far preferable to such dishonor." He paused before continuing, his voice becoming softer, more philosophical. "We are but pawns of fate, General. There is little enough of our destiny we can control, but loyalty and courage are two that we can."

Khaled could feel Cain's guilt, the Marine's genuine sorrow that those who had come to his aid and stood by him were now trapped, facing an enemy far stronger than they had imagined. "Who could have thought that I would fight my final battle – if such this is destined to be – alongside Alliance Marines?" Khaled breathed deeply. "Yet, if the hour of my death is nigh, I could ask for no more honorable companions by my side."

"Nor I, Lord Khaled. It has been a privilege to ally with you and with your warriors, both out on the Rim against the First Imperium and here on Armstrong." He still felt a pang of guilt. The First Imperium was mankind's enemy, a force that struck from deep space. It was only fair and just that the Powers faced that grievous threat together. But Gavin Stark and his Shadow Legions were a creation of the Alliance...at least more so than any other Power. Cain wondered how he would feel if he and his Marines faced death fighting the overwhelming forces of a madman from the Caliphate. Would he be as gracious and supportive as Khaled? He wanted to believe he would, but he wasn't sure.

Cain's expression hardened. "Still, I am not ready to give up the fight just yet." He stared coldly into Khaled's eyes, and the Janissary commander returned his feral gaze. "We have a little more than two days before the enemy fleet arrives...closer to three before they can get new forces landed and into action. I propose we use that time to the best possible effect."

Khaled stared back, his head moving slightly in a barely perceptible nod of agreement. "By all means, General Cain. We must cripple the forces currently on the ground before their reserves can land. We must attack immediately and with everything we have. And we must press on, day or night...regardless of losses or fatigue." Khaled stared right at Cain. "By the time the reserves land, we must destroy or break every enemy formation already on Armstrong. Then we can concentrate on the new arrivals."

Cain was silent for a moment, unmoving, his eyes locked on Khaled's. "We have no time to waste," he finally said grimly. "We attack in one hour."

Gavin Stark sat in the command chair on Spectre's small,

cramped bridge. The seat was tight and uncomfortable, and he had to be careful when he rose not to bang his head on the large girder just above. Spectre had not been built for comfort.

The vessel was a technological marvel, the result of a long Alliance Intelligence R&D project, one Stark had completed in great secrecy. She was a small ship, streamlined to enable landings directly on a planet's surface. She was fast too, nearly as speedy as Roderick Vance's Torch transports. But that wasn't what truly made Spectre an amazing development…or one so useful to Stark.

The small vessel was the ultimate development in stealth technology, a ship nearly undetectable to any known scanning technology. She could even hide from normal vision. Her hull was covered with cameras that transmitted the view to the opposite side, creating an almost perfect illusion of total invisibility.

Stark didn't pretend to understand the amazing technology behind the ship's incredible capabilities…and now no one else would either. Once he had his prototype and the complete schematics to guide his technicians in building more of the class, he disposed of the team of scientists who'd created the Spectre project. He'd penetrated enough enemy research programs to know anyone was breakable. Torture, blackmail, threats, bribery…he'd seen up close just how they all worked, even on the toughest subjects. There was a way to break anyone. And once they were broken, they hemorrhaged information. There was no point in taking unnecessary risks. Dead men were reliably silent. Live ones were loose ends. And Stark hated loose ends.

He was a day in front of the rest of the fleet, darting toward the planet. His scanners had picked up a small enemy task force in orbit. Stark had been a little concerned about giving his stealth ship that kind of up close test. But the enemy ships broke orbit and fled toward the Vega warp gate shortly after Stark's main force entered the system.

The Shadow fleet was carrying 34,000 fresh troops, enough he figured, to wipe out those hellspawn Marines once and for all. Soon they would land, and when they did, their orders were clear. They would attack, and they would keep fighting without a break until every Marine on Armstrong was dead or a prisoner.

But Stark had his own agenda. Since no one he'd sent had managed to get the job done, he was going to see to Erik Cain's death himself. He was becoming obsessed with Cain, the repeated, failed attempts to kill the Marine general consuming his thoughts. Cain, the Marine who had invaded his fortress headquarters and ripped Augustus Garret from his grasp. Cain, who had somehow repulsed every assault Rafael Samuels and the Shadow legions had launched against his ragtag remnant of the Marine Corps.

The continuing battle on Armstrong, despite the massive superiority of the Shadow forces, only inflamed his rage. Cain was a loose cannon, an adversary with the capacity to surprise Stark, to prevail against seemingly hopeless odds. And that was the one thing Stark couldn't tolerate. An enemy he couldn't predict was dangerous…a risk that had to be eliminated.

"We are about to enter orbit, sir." Captain Yantz had skippered Stark's personal transport for years, and the spymaster took the loyal agent with him into the Shadow corps. "Do you want to land immediately?"

Stark was lost in his thoughts about Cain, but Yantz' words grabbed his focus. "Yes, Captain," he said slowly, deliberately. "Bring us down just behind General Samuels' lines." He felt the anger and tension growing inside him. He turned and muttered quietly to himself. "It is time to deal with Erik Cain once and for all."

Explosions rocked the depths of the Sentinel, the shattered remnants of massive trees falling everywhere along the line. The twisted, battered trunks stretched across the field in hundred meter sections, blackened and twisted, lying where they had fallen and slowing the advance.

The Janissaries had been attacking nonstop since dawn, landing hammer blow after hammer blow on the wavering enemy lines. The Shadow forces fought back ferociously, but they were exhausted and low on supplies. They were being driven back… slowly, steadily.

Commander Farooq pushed the attacking Janissaries relentlessly, driving them against one enemy position after another.
Cain and Khaled had put him in command of the 11,000 Janissaries and 2,000 Marines of the left flank with orders to attack…
and attack, and attack. There was no time to rest, nor to regroup.
The Marines and Janissaries had less than two days to destroy
the enemy forces, and the morale of the Shadow legions was
almost impossible to break.

"Agha Sedik, commence your advance at once." Farooq's
voice was deliberative, cold.

"Yes, Pasha…at once." Sedik was Farooq's most reliable
Agha, roughly comparable to a Marine brigadier. Sedik was
leading three fresh ortas in a wide flanking maneuver. Once he
was behind the enemy position, Farooq would launch the entire
line in an all-out attack, driving the Shadow forces back onto
them. It was a risky maneuver, especially for Sedik's forces, but
Farooq didn't have time to spare. He knew they were fighting a
battle of annihilation, and anything less than the total destruction of the enemy in the next 40 hours would be a failure.

His forces had been pushing steadily forward, but the Sentinel was far from ideal ground for an offensive, especially when
time was so short. Every time his people had to stop to clear
the fallen trees from their paths, they lost precious minutes. But
they couldn't do anything about the terrain…the enemy was in
the Sentinel, so the battle was there as well. Whatever difficulties the ground put in their way, the Janissaries would have to
overcome with training, skill, and raw determination.

The enemy was withdrawing to the south, and Farooq
intended to stay right on top of them, despite the challenges
of the terrain. The Shadow forces were heading toward the
Graywater. That great river could be a highly effective defensive
barrier…or a deathtrap. It largely depended on timing. If the
Shadow forces got there in time to effect a crossing, they could
prolong the fighting indefinitely…and with enemy reserves on
the way, that would be a disaster for the Janissaries and Marines.
On the other hand, if Farooq stayed close enough to attack
while the enemy's back was still to the river, he might bag the

whole army.

"C'mon, Sedik," Farooq whispered anxiously to himself. "Get your people moving. We don't have a second to spare."

"You have squandered 40,000 elite soldiers here, and the Marines are still defeating you." Stark was glaring at Samuels as he spoke, his voice icy. "Are you truly so incapable that you fail despite all the advantages I have provided you?"

"We had the Marines on the run, sir, but then the Janissaries arrived." Samuels was clearly afraid. He'd seen more than once how Stark punished failure. And for all his own inflated ego, deep down, Rafael Samuels knew he had failed., that Erik Cain had outmaneuvered and outfought him.

Stark had been surprised to find the Janissaries on Armstrong. After all the trouble he went through to get the Caliphate embroiled in a war with the Alliance, he still ended up facing 25,000 of the Caliph's elite soldiers backing up Cain's Marines. He couldn't understand it at first, but then he realized the Caliphate must have botched their proscriptions, allowing the intended targets to escape and take flight...right into the arms of the Marines. It was almost too much to believe.

He'd considered the whole move by the Caliphate against its officers a stupid exercise of pointless paranoia. He'd had nothing to do with it, and he hadn't expected it to have a significant effect on his plans. Instead, he ended up with 25,000 rogue Janissaries on Armstrong and a Caliphate fleet out there somewhere...probably also allied with the Alliance. It was damned bad luck.

Still, even with the Janissaries, his Shadow forces should have been strong enough to win the battle. He knew it was Samuels' incompetence as much as any other factor that had let victory slip away for so long. "I do not suffer excuses, General Samuels...certainly not ones without merit." His voice dripped with menace. "You had more than enough time and force to secure the planet before the Janissaries arrived. They were only allowed the opportunity to intervene by your incompetence. And even after they landed, you still had numerical superiority."

Stark stared at Samuels, death in his eyes. "Yet you were driven back almost from the moment the enemy was reinforced."

Samuels stood, silently enduring Stark's tirade. He suppressed his own anger. Samuels was a bully by nature, not one to endure abuse from anyone. But he didn't have anywhere near enough courage to stand up to Gavin Stark. He knew Stark might order him killed at any moment, and showing his rage would only seal his fate. He opened his mouth, planning to explain that the Shadow troopers were no match for the Marines on equal terms, but he caught himself before he said anything. Any excuse or attempt to shift blame would only enrage Stark further. "I'm sorry, sir. I have done all I could."

"Well, that wasn't enough, was it?" Stark glared at Samuels. "But, fortunately, we have another opportunity. I have brought additional reinforcements to Armstrong. They are even now approaching the planet."

Samuels felt a small wave of relief. Gavin Stark was fundamentally unpredictable, but it didn't sound like he was planning to dispose of his ground commander just yet. He knew the coming battle was crucial, not only to Stark's plans...but to his own survival as well. Perhaps he could yet redeem himself. He had to hold out until the reserves landed. And then he had to lead the combined forces to victory against the Marines and their Janissary allies. It was a battle to which he would give his all. He knew another failure would seal his fate.

"The reinforcements will be here in approximately 40 hours." Stark's eyes were locked on Samuels as he spoke. I suggest you find a way to contain the enemy offensive until they have landed." It was a suggestion that carried the menace of death on it.

Stark continued, his tone becoming harder, angrier. "But before the reserve divisions arrive, we have another job to do." He paused, his face frozen with hatred. "Where is Erik Cain?"

Chapter 26

AS Yorktown
Kruger 60 System
Approaching Gamma Pavonis Warp Gate

"We will begin transiting the warp gate in less than an hour." Camille Harmon sat at the small table in her quarters, looking across at Cate Gilson and General Holm. "I don't expect we'll need the couches for our deceleration, but I'd like you to have your people ready on short notice, just in case."

"That's not a problem, Camille." Holm nodded as he spoke. He turned toward Gilson. "In fact, Cate, I want them all doubly ready. We have no idea what we're going to find on Armstrong, and we need to be prepared to hit the ground immediately." He paused. "I hope they enjoyed some rest on the trip, because it may be all they get for a while." There was a hint of regret in his voice. After the brutal campaign on Arcadia, he knew his Marines deserved a much longer break than they were likely to get.

Gilson glanced over at Holm and nodded. "They'll be ready, sir." Most of the Marines in the fleet's transports were Gilson's, though Holm's old vets were there too. Gilson's tone displayed no emotion like Holm's did, though he knew she was as worried about her people as he was. He was just as sure she'd never show it. As far as Cate Gilson was concerned, her people would be ready for whatever they had to do...or God help them. Holm knew that some of her hard edge was a façade, but he'd never been able to get a feel for just how much of it.

Sam Thomas was another one who had surprised Holm...

or maybe not. Perhaps he'd just done what Holm had expected all along. His people had distinguished themselves enormously in the fighting on Arcadia. Holm initially ordered the old vets to stay behind when he left for Armstrong, but Thomas would have none of it. He'd diligently and obediently followed Holm's orders without argument until the Commandant told him to sit out the rest of the fight. Then Holm got a caustic blast of the old Colonel Thomas he remembered from the Second Frontier War days. He felt guilty about exposing the old veterans to more danger, but when he polled them, they backed up Thomas to a man. In the end, Holm relented. The old Marines had earned the right to stay in the fight if that's what they wanted, and he knew he didn't have the moral authority to overrule them.

Holm was anxious to get to Armstrong. He was concerned about the status of the battle and the thousands of Marines fighting there...and he was worried about Erik Cain. He thought of the brilliant but difficult subordinate as far more than a colleague. Career had been everything to Elias Holm, and he'd endured all the sacrifices that choice had cost him... love, home, family. But part of that void had now been filled, and he thought of Cain as the son he never had.

He was deeply concerned about all his Marines fighting the battle for Armstrong, but his thoughts kept coming back to Cain. Holm knew the younger Marine was wild and reckless, that he'd put himself in almost any imaginable danger to win a fight. He also knew Cain's luck would run out one day...that he would end up dead in a trench on the front lines, somewhere he'd had no place to be. He had tried to knock some sense into Cain more than once, but in the end he came to realize that his protégé's intransigence and his strength came from the same place. For Erik Cain there couldn't be one without the other. He was who he was, and there was no changing that. The cantankerous Marine was stubborn as a dozen mules, and he always would be. All Holm could do was accept reality and hope that Cain's luck held until he got there with help.

The 5,200 Marines on the fleet's transports were exhausted, but they were also elated at the victory on Arcadia. The invading army had been completely destroyed, and Kara Sanders and her people were back in control of the planet. The three officers knew it was only one small triumph, that the status of the war as a whole was still very much in doubt. But winning any conflict started with the first victory. There were a million and a half people on Arcadia who were free again, and there was no bad side to that.

They'd left all the wounded behind under the command of James Teller. As they recovered and returned to duty, they would support Sanders' army and hold Arcadia against any new threats. As pleased as everyone was at the liberation of the planet, they were well aware the war was far from over. They knew another enemy force could attack the planet at any time.

There was something else troubling Holm, something that cast a pall over the victory. His people had pushed the enemy back onto Kara Sanders' forces during the climactic battle. Hit from two sides by vicious and relentless attacks, the morale of the Shadow forces finally broke, and the enemy soldiers ran for their lives. Holm had expected to take thousands of prisoners...but in the end there wasn't even one. All along the line of the enemy's flight, the Marines discovered something terrible, a hideous glance into the depth of evil behind their enemy. The Shadow soldiers lay strewn all about their line of rout. Dead. Poisoned by the AIs controlling their suits.

Holm was horrified at the discovery. He had no love for the enemy soldiers...not after the losses they had inflicted on his own people. But they had fought bravely and with great discipline, ignoring casualties and fatigue. It was sobering to imagine an enemy so evil it would murder its own wounded and fleeing soldiers...even after they had taken 75% casualties in the fight. He wondered what it would cost to defeat such an enemy...and whether he had the strength to see it done.

"We have no idea what we will discover when we transit into Armstrong's system." Harmon interrupted Holm's thoughts. "But the lead elements are going through in exactly..." – she paused and glanced at the chronometer on the wall – "...33 minutes. I'd expect Yorktown to be roughly 40 minutes behind the vanguard." She glanced at each of her guests in turn. "So," she continued, "I suggest we all see to our responsibilities while we still have time."

Harmon rose, followed almost immediately by Gilson and Holm. "I suspect you have more to do than we do, Camille." Gilson spoke softly to her friend as she started toward the door. She turned and looked back at Holm. "But I'll get our people on pre-launch protocols, sir." She took a few steps and turned back one last time. "They'll be ready to do whatever they have to." A short pause then: "As always."

"Battlestations." Camille Harmon's tone was cold, emotionless. "The fleet will prepare for combat." Yorktown had just emerged from the warp gate to find the fleet's lead elements on alert. The scouts had transited almost an hour before, and they were just getting scanner readings from another fleet about one lighthour insystem.

"Yes, Admiral." Lieutenant Commander Givens punched the alert code, and Yorktown's battlestations lamps cast a reddish glow across the bridge. A few seconds passed, then: "All fleet units acknowledge alert status, Admiral."

"Very well." Harmon's eyes stared right at the main scanner. The reports were still coming in, but it was already clear she was facing a stronger force than her own. The scanners were picking up Alliance transponders, but not from all of the ships. Harmon wasn't sure it was a hostile force yet, but she wasn't taking any chances.

The bridge doors zipped open and General Holm breezed through. "What do we have, Admiral?" Holm was normally informal with Harmon, but not on her flag bridge in front of her staff.

"Unknown force, General. We're still working on IDing them." She was staring at her workstation as she spoke, monitoring the incoming data. "I will defer to your judgment, General, but we may want to leave the troopships in Kruger 60 until we have more data." Harmon had insisted on bringing the battlefleet through before transiting the poorly armed and protected troopships. The dozen vessels carrying the Marines, and their cruiser escorts, were waiting for the word to transit.

Holm paused, his eyes moving toward the main display. He could see some of the individual ship IDs, and he knew immediately. "That is Gavin Stark's fleet." Holm had been with Garret when his fleet had tangled with Stark's Shadow forces. "I recognize some of the ships." He stepped closer to Harmon and lowered his voice. "And that's not all of what he has. There's more out there."

Harmon looked straight ahead and sighed. "Well," she said softly, "it doesn't really matter. Cain and his people are stuck on the planet, and we can't leave without knowing their status." She turned her head and looked right at Holm. "So, whatever Gavin Stark has out there, we're going to fight him."

Holm nodded silently, touched by Harmon's devotion to the forces on Armstrong. He knew she was putting her own people at grave risk to aid Cain and his Marines. "I think we should bring the transports through now, though, Admiral." He was staring at the tactical display. "The enemy is going to have to alter their vector away from the planet to intercept your fleet. We can beat them to the planet with our transports if we don't waste any time."

Harmon looked over at Holm. "That's a little risky, isn't it, Elias?"

Holm smiled. "My people are down there, Camille, fighting as we speak. Your crews are risking themselves against a superior enemy fleet...I'll be damned if my Marines will hide on the other side of the warp gate while all that goes down."

Harmon nodded. "I understand, Elias. I will issue the orders."

"Thank you." Holm took a deep breath. "One more thing... if I can borrow a shuttle to get over to the transports when they come through? I'd like to go in with the Marines."

Liang stared at the screen. The Alliance ships had stopped transiting into the system. That wasn't a guarantee that there were no reserves on the other side of the warp gate, but it was a good bet. The ships in the system had scanned his fleet by now, and they knew they were outnumbered. They would have sent for reserves if they had them.

At first he'd been afraid Garret's fleet had caught up with him, but now it was looking like something else. He faced a sizable force, but one significantly smaller than his own....and certainly than Garret's. His worries about Garret subsided; he could see there were too few ships for the enemy force to be the main Alliance fleet. He felt a wave of relief. He wouldn't admit it to anyone, but Liang was terrified of facing Garret again. The mythology surrounding the Alliance admiral had grown to new levels after he obliterated the CAC fleet. Liang, three times defeated by Garret in his career, had come to believe the legends...that Augustus Garret was invincible.

"The enemy appears to be moving into a battle formation, Admiral."

"Very well," Liang snapped at the tactical officer. He took a deep breath. He'd have preferred to avoid combat, and he would have allowed the enemy to flee back to Kruger 60 unmolested. But it looked like they wanted a fight.

He was worried about more than just Augustus Garret. The Alliance navy had the highest standards of any power's fleet, and its veteran personnel were feared by all the forces who had opposed them. Liang's crews, on the other hand, were whatever Stark had been able to scrape up. Some of them were experienced...ex-naval personnel recruited from the various human navies. Others were barely better than a pack of pirates, drawn into Stark's service by the promise of rich rewards.

Liang wondered if Stark had tried to clone naval crews as well as Marines. Perhaps he simply didn't have time, the admiral thought. An infantry force was fairly straightforward, while a naval crew required dozens of different specialists. But, whatever the reason, the naval crews were definitely the weak link in the Shadow forces.

Liang frowned. He might not be facing Garret...and he certainly had the numerical advantage. But his gut told him not to take this fight for granted. Garret's lieutenants were not to be underestimated, and their crews were all veterans of the First Imperium War, far more adept at their craft than his own spotty recruits.

"Bring the fleet to full alert." Whatever happened, he was going to have to fight this new force before he could land the ground troops. The Alliance entry point at the Kruger 60 warp gate was much closer to Armstrong than the current position of his fleet. His forces would be engaged long before they reached the planet. He turned his head and snapped, "And order the transports to decelerate immediately. I want them to fall back 60 light seconds behind the main fleet and reduce velocity to 0.005c." He knew Stark would have him nailed up by his feet if he got those troopships and their cargo of Shadow Legion soldiers blown to bits in space. Pulling them back and reducing their inbound velocity would facilitate a quick escape if necessary...at the cost of adding days to their estimated arrival at the planet.

"Yes, Admiral."

Liang stared straight ahead, trying to ignore the knots in his stomach. "And bring the fleet to battlestations."

"Estimate four minutes until enemy missiles enter shotgun range, Admiral." Givens' voice was deliberate, focused. He knew Harmon was trying to thread a needle with her own launch.

"Launch all missiles." Harmon had held back her first volley, waiting until the last possible moment. The fleet was moving at .03c, and every minute brought them closer to the enemy and increased the accuracy of the strike.

But she couldn't wait any longer, or her own defenses would degrade her barrage. In four minutes her ships would open up with their shotguns, filling space all around the fleet with clouds of metal shards moving at 3-5% of lightspeed. At that velocity, even a tiny piece of depleted uranium could obliterate an incoming missile....or an outgoing one.

"Yes, Admiral." Givens pressed a button, sending the launch order to the entire fleet.

Yorktown shook a few seconds later as it launched its externally mounted missiles. Harmon knew the same thing was happening on all the ships in the fleet, and she waited half a minute to allow her units to finish their launches. "Put me on fleetcom, Commander." Harmon's voice was hard, cold.

"Yes, Admiral." Givens worked his controls. "You are connected, Admiral Harmon."

"Attention all fleet personnel. This is Admiral Harmon. As you all know, we are facing an enemy that outnumbers us by a considerable margin." She was staring straight ahead as she spoke, eyes fixed on the main screen. "But we have never allowed that to deter us from our duty." She paused for a few seconds. "We are going to exceed even our top performance in this battle. I expect the absolute best every one of you has to offer, and I will accept nothing less. We are going to launch our second volley in 8 minutes. That means we have to clear the external racks by then…and we need to do it while the enemy strike is coming in and our interdiction efforts are underway." She paused again, for only an instant this time. "You all have my complete confidence. Now let's get to work." She cut the line abruptly.

Throughout Harmon's fleet, her crews flew into a frenzy, maintenance staff clearing away the external racks while gunners manned the shotguns and other defensive systems targeting the incoming enemy missiles. She had asked more from her people than conventional wisdom deemed possible. But Camille Harmon had learned her craft from Augustus Garret, and the word impossible wasn't in her vocabulary.

She sat in her chair, emotionless…as she had been since the day she led her ships through the X2-X1 warp gate, leaving her son behind with Terrance Compton and thousands of Alliance naval crew. But now a small grin formed on the corner of her mouth, its origin deep within the darkest part of her soul. I am here, Gavin Stark, to face your fleet. And I am Death Incarnate.

Holm twisted and turned, trying vainly to get comfortable. The acceleration couches could keep a man alive at g forces that would smash him into a broken and bloody piece of meat, but no one ever said they were comfortable. But Holm wanted to get to Armstrong as quickly as possible, and that meant accelerating halfway and decelerating the other half. Now they were just about there.

He'd ordered the ship's AI to feed him updates on the naval battle taking place in the middle of the system. Harmon's people were outnumbered...almost 2-1...but Garret was still betting on her coming out on top of the enemy. She was one of the fleet admiral's very best lieutenants...the best since Terrance Compton was lost out at X2. The two forces had exchanged several missile volleys, but they hadn't closed to energy weapons range yet. Harmon's direction of the close-in point defense had been flawless, and so far the Alliance fleet had taken less damage than it inflicted.

"Prepare for depressurization." The transport's AI made the announcement, interrupting Holm's thoughts. The task force was approaching Armstrong, and the ships were reducing thrust prior to orbital insertion. Holm lay back, feeling the crushed, bloated feeling slowly dissipate as the AI normalized the pressure in the chamber and administered drugs to counteract the pressure-equalization cocktail it had injected at the start of the journey. Holm's mind was still a little fuzzy, but then he felt another small pinprick – a shot of stims - and his head cleared up immediately.

"Get me General Gilson," he snapped out at the AI, suddenly feeling more energetic and aware. The stims were helping push out the last vestiges of the hallucinogenic side effects caused by the drugs injected during acceleration and deceleration.

"Yes, General Holm." The troop transport AIs had relatively rudimentary personality systems. The tone of their voices sounded human enough, but the unnatural cadence gave them away. "General Gilson on your line, sir."

"Yes, General?" Gilson sounded a little woozy. Her ship was a few seconds behind Garret's in coming out of heavy deceleration, and he could tell she was still feeling residual effects.

"I'm launching a spread of scanner drones to get an idea

what's going on down there. I want you to get your people ready
to land as soon as the reports come in."

"Yes, sir." There was a noticeable delay in the communication. Gilson was on a ship 60,000 kilometers from Holm's. Not
a sufficient distance to meaningfully interfere with communication, but enough for a noticeable hitch. "We'll be ready to go."

"Very well. Garret out." He looked around the room at
Marines climbing out of their acceleration couches, stagger-
ing around trying to regain their balance as quickly as possible.
"Let's go, Marines," Garret yelled, clapping his hands as he did.
"Shake the shit out of your heads. Our comrades are facing
God knows what, and we're going to get out asses down there
to help."

Liang sat in his command chair, staring at his screen in disbelief. It just wasn't possible. The Alliance fleet had held its
missile fire until the last possible instant…and then released 4
volleys in less than 20 minutes. He couldn't understand how
the enemy had managed to clear their external missile racks so
quickly while fighting off his own incoming volleys. Yet they
had defended against his missiles very effectively while savaging
his fleet with their own, perfectly-targeted barrages. Despite his
advantage in hulls and missiles, he was in far worse shape than
his adversaries.

What do I do, he wondered…do I stand and fight, or do I
run for it and preserve the fleet? His orders were crystal clear.
He was not to risk a catastrophic defeat under any circumstances.
Preserving the fleet was his primary consideration.

But Gavin Stark was on Armstrong by now, and breaking
off and fleeing the system meant leaving him behind. How
would Stark react if his lieutenant fled and abandoned him on
the planet? Would Spectre be able to escape the system if the
fleet withdrew? In theory, the stealth vessel should be able to
sneak out undetected, but it really hadn't had much testing.

Liang imagined – for a brief instant – what would happen
if Stark was lost. The Shadow forces would still be there, along
with all Stark's preparations. Would Liang have the chance

to take control? To take Stark's place and make himself an emperor?

It was a seductive thought, but Liang knew he didn't have the capability or the tools to hold Stark's immense operation together. Liang hated Stark; he feared Stark…but he had no illusions about the man's superhuman genius. There were former Alliance Intelligence spies everywhere, and Stark was the only man they would follow. And Liang shuddered at the thought of what would happen if he made his own bid for power and Stark got off Armstrong and returned. Gavin Stark knew an almost infinite number of ways to dispose of enemies…most of them very unpleasant.

Liang made his choice. He knew what would happen if he got Stark's fleet shot to pieces, and it wasn't likely to be a very pleasant outcome for him. His overriding order was to preserve the fleet at all costs. So he had two choices. Stand and fight it out to the end, or run for it now while he still had time to disengage.

Even with the damage he had sustained, his fleet was still stronger than the Alliance force. But Liang felt a sense of hopelessness. When he'd seen the size of the enemy fleet, he had discounted Garret's presence. But the enemy fought the way they did under their legendary commander. Was it possible Garret was on the enemy flagship after all? Perhaps he had detached a portion of his fleet for another purpose, and it was him on that enemy battleship leading a reduced force.

He turned and looked back at his tactical officer. Liang didn't have confidence in his people…and he knew how good the Alliance spacers were. And if that was Garret out there, he'd not only destroy the Shadow fleet, he'd chase down the troop transports and destroy the reserve legions too.

Liang swallowed hard. "The fleet will withdraw at full speed. All personnel to the couches. Maximum acceleration in ten minutes." Yes, he thought…I will live to fight another day. Or at least until my reckoning with Gavin Stark.

Chapter 27

City of Nancy
French Sector, Europa Federalis
Earth – Sol III

Hans Werner was sweating like a pig. The heavy rubberized material of his protective suit was stifling. He could feel the sweat pouring down his neck and back. He wanted the rip his way out of the bulky coverings, suck in a breath of fresh, cool air…but he didn't dare. The Europans had escalated things late in the battle for Nancy, bombarding his advancing troops with chemical weapons in a last ditch attempt to hold the city.

His detectors showed a non-lethal, but still potentially dangerous concentration of nerve gas in the city itself, so his forces were all operating under full chemical warfare protocols…even though the fighting had ended, and the enemy was in headlong retreat.

His forces had taken Nancy, but the battle had been a brutal one. He'd hesitated before reporting the chemical attack, knowing exactly what HQ's response would be. Most of the major powers had automatic response policies in place, making escalation unavoidable when one side employed a proscribed weapon. Werner was now authorized – no, expected - to use his own chemical weaponry…and the high command was rushing him additional enhanced ordnance.

The hard-fought victory had earned Werner his third star, and an upgrade for his hastily-assembled and heretofore haphazardly organized force. He now officially commanded the 12th Army, and reinforcements were working their way forward to bring his formations back up to strength.

He climbed up and over a pile of wreckage that had been part of someone's home a few days before. He knew he shouldn't be up this far. One enemy sniper left behind could deprive the army of its commander. But in his mind he was still a lieutenant-colonel commanding a single battalion, and he had a hard time adapting to the exalted rank his well-timed successes had bought him.

He scrambled down the pile of rubble and spotted a cluster of dead soldiers...and two who were still alive. He pulled himself back up onto the mound of debris, looking toward a crew searching for wounded. "Over here...there's two wounded over here." His voice was dry and hoarse from yelling. He knew he was dehydrated, but it was such a pain in the ass to get a drink in the CBN suits, he tended to ignore the thirst as long as he could.

He pointed as the soldiers scrambled toward his position carrying two stretchers. The streets were too pockmarked and full of wreckage to get the transports through, so his troopers were carrying the wounded to the edge of town and loading them onto the trucks there. Werner had moved the field hospitals back, farther away from the chemical weapons zone. He knew every extra kilometer cost lives, but he couldn't take the chance that one of the hospitals might get hit with a gas attack.

The city had been badly damaged in the fighting, at least half its buildings now little more than shattered facades and piles of smoking rubble. It was hard to tell, but it looked to him like Nancy had been a pleasant community, without the dense ring of slums that surrounded most cities in both Europa Federalis and the CEL. Whatever it had been, he thought sadly, it was mostly a ruin now.

That ruin had cost him 50,000 casualties. The field hospitals were bursting at the seams, and his support teams were scouring the battlefield, looking for disabled tanks they could get back in working order. His soldiers were exhausted and mourning their legions of dead. But they weren't going to get a rest. He already had his orders. The new 12th Army was to move north toward Metz and take the ancient fortress-city, opening the way for an advance against the Europan capital at Paris.

He had walked among the troops, rallying them and urging them forward. The CEL's military hadn't had any real veterans when the war began…no nation's had. Yet his people had pushed relentlessly forward, fighting battle after battle and suffering devastating losses. He didn't know how he was going to keep them going. He'd been assigned internal security companies, special formations intended to follow the army and round up and summarily execute any soldiers who ran, but he had no intention of deploying them. His people deserved better.

But that meant he'd have to keep them moving himself. If the army failed to advance, the high command would compel the use of brutal force to push them. And the thought of his soldiers rounded up by death squads and executed in front of their units was more than he could bear to imagine.

Jim Larson crouched down in his foxhole, peering cautiously over the edge. He was waist-deep in muddy water, holding his rifle out over the soggy ground. He'd been one of the lucky ones in the convoy…his ship had escaped the nuclear attack and landed safely at Manila. But he had friends who weren't so fortunate. At least half a dozen guys he knew well from the barracks were on one of the destroyed vessels. He hadn't had time to mourn…or even think much about it, though he knew intellectually, at least, that they were dead, lying 4,000 meters below the ocean in a dark, watery tomb.

His unit had been hustled off the ship and loaded right onto transports bound for the front. Three hours after landing he was crawling through the sopping mud, falling back the way he had come along with the rest of the army.

Crawling through a steaming, muddy, insect-infested jungle…he didn't think it could get much worse than that, but now they'd gotten the orders to don their CBN suits. He reached around, pulling the rubber pouch off his pack and unzipping it. He couldn't imagine how hot it would be inside the heavy rubber of the protective suit, but he knew damned sure he didn't want to be caught without it if the enemy hit with enhanced weapons.

He climbed clumsily into the suit, splashing muddy water inside as he did. He was right...it was hot as hell, and wet and heavy too. He zipped it up and took a deep breath, inhaling the industrial smell of new rubber and the pungent odor of his air filter. If something had been designed specifically for discomfort, he thought, it couldn't have hit the mark better than this piece of shit.

"Larson, team status?" It was Sergeant Garcia, the squad leader.

Larson turned his head, trying to check to see if the four privates in his team had gotten their gear on properly. He should have done it already, but it had taken him forever to get his own suit on, and he'd completely forgotten.

"Yes, Sergeant. We're all set." It was a lie. Grover and Litton were both still struggling to climb into the unwieldy suits. But Larson didn't want an ass-chewing, and he figured the two slowpoke privates would pull it together in another few seconds. They did, but it took a few minutes, not seconds.

He flipped to his team com line. "Let's go you two fucking idiots! How many times did you practice putting those suits on?"

The two snapped back excuses while frantically slipping resisting limbs into the heavy rubber. Larson was staring back at them when he heard the barrage begin. It was coming from near Manila, from the heavy batteries emplaced there. The shells sounded strange to him, different than the explosive rounds he'd heard since arriving at the front. Then the impacts...soft, muffled. Not like high explosives at all.

He wondered for a few seconds then suddenly he realized. The Alliance forces were firing nerve gas at the CAC positions. He self-consciously checked the seals on his suit. If the Alliance was using gas, it wouldn't be long before the CAC responded in kind.

Larson laughed caustically. "And you didn't think it could get any worse," he muttered softly to himself.

"Squadron 117 reporting. Approaching southern tip of Manhattan Island." Squadron Captain Raymond Marston gripped the controls of the lead gunship as he guided the squadron into attack position. "Request authorization to commence attack run."

Marston was looking ahead, over the shattered wreck of the Statue of Liberty toward Manhattan itself. The crumbling skyscrapers of the abandoned financial district blocked his view of The Crater, but he knew it was there. That had almost certainly been the deadliest day in New York history...perhaps until today, he thought darkly.

Marston was a member of the Political Class' bottom rung, and the lowest-ranked of the privileged were often the most arrogant, clinging desperately to their status. So it was with Marston, and he regarded the Cogs now rioting outside the walls of the Protected Zone with utter contempt. One thing he was certain about...in a few minutes they would learn their place again.

"Squadron 117, this is central command. You are cleared to begin your attack."

"Alright, people. We're going in." He pushed forward on the throttle, guiding the heavy gunship forward. The large aircraft zipped over the waves, and angled around the ghostly towers, streaking northward. Marston could see the surging masses camped just south of the southern wall of the Zone. They were milling around, but there were small groups making runs at the Wall and taking potshots at the police manning the defenses.

"All weapons armed, Captain. The squadron reports ready for action." Sergeant Sanger was the chief gunner on Marston's bird, a job that came with the task of monitoring the status of the other ships of the squadron. Sanger's voice was strange, tense, angry...but Marston was too focused on the mob of Cogs to notice.

The ship whipped around the financial district towers, flying over the Crater and swinging around 180 degrees to set up the east to west attack run. The crew felt the g forces as the craft swung around over the East River and began descending rapidly.

"Commence firing...all ships." Marston's voice was anxious,

excited. He hated the Cogs, and resented their willingness to rise up against their betters. Now they were going to get their lesson.

He flew the gunship just above the mob, but the fire from the squadron was sporadic...and nothing at all from his own craft. "I said commence fire, Sergeant!" His tone was sharp and angry.

He heard the quad autocannons open up, spraying the mob with 4,000 rounds per second. On the ground, the helpless Cogs died in their thousands, bodies torn to shreds by the heavy 20mm rounds. The crowd panicked, a million terrified Cogs running in every direction, fleeing the death raining down from above.

Marston smiled as he brought the gunship around for another run. He repositioned, lining up the run over the densest group. "Fire!" he screamed. Nothing. "Fire," Marston repeated. Still nothing. He turned around and opened his mouth to yell again when he froze. Sanger was staring right at him, a pistol in his extended hand.

"No, sir." Sanger was in tears. "We're not going to massacre any more of these people."

"Sergeant, you will put that gun away at once and follow my orders."

"No, Captain...I won't." Sanger stared back at the enraged officer. His hand was shaking, but he didn't back down. "We're not murdering anymore people." Marston was from the Political Class, but his crew were all Cogs.

Marston looked at the other two crew members. "Arrest the sergeant immediately." No one moved.

"I order you to arrest Sergeant Sanger! Corporal Fring! Corporal Javin!" Marston was apoplectic with rage, but the two crewman just sat at their stations.

Marston felt the rage boiling over. He lunged from his chair toward Sanger, reaching for the pistol. The sergeant stared right into his eyes and fired twice, both shots slamming into his chest. The stunned captain fell back against the controls, blood pouring from the two wounds.

He reached his hand out behind him, vainly struggling to grab the controls, but he had no strength. The ship spiraled out of control and slammed into the ground, erupting into a large fireball.

The crowd cheered as the gunship came down, thousands running toward the crash site. Thousands more stood transfixed, looking up into the sky as each of the gunships in turn spiraled out of control, their Cog crews following Sanger's example and killing or disabling their Political Class officers.

Two of the crews managed to take the controls and bring their craft down safely. The other ten crashed hard...and as each one slammed into the ground the mob howled with feral satisfaction.

Chapter 28

North of Astria
Planet Armstrong
Gamma Pavonis II

"General Holm…it really is you." Cain couldn't keep the emotion out of his voice. "It's so good to see you." He jogged the last few meters toward the Commandant. "I can't tell you how glad I am you're here, sir."

Cain felt like he'd been punched in the gut when the scanners picked up landers coming in a full day ahead of projections. His people were still pushing the enemy back toward the Graywater, and they needed every second of that day to have any chance to face a new invasion force. Then, he got the report he couldn't believe. The troops coming down were Alliance Marines, not Shadow Legions. And the biggest shock of all…General Holm was in command.

"It's good to see you too, Erik." Holm could hear the exhaustion in Cain's voice, the hopelessness. No one except Sarah Linden knew Erik Cain as well as Holm. "From what I'm hearing, Armstrong is going to occupy a place of honor in your battle history." He paused. "Seriously, Erik…you've done a tremendous job here."

Cain looked down at the ground. "Another bloodbath… that much, at least, fits my profile." He sighed and glanced back up a t Holm. "But how did you get here, sir? We had a report of enemy transports inbound."

Holm was going to respond to the bloodbath remark, but he caught himself. He'd known Cain long enough to realize there was no way to change his point of view. Erik would blame himself for the losses while resisting any credit for holding out against overwhelming enemy forces. It was just how he was wired.

"We came in from Kruger-60…a lot closer to the planet than the enemy's entry point. Camille Harmon is fighting the enemy fleet as we speak, and we made a run with the transports to get here as quickly as we could."

"Well, I still can't believe it is you, General." Cain's voice was a mix of confusion and relief. "But I'm sure glad you're here."

"It looks like you already got some help." Holm had been surprised to find Janissaries fighting on Armstrong. "How did that happen?"

"Long story, sir. The short version is, the Caliphate tried to execute most of its top field commanders on jacked up treason charges. Ali Khaled and Admiral Abbas took the fleet and the Janissary corps renegade and fled Caliphate space." Cain's voice was matter-of-fact, despite the bizarre nature of the story. "Apparently, they spent a considerable time trying to find Admiral Garret and, when they were unable to locate him, they decided to intervene on one of the worlds where we were fighting." He paused and allowed himself a tiny smile. "I believe they came to Armstrong instead of Arcadia or Columbia by sheer luck, sir. Perhaps the Caliphate version of a coin toss."

"Well, it looks like they got here just in time, Erik."

Cain let out a long breath. "That is an understatement, sir. The Janissaries really saved us. It was a miracle." He turned his head, looking off to the south. "We'd all be dead by now if they hadn't come…" – his voice became grimmer – "…and they're still bearing the brunt of the battle as we speak. My people are worn down to their last strength."

"Well, Erik, I've got Cate Gilson and 5,000 Marine veterans with me." Holm offered Cain a smile. "So let's get them into the fight before Khaled and his boys finish things without us."

"Everyone is exhausted and low on supplies, Commander Bayram." Farooq's voice was raw, harsh. They had the enemy on the run, but if they gave the Shadow forces any respite at all, Farooq knew they'd slip across the Graywater and reform. That would prolong the battle indefinitely. "Do not trouble me with excuses. You are to attack again. Immediately. And again, if necessary, but you are not to stop until you reach the river." Farooq was crouched behind one of the massive trees. He'd moved too far forward, as he often did, and the enemy fire was heavy. "If you feel that you are incapable of executing my commands, tell me now so I can replace you with someone who knows how to follow orders. Do you understand me?" Farooq knew they had a chance to end the Armstrong bloodbath if they pushed hard enough, and he wasn't about to let lackluster commanders throw the opportunity away.

"Yes," came the sullen reply. "I understand, sir." Bayram was not Farooq's favorite officer, not by a longshot. He considered the orta commander to be lazy and a poor example for his men. Bayram wasn't exactly a coward; not even Farooq would say he was. But he was insufficiently audacious by Farooq's fanatical standards. He shrunk from challenges and lacked the aggressiveness of his more capable peers. He preferred simpler, safer strategies, and he never understood the time and place for bold action.

"Then see to your duties, Commander." Farooq cut the line. His eyes moved to the tactical display projected inside his visor. His forces were less than 2 kilometers from the river on the left of the line, and General Merrick's command on the extreme right was even closer. In another few minutes, the enemy would be penned in…pressed up against the river with no alternate escape route. Then it would be time for the final push.

The opportunity would be extraordinary but also brief. The enemy infantry was fully armored, and they could cross the Graywater submerged if they had to, making their way slowly across the bottom to the south bank. But their retreat would be delayed by the crossing…and the Marines and Janissaries would have a chance to hit them hard while they were disordered and backed up on the riverbank.

Farooq flipped his com to the general frequency. "Attention

all units." He spoke Arabic, but the Marines under his command heard perfect English, courtesy of their AIs. "We have driven the enemy back over a hundred kilometers from our last ditch defense line…through the streets of Astria…from one end to another of the Sentinel." His volume was rising slowly as he spoke. "Now we find ourselves at the moment of truth. The enemy is trapped against the river, exposed to our attack."

He pulled his rifle out of the harness as he spoke, sliding a clip into the magazine and prepping the weapon for action. He was about to order the final attack, and one thing was absolutely certain. He was going in with the troops.

"The time is now. Now. We either give all we have to the battle, or we watch our enemy, so closely pursued, so hard fought, slip away across the river. It is up to us, my soldiers. We attack the enemy now…or we watch them regroup and reform. Then this battle will go on for months, and thousands more of our comrades will die."

Farooq felt the tension in his legs, the impulse to lurch forward and run into battle. "Marines and Janissaries…the plan is simple. Attack! Throw yourselves at the enemy! Drive them into the river! And don't stop until the war on Armstrong is won!"

Farooq thrust himself forward, running through the thinning trees and into the band of open plain between the forest and the river…the ground Erin McDaniels' Obliterators had consecrated with their blood weeks before, when the battle on Armstrong was young.

"Attack. Janissaries…Marines…attack! Follow me!"

"The battle here is lost, General." Stark was staring at Rafael Samuels, his eyes as cold and deep as space itself. "It would appear that the Alliance naval forces in the system have driven Admiral Liang away…along with our reinforcements."

Samuels stared back, expending every ounce of courage he could muster to meet Stark's withering gaze. "We still have considerable forces under arms." He was reaching, and he knew it. There was, indeed, a large body of troops still in the field, but they were scattered and disorganized. They had lost three-fourths of their number, and the survivors were broken. None of Samuels' units remained combat effective, and there was no chance the Marines and Janissaries were going to allow them time to regroup.

"No, General. There is no time." Stark's voice was calm, not at all what Samuels had been expecting. "The battle is lost, and if we do not act immediately, the survivors will be captured."

Samuels understood immediately. He'd reluctantly followed the directive to terminate the badly wounded, though as he saw the troops continue to fight so steadfastly and obediently, he regretted the policy. They deserved better. But now Stark was talking about murdering 15,000 of his soldiers...survivors of one of the toughest battles ever fought. "Sir..."

Stark's eyes bored into Samuels' like lasers. "Do you have a way to get them off-planet, General?" He paused, continuing when Samuels didn't respond. "So what do we do then? Allow them to be captured and studied by the enemy? Do you wish to face another clone army? Do you want the enemy to discover weaknesses in the Shadow troops and use them against us? Do you want the enemy to figure out how to undo our conditioning?" He paused then added, "Do you think the people we are fighting are stupid, General? Do you think they will fail to exploit opportunities that we give them?"

Samuels stood stone-still, staring back wordlessly at Stark. The spymaster's logic was flawless, his justifications for massacring his own soldiers utterly logical. But there was more to consider than just simple facts. Those men had earned better treatment. They had fought bravely, and almost 3 out of 4 had been left behind, dead on the field.

"No answers. Just as I expected." Stark's voice was still calm, but there was a hint of disgust there now. "As with all who make their decisions based on arbitrary morality and emotion, you cannot respond with facts." Stark paused for perhaps ten seconds. "So, General, if you have nothing of substance to offer to the discussion, kindly give the order."

Samuels felt the urge to resist, to refuse Stark's command.

But he knew he was inextricably tied to his psychopathic master. There had been a time when he'd had the chance to escape, he thought, but it was long past. There was nothing left of General Rafael Samuels, Commandant of the Marine Corps...nothing but the craven creature standing before Gavin Stark, doing his bidding. He tried to hold back the tears he felt welling up in his eyes as he muttered the command to his AI. "Execute clean sweep." It was just one more treachery for him, and not the worst. Samuels wished he could go back and do things differently, but he had chosen his path, and now he was stuck with it.

"Thank you, General." Stark spoke softly, almost sympathetically.

Samuels couldn't remember the last time the Shadow commander had sounded so reasonable. He turned his head, trying to hide the tears streaming down his cheeks. All across the battlefield, the Shadow legions, his soldiers, were dying, poisoned by their own AIs on his order.

"Go, General." Stark's voice...still sounding almost sympathetic. "Take some time to yourself. I know that was difficult."

"Thank you, sir." Samuels saluted and turned around, walking slowly back toward his tent. He was still surprised by Stark's empathy.

Take all the time you want, General, Stark thought as he watched Samuels walk away. He pulled a small remote from his pocket and pressed one of the buttons. He smiled as he saw Samuels stop in his tracks, hesitating for a few confused seconds before he fell forward, his immense, armored bulk dropping hard to the ground.

Stark put the controller back in his pocket and stared at Samuels' body. "That's the reward for failure, General." He turned and walked slowly away. "One you richly deserved."

One less loose end, he thought with grim satisfaction. Now for Erik Cain.

"It was the same here as on Arcadia." Holm spoke, the shock clear in his shaken voice. "But there were so many more of them here. There must have been 15,000 enemy troops still standing…and they murdered them all?" He turned to face Cain. "What kind of enemy kills its own soldiers in such numbers? Especially after they fought the way they did here."

"I can't understand it, sir." Cain paused. He knew he wasn't being completely honest with Holm. In truth, the more he thought about it, the less unexpected he found it. Stealth and secrecy was enormously important to the enemy, and he understood why Stark employed such draconian policies. He was angry that he'd allowed himself to be surprised at all at what Gavin Stark would do to win the war…and ashamed that he understood their enemy's motivations so well. But he lied to Holm, unwilling to risk the general thinking less of him. The Commandant was genuinely shocked at a type of evil he couldn't comprehend. But Cain could.

He was beginning to wonder how much difference there really was between him and Gavin Stark. He'd never murdered his wounded soldiers, but he had sent Clarkson's Obliterators on a suicide mission…an attack he knew few, if any, of them would survive. Others saw the difference between those acts clearly, but the distinction was blurring for Cain. He knew he had as much blood on his hands as Stark did, and the only difference was that his cause was just, and Stark's wasn't. How many mass-murderers, he wondered sadly, have justified their actions in exactly that way? Morality had always been a pliable concept to most men, malleable enough to justify desired actions while condemning those of adversaries.

"At least you managed to take some live prisoners, Erik. How many did you get in total?"

"Ten, sir. Plus Anderson-45." Cain welcomed a change of subject, however slight. "I've had everyone on alert to get wounded soldiers out of their armor immediately." He paused, casting his gaze toward the ground. "But the prisoners are in rough shape, sir. They were wounded already, and the men had to cut them out of their suits with blades." His tone darkened. "We'll be lucky if half of them survive."

"They'd all be dead if your people hadn't gotten to them, Erik." Holm reached out and put his hand on Cain's shoulder.

"I know you're beating yourself up, but you did one hell of a good job here, son. Our profession demands sacrifice. You may send those men and women into the firestorm, but you didn't create it. You didn't cause this war…or any of the others you've fought. Somebody has to stand against people like Gavin Stark, or mankind will plunge into a dark age that would make today's Alliance seem like utopia."

"I know, sir." Cain sighed. "But I've lost so many. How many people can one man kill and not be evil?"

"You don't kill them, Erik. You lead them into difficult situations." Holm paused. "Ok, sometimes you send them into the fire, but you do what has to be done." Holm knew Cain had an easier time when he went in with his Marines. Sitting back in HQ and sending a unit on a hopeless mission tore him apart. But sometimes there just wasn't a choice. It was part of his duty now that he wore stars on his shoulders and not a sergeant's stripes. But he had never full accepted that fact.

Cain was about to reply when Merrick walked up with Ali Khaled and Commander Farooq. With the conclusion of the fighting, they had all shed their armor, enjoying the fresh air while their suits were refurbished and reloaded. Merrick was wearing the same Marine-standard fatigues as Holm and Cain. The Janissary commanders were clad in their considerably more ornate off-duty uniforms.

"Cate Gilson's handling the wrap up, sirs." Merrick snapped off a quick salute to Holm and Cain, and he offered the Janissary commanders a respectful bow. "The last of the wounded are on the way to the main field hospital. It appears there are no live enemy troops remaining on Armstrong." His voice softened. "Still no new prisoners, sir. Two of the ones we had died, but Sarah told me she thought she could save the others. That makes nine, including Anderson-45."

"How is Anderson-45 doing, Isaac?" Cain turned his glance to Merrick.

"He's good, sir. He's great physically…and Sarah was making substantial progress breaking down his conditioning, at least before she had to get back to the hospital to deal with the wounded from the final push." He hesitated then added, "I think we might get through to him. I don't relish the thought of starting from scratch with the others, but I think Anderson-45 will prove to be very helpful."

"Well, that's good news, Isaac. Let's hope you're right." Holm was nodding his head as he spoke. "We weren't able to get any prisoners on Arcadia. Maybe now we can figure out what makes Stark's soldiers tick." Holm turned from Merrick toward the Caliphate officers. He'd gone right into action after he arrived, and this was the first time he'd seen them. "Lord Khaled, Commander Farooq...it is a great pleasure to see you both. Fortune to you and to those who follow you." Holm offered the standard Caliphate greeting.

"And fortune to you, General Holm, and to those who serve you." Khaled finished the salutation and then extended his hand. "Please accept our warm regards. It is good to see you again."

Holm reached out and grasped the Caliphate lord's hand. Then he turned and offered his to Farooq. "I cannot thank either of you enough for what you have done here."

"There is no need for thanks between good friends, General. And as fate's fickle nature would have it, it appears that old enemies have indeed become good friends."

"Very good friends. Honorable friends." Holm offered the Janissary officers a warm smile. "And I fear we will all have need of such comrades in the weeks ahead."

Stark crept through the tall weeds, working his way closer to the cluster of Alliance and Caliphate officers. Armstrong was lost and, with the victorious Alliance fleet approaching the planet, there had been no way to extricate any of the legions. Stark ordered them all put down to avoid capture. It was a terrible waste, but nothing was more important than protecting the secrets of his cloning technology and neural download process.

Spectre was ready to go as soon as he returned. The stealth ship wouldn't have any trouble slipping past the Alliance fleet and getting back to HQ. He'd have a reckoning with Admiral Liang when he got there. He was angry that the fool had not defeated the Alliance fleet, but his rage was tempered. As long as Liang got away with most of his ships and troopships intact, it wasn't a disaster. Armstrong was never critical. Even in defeat, it had served well to bleed the Marines white. The Shadow legions lost far more troops, of course, but then Stark had more to begin with. He could sacrifice thousands of his manufactured soldiers to destroy the Marines. And another battle like Armstrong would be the last Cain and his pitiful band of survivors ever fought.

The Janissaries were an unexpected wrinkle, something none of his projections had considered. When he got back to Omega Base he'd have to revise some strategies to deal with the unexpected intervention. Handling another 25,000 first rate troops wouldn't be easy, but it was doable.

But first he had unfinished business. He glanced over his shoulder. He had two agents with him...everyone else was already aboard Spectre, ready to lift off as soon as he returned. He motioned for his companions to remain in place, and he gripped the cool plastic of his weapon's stock, methodically checking the sight for the third time in ten minutes.

Stark felt nervous, and he could feel the sweat on his neck. He could never admit it to himself, but he was scared to go up against Erik Cain. The Marine was the most dangerous enemy he'd ever faced off against. He had always used his opponents' weaknesses against them. Their compassion, ethics...the squeamishness to do whatever was necessary to win. But Stark didn't think he could count on Erik Cain displaying those vulnerabilities. In the end, he believed the Marines' crazy but ever-victorious general would do anything necessary to win the ultimate victory. And that made him a very dangerous foe.

He glanced at his handheld scanner. Just ahead...only a few more meters and he'd be able to see them. He slowed to a crawl, careful not to step on a branch or even breathe too heavily. He climbed up a small rise and peered over the crest. There they were...a small group of senior officers standing around, unarmored. And there was Erik Cain, right in the middle. This was

going to be too easy, Stark thought with satisfaction, though
he maintained his deadly focus. He refused to underestimate
Cain...or any of his enemies. He had done that before, with
disastrous results.

Stark raised his rifle slowly, the movement almost impercep-
tible. He looked through the AI-assisted sight, checking and
double-checking his targeting. He'd kill all the officers if he
could, but there were a dozen guards just behind the command
group. He knew he might only get one shot before he had to
flee. And he was going to put that shot in Erik Cain's head.

"Still, we held both Arcadia and Armstrong, and that is
something to be pleased about." Holm was trying to sound
upbeat, but it wasn't easy. Not after the losses they had suffered. Not when at least 20 other Alliance worlds were still
occupied. He didn't begin to understand how they were going
to fight almost two dozen more battles against an enemy like the
Shadow legions, not to mention deal with the escalating problems on Earth. And he was still shaken by the enemy's homi-
cidal end game, just as he had been on Arcadia.

Cain nodded. "We paid a heavy price for these two rocks. I
hope they're worth it." He sighed. "But now we need to decide
what's next. We need to connect with Admiral Garret and put
together a plan to drive the enemy from the other worlds." Cain
paused. He knew mounting 20 successful invasions was a fan-
tasy. The Corps was in ruins, nothing left save a few shattered
remnants of one of the greatest fighting forces mankind had
ever fielded. They were all veterans - even the trainees who'd
been activated to fight on Armstrong deserved that distinction
now – but they were hopelessly outnumbered. And it would
take years to rebuild...time they didn't have.

"You may count on my people, General Holm." Khaled
moved his head slowly in Holm's direction. "As General Cain
said, there remains much to do before we have a chance of stopping our enemy."

"Thank you, Lord Khaled." Holm's voice was emotional.
The promise of the Janissary commander to join the Marines'

cause - one they all knew might be hopeless – affected him deeply. "We are profoundly grateful to count your people among our friends." He still found it odd thinking of the Janissaries as allies. For a century they had been the most hated and feared enemy of the Alliance Marines. But they had proven their friendship and risen above old hatreds for their own part, and Holm would accept no less from his Marines…and himself. Indeed, he was surprised how quickly he too was forgetting the old anger and hatred. It felt almost as if those old battles had been a dream.

"We should never have been enemies, General. I fear our governments are to blame for those decades of needless slaughter." Khaled was usually circumspect about discussing politics, but recent events had deeply affected his opinions. He was angry about the proscriptions…and that outrage was morphing into hatred for the immoral government that issued the orders. He was lightyears away from those responsible, but he'd sworn that if fate afforded him the chance, one day there would be a heavy reckoning. "However, we warriors will stand together, General, and when this is over, we will put the politicians in their places."

Holm smiled. "Perhaps, Lord Khaled." Holm wasn't quite ready yet to rebel outright against Alliance Gov, though he rather suspected Cain would do it without a second thought. "But for now…" Holm caught something in the corner of his eye. Movement. Something was wrong. He turned his head slowly, angling for a closer look. He paused for an instant, staring…and then forty years of combat reflexes took over.

"Down!" he screamed as he lunged for Cain, slamming hard into his shocked protégé, pushing him to the ground just as they all heard a loud crack. A spray of blood exploded from Cain's leg as he fell to the ground. Holm was twisting in the air, falling on top of Cain when another shot ripped through the air. Holm's head twisted violently, and his body was pushed over Cain's, falling hard to the ground two meters from his friend.

Cain was lying on the cool grass, stunned, his leg burning like fire, uncertain at first what had happened. He could see Khaled and Merrick rushing to his left, panicked looks on their faces. There was more firing, too…coming from the security detachment this time. What were they shooting at, he wondered, as he tried unsuccessfully to force himself up, grabbing his sidearm as he did…what was happening?

He saw the guards rushing toward a small cluster of heavy brush, firing away at full auto as they ran. He was about to try to get up again and follow them when he realized…

"General?" He spun his upper body around, and he crawled over to where Holm lay. The Commandant was on the ground, surrounded by Merrick and the two Janissary commanders, all on their knees, crouched over the stricken Marine.

Cain felt his stomach clench as he held himself partway up and stared down at his friend, his mentor. Cain's eyes filled with tears as he screamed urgently, "General? General Holm…"

Chapter 29

Outskirts of Astria
Planet Armstrong
Gamma Pavonis II

The silence of the ice-blue morning was shattered by the wailing of the pipes, the haunting notes of Amazing Grace floating through the clear cold sky. The Corps was assembled, those few who remained after the savage bloodbaths that had decimated its ranks. These veteran warriors were somber and heartbroken. Soon they would be dispatched to other worlds, to continue the war…to face an enemy that hopelessly outnumbered them. To grimly fight another hopeless war. But first, they were gathered to bid farewell to their leader, the very heart and soul of the Marines.

Not a word was spoken; not a sound broke the stillness save those mournful tones, and on the faces of these thousands there was not a dry eye. Men and women who had marched stone-faced into the fiery hells of a hundred bloody battles wept openly, unable to hold back the crashing waves of grief. For this time, among the thousands of dead from their desperate battles, lay a man they had all loved and respected, one who had led them across the galaxy, who had always been there to pull them through their endless struggles.

Elias Garrison Holm had fought everywhere man's hand had touched, and he had led his Marines wherever battle called them. He had saved the Corps from destruction and the shame and despair of Rafael Samuels' treachery. He'd given the Marines back their pride and rallied them to face one dire threat after another.

He had nurtured the newest Marines, many ripped from incomplete training programs to join the battle lines far too early, and he had shared an unspoken connection with the old sweats, the veterans who'd followed him from battle to battle over the years, even decades. They were gone now, most of the old guard. They had poured their life's blood into the cold sands of a hundred worlds, stood in the breach and held back the foe, the forces of destruction that would have consumed civilization. Now Holm was with them, gone to command the legions of lost brothers and sisters in whatever Valhalla awaited fallen Marines.

Erik Cain stood rigidly at attention, staring at the flag-draped coffin of his friend, his mentor. His wounded leg throbbed, but he was aware of it more as a detached fact...an awareness of pain that seemed so unimportant it was almost unreal. Elias Holm had been more than a commander to Cain, more than a father. Cain couldn't describe what Holm had meant to him. Words failed; thoughts failed. There was only a raw ache, an emptiness he knew could never be filled.

Cain had seen things no man should see, sent untold thousands to their deaths on worlds throughout human space, his stony resolve through endless horrors a legend in the Corps. But now that monolith was broken, and tears streamed silently down his cheeks. His hand was pressed to his forehead, firm and unmoving in a perfect salute. A last tribute to his fallen leader.

Sarah Linden stood a few meters behind Erik, an image of icy perfection, her black dress uniform perfectly pressed. But it was a façade, her face a mask of pain, wet with tears. She'd been devastated already, wracked with grief and guilt over the death of her sister, Alex. The loss of Holm so soon afterward was too much to bear, and she felt empty...dead inside.

Despite her own agony she wanted to go to Cain, to comfort him somehow. She, more than anyone here, knew just how badly he was wounded, the hurt he was feeling...pain he would keep to himself until his time came to join his fallen commander. She wanted to ease his suffering, but she just stood rigidly, looking out over the ceremony in stony silence. There was nothing to do; she knew that. Part of loving Erik Cain was accepting the immovable rigidity of the man.

The Marine guard stood unmoving, at rigid attention, polished rifles held perfectly aloft. This was no normal detachment, but an assemblage of veteran non-coms from Holm's many battles. Gray-haired and grim faced, many of these warriors had fought under Holm since the early days of the Third Frontier War, following him unquestioningly wherever the bugle sounded. They were the few, the last survivors of a dying breed now almost lost. They were among the toughest and strongest subjects the human race had ever produced, but now they were broken inside, wracked by a grief they could hardly contain.

Ali Khaled stood off to the side along with Farooq. They had come to pay their respects to the great leader, but they took their place at the periphery, not wishing to upset or offend the Marines. Both Caliphate leaders had tremendous respect for Holm, but they were aware that they had spent most of their lives as his enemy...as the enemy of all those gathered here, and they had elected to pay their respects quietly and without fanfare.

Cain stepped forward, leaning on his cane and willing every shred of strength remaining within him to make the walk to the dais. Sarah had treated his wound, but he still moved slowly, painfully. Catherine Gilson had offered to give the eulogy, to spare Erik the weight of the task. The two had inherited the Corps from Holm, and both were heartbroken by his loss. But Gilson knew Erik's agony was something even beyond her own, and she couldn't imagine what it would cost him to mount that podium and shoulder this burden. But Cain had said no. He owed this to Holm, he and he alone. He was the son to the man with no family, who'd given his life to the Corps, just as the fallen general had been a father to Cain. Erik would not let himself fail in this final duty. That would be unthinkable.

He stood behind the podium, silent, looking out over the assembled multitudes. He felt the yawning pit inside him, and for a moment he couldn't bring the words. Bidding farewell to friends was part of a Marine's life; Cain knew that well enough. It would have been difficult under any circumstances to say goodbye to Holm, but this was worse even than any scenario Cain had imagined. The valiant general hadn't died leading a heroic attack or standing firm in the breach, holding back the enemy. He'd been murdered, shot down in the open after the battle had been won. He'd died saving Cain from an assassin's bullet. Killed by a sociopath so evil, even Cain's cold-blooded mind failed utterly to comprehend his motivations.

He reached down, summoned all that remained of the strength that had sustained him through the horrific battles he had fought. His hands gripped the podium, and he stared out at the silent masses. Finally, slowly, he forced the words from his quivering lips.

"We are here to bid farewell to a great man, a man to whom no poor words I can muster will do justice. Elias Garrison Holm was more than a general, more than a Commandant. He was an example for all of us, the perfect warrior...noble, honorable, a father to every Marine." Cain's voice was cracking, struggling, but he pressed on. "He saved the Corps from treachery and destruction, and with his own force of will he pulled us from the brink, led us through our darkest hour, gave us back our pride, our dignity...reminded us that we are Marines...and what that truly means."

His fingers tightened on the edges of the podium, but he continued his speech. His voice was halting...but he went on. "He was a Marine, and a Marine he shall always be. Wherever we go into battle, wherever our successors and those Marines who come after us carry the flag, he will be there. As long as the Corps endures, General Elias Holm will never be truly gone."

Cain paused, staring out at the crowd. There was silence over the field, save for the sounds of men and women sobbing softly. Tears streamed down Cain's cheeks as he stood there, drawing on what little strength remained to him.

"General Holm was a Marine's Marine, from the day the Corps adopted him as a lost teenager, as it did so many of us, until the moment he fell…and he remains such, down whatever paths he now treads." Cain sucked in a deep breath of air, and forced himself to go on. "Farewell, General Holm, Commandant, mentor…friend." He forced himself to stare out again, panning his eyes across the multitudes. "A grateful Corps offers you its heartfelt thanks…its everlasting gratitude and admiration. Rest, General…rest in the peace you have so profoundly earned."

Cain bolted to rigid attention and snapped his hand to his forehead in a salute as crisp and flawless as the one he'd offered moments before. Despite his rank and years of service, Cain's salutes had always been notoriously poor. But not today.

Every man and woman present answered Cain's salute and held it, as he did, while a single bugle sounded the mournful notes of taps. Finally, he let his hand drop to his side and walked silently from the podium, to the platform where Holm's coffin lay, draped in the flag of the Alliance. He stood silently, hundreds of eyes upon him, then he pulled the sword from his side and lay it on top of the casket. It was the blade he'd been given at his graduation from the Academy so many years before. Now it was a tribute to his lost friend.

Cain turned and walked slowly from the field. He could feel a change inside with each step. The grief was still there, as he knew it would always be. But it was changing, becoming harder, colder. Erik Cain was a fearless warrior, a relentless force in battle. But this was something different, something new. It was as frigid as space itself. There was no roiling anger, no quivering rage that would quickly burn out. It was a silent, frozen hatred in his heart so strong it scared even him.

It was early…very early. The first tentative rays of light were moving across the horizon, and in the dawn haze a group of Marines, senior officers all, were gathered atop a small hill outside the war torn city of Astria. They'd come together the day before to bid farewell to a friend, a leader whose legend, they knew, would never truly die. Each of them was touched in his own way by the loss of a man who'd been a mentor to them all, and none of them would ever be the same after his loss.

They'd been up all night, drinking to Holm's memory and telling stories – mostly true - of past battles, just as they all knew he would have wanted. They could almost feel him watching them, and if a tale grew a bit in drama, if an enemy became more numerous or a situation more dire in the retelling, all were sure Elias Holm would have been the first to roar with laughter and slap the back of the storyteller.

Last night had been for reminiscing, for the past. Today they were met for another reason, one looking forward and not back. They were here to plan their next moves in the war...and to plot their vengeance.

"Gavin Stark will pay for what he's done. There isn't a man or woman in the Corps who will rest until he has...who wouldn't give their lives to destroy him." Catherine Gilson wore a freshly-pressed uniform, looking surprisingly sharp and alert for someone they all knew had been toasting Holm until only a few hours before. "But we must win the war too. Stark is fighting a battle for dominance over mankind...and that struggle isn't over. We've won a few fights, but his forces are entrenched throughout occupied space." She paused and panned her eyes across the small cluster of officers. "We must never forget... we could still lose this war. Indeed, we are still at an extreme disadvantage. And it could still lead to Armageddon on Earth."

Everyone nodded in somber agreement...everyone save Erik Cain. He stood stone-still, staring straight at Gilson, but he not really seeing her. His thoughts were elsewhere, and they were dark. Cain didn't care about fighting Stark's manufactured soldiers, and he didn't give a shit whether Earth plunged deeper into its last war. He'd spent a lifetime fighting...watching good men and women die. He'd told himself they were lost for a good cause, that mankind was worth saving. The fight against the First Imperium, watching the forces of humanity unite and fight together in a common cause had helped him believe that... for a time. But now that faith was gone. The dead from the First Imperium War hadn't even been buried before the Powers were fighting again...and a psychopath like Gavin Stark had managed to work himself a hair's breadth from total domination. Cain didn't believe in anything anymore. Nothing but vengeance.

The discussion continued, but he heard none of it. He was thinking about Gavin Stark, about where their hateful enemy had fled to continue his struggle. He felt hatred coursing through his veins, but also caution. Stark was one of the evilest creatures ever produced by Earth, but he was also one of the most dangerous. Unfocused anger wasn't going to destroy him. If Cain let uncontrolled rage dictate his actions he would hand Stark the final victory. Cain had to be as dark, as focused…as sociopathic as his enemy. To destroy Stark, Erik Cain would shed the last shreds of his own humanity…he would become like his enemy.

"Erik?" A familiar voice was calling to him. "Erik?" Louder.

"Yes?" The voice had been Gilson's. Cain saw her now, his consciousness drifting sluggishly back to the current time and place.

"Are we agreed then?" She was looking into his eyes, slowly realizing that he hadn't heard a word she'd said. "We defeat the rest of the Shadow Legions and stabilize the situation on Earth first. Then we hunt down Gavin Stark." The group was silent, a few of them nodding as they stared at Cain.

He returned Gilson's stare, but he didn't answer.

"Erik, I know how you feel, but duty is first." Her voice was urgent, tense. "No one would have believed that more than General Holm." Her eyes bored into his. "You know that."

Cain remained silent for a few more seconds. When he spoke his voice was soft, not the raging tirade they all expected. "And what did that get him, Cate? What has it gotten any of the thousands who've died?"

Gilson didn't answer; she just stood opposite Cain and held his gaze. She couldn't order him to follow the consensus…the two had received their 4th stars simultaneously, General Holm's way of making them equals. It made sense as long as he'd been alive to assume overall command, but now it left the succession in doubt. Finally, she said, "Erik, we have to win the war first. You're hurting now, but you know what we have to do."

"You do it, Cate. The Corps is yours." There was a hollow-ness in his voice…as if he were already elsewhere. "You take command. You can lead the Marines every bit as well as I can." He reached up to his shoulder, pulling the four small platinum stars off his jacket. He took her hand and placed the insignia on her palm. "I can't wear these where I am going." Then he turned and started to walk away.

"Erik!"

He stopped and glanced back. "You command the Corps, Cate." He stared at her for a few seconds. "You take care of our Marines." He paused, turning away and taking another step. "And I'll take care of Gavin Stark."

Cain walked silently down the grassy knoll, the peaceful spot on the Academy grounds where Elias Holm would rest for eternity, keeping watch on his beloved Corps. Sarah walked wordlessly beside him. She knew he needed to be left alone, that nothing she could say would help him. She wasn't even sure she had any comfort left to offer. Sarah had long been the more optimistic of the two, the lighter counterpart to the darkness that had always been part of Cain's soul. But now her own thoughts were just as grim. Holm had been as dear to her as anyone in the Corps, and his loss, coming so soon after the tragedy with Alex, was more than she could bear. She was lost and confused, and felt as if she had nothing left to give anyone.

She knew she couldn't do anything to ease Erik's burden, even if she'd had the strength to try. He had to tread a dark path, one she knew would take him away from her…one that might finally claim him. She tried not to think about that, though. Losing Erik was more then she could imagine. But now his hand held hers with a firmness that told her all she needed to know about what he meant to him. They didn't need words between them, these two, and she silently drew from him the strength she needed to go on, to deal with her own heartbreak and despair.

Cain stopped and turned back, taking one last look at the small, marble statue that marked Elias Holm's grave. Goodbye, sir…Elias, he thought…you were the best man I ever knew.

Erik Cain didn't know how he would learn to live with the grief…or where he would dig up the strength to see this war through to a victorious conclusion. But he knew one thing with utter certainty. He would find Gavin Stark…wherever he ran, down whatever rathole the miserable coward tried to hide. He would do whatever was necessary, without hesitation, without remorse. He would follow Stark to the ends of the universe if needs be, but he'd never cease, never slow in his hunt. He would have vengeance for Holm, and no force in the universe would stop him. He would leave Earth in her ashes if that's what it took, destroy a dozen worlds, lose whatever scraps were left of his soul to the fires of hell…but Stark would not escape his wrath.

His hands were clenched in trembling fists, hatred consuming him with each step. He would find Gavin Stark…and he would kill him. Whatever the cost. *Whatever the cost.*

Coming Summer 2014:

The Farthest Stars

Book I of the new series...Crimson Worlds: Refugees

Terrence Compton and half of humanity's Grand Fleet are trapped, cut off from home and relentlessly pursued by the forces of the First Imperium. Crimson Worlds: Refugees is a new series, continuing Compton's story after the end of To Hell's Heart.

Coming Autumn 2014:

Crimson Worlds IX: The Fall

The stunning conclusion to the original Crimson Worlds series.

Crimson Worlds Series

Marines (Crimson Worlds I)
The Cost of Victory (Crimson Worlds II)
A Little Rebellion (Crimson Worlds III)
The First Imperium (Crimson Worlds IV)
The Line Must Hold (Crimson Worlds V)
To Hell's Heart (Crimson Worlds VI)
The Shadow Legions(Crimson Worlds VII)
Even Legends Die (Crimson Worlds VIII)

The Fall (Crimson Worlds IX)
(October 2014)

War Stories (Crimson World Prequels)

Also By Jay Allan

The Dragon's Banner

Gehenna Dawn (Portal Worlds I)

The Ten Thousand (Portal Worlds II)
(July 2014)

www.crimsonworlds.com

Made in the
USA
Middletown, DE